FREEING SERAPHINA

TIAGO DE SILVA

This is a work of fiction. Names, characters, business, events and incidents are the products of the author's imagination. Any resemblance to actual persons, living or dead, or actual events is purely coincidental

Copyright © 2019 Tiago De Silva (also known as Santiago De Silva)

All rights reserved. No part of this publication may be reproduced, distributed, or transmitted in any form or by any means, including photocopying, recording, or other electronic or mechanical methods, without the prior written permission of the publisher, except in the case of brief quotations embodied in reviews and certain other non-commercial uses permitted by copyright law.

For orders, please visit Amazon.com.

This book is dedicated to the teachers and mentors in my life who have contributed so generously to me – Mrs Main, Kylie Salisbury, Susan Phillips, Paul Walker, Peter Wise, Paul Berry, Samantha Wall, Emily Fletcher, Octavio Salvado, and Lina Zapata. I also dedicate this book to Violet Rose, and the adventures we are going to have getting to know one another in this lifetime.

A note to those seeking their highest path in life – my heart is with you. I have nothing but pure admiration and love for you, and I wish you an amazing journey through this gift called life.

ONE

Now was her chance. A wall of young women blocked the guards' view of her. She had gone over the motions repeatedly in her mind, and forced open one of the leg shackles, feeling the strain in her arms and shoulders, squeezing every drop of effort from her muscles. She got the other one free and scooped the chains up in her arms.j

She was still fast. As she bolted towards the trees, she dared not look back, even when she heard shouting after a few moments. They were chasing her, she was sure of it. She felt her heart pounding in her chest, and her breaths started to get shorter. Her body began to crumble under the effort of sprinting, while carrying the extra weight of her chains and shackles.

The edge of the forest was so close. She focused and pumped her long legs once more. Keep going, she thought. She could hear them now. They were still a long way behind her, but she could not outrun them for much longer. Not with these chains.

She ducked under the canopy of a tree. The cool darkness of the forest soothed her body, but there was no time to luxuriate. Opting to ignore the nearest tree, she kept running and threw the metal chains over her shoulder. The weight nearly yanked her to the ground, but she stayed upright. Looking over her shoulder, she could see the guards were almost in the forest. She clambered up the tree, her arms and hands moving before her eyes with dizzying speed.

Finally, she got high enough and heard the men crashing through the leaves below her. Careful not to make a sound, she looked down at the three of them, and stayed completely still...

✱✱✱

Seraphina opened her eyes with a start.

Heavy chains were pulled tight around her wrists. Her eyelids felt heavy as she opened them. It was pitch-black. She tried to wriggle into a more comfortable position, but it was useless. Gruff voices echoed in the distance, speaking a language she didn't understand. There was whimpering nearby. Someone else was there!

'Hello?'

'Shhh!' came the angry, whispered reply.

Seraphina stayed still and silent.

A tear rolled down her cheek, and she wiped it away. Then another. Before long, she was sobbing. There was a dank smell in the room, and the air around her face was cool. Her body felt warm though, as if heat were rising from the floor.

'Shhh!' said the same voice 'They'll come in here. Be quiet!'

It was too late. A loud sound, and the huge door opened. Seraphina flinched at the light then focused for a moment on the silhouette of a large man. Blinking, she took in the rest of the room. Her mouth opened, and she scanned the room, counting. At least forty. Forty women and girls, all bound just like she was. A barely audible gasp escaped her lips.

The man yelled some words she did not understand and held up a weapon of some kind. Squinting, Seraphina could make out a thick handle and long, heavy threads flowing down from it. A whip. The room was silent. Not even the sound of breathing could be heard. He stood there for a moment. Seraphina could not see his eyes, but she could feel his gaze. Then he turned and left the room in one motion, slamming the door behind him. The sound of a bolt being slid home followed, and the room was engulfed in darkness again.

Seraphina had caught a glimpse of the girl next to her when the man had come in. She waited a couple of minutes, then, with her shoulder, gave her neighbour a gentle nudge.

'What do you want?' the girl whispered.

'Where are we?' asked Seraphina, as quietly as she could.

'None of us know.'

'How long have you been here?'

'Months. You came in only a couple of days ago.'

'I've been sleeping for a couple of days?'

'More or less. It's time to sleep now, it's nighttime.'

'How do you know?' asked Seraphina.

'They take us out every day for an hour, just before sunset. That was a couple of hours ago. Now go to sleep.'

'What's your name?'

'If I tell you, do you promise to stop talking and go to sleep?'

'Yes. I'm Seraphina.'

'Seraphina, I'm Rhea. Good night.'

She remembered now. The ship being boarded. The huge men taking her and putting her below deck. She remembered the drink they kept forcing her to take, and the memory of its aroma caused her to retch. Like wine, but with a foul, pungent smell. Most of what she remembered was having the cup held to her mouth, and her nostrils held shut until she drank it. She clenched her fists to fight off the nausea then thought of Quintus. *Had he been hurt? Had they taken him too? What about Cicero?*

Finally, her racing mind gave way to exhaustion, and Seraphina passed out.

TWO

His name was Karsas, and he was a beast of a man. He stood nearly seven-foot tall. His legs resembled tree trunks more than limbs. The shorter tunic he almost always wore was typical for a warrior. It strained against his thick chest muscles and ample belly. A large, black eyepatch adorned his right eye, and he glared with fury out of his left at anyone who stared for too long. The eye had been lost many years ago, in some long-forgotten skirmish, in a land far away from the stinking pit he was now consigned to.

To say that Sarmatia was not glamorous would be a gross understatement, but Karsas had long since learned to accept his lot in life. A vagabond since he was a boy, he had endured far rougher circumstances in his life. At least here he was in charge, and that was far more pleasant than being an underling in a more esteemed location. He despised being subordinate by nature, and he would never find a gracious master in his chosen profession. When his uncle had sent him to run things here, he was relieved that, for the most part, he would be in a position of authority.

In his lifetime, he had trafficked all manner of stolen goods. Textiles, livestock, wine, occasionally gemstones or even gold. A decade ago, he and his band of brothers had discovered the most lucrative stock of all to trade—human beings. It had begun quite by accident, during a gold deal with a shady Roman official. In passing conversation, the official had made mention of how much gold he had paid for his slaves. Karsas' uncle, a brute of a man named Gadas, became fixated with the idea.

Only a ship loaded to the brim with gold would be more profitable than a boatload of slaves, and such ships were rare indeed. People, on the other hand, were readily available. They could be taken at will and, if the right targets were selected, with minimal resistance or consequences. Over time, they learned that by far the most valuable slaves were beautiful girls and young women. These became their sole focus, and, since then, they had never known such riches.

He lay on a comfortable lounger, while a couple of his own slaves attended to him. One danced, another fed him. He stretched his thick arms back, bringing his hands behind his head, and followed that with a deep sigh. One of the benefits of his position was that he could take a girl or two for his own amusement. He felt himself getting bored of the current roster. The beauty they had picked up only a day or two ago would be his, he had decided. *Once she was properly cleaned up and processed*, he thought to himself.

The processing period was important. Firstly, they had to clean the girls up from whatever ordeal had resulted in their capture. Second, and most important, any resistance had to be broken. This was achieved by keeping them in darkness, with very little sustenance, unable to move or speak. Once suitably docile, they were allowed out once a day to eat and get some fresh air. After all, the goods had to be kept in a saleable condition. The remote location of the prison meant there were lengthy intervals between when they could sell the girls, but the huge payoffs made their efforts worthwhile.

He had marvelled at the allure of the young Hebrew woman. Hers was an unusual capture. They had come across the small Roman ship carrying an obviously important official, but no guards. It was a risk, but one he had decided to take. Roman officials were occasional customers of the pirates, though they usually dealt with middlemen. There was very little chance the man would ever see Karsas and his crew again, and they had not harmed him.

Karsas had become enamoured with her. Yes, she would be his.

THREE

The sky was blue and bright. Too bright in fact. Seraphina squinted as she experienced her first taste of daylight in three days. The weight of the metal binding her hands together dragged her arms down. This was accompanied by a dull pain in her shoulders and upper back. In the dark room where they were being held, she sat and the floor supported the weight of her chains. Standing outside, they pulled down on her entire upper body. As if this wasn't enough, leg shackles were attached to each girl.

The aches travelled up and down her limbs as she started walking. She stretched her fingers in an effort to counter the stiffness in her body. Despite this, Seraphina felt a smile cross her lips as the warmth of the sun brushed her skin. She tilted her head backwards a little, breathing in the fresh air, and was happy to be outside. It was an odd mood, given the circumstances, but one that seemed to be shared by the other girls. They looked relaxed. Another whispered conversation with Rhea that morning had revealed that this was the time of day when they were fed too. Having not eaten for two days, Seraphina was all too eager to eat whatever she was given.

As they were marched out of the building in single file, Seraphina's eyes adjusted to the light. She glanced around and immediately felt the stares of her captors as she did so. A lump formed in her throat and Seraphina noticed all the other girls looking directly ahead. She closed her eyes for a moment, and did the same, concentrating on the back of the girl in front of her.

The girls were all young and of slight build. They wore the same crude dress as Seraphina; almost a uniform. The only distinguishing factors were their height and hair colour.

They were in a vast green field, peppered with large boulders. The field was almost encircled by a thick layer of trees. There was, no doubt, a deep forest around them, and their prison behind. Seraphina dared not look behind her.

An involuntary deep inward breath, and she could feel the tears coming. She held them back, shaking, and continued to walk forward, in step with the other girls. She had no idea where they were, or what these men intended to do with them. Despite that, there was an unmistakeable feeling that they were the only people around for many miles, and that whatever her fate was to be, it could be nothing good.

Seraphina took another deep breath, this time of her own volition. She straightened her spine and walked tall in the direction the other girls were heading. Rhea was behind her, and she was grateful to have made something of a friend in this situation.

As the line of girls began to come to a halt, each took a seat on a boulder. This was done without prompting, and Seraphina followed their lead. At the same time, three men walked towards them, a huge knapsack slung over each of their shoulders. They looked Greek, Seraphina observed, but with two notable differences. One, they were huge men. Not tall and taut like the soldiers she remembered in Alexandria, but with much thicker muscles, more hair on their bodies, and big, heavy stomachs. They stomped the ground with each step. The other difference was their language. They were not speaking Greek, and Seraphina had never encountered the language the men used.

They were fearsome, robust men. After leaving the knapsacks in a row in front of the girls, they hulked back towards the prison. For a moment, no one moved. Just as Seraphina made a move towards the knapsacks, Rhea gestured with her hand to stay still. The three girls who had been at the front of the line each took a place behind a knapsack. One by one, they were opened. Seraphina gasped as the remaining girls moved towards the food.

Abundant, delicious food was spread before them. Fruits, meats, vegetables, breads, and cheeses. Recovering quickly from her initial shock, and feeling her hunger, Seraphina dashed towards the food. The girls ate with their hands. Some rapidly, some slowly. All were grateful for the meal. For the time being, the presence of their captors was forgotten. Idle conversations were started, and there was even some laughter.

Seraphina popped a piece of bread with cheese on top into her mouth. She closed her eyes and let out a little moan. The bread was surprisingly fresh, the cheese rich. After she had filled her belly, Seraphina could not help but notice the oddness of the scene, given the circumstances. She stayed quiet initially, but after a while, spoke with Rhea. If not for the wretched restraints around their hands and feet, they would appear to be leisurely enjoying a meal outside on a beautiful day.

FOUR

Grey.

That was all he could see.

For a moment, he could not remember where he was. One of his assistants came to check on him, and the boat rocked slightly. Cicero sat up and took the water his assistant was offering. He stared through the water for a few moments as he felt the slow waves continue to rock the boat back and forth, back and forth. The water had a heavy, almost metallic appearance to it; its colour like faded cobalt. Cicero shifted his gaze up to the port town then closed his eyes and clenched his fist. Did it really happen? Had it all been a nightmare?

Looking around the ship, he got his answer. It was not a nightmare. There was no Seraphina and no Quintus. For days now, he had gone through the same ritual, hoping. It was always the same though. Opening his eyes, he could see Ostia in the distance, its familiar docks almost imperceptible through the mist.

They had made it back to Rome.

He shook his head to himself as he replayed events in his mind. The pirates had appeared so suddenly and, even after they boarded, Cicero thought he could handle matters. He offered them all the money they had on board. It had not been enough. He threw the water to the ground, and his head dropped. The senator started shaking his head again and could feel his heart beat faster.

'Senator,' said the assistant.

No response.

'Senator,' he repeated.

The senator looked up.

'We'll be landing at Ostia soon, sir. Are you alright?'

Cicero nodded to put the young man at ease. In truth, he could not fathom the question. He had been away from Rome for four months. Four eventful months at that. He would now return to his day-to-day duties in Rome which were considerable. The guilt niggled away at the great senator, but he knew he could do nothing. He had to let it go and hope that fate would deliver his friends, Seraphina and Quintus, wherever they may be, from the hands of those terrible, terrible brigands.

He would have to send word to Alexandria about what had happened.

FIVE

Weeks passed, and Seraphina slipped into the routine shared by the other girls. Little by little, she befriended them. More than anyone else, she grew closer to Rhea. Rhea was a dainty creature, only standing as tall as Seraphina's chest. She had light-brown hair, with a few blonde streaks. While petite, her figure was also womanly and curvaceous. In the mornings, or when they were let out into the field, Rhea would have a wide smile on her face. Each time they talked, Seraphina noticed how, after a few moments, this would be replaced by a downward gaze and a serious frown.

They sat next to each other each day when they ate and even managed the occasional bout of laughter together. The green of the grass, and its softness against their bodies when they sat, was a source of great comfort during otherwise dreary days.

Seraphina made an effort to enjoy something about the time outdoors each day. The blue sky, the warmth of the sun, or the sight of a passing bird. Anything would do. She may have appeared placid, but she knew something had to be done.

Thinking practically helped keep her rage at bay. Gaining the trust of the other girls was imperative. She also observed her captors. Their behaviour was curious. They were hard men, and their viciousness was evident from every angle—their mannerisms, the way they spoke, and even the way they would fight amongst themselves on an almost daily basis. They regularly threatened the girls, though none seemed to understand the language they spoke. It remained a mystery to Seraphina.

This cruel behaviour contrasted with the fact that the guards—as the girls had come to call them—never raised a hand to any of the girls. They were well fed, and the daylight breaks were a relaxed time of day. The needs of the girls were attended to, as well as they could be. Moreover, they took unusually good care when removing the metal restraints and putting them back on, displaying a delicateness that belied everything else Seraphina observed about the guards.

Seraphina could not deduce what was in store for her and her fellow prisoners. It did not matter though. They were being held against their will. As they were seated out on the field for another day's meal, Seraphina gazed towards the building that had become her prison. The guards were not watching with any serious interest and busied themselves with conversations over their own food. For a moment, she locked eyes with Rhea who then followed Seraphina's gaze around the group.

'Everyone. Keep smiling and eating as usual,' said Seraphina.

Most of the girls failed to follow this directive, and they all looked at Seraphina.

'Stop looking at me' she said. 'Just keep eating, act as if we are all getting along, and listen to me.'

'Why should we?' asked one of the girls by the name of Korinna. She was as tall as Seraphina and had a fierce look to her; bright red hair that fell in thick locks almost to her waist and piercing blue eyes. Her alabaster skin had been unaffected by the sun. While Korinna's face was naturally pretty, she perpetually wore a frown or some other equally unpleasant expression that made it hard to appreciate.

Not surprising given the circumstances, thought Seraphina. At least they had all stopped looking at her.

'We all need to talk,' said Seraphina.

'So, talk,' replied Korinna.

'Not here. Tonight, after the guards have gone to sleep. We can whisper.'

Korinna stiffened. 'You're going to get us all into trouble. What do you want to talk about?'

'It's important,' said Seraphina, looking around the circle of girls. Most managed to remain nonchalant, but some had begun to sit up and take notice of the conversation. 'We can't do it here,' continued Seraphina. 'They aren't watching us closely, but they'll notice if we're talking about something serious.'

Korinna shook her head and went back to eating.

'Please,' said Seraphina. 'Stay up tonight, so you can hear what I have to say.'

The girls finished their meal in silence.

SIX

He seemed the kindest of their captors. The youngest too. Ourgious was checking the restraints of each of the girls, making sure they were firmly locked in place. He was a tall man, though most of his colleagues dwarfed him. He was lean and clean-shaven, and this also set him apart from the rest of the pirates, most of whom were only a slightly smaller version of their leader. Once everything had been inspected, he closed the door, taking no notice of the girls' faces. Ourgious locked the bolt into place and walked into another room where Karsas was waiting.

'How many?' asked Karsas.

'Forty,' came the reply from Ourgious, the young pirate. 'It has not changed.'

'I have to check these things, or no one will.'

'They dare not try to escape.'

'When is the dealer coming?'

Ourgious smirked. Karsas had a good sense of humour and referred to anyone they sold girls to as a 'dealer'.

'In the next few weeks.'

'They're all secure in there?' asked Karsas, nodding towards the heavy wooden door.

'They are, sir.'

'Thank you, Ourgious. Good night.'

'Good night, sir.'

Seraphina strained to listen. She could barely hear the words, much less understand them. The talking had seemed to stop. The sound of steps, heavy at first, then faded into the distance. After several minutes, she could hear nothing. Seraphina felt the usual quiver of her body as the complete darkness was now joined by silence.

'Are you all awake?' asked Seraphina.

'Shhh. Go to sleep,' someone replied from across the room. It was Korinna, without a doubt.

'Stop it, Korinna,' whispered Rhea. 'Just listen to what she has to say.'

Silence.

'If you're awake, sniff a short breath out of your nostrils, like this.' Seraphina made a tiny sound as her top lip reached towards her nose and she exhaled.

A few sniffs in response. *Good*, thought Seraphina.

'Alright. Now, to begin with, whatever gets said, let's make sure we keep it to a whisper. I think they go to sleep at night, but there's no telling how close they stay, or if someone could be listening. Sniff if you understand.'

A few more sniffs.

'I don't know why we are here, or what these men have planned for us. Frankly, I don't care, but I don't plan to live out the rest of my days in this room as a prisoner. So, we should start talking to each other and come up with a plan.'

Seraphina paused for a moment. When no one said anything, she continued. 'Our meal times are the best time to talk. The guards leave us alone, and if we look like we are eating and making simple conversation, they don't even seem to look our way. So, the day after tomorrow, I want to start talking. To see what we know about these men, and what we might do to be able to get out of here.'

'You're crazy,' said another girl. 'They'll kill us.'

'What do you mean?' asked Rhea. 'How do you know that?'

'I've seen men like this before. When I was free. Some of them lived in my town. I can recognise them from how they speak.'

'Where was that?' asked Seraphina. 'You can understand their language?'

'Phanagoria. They are brutes. Trust me. They will kill every one of us. I don't understand what they are saying, but I recognise the dialect.'

'Who are you?'

'Philomena,' came the reply.

Interesting, thought Seraphina. The diminutive girl had not said but two words to Seraphina up to this point. Maybe she was less shy in the darkness.

'Here is what I suggest,' said Seraphina. 'For those who want to talk and see what we can do to help ourselves, we can start talking at mealtimes. We must not give any indication that we are talking about serious matters, or that anything is amiss. If you don't want to join in on these discussions, please ignore us and enjoy your food and your own conversations. Is that fair? Sniff again if you agree.'

Several sniffs came immediately. Others thought about it for a few seconds, and Seraphina heard a few more sniffs. She counted about thirty who had responded.

Not bad, she thought. 'Thank you all. I know how afraid you must be.'

'You're welcome,' said Korinna. 'Now, go to sleep.'

SEVEN

Each day, the girls were marched into the field for fresh air and food. Seraphina couldn't be sure, but she sensed they came to collect them at the same time each day. Most of the other girls kept their heads down. Seraphina tried to do the same, and gazed upwards with her eyes only, remembering to appreciate the beauty of the nature around her. It wasn't doing any good today. She was trying to keep her face straight. She didn't want to show her anger, her seething rage.

The ritual of the food being left, and the same three girls unpacking it was followed. Then the rest of the girls sat, forming a circle, and started to eat and talk. The nearest guard was at least five hundred cubits away. It was time.

The food calmed her. Seraphina took a long glance at the nearest part of the forest, observing the tall, thick trees. 'So, who has been here the longest?' she asked.

'Me,' answered Korinna.

That figures, thought Seraphina. 'How long has it been?'

Korinna shrugged, 'I don't know. Maybe two months. I don't count the days in here.'

'Is every day the same?'

'Yes. There's no way you can escape from here, Seraphina.'

'How do you know? Have you tried?'

'No. There's no opportunity. This is the only time we are out of that locked room, and we are completely chained. I find it hard just to walk out here with these things on,' said Korinna, gesturing towards her shackles.

The other girls followed the conversation, but not one uttered a word. They continued to eat and smile as if they were idly chatting. Seraphina smiled at them. At least they did not look suspicious. Looking down at her own legs, she could see the way the leg restraints wove together with a metal hoop that sat in front of her stomach. Separate chains wrapped around the same hoop bound her hands. She had been watching the way the guards removed the leg restraints when they left her to bathe. It was easy for a strong man with two free hands to do, as a lot of pressure had to be exerted on the hinge of the shackle. The latch could then be lifted, freeing the leg. Trying to do so herself would cause a lot of noise, with the movement of the chains around her arms.

Korinna interrupted her thoughts. 'Even if you could escape, where would you go? I have no idea where we are, but I see nothing for miles except forest and plains.'

'I don't know,' said Seraphina, shrugging. Her eyes remained on her leg chains. *Perhaps if I could free one leg, I could make a run for those trees*, she thought.

Korinna returned her attention to eating and talking to some of the girls around her. Rhea brought a fig to her mouth, her gaze on Seraphina's shackled legs. Rhea then looked at her friend's eyes, which alternated between the chains around her arms and the guards in the distance. Eating very slowly, she continued to watch as Seraphina, looking at the guards in the distance, leaned forward, her hands outstretched towards her ankle. The chains made a big clang, and as one of the guards looked over, Seraphina made a pretence of stretching one side of her body, and then the other, turning her head away from the direction of the guards.

She took a piece of cheese and looked at Rhea, smiling.

'What are you thinking?' asked Rhea.

'I wanted to see how they would react if I moved too much,' said Seraphina.

'I think they are still looking at you.'

As she went to pick up something else to eat, Seraphina moved very slowly. Turning her gaze up only for a moment as she feigned interest in the food, she saw that two of the guards were indeed glaring in her direction. Popping a piece of cheese into her mouth, she turned back to Rhea and asked her a question about her family. They started a banal conversation which Seraphina did not pay attention to for the most part.

A plan had formed. She had spent so much of her life living in secret. She would not spend the rest of it living in captivity.

EIGHT

Karsas fumed. His anger was palpable, and neither Ourgious nor any of the other pirates dared break the silence. The leader was used to having the room to himself as his private office, and the fact that several large, sweaty men were squashed into the small room only compounded his irritation.

'Where is this man?' he yelled again. 'I have forty girls here. Forty! We cannot hold any more, which means we simply have to sit here until he comes and takes some of them.'

Karsas banged his fist on the table over and over, each strike louder than the one before. Beads of sweat trickled down his forehead, as they did on the brows of his men, who stood lining the wall, shoulder to shoulder. Only Ourgious' face was dry.

'What do we do, just sit here, babysitting these girls forever?' He was not really asking for a response, but rather just wanted to vent his rage. The men sat there, quiet, and somewhat fearful.

The banging stopped. Karsas adjusted his tone and asked, 'Does anyone have any ideas?'

Ourgious looked around the room then spoke. 'Sir, you are right.

We can only wait. This man is supposed to be reliable, and I was told he would take all forty girls. Not just a few or even half, but all of them.'

Karsas grimaced and folded his arms then, looking down at the table, he nodded his head.

'He'd better get here soon, or some of you will be marching these girls to Byzantium,' said Karsas, looking around the room.

This remark caused a slight panic as many of the guards looked up from the floor, seeing his wide bloodshot eyes and the scowl on his face.

'Sir, he will come. I am sure of it,' said Ourgious.

Karsas allowed the scowl to fade from his face. While there was no hierarchy in this band of pirates, Ourgious was the closest thing he had to a right-hand man. He was reliable, intelligent, and tended to act more from reason than anger or impulse. Karsas nodded again and unfolded his arms.

'Very well. Is there anything else to report?'

'There is one thing, sir,' continued Ourgious.

'What is it?'

'That Hebrew girl. I think we need to keep an eye on her.'

'What do you mean?'

'Well,' started Ourgious, 'I have been watching her. When she knows someone is looking, she behaves just as the other girls do. When I'm watching from a distance, as they walk out into the field and eat each day, I notice various things.'

'Such as?'

'She is always looking around, taking measure of her surroundings. She even looks happy on occasion, though I can understand the relief of being outside each day.'

'So what?' said Karsas gruffly.

'Well, I just have a feeling we should keep an eye on her.'

Karsas waved him off. 'Look, just make sure they are in good condition for when the dealer comes. If they misbehave in any way, yell at them. That always seems to scare them. No one has ever escaped from here, Ourgious. Where would she go?'

'I just wanted to tell you what I was thinking, sir.'

'Very well. Make sure they are always properly shackled, especially when they go outside each day. The most important thing is that they are kept clean and fed. I don't want this man coming here and refusing to take some of the girls because you lot have failed to do your job. Keep your focus on that, and there will be a pretty sum of money for us to split after he comes.'

'Yes, sir,' said each of the men in response.

Not one of the men believed it would be a fair split, but they understood that was the way of things.

NINE

Seraphina was chained in the far corner of the room from where the door was. Hearing the metal latch unlock, she knew it was once again time to go outside. As she was one of the last to have her chains detached from the wall, there was always time from when the door opened and light flooded the room to when she was taken outside.

She looked again at the shackle around her right ankle. For the past few days, every time she had been able to, Seraphina would look down and mentally clasp the hinge tighter, and lift the latch, freeing her leg. Then the other. Repeatedly, she went through the movements in her head. She felt Rhea watching her and looked back up towards the guard. He was busy unhooking one of the girls from the wall. Seraphina dared not speak to Rhea with a guard so close by but wanted her to look away. Catching Rhea's gaze and nodding towards the guard with a stern look Seraphina managed to get Rhea to stop looking at her without catching the attention of the guard.

Coming out of the building, Seraphina kept her head down, the same as the other girls, and her gaze neutral. She and the other girls waited patiently as the knapsacks of food arrived, the guards left, and the food was set out for everyone to eat. The rest of the girls got up and made their way to their usual spot. As they did this, their bodies obscured Seraphina from the view of the guards for a few moments.

It was time. Bending down, she strained with all the might of her body against the pressure of the spring in the shackle. She lifted the latch without a sound and took a deep breath in, feeling the strain in her entire upper body as she untensed. Seraphina summoned every ounce of energy she had and managed to unlatch the other shackle. Her legs were free!

Taking the leg shackles in her hands, she dashed towards the trees. None of the girls had even seen her move. Likewise, the guards who had delivered the food were oblivious, their backs turned to the girls as they walked back to the building. It took a few moments for anyone to notice, and even then, Ourgious could not believe what he was seeing. The girl was moving so fast. Was that the Hebrew girl? He shouted and waved at the returning guards, who did not understand what the commotion was.

Seraphina neared the trees by the time they reacted. The three men turned and ran towards the forest in pursuit. Even carrying shackles and with her hands chained, Seraphina easily outran them. Ourgious and the remaining guards sprinted from the building, their weapons drawn. The girls watched the scene unfold in shock. Rhea raised a hand to her mouth as she watched her friend disappear into the thickness of the trees. Two of the guards stopped where the remaining girls were, and yelled at them, gesturing for them to sit down and eat. Without understanding what was being said, the girls quickly realised what they were being told to do. They complied without hesitation.

Ourgious and the remaining men followed Seraphina into the dark cover of the trees. In the distance, Karsas stood atop the building and watched his men vanish into the forest.

TEN

He knew it. He just knew it. The girl was trouble. Ourgious had warned Karsas but to no avail. He shook his head and looked up, opening his eyes wide. The thick forest trees cast shadows over most of what he could see. He cast his eyes towards the ground. Nothing but leaves. No tracks to follow but judging by the noise of the rustling leaves under their feet, they would know if she was still running. Then again, she could already be out of earshot. Ourgious had been shocked by her speed. He ordered the men to spread out and move fast.

'Who are you to give us orders?' asked one of the men.

Grabbing him by the scruff of his neck, Ourgious said, 'Just do as I say.'

Another man then pushed Ourgious in the back, and the men began to bicker and fight. *This is ridiculous*, thought Ourgious. *This girl is getting away, and here we are fighting each other*. He still could not believe how fast she had moved. He had never seen anything like it. Even though Ourgious knew she was a problem, he would never have anticipated this. Stuck between several men arguing with him, his anger finally got the better of him.

He forced all three men to the ground and drew his sword. Pointing it at their necks, he said, 'Do as I say, and find the girl, or none of you will leave this forest alive.'

'There is no need for that, Ourgious,' came a voice from behind them.

Ourgious turned to see Karsas facing them, sitting on his horse. 'Men. Go,' he commanded the three lying on the ground. They quickly set off in separate directions. Karsas approached Ourgious. He looked surprisingly calm, given the circumstances. Ourgious still had his sword drawn, and his arm began to shake. The horse came to a standstill and Ourgious looked up, his top lip quivering. Karsas dismounted the horse and came eye to eye with Ourgious.

'I am sorry,' said Karsas.

'Excuse me, sir?' asked Ourgious.

'I am sorry for not listening to you. You were right.'

Ourgious nodded, sheathing his sword.

'Take my horse. Find the girl. She may be a little more trouble than the others, but she could be very valuable.'

'Yes, sir. Will you walk back?'

'I will be fine, Ourgious. Go. Now.'

Ourgious jumped on the horse and rode off.

ELEVEN

Cicero had plenty to keep his mind occupied. He was still recovering from the ordeal at sea, but more than that, he had political worries. His flight from Rome and subsequent support of Pompey's forces had put him into disfavour with Caesar. Even though the great dictator had eventually prevailed in the conflict, Cicero was not sure of his fate.

He saw his friend and long-time colleague, Porcius, waiting for him on the steps of the basilica. Cicero crossed the street, dodging a reckless chariot driver just in time. The driver continued as though nothing had happened. Cicero watched the chariot speed away, shaking his head. He walked up the stairs and greeted his friend.

'Crazy chariot drivers' said Cicero.

'Just another day in Rome' quipped Porcius.

Once inside the basilica and upstairs, the roar of the commotion outside dimmed. Ornate, grey marble surrounded them, and Cicero admired the floor-to-ceiling columns as Porcius chattered. Porcius was a diminutive man, but only in stature. His meagre build, simple face, and clean-cut appearance had seen the demise of many political foes. When first meeting Porcius, it could almost seem as if one were talking to an innocent adolescent. It was part of his guile. Whereas Cicero had built a career on diligence and integrity, Porcius had mastered the political game. He flirted with the boundaries of what was ethical and had enjoyed a career almost as long as the former consul's.

The two had known one another for years, but Cicero's misjudgement had even affected that relationship. As they walked and talked, Cicero listened more than he spoke. There was an edge to Porcius' tone, and it made Cicero choose his words carefully.

The pair continued to walk, and after a few moments, Cicero noticed someone in front of them. The tall, lean stature was unmistakeable. He was wearing his usual coloured toga, the maroon making for a sharp contrast with the white. As he looked up past the strong, square jaw and the famous, prominent nose, his eyes met those of the great Julius Caesar. The dictator's serious expression gave way, and the corners of his mouth turned up into a smile. Cicero leaned back, and his eyes widened.

Standing straight, Porcius said 'Ave Caesar!'

'Ave Caesar,' followed Cicero, somewhat more shakily.

Caesar outstretched his arms, taking Cicero's shoulders with his hands.

'My dear Cicero, I heard about your calamity at sea,' said Caesar.

'Yes, my lord.' Those were not the words he had expected from the dictator.

'I am glad you are out of that danger. Did I hear correctly that you lost some of your crew?'

'Yes, a young la—'

'Well,' interrupted Caesar, 'you are home now. Safe and sound.'

Cicero nodded.

'Is there something on your mind, dear Cicero?' asked Caesar.

Cicero could not help but notice the smile on Porcius' face. He grinned at Caesar and when Cicero returned his gaze to Caesar's face, the dictator was barely containing his laughter.

'Do not worry. I have decided to pardon your miscalculation. I have given the matter some thought and decided it was not treachery that you committed, but rather a lack of judgement that caused your actions.'

'That is very gracious of you, sir,' said Cicero.

'It is done,' said Caesar. 'Besides, we have more important matters to attend to.'

'Oh?'

'We must stabilise the Republic. There has been far too much conflict, and the people must not lose confidence in us.'

'I agree, sir.'

'I can count on you, then?'

'Of course, sir,' said Cicero.

'Very well. Now, tell me about these pirates.'

Caesar led Cicero off, as he regaled him with what had happened on the ship. Porcius followed at a distance, saying nothing.

TWELVE

The leaves covered the ground below, with shades of green, brown, and golden yellow. The air was a little heavier, perhaps due to the dampness of the forest. Seraphina had watched everything from one of the trees. As soon as she had gotten into the forest, she had climbed as high as possible. The moment she caught sight of the guards again, she did not make another move. Holding the branch and the chains tightly, Seraphina could not believe her eyes when the men started fighting. The largest of them, who she presumed to be the leader, appeared to order them into the forest to find her. Before he walked back to the prison, he looked straight up at the sky. It had terrified her for a moment as she thought he had seen her. It turned out to be nothing, as he returned to the field without hesitation.

The guards were still out there, somewhere amongst the trees. Seraphina had seen none of them for over an hour now. She had not even spotted the man on the horse. So, she waited. Surely, they would give up before it got dark.

Pressing her feet against the thick wood beneath her, Seraphina rested her back against one of the tree branches. She sighed, able to relax for the first time in weeks. Her period of captivity had forced her not to think about Quintus. She knew it would upset her and considering all the scenarios of what may have happened to him was more than she could take. In that tree, she could hold it back no longer, and devolved into a state of weep and worry.

They were only going to take her, she thought. Cicero and the crew were powerless to resist. Then Quintus fought. That was her last clear memory before she was knocked out cold. *Where was he? Where was her love, her dear Quintus?*

Shaking her head, she saw the last of the sun's light in the distance. Looking directly at it, she remembered the first time she had tried to meditate in the library. The candlelight. That night by the water. Then all that followed. It seemed like a lifetime ago, when in fact it was only months that had passed since her life was thrown into such disarray.

Leaves rustled nearby. Seraphina froze and even stopped breathing for a moment or two. Then, she heard the familiar voices of the guards. Not moving a muscle, she listened intently. She still had no idea what language they were speaking, and it bothered her to no end. Rolling her eyes at herself, Seraphina concentrated on being still and silent. They walked past the tree she was in, through the edge of the forest, and back into the field. There was no sign of the fourth man though, the one on the horse.

Her breath relaxed and returned to normal. *Where was he?* Her head dropped for a moment as her eyes closed, and her neck jerked back, a reaction to the sudden tiredness. Opening her eyes as wide as she could, Seraphina took in a deep breath through her nostrils and held it in. She remembered reading somewhere that this would help her stay awake. One of those Hindu texts perhaps. Another deep breath, and thoughts of her life in Alexandria swept over her. A tear came to her eye, and she remembered how much she missed Afiz. Clenching her fists, she shook her body a little, determined to stay awake.

THIRTEEN

She was running. Flying across Alexandria's rooftops, somersaulting through the air. Maximus dashed alongside her, and the two were having a wonderful time as usual. Seraphina felt the smile on her face as the air rushed on to her skin. Her long, lustrous hair trailed behind her, and she saw the huge jump ahead. Launching herself off the edge of the building, her foot faltered. She was falling, and the buildings disappeared. So did Maximus.

She screamed, but no sound came out. Seraphina kept falling and falling.

She hit the ground with a thud and opened her eyes. A bed of leaves, and hard ground beneath her body. It had been a dream. Rubbing her head, she felt something around her ankles. Looking up, she saw the young guard smiling at her, as he snapped the restraints back into place. Seraphina went to push him away, but he easily caught her arms and bound them with the chains. This time, they were so tight that she could barely move.

Her head dropped, and she gave up resisting. The guard continued to smile at her, not saying a word. He easily lifted her up on to the horse and tied the reins around the chains binding her wrists. The guard led the horse with Seraphina tied in place out of the forest. It was dark, and a million stars lit the sky. He stopped for a moment when he saw the sky. Seraphina sat on the horse, watching the same beautiful sight. It reminded her of those quiet nights spent with Maximus by the water, with nothing but a starlit sky to keep them company.

Looking down at the guard, she asked, 'What's your name?'

'Ourgious,' replied the guard. 'What's yours?'

'Seraphina' she answered without thinking. She was surprised. He understood Greek. 'Why are you keeping us?'

Ourgious held his hand up. There would be no more conversation. They returned in silence to the prison, and Seraphina was secured in her very own room. The door shut slowly in front of her, and Seraphina was alone in the darkness. Tears streamed down her face for a few moments, and she finally passed out from exhaustion.

FOURTEEN

The other girls were given no indication of Seraphina's fate. She was not taken outside each day for meals, and they dared not speak to the guards. Rhea had not talked to anyone in days. When inside, she cried and slept. When outside, she ate by herself in silence. It had been a week, and she could not help but worry about her friend.

Seraphina thought of Rhea too, and the isolation was beginning to take its toll. Her new quarters had yielded something interesting, however. She could hear the guards meeting and speaking on a regular basis with their leader. It didn't help much, though. Seraphina still could not understand a word of what they were saying. Nevertheless, she listened and listened. There was nothing else to do. Once a day, she was fed in her cell, and she was not allowed outside.

One day, she detected an unfamiliar voice, a softer tone, and as Seraphina awoke from her slumber, she noticed the man was speaking Greek.

'Are the girls ready?' asked the stranger.

'Yes,' came the leader's reply. 'You are over a month late, you know.'

'Karsas, I am a busy man. Would you prefer I leave?'

'No, no. We were waiting for you, is all.'

'That's what you are to do, pirate. Wait until people like me come and buy what you have to sell.'

Karsas grunted in response.

'How many are there?'

'Thirty-nine.'

'I was told forty, Karsas. I was expecting forty.'

'We had some trouble with one. I doubt you would be interested in her.'

'I'd like to see her nonetheless,' replied the stranger.

'What's your name?' asked Karsas.

'You do not need to know my name. Now, when can I see these girls?'

Another grunt. Then he said, 'Later today, when we take them outside to eat.'

'I trust you have kept them in good condition.'

'Of course. We do know what we're doing here.'

'We shall see.'

'Do you have the gold?'

'Of course. Will this be enough?' asked the stranger, as Seraphina heard a loud thud, followed by the gentle sound of metal clinking.

'Yes, sir,' replied Karsas, his tone softening remarkably. 'Where will they go?'

'I have many customers in Rome and Athens who will pay good money for them. The most beautiful ones first, as I'm sure you know.'

'Right, well it will be good to get them out of here. Go and rest, Greek, and my men will send for you this afternoon, so you can inspect the merchandise.'

'Very well, Karsas.'

It sounded like the Greek man had left the room. *So, they can speak Greek*, thought Seraphina. More important than that, it confirmed her suspicions that she and the other girls were to be sold as slaves! She struggled in her shackles, feeling that her legs were no more tightly restrained than before. She could not move her arms at all though.

Seraphina sat there, staring into the darkness. *No matter what*, she thought, *I would rather die than be a slave.*

FIFTEEN

It was nighttime, and Seraphina was starving. The quality of the food had diminished after her attempt to escape, but she still looked forward to eating each day. She had a private cell now, but there was nothing comfortable about it. Her legs nearly stretched to the door, and the room was not kept as clean as the one where she had been held with the other girls. There were scatterings of dirt, and large ants scurried across the floor. Due to the darkness, she felt them more than she saw them. Each time an insect crawled across her skin, she wriggled and huffed. Thoughts of the Greek man and his intended fate for her and the other girls consumed her. Something had to be done. Seraphina just did not know what.

    The door to her cell opened, and in came one of the guards to feed her. The same one as usual. A thickly-built beast of a man who never spoke—not that Seraphina desired a conversation. He came in, checked her restraints, and started to feed her. As he stuffed the food in her mouth, Seraphina recoiled, taking time to chew each mouthful. The guard grunted with his usual heaving, stinking breaths, his eyebrows lowered, and a frown on his face.

It was not a pleasant sight, but at least some light came into the room during this time of day. Seraphina was grateful for that. It helped her think, and she ate as slowly as possible. This continued to test the patience of the guard, but Seraphina was in her own world.

Did the Greek see the girls this afternoon?

When will he take them?

Will he want to see me, and take me too?

She felt her heart racing, and her whole body rising and falling with each breath. The guard looked her over and finished feeding her. As he got up and turned towards the door, Seraphina tensed her upper body and launched her legs into the air. She caught him by the neck with her leg shackles, and he crashed to the ground with a thud. Before he could make a sound, Seraphina wrapped her thighs around his neck as hard as she could. Seraphina heard the man choke, and she squeezed tighter.

She was uncertain of what to do next. If she asked him to undo her leg shackles, her grip on his neck would be released and he could free himself.

'Don't say a word,' she whispered.

He responded in their usual language. Nothing she could understand.

'I know you speak Greek. Now stay quiet!'

Seraphina relaxed her thighs, and the guard gasped for air. She raised her legs and hit him on the back of the head as hard as she could with the shackle. He did not move, but she could hear him breathing. Her heart was pounding in her chest.

Seraphina then looked up at the hook to which her arms were chained to the wall. She launched her legs towards it, the sliver of light through the doorway aiding her efforts. She missed.

She sat up and leaned as far forward as she could. Seraphina threw her weight back, and once again brought her legs over her head. The leg shackle landed on the hook! Pulling with her legs, the shackle dragged the arm chains off the edge of the hook. Seraphina held up her hands, catching the chains just above her forehead. An involuntary grunt escaped her mouth as she strained forward, remembering how much effort the leg shackles had required on her first escape attempt. She heaved, desperate not to wake the unconscious guard, and managed to get them off.

She pulled one arm free from the chains, scraping skin off her arm as she did so. Through gritted teeth, Seraphina rid herself of the chains with her free hand. A drop of blood fell from her arm. As it hit the ground, a door opened in the distance. Looking down at the unconscious guard, Seraphina noticed a bloodied bruise on his head, where she had knocked him out. She could also see a club hanging from his belt. It was a nasty weapon, with spikes protruding from the heavy stone head.

She took it in hand, careful not to disturb the guard any more than was necessary. Seraphina rocked her forearm back and forth a couple of times, feeling the weight of the weapon. She stepped out into the hallway. Looking left and right, she saw the door to the cell where the other girls were being held. Footsteps. Someone was coming. Stepping back from the cells and to the edge of the hall, she tilted her head to see who was there.

It was Ourgious! He was walking towards her with Rhea. She wrapped both hands around the handle of the club, wondering how hard she could swing it. A moment later, she had her answer. He came around the corner first, and never had a chance. Seraphina swung up at his head with the club. The head of the club landed perfectly on the right side of his jaw. Ourgious' head jerked away, involuntarily spitting blood and what looked like a tooth against the wall. Rhea's height, or lack thereof, saved her from being spattered with blood. He crumpled to the floor, as Rhea gasped, looking at the thin streak of blood now decorating the wall. Seraphina held a finger to her mouth as she stared into Rhea's eyes. Rhea nodded.

Seraphina crouched down and started removing the shackles from Rhea's leg. She felt a hand wrapped around her ankle and let out a scream, then quickly brought her hand to her mouth. Then Ourgious yelled something. Seraphina picked up the club and swung it at his arm. Both girls heard Ourgious' forearm breaking, and the wounded guard screamed in agony. Seraphina swung again at his head, knocking him out cold. Seraphina looked at the club head for a moment, taken aback by her violence. In the light of the hallway, the sight was even more gruesome. Ourgious' arm had started to turn purple and Seraphina could see the blood-soaked indentations where the spikes of the club had driven into his head.

'Seraphina!' exclaimed Rhea.

She returned her attention to Rhea's shackles. 'There,' said Seraphina, releasing Rhea's legs. 'Let's go.'

The girls did not wait to see who Ourgious had been calling for. They ran out towards the field. Once outside, Seraphina told Rhea to wait. Running off to one side of the building, she found what she was looking for. The sturdy horse looked in her direction. Taking the reins, Seraphina mimicked Ourgious' movements from earlier, leading the animal back to where Rhea was waiting.

'Get on,' said Seraphina, as she crouched down to help Rhea up.

Once Seraphina was on the horse, she looked back at Rhea.

'Hold on to me as tight as you can. I've never done this before.'

'Wha—' said Rhea.

Seraphina slapped the reins down on the horse as hard as she could, and they galloped off into the night.

SIXTEEN

Thump, thump, thump. Karsas woke, sat up in his bed, and stared at the wall. He listened for the source of the sound. Blinking his eyes, and casting his gaze around the small bedroom, it took a few moments before it registered that someone was knocking on his door. Looking out of his window, he saw nothing but night sky and stars. He waited a moment, then rested his head again.

More thumping. This time, he threw off his sheets and rolled off the bed on to his feet. Then, stomping his way out of his room, he picked up the axe by his bedroom door without breaking stride. Who would be here at this hour? He swung the door open, the axe raised behind his head.

'Who is there?' said Karsas.

'It's me, sir. Ourgious.'

Setting the axe down, Karsas reached for the lamp sitting by the doorway and held it up.

'What are you do—' Karsas started to say, but he stopped talking upon seeing Ourgious' face. He could barely recognise him behind the blood and bruises.

'What happened?'

'The Hebrew girl. She escaped. Again.'

Karsas thought for a moment of picking up the axe and swinging it at the man's head. He decided he would listen first. Ourgious stepped into his house, and Karsas stepped back for a moment.

'And who said you could come in?'

'Please, sir,' said Ourgious, 'I need to sit. I had to walk here.'

'Why didn't you take the horse?'

'She took the horse, sir.'

Karsas relented and had Ourgious sit down.

'Tell me what happened.'

Ourgious was having difficulty speaking, and Karsas noticed he was holding his arm.

'What's wrong with your arm?' interrupted Karsas, as Ourgious began telling him the story.

'She hit it with a club. I think it might be broken.'

'By Zeus. Okay, tell me everything.'

Ourgious told how the Hebrew girl had attacked him. He almost referred to her by name at one point, and Karsas gave him a strange look when he paused. Karsas listened and could tell he had been completely taken by surprise. He flinched when Ourgious spoke of the unconscious guard he found in the cell.

'Who is this girl?' said Karsas.

'I don't know, sir, but she runs fast, swings a club like a warrior, and can even ride a horse. Very unlike the rest of these girls.'

Karsas grinned and stroked his chin for a moment.

'Look, Ourgious, stay here for now. My servants will attend to you and get you cleaned up. See what they can do about that arm.'

'Yes, sir. I am so sorry about this.'

'We shall deal with it later. What about Asaros?' asked Karsas, referring to the other guard.

'He was still unconscious. I made sure he was still breathing, and then came here to tell you.'

'The other girls are secure?'

'Yes.'

'Anything else?'

'I was bringing a girl back from the toilet when the Hebrew attacked me.'

Karsas' hand gripped his forehead. 'Oh, no.' He looked at Ourgious and watched his head drop.

'Two of them escaped?' he growled.

Ourgious nodded.

SEVENTEEN

There was a hint of light. As Seraphina looked ahead through the tall tree trunks, morning began to break. The faint rays of the morning sun gave off a hint of warmth, which was welcome. Thankfully, the ground was dry, but the night had been cold. Rhea was asleep on her back, but Seraphina was wide awake. She had felt her chest pulsing, then her arms. Her head. Her whole body, it felt at times. They had been riding through the forest for hours, not stopping once. Something reflected in the distance, and Seraphina saw a small lake directly ahead. She came to a stop beside a tree. Careful not to wake Rhea, she slipped off the horse, resting her friend's head on a ridge of the horse's spine.

Rhea had cried, screamed, and yelled for what seemed like an eternity when they first rode away from the prison. Seraphina had tried calming her, shouting at her, and singing to her. Nothing had worked. She had been grateful when Rhea had finally fallen asleep. Seraphina looked at Rhea's peaceful face. *She was just scared*, thought Seraphina. Looking down at her own hands, Seraphina saw they were shaking. A lot.

She tried some deep breathing to stop the shaking, but it was not working. She wondered about Ourgious. There had been no time to check if he was dead or alive. What she really wondered about is whether she had killed a man. Pressing her hands on her knees, she finally got them to stop shaking.

She walked slowly to the edge of the lake. The water was clear, and one hand after another, she lowered her arms into the water. Smelling the water first, she took a drink. It was fresh and tasted good. Seraphina drank some more and heard her friend stirring. The horse began to move too, and Seraphina rushed to tie the reins to the tree. Maybe she wasn't as awake as she thought. Putting her hand over her chest to calm herself once again, she saw Rhea staring at her.

The Greek girl shook her head and looked around. 'Whe … Wha …' she stammered. Looking down at her hands, still bound in chains, she finally got some words out. 'Can you help me with these, Seraphina?'

Seraphina helped her down from the horse and freed her hands from the chains. The two embraced for some time, and they both started to breathe slower.

'Where are we?' asked Rhea.

'I have no idea,' answered Seraphina.

'Did that really happen?'

Seraphina let out a chuckle. It relaxed her more, and she told Rhea what had happened in her cell, and how she had seen Ourgious and her coming down the hallway. Rhea stood in silence the whole time, shaking her head.

'So, here we are,' said Seraphina.

'Now what?'

Seraphina shrugged. 'I have no idea. Come and drink some water.'

The two young women drank water from the lake, as the rising sun shone on them. Rhea rubbed her shoulders and a slight smile formed on her face. Seraphina stretched her arms towards the sky, grateful for the warmth.

EIGHTEEN

Seraphina's complexion gave her a very multicultural look. At various times in her life, she had been thought of as Egyptian, Hebrew, and Greek. Being a chameleon had proved useful of late. The two young women had found a village on the edge of the forest and had spent the last week enjoying the hospitality of the locals. The village was made up of small buildings and large tents. Both Seraphina and Rhea were impressed as they watched the villagers gather resources from the forest – wood, herbs, and fruits. They spent their days talking to the villagers and regaining their strength.

Seraphina had formed the story that they had been part of a trade caravan. Having recently found themselves out of work, the pair had made their way on the horse they were given and hoped to make it to Rome to find more work.

'Rome?' one of the women had said, raising her eyebrows. 'We are a long way from Rome.'

'We got a little lost,' said Seraphina. 'Where is the nearest city?'

'We are on the outskirts of Tanais.'

Tanais. Seraphina remembered it from her geography studies. They were a long way from Rome, indeed. She had no idea how she would get there. Rhea was no help. The poor girl had been slowly unravelling and was barely keeping their story straight. She only spoke of getting home to her family in Byzantium. Rhea wept night and day, and Seraphina felt for her. Seraphina went into the room they were sharing and sat on Rhea's bed as she lay there.

'Rhea, what did you do in Byzantium?' asked Seraphina.

Rhea rolled over, turning to face Seraphina. 'I helped manage my family's lands, why?'

'I'm curious. What do you mean by manage?'

'I kept records of the amounts paid by tenants, and amounts we had to pay for maintenance, taxes, and so on.'

Seraphina raised her eyebrows. 'That's a useful skill, Rhea.'

'Why are you asking me this?'

'I have to get to Rome. You want to go to Byzantium. I have been thinking about this.'

'And?'

'I think we should go to Tanais and find a way of getting you to Byzantium.'

'Can't you come with me?' pleaded Rhea.

Seraphina shook her head. 'No, I'm sorry but I can't. It's a long way, and I have to get to Rome.' Seraphina was unsure if Byzantium was in the same direction as Rome, but her recollection told her that Rhea would be alone for at least part of the journey.

Rhea nodded her head and sniffled. 'I understand, but how will I get to Byzantium?'

'Maybe you can work for someone and earn the money to get home. I honestly don't know.'

'Very well. Perhaps we can talk to these women. They have helped us so much.'

'Perhaps.'

Part of Seraphina wanted to go home as well, to Alexandria. She would be reunited with Afiz and Maximus. Who knows, maybe even

Quintus had found his way back there. Indulging the thought for a moment, she knew that she had to get to Rome. She would find Cicero and somehow convince him to help the rest of those girls stuck on the other side of the forest in that terrible place.

NINETEEN

It was a large tent, not unlike ones Seraphina had seen in Alexandria. She had been told to enter and wait to be spoken to. Seraphina did as she was told. The tent was sparsely furnished, with a set of table and chairs to one side, and a large sleeping mat on the other. She could see the milky white cloth of the tent had not a single blemish on it, and she admired the height of the tent as well as its perfect symmetry. Drawing her gaze down from the ceiling to the rear and centre of the tent, there stood another chair. This one was taller than the others, with a few steps leading up to the seat, like rungs of a ladder.

The woman's name was Tamura, and she was the matriarch of the village. Contrasting with the warm nature of her people, she was a stern and strict type, who wore a perpetual frown on her heavy face. Her squat frame matched her round head, and her dark hair was pulled back and tied behind her neck in some fashion. The chair seemed to struggle under her weight. Tamura's mood matched her appearance, and Seraphina would have preferred to be elsewhere at that moment.

Tamura had been told about the pair of girls who had arrived but a week ago. She examined the young woman in front of her without saying anything. There was a strange look to her. Her features, her complexion. Yet she spoke perfect Greek, so Tamura's curiosity did not extend too far. She told Seraphina to sit.

'What do you want, child?' boomed Tamura, causing Seraphina to flinch.

'I was told to come and ask you for help,' said Seraphina.

'With what?'

'My friend, Rhea. She needs to get back to Byzantium.'

'And what am I to do about that, child?'

She spat the word 'child' out as if it were an insult. Seraphina continued, 'well, she is a good accountant, and should be able to earn her way. I'm not asking for any type of special treatment, my lady. I was hoping you could advise me on the best way to help my friend get home.'

'Why is she not here speaking for herself?'

'She is not well,' said Seraphina. 'I think it's important to get her home to her family.'

'Where will you go?'

'Home. To Alexandria.' Seraphina thought it best not to tell this woman everything.

'In Egypt? How did the two of you come to know one another?'

'I was working in Byzantium,' lied Seraphina. 'I met Rhea there when we both came across the caravan that we recently finished working on.'

'I see,' said Tamura. 'Very well. I believe one of our men is going to Byzantium in the next month or so. His brother has a business there. I will arrange for your friend to go with him. She will pay for passage either with work here, or there in Byzantium.'

'Thank you, my lady.'

'Understand, child,' Tamura said as she pointed a finger in Seraphina's direction, 'that she must complete the work she agrees to, even once she is in Byzantium.'

'I understand, and I will make sure she understands this too.'

'Good. You have your horse, so you can leave at once for Alexandria.' Seraphina hesitated for a moment. 'Do you have any problem with that, child?'

'No, but—'

'My people have been very good to you, and we will take care of your friend until she goes to Byzantium. We will not continue to house and feed you in the meantime, however.'

Fair enough, thought Seraphina. 'Yes, my lady. I understand.'

'Goodbye, child.'

TWENTY

Seraphina had spoken to Rhea and the women they were staying with. They were so kind, but there was a feeling Seraphina could not shake. It was about Tamura, the gruff old woman. She had undoubtedly helped them, especially Rhea. Seraphina tried to tell herself this, and that the best thing for Rhea was to go home. There was something amiss, though. She even spoke to the man who was to take Rhea to Byzantium, and he seemed a good and decent person.

The villagers helped Seraphina with some supplies for her journey.

'How will you get home, Seraphina?' asked one of the women.

'I will work my way. I always do.'

'Be careful, Seraphina. There are bandits across these lands. They would relish the opportunity to take advantage of a young woman.'

Seraphina nodded, 'I will be careful, I promise.'

Once everything was prepared, Seraphina went inside to say goodbye to Rhea. Tearful as always, Rhea hugged her tightly.

'Thank you so much, Seraphina.'

'You are welcome. Please take good care of yourself, alright?'

Rhea nodded and sniffled. 'I will, I promise.' She looked down at the floor.

'What's wrong?' asked Seraphina.

'I still can't believe what you did to save me from that place. I'll never forget it and hope I can repay you some day. Thank you again.'

'The best thanks I could get is you going home and enjoying your life. You deserve that, Rhea.'

'I love you, Seraphina.'

'I love you too, Rhea. I must go now.'

'Be safe, please.'

Seraphina smiled at her friend for the last time and got on her horse. He felt sturdy underneath her, and Seraphina looked up to the sky, a brief smile crossing her face. Riding out of the village, she headed west. She gripped the reins more tightly, and her jaw hardened. She wanted to look back at Rhea, but at that moment, it felt hard to move. She focused on the horse and its reins and kept her gaze fixed in front of her. She dared not think about how she was going to achieve her goal. It seemed impossible.

TWENTY ONE

After a few hours, she noticed the coast and the sea on her left. Seraphina decided to ride alongside the coast, and only to ride during the day. She was mindful of the advice she had been given, and the last thing she wanted was to attract bandits. Just in case, she had kept the guard's club. It was now stowed safely out of sight with the supplies the kind villagers had given her.

She came to a gap in the treeline and stopped. The view of the sea was beautiful. Off to the right, she could see a large peninsula protruding into the water. In the distance, there were boats and what looked like a settlement or two. Her mind was not fully in the present moment. Seraphina could almost hear Afiz scolding her for her thoughts being elsewhere. She couldn't help it though. She worried about Rhea, and her mind kept coming back to Tamura. *It was fine*, she thought. Rhea would be home soon, and she would never see Tamura or her village again.

Behind her was a clearing. A perfect circle of trees surrounding a very flat bed of grass. It was out of place when compared to the rest of her surroundings. Seraphina walked around the circle, touching the bark of each of the trees. As she did this, she breathed in and out through her nostrils. Deeply. It soothed her, and she circled the trees a few more times. The fresh breeze from the sea splashed against her face, and a moment of calm came over her. It was an unfamiliar feeling, given recent events. When she thought about it, the last time she had been calm was months ago. In Alexandria, before she had remembered her parents or any of her past.

Taking her gaze away from the trees, Seraphina looked towards the middle of the clearing. The centre was flat, in the shape of a circle. There was very little grass on the circle, and she walked towards it. Once she could see more closely, her body swayed back away. A pattern was etched into the ground. It was as if a series of concentric circles had been drawn from the centre moving outwards, but different parts of each circle were missing. Seraphina had never come across such a sign, or symbol. Whatever it was, it had not been formed by accident.

She stared at it a little longer, and then looked around. The breeze had died down, and it was very quiet. Even though it was the middle of the day, an eerie feeling came over Seraphina. She could feel her skin tingle, and she marched straight towards the horse to untie him and get away from this place. Grabbing the reins, she looked back at the clearing. There was something compelling about the clearing. Seraphina dropped the reins and folded her arms, pacing back towards the circle. She stood over it, then turned and looked at the sea. Everything was still.

Lowering herself to the ground, with legs crossed, she meditated. Just as she had learned to from reading the texts of the Hindus, Seraphina focused. She looked behind closed eyelids to the point between her eyebrows. Then, in her mind, she made the same sound over, and over again. That point became bright, and she started to notice colours. Blue, green, then blue again, and then some red. She allowed the light show in her mind to continue and ensured the sound of the mantra kept ringing in her heart, and in her mind.

Seraphina felt calm in her entire being, and the colours she saw were replaced by white. It started as a light in the same place, and soon expanded to being all she could see. She held her gaze in the same place, and the white became increasingly intense. Then the brightness became so strong that it seemed to push her. Losing her balance, she fell back and opened her eyes. She turned her head to the left and right. It was dark.

She placed her hands on the ground and could feel the hard grass. The light of the stars showed the same pattern on the ground as had been there before. Looking towards the sea, she could see the moonlight reflecting off the water. The silhouette of the large horse was there. Everything was as it had been, except hours had passed. Seraphina pushed herself off the ground and stood up. Palms facing the ground, she took one step. Then another. *Okay, that was weird*, she thought. *Maybe I fell asleep.*

Except she did not feel as though she had slept at all. She shrugged and shook her body. Walking up to the horse, she admired the deep brown that extended from the points of his ears, along his mane, to the tip of his tail. He was a huge, strong creature. For a few moments, she stroked the white fur that ran down the middle of his face. The same colour coated his belly and lower legs. Seraphina smiled, as he seemed to enjoy the attention.

'I think it's time I gave you a name,' said Seraphina. Looking out at the water, and then up at the sky, she returned her attention to the horse. 'Luna. How about that?'

TWENTY TWO

Seraphina felt the prong in her stomach. It jerked her out of sleep, and before she opened her eyes, her arms were folded over her belly in defence. Looking up, all she saw was the shadow of a man in the morning sunlight. She rolled away and got to her feet. She raised her hands. The assault had stopped for now. Then, a deep stern voice saying words she did not understand.

What a way to wake up. Her eyes adjusted to the light, and she saw her assailant. A tall, thin man in odd-looking clothes. His skin was wrinkled and swarthy, but his eyes were wide and engaging. They were the colour of hazelnuts. His hair was a much darker shade of brown, thin and unkempt. It was a full head of hair, though baldness looked to be lurking in the man's near future. He looked somewhat Egyptian, Seraphina decided. On second glance, she could see his garments were of a more traditional style. She had seen older Egyptian men wear such things in Alexandria.

'What are you doing, striking me like that?' asked Seraphina.

'What am I doing?' said the old man. 'What are you doing, sleeping in my home?'

'What home? This is grassland. I see no home.'

'You didn't notice anything different about this place?' asked the old man, gesturing with his staff to the same spot where Seraphina had meditated. The same spot where, in fact, she had fallen asleep.

'I don't even rem—I mean, I saw it, but … Who are you?' demanded Seraphina.

The old man shook his head. 'You have some nerve, child.'

It was too much. The pirates. The prison. Escaping. Now this strange old man poking her in the stomach with his staff, saying something about his home being a circle on the ground. Seraphina walked away. She found a tree, and sat against it, looking off into the distance.

The old man watched her and calmed himself. Seraphina glanced at him. Seeing the amused look on his face, she turned away again in a huff. Taking his time, the man paced towards her and halted before getting too close.

'I am sorry, child.'

'Don't call me child! My name is Seraphina.'

'I am sorry, Seraphina. This is my home, at least the home I have made for myself. There are many bandits in these lands, and I was surprised to see you sleeping on my shrine. No one ever comes here.'

'Do I look like a bandit?' snapped Seraphina.

The old man crouched and apologised again. 'I am Keb. I can imagine that was quite a shock. Maybe I can help you. What brings you here?'

His tone had softened a lot. Seraphina unclenched, releasing her arms from her knees. 'It's a very long story, Keb. What kind of name is that?'

'Egyptian. You should know,' replied Keb, smirking with a knowing twinkle in his eye.

Seraphina smiled. Keb offered his hand. 'Come on, get up. Let's go and sit by the water.' Seraphina took his hand and got to her feet. The two of them walked alongside each other towards the edge of the sea.

'How did you know I'm Egyptian?' asked Seraphina.

'I didn't say you were Egyptian. I just said you'd know an Egyptian name, or an Egyptian man if you saw one.'

Seraphina said nothing. She looked over the vast sea, which disappeared over the horizon.

'You have been through a lot, haven't you?'

Seraphina put her hands on her hips and stared at Keb with a slight frown on her face.

'I'll let you tell me when you want to,' he said, looking out at the sea.

'It's a very long story.'

'All in good time, my child … I mean, Seraphina.'

Seraphina laughed at this and turned to look back at the clearing. She felt Keb watching her and was reluctant to face him.

'Something strange happened here, didn't it?' he asked.

Seraphina looked directly into his eyes this time. 'Who are you, really?'

'Just an old man living in the woods. Some say a crazy old man, though I suppose it has been a long time since anyone has really spoken of me.'

'What do you do out here?'

'Go on adventures,' Keb replied.

'What kind of adventures?'

'You should know.' Another smirk.

'Alright. You must stop that. Don't be cryptic and tell me what you mean.'

'Tell me what happened here yesterday, and you'll know exactly what I mean. Yet, you already know, don't you?'

Seraphina walked back towards the clearing. In the same way as she had yesterday, she walked around. Touching each of the trees, that same sense of calm came over her.

'What is this place?'

'I told you. It is the place where I've built my home.' Seeing Seraphina's eyes widen, he held up a hand. 'I am not being cryptic. What you sense here is a result of what I have built. How I have built my home.

In time, I can explain. That is, if you want to know.'

'Perhaps.'

'So, you never told me, what are you doing here?'

'I am on my way to Rome,' said Seraphina. Straightaway, she covered her mouth with her hand.

'You can trust me, Seraphina.'

'How? I don't know you. A few minutes ago, you were attacking me with that thing,' she said, pointing to Keb's staff.

'Why do you need to go to Rome?'

Seraphina shook her head. 'Really, I must be going.'

'Maybe I can help you. It doesn't look like you have many supplies, and I know these lands very well. I can give you some guidance that will keep you safe.'

'You know the lands from here to Rome?'

'Your journey is a dangerous one. Trust me and let me help you. Give me a day to show you what I mean, and then you can decide.'

That seems fair, she thought. 'Very well, Keb. I can spare a day. Besides, I could use the advice.'

'Splendid decision, my dear Seraphina. Before we get started, how about we have something to eat?'

'Yes, please. I'm starving.'

The smirk was back. 'Great. What would you like?'

TWENTY THREE

She limped into the house. Her father, seeing her, came straight to her aid. He supported her weight and helped her to a seat.

'Thank you, father,' said Seraphina.

Josef smiled at his daughter. 'Leaping off buildings again, my darling?'

Seraphina giggled. 'Maybe.'

'She thinks she can fly,' came a voice from the kitchen. Her mother walked out to examine her daughter, wiping her hands with a cloth, and smiling at Seraphina.

'She can,' said Josef.

'You only encourage her,' Rebekah shot back at her husband.

'Well, if encouraging her to be an adventurer is my lot in life, then so be it.'

Rebekah could not help but smile at this. Her gaze lingered on him as he left the room, heading towards the back of the house and his workshop. She took a seat next to her daughter.

'Alright. Let me have a look at you,' she said, lifting Seraphina's foot on to her knee.

'Argh,' said Seraphina.

'Don't be such a baby. You're not a child anymore, Seraphina. You're a young woman now.'

'Yes, Mother. I know.'

'Look at your knee!' she said, cleaning up the dried blood with a damp towel. Trailing her gaze down her daughter's leg, she felt the heaviness in her ankle. 'Is this swollen?'

'Well, I was limping for a reason,' sniped Seraphina, grinning at her mother.

Rebekah shook her head and smiled. She dabbed at the bloodied spots until her leg was clean. Then, she unrolled a longer piece of fabric, looking at it from end to end. Finding the end she wanted, she placed it on Seraphina's ankle.

'Argh.'

'You actually fell off a rooftop?' asked Rebekah, wrapping the bandage around her daughter's ankle.

'Tripped, actually. I didn't see the edge properly.' She winced a little. The bandage was tight, but she knew it needed to be.

'You're not in bad shape, considering. Was it a high building?'

Seraphina nodded.

'There,' said Rebekah. 'All done.'

'Thank you, Mother,' said Seraphina, moving to get up.

'Just a moment, darling.'

'What?'

Rebekah looked at her daughter, who relaxed back into her seat.

'Your father and I will have very little to do with how your life goes from this point. I want you to remember two things. One, if you ever need to remember us, just hold this,' said Rebekah, holding on to the silver ring hanging from her neck. 'Second, and more important, learn to slow down and take in the lessons that life has to offer.'

...

Seraphina's eyes sprang open and her hand went straight to her chest. She held the ring in her hand and took a moment to remember where she was. Keb was asleep near the sea, and Luna was chewing some grass. Gazing to the ground and blinking, she felt the ring between her fingers.

As she came out of her slumber, she realised it had been a dream. There had been many memories of her parents. This one was different. A dream in which she was fully grown, just as she was in this very moment. It was no memory! Her mother had been speaking to her in the dream. Something about slowing down. Bringing the ring in front of her face, she read the familiar inscription.

Our love.

Seraphina looked around. Everything was unfamiliar. The sea. Luna, her new companion. Keb, the old man whose sanity she was not yet sure of. She missed her parents more than ever.

TWENTY FOUR

Seraphina was just about to go back to sleep when she noticed that Keb was waking up. *Why was he getting up in the middle of the night?* Watching him, she wondered if she was still dreaming. He stood up and started to blast air out of his mouth. Loudly. He was taking breaths in then blasting them out while throwing his body forward. Then he held his arms out to his side and, with his whole body shaking, breathed rapidly.

Seraphina scratched her head. She started walking towards him, then got the feeling that he was not to be disturbed. Next was a series of movements. Most of them were very slow. He was breathing audibly through most of them. It was strange as anything, yet also fascinating. Seraphina sat next to Luna, stroking his face, and watching the old Egyptian man do his odd form of exercise.

Now he was sitting. With this came another series of movements, and finally he lay down. He was not moving at all. For a moment, Seraphina wondered if he was dead. There was no indication that he was even breathing. After a few minutes, she got up to check on him and just then, he popped back up. Seraphina went back to her seat and wondered what he would do next.

It was even more odd. His hands were formed into a shape, and he was moving them up and down in sync with his breathing, saying different words as he moved. Well, not saying. Not quite singing though. Something in between. She tried to listen.

'Lammm,' came the sound from Keb again. 'Yammm.'

Keb came into stillness again. This time he was sitting upright. He stayed this way for quite some time. Seraphina had never seen someone remain so still. She looked past Keb, to the sea, and a long breath left her as she sighed. Another welcome moment of calm. There was even a smile on her face. Then she looked off to her right, to the west. Rome was out there somewhere. *How on earth am I going to get there?*

'Good morning, Seraphina,' said Keb.

She looked up, and he was standing in front of her, smiling. 'Good morning.'

'How did you sleep?'

'Quite well, thank you,' she replied, getting to her feet.

'How's your horse faring? He looks happy when you stroke him like that.'

'I think he's alright.' For now, Seraphina had decided not to tell Keb too much.

'I'm surprised you are awake so early.'

'Well, something woke me up. Then I saw what you were doing down there by the water.'

Keb nodded, his eyebrows raised.

'What was that?'

'That…is an ancient science.'

'I see. Does it have a name?'

'Not that I know of.'

'You said it's a science. It is not one I've ever read of. What's its function?'

'How many sciences have you read of?' asked Keb.

'Many. I have spent most of my life studying the sciences of our world.'

'The sciences of our universe, too?'

Seraphina raised her eyebrows. 'I'm not sure,' said Seraphina with a shake of her head. 'So, what does this science do?'

'It energises me.'

'Is that all?'

'Far from it, but it is not something so easily explained. In fact, it is best experienced for oneself. Having knowledge of this science will never be as rewarding as learning how to practice it and use its benefits.'

'Does it have anything to do with where our food came from yesterday?' asked Seraphina.

'That's an interesting question. Why do you ask?'

Seraphina looked around and gestured with her hand. 'There's nothing here. You have no weapons for hunting or tools for preparing and lighting a fire.' Looking to the sea, she continued, 'we didn't eat fish yesterday, rather some other type of meat. Rich and gamey, not unlike lamb. Those vegetables were cooked perfectly as well.'

'Did you enjoy the food?'

'I did.'

'Are you glad you stayed for a day?'

'Yes, Keb, but I'm not sure—'

'If I helped you?' he interrupted.

'Well, yes.'

Keb looked into her eyes. 'That is for you to decide, Seraphina. You have a big journey ahead of you, and I'm not only talking about the distance between here and Rome. There is much inside of you that must be traversed. To prepare you.'

'To prepare me for what?'

'For the life you want for yourself. That you see for yourself.'

Seraphina frowned at him. 'How do you know what I want for myself? What I see for myself? You don't know anything about me.' Her voice was raised now.

'I don't know, Seraphina,' said Keb, keeping his tone gentle. 'You do, and it is important for you to deal with your past before you can get there.'

Seraphina shook her head. 'You don't know what you're talking about, old man.'

'Believe me, I do,' Keb said, reaching out and placing a hand on her shoulder. 'I may not know everything there is to know about you, but I see real strength in you. Spirit. And pain. That strength and spirit that I see, that everyone sees, will never be what it can be unless you let go of your pain.'

She had no words. Not for the first time, she wondered who this old man was. She shook her head as she glared at him. Clenching her fists, she tried to get some words out.

'What were you dreaming about?' asked Keb.

The question disarmed her. 'My mother,' she answered.

'Has it been a long time since you saw her?'

'You could say that.'

'How long?'

'I haven't seen either of my parents since I was six years old.'

'Oh, I'm sorry, Seraphina.'

'It's alright,' said Seraphina, looking down at the ground as if she were looking through it.

A few moments passed, and Seraphina took a seat on the ground. Keb sensed they had talked enough for the time being. He sat next to her, not too close, and aside from the sounds of nature around them, there was silence.

TWENTY FIVE

Seraphina smelled the delicious stew as Keb placed the bowl in her hands. A plate of bread sat between them, and she looked at Keb for some sign they could start.

'Please, eat,' he said, smiling at her.

She devoured the stew and most of the bread. *At least my appetite isn't suffering*, she thought. Keb ate at a much calmer pace, closing his eyes during each mouthful. A contented smile came across his face every few moments. Seraphina stared at her empty bowl, and then looked back at Keb. He was enthralled by the meal. *Maybe I could stand to eat a little slower myself.*

Next time, she thought. Her mind then shifted gears and she realised she had stayed longer than a day. She needed to get to Rome. Then she brought her attention back to the bowl. It was made of the same bark on the trees around them. Same with the plate that the bread sat on. It looked as though the bark had been bent, and then several pieces of it pressed together to make the bowl. The plate was a much simpler effort.

'Did you make these?' asked Seraphina.

Keb opened his eyes, coming out of his trance.

'Sorry,' said Seraphina. 'I didn't mean to interrupt.'

'That's quite alright. What did you say?'

'I asked if you made these.'

'Yes, I did. Do you like them?'

'They are lovely. Rustic.' She giggled at her own sense of humour.

'Why thank you,' said Keb, smiling across at his dinner companion.

Seraphina let Keb finish the rest of his meal in silence. She looked the bowl over once more then walked over to Luna. As usual, he was happy eating his grass and keeping an eye on the sea. Seraphina had adopted the habit of walking him along the shore every morning. She marvelled at the gentle nature of the huge steed. Seraphina looked at him and stroked his face in the way he had become accustomed to. Luna was the latest in a series of unlikely friends she had made.

Her thoughts turned to Quintus at that moment. She was beginning to think about him less often. This caused an inescapable feeling of guilt. The two had fallen in love, no doubt. Quintus had made the decision to stand against his father, who was his only family. He had lost his dear uncle, and then his father. He had not hesitated to join Seraphina on the voyage to Rome, and now she had no idea where he was. Even that was because those horrible men wanted to kidnap her.

Seraphina kept telling herself that Quintus was safe with Cicero, and they had made it to Rome. As she said this to herself, her head would shake involuntarily. She continued to hope, and besides, there was nothing she could do.

'Wasn't that delicious?' said Keb, coming towards Seraphina and Luna from the clearing.

'It was.' Keb was looking at her with that grin on his face again. 'So, are you going to tell me where this food is coming from? I know you're not gathering it and cooking it. That was chicken we had tonight. I'm quite sure I didn't see you chasing chickens earlier today.'

Keb laughed at this. 'Maybe I did, and you weren't paying attention.'

'Keb, please tell me.'

'Is this why you're staying? To find out how I'm providing this delicious food.'

'Well,' laughed Seraphina, 'that, and the fact that I'm very hungry. Who knows when I'll eat this well again?'

Keb laughed again. 'Very well, I'll tell you. Remember the science I spoke of the other day?'

Seraphina nodded.

'Well,' continued Keb, 'it is a spiritual science. It centres around how to move energy, both within our bodies and in the external world. The whole universe is made up of energy, did you know that?'

Seraphina shook her head. She had read about such ideas in one text or another, but it had never made much sense to her.

'I have been learning and practising this science since I was a small boy. Over time, one can master the ability to move energy in a multitude of ways.'

'Are you telling me ...'

'Just let me explain,' Keb tried to interrupt.

'... that you are conjuring this food out of nothing?' Seraphina asked incredulously.

Keb held his hands up, gesturing for Seraphina to stop. 'It is not so simple. There is no nothing.'

'Maybe we should sit,' said Seraphina.

'Good idea,' said Keb. He gestured with his palms turned upwards, and continued, 'this air, it is not nothing. It is made up of the same energy as that sea over there, the trees over here, Luna over there, and everything around us.' He motioned to each in turn as he spoke.

Seraphina leaned forward, hands on her knees, trying to think. She rocked back and forth. On one hand, what this man was saying was crazy. On the other, she noticed a sensation deep inside that said there was some truth to his words.

'Perhaps I should have started with something small,' said Keb. 'I know this is a lot to consider.'

'It's alright, Keb.' Seraphina was still rocking back and forth. She eyed everything around her with suspicion, as if it had all somehow changed in the last few moments.

Keb could not help but be amused. 'Try not to analyse my words, Seraphina. Instead, sit still and try to feel or otherwise sense if there is truth in what I'm saying.'

Seraphina's gaze softened, as did her countenance. The rocking slowed, and she took in her surroundings.

'It may help to close your eyes,' said Keb.

She looked to him then closed her eyes. Her body became still, and her breath deepened. *Sure, everything feels the same now*, she thought. Then she opened her eyes. Keb looked at her, and she closed her eyes again.

'I don't know, Keb. It's a bit much. I feel more comfortable with the idea that you were secretly chasing chickens this afternoon. Are you sure you weren't?' she asked, with her eyes still closed.

'You do have quite the sense of humour.'

'I thought I had a good imagination, too. Clearly, it has its limits.'

Keb laughed again. 'That's probably enough for today.'

'Enough of what?'

'All your questions will be answered in good time. For now, it's time for us to sleep.'

'Very well. So, I can stay another day?'

'Don't you need to get moving? To Rome?'

Seraphina nodded. 'I do, but...'

'You are welcome to stay as long as you wish.'

'Thank you,' she said, smiling.

'It's my pleasure. Good night, Seraphina.'

TWENTY SIX

The lack of movement was bothering her. Her time in the prison had been very restrictive and the past couple of days here with Keb had mainly been restricted to walking Luna in the mornings. Then there were her talks with Keb, which typically involved long strolls along the seashore.

Keb was not awake yet. Even Luna was still deep in slumber. Seraphina got up and started to run along the coastline. The ground was uneven and very different from the streets of Alexandria. *If I'm going to stay here,* she thought, *I had better get to know the land a little.* It felt good to run, and after some time, she had worked up to a light sprint. There was precious little to jump off, though. The occasional rock or mound, but nothing she could really leap off. Ahead, she saw a low hanging branch, and she grabbed at it.

Her speed swung her up into the air, and the weight of her legs pulled her arms off the branch. She somersaulted through the air, with no idea of where she would land. Seraphina sensed something solid underneath her feet and she pressed down into it. Holding her arms out to the side, she balanced and looked out to the horizon. She hopped down, taking a seat on the tree branch she had landed on.

She always felt good when she moved like that, and a big smile adorned her face. Her fingers came to her chest, grasping the silver ring that hung around her neck. Seraphina could feel the letters inscribed on it, and she said a prayer for her parents and for Quintus, Afiz, and Maximus. As often as she thought about Quintus, she wondered where he was. Maybe he had found his way back to Alexandria. He could be with Afiz and Maximus at this very moment. The thought comforted her, and she allowed her mind to settle.

'What are you doing up there?' came a whisper from the ground below, interrupting the silence.

Seraphina looked down to see Keb staring up. The look on his face mimicked the way she had often looked at him since they had met.

'I just found my way up here,' she said.

'It's very high up there. Maybe you should come down.'

'In a moment, I will.'

Seraphina smiled. Keb reminded her of Afiz in some ways. There was a caring nature there. That was something she appreciated, particularly considering recent events. She dropped down to a lower branch, then leaned back and swung towards the ground, landing on her feet.

'Quite the gymnast, aren't you?'

'It has always been a hobby of mine,' said Seraphina.

'So,' said Keb, starting to walk, 'tell me what is taking you to Rome.'

Seraphina followed him. She wanted to talk about it. Maybe there was danger, but, for now, she trusted Keb. The catharsis of having someone listen was worth it.

She gave the full story for context. Starting with her life in Alexandria, she spoke of the recovered memories of her parents, and everything that had happened with Quintus and Rufio.

'Fascinating,' said Keb.

'I'm nowhere near finished.'

'Sorry to interrupt.'

She continued to her meeting with Cicero, and the plan to head to Rome. Then the pirate attack, and where she had found herself in

Tanais. Finally, she spoke of the initial escape attempt, getting away with Rhea and to how she had come to be in her present situation.

Keb's eyes were wide, his eyebrows raised. 'That is incredible. I sensed you had been through a lot, but I had no idea of just how much you'd endured.'

'Yes. So now I don't know where Quintus is, or if he and Cicero even survived the attack. Rhea should be safe for now.'

'And you're going to Rome to find Cicero and hopefully Quintus too?'

'Correct. I also want to tell them about the prison, the pirates, and the other girls.'

'You want to rescue them?' asked Keb.

'Well.' Seraphina paused for a moment. 'Yes. Yes, I do. They're kidnapping girls and selling them into slavery. It doesn't seem like this is the first time. I heard them speak to a slave trader ...'

'And?'

'It seemed like this is something they've been doing for quite some time.'

'I see. So, what's your plan?' Keb had stopped walking now, engrossed by Seraphina's story.

Seraphina stopped too. 'Get to Rome, find Cicero, and convince him to help. I didn't get to know him all that well, but I sensed he's an influential man.'

'Let's hope so, for the sake of those girls.'

'What do you think?'

'Of what?'

'Of my plan,' said Seraphina, shrugging, and turning her hands upwards.

Keb folded his arms across his chest. 'Well, the getting to Rome part may prove the hardest of all.'

'You said before that there's a lot of danger between here and there.'

'Yes, and I've encountered some of it in the past.'

'What do you suggest?'

'A disguise,' said Keb with his signature grin.

'A disguise? Disguised as what? Or who?'

'A boy. You will encounter much less trouble if you appear as a young man. Even better, a young man who is armed.'

Seraphina shook her head in disbelief. 'How will I disguise myself as a boy?'

'I have a few ideas. You'll need to lower the tone of your voice as well.'

She looked at Luna, resting in the distance. 'This is crazy,' she said, thinking aloud.

'You're right, Seraphina, but no less crazy than what you've come through so far. How important is it for you to get to Rome?'

'I must get there,' she said, looking back towards Keb. I need to know what happened to Quintus. If Cicero is alive, that's where he will be.'

'Then you must go.'

'When?'

'Tomorrow, at first light.'

'What will we do today?' asked Seraphina.

'I'm going to get you ready.'

TWENTY SEVEN

Seraphina lay still and kept her eyes closed. Keb had been moving around her for what felt like hours now. He would place his palms on some part of her, hum, and breathe. Then he would tap her on different joints with his fingers. She had no idea what he was doing but endured it, nevertheless.

'Alright,' he said. 'You can get up now.'

Finally, thought Seraphina.

'You're strong enough to make the journey.'

'Why, thank you, Keb,' she said, smiling.

'I did remove some energy blockages I found, and you will probably notice the effect of that over the next couple of days.'

'Energy blockages?'

'Everything is energy, remember?' said Keb.

'Yes, but what blockages did I have?'

'I don't want to overload you with information before you travel. We have many other things to do to get you ready. I just wanted you to know.'

'Are you talking about the energy centres along my spine?' she asked.

Keb's mouth dropped open. 'How did you—'

'I remember reading about it once. Not long before I left Alexandria, I took a lot of interest in Hindu texts.'

Keb nodded as she spoke.

Seraphina continued, 'that's how I learned to meditate. I recall something about how all human beings derive their energy from the spine. There are specific points along the spine that contain energy centres. Am I getting this right?'

'Yes.'

'I had thought those texts were speaking of energy in the sense of what we need to move, to digest food, and other things we do each day. You know, so we don't become tired halfway through the day and need to sleep.'

'That is correct, but what you read also refers to the energy that flows through all of nature. The energy centres you speak of each have a specific purpose.'

Seraphina tilted her head. 'A specific purpose?'

'Yes. One affects how we think. Another, how we express ourselves. Then, how we love.' Keb pointed to his chest as he said this.

'They're the same in every person?'

'Correct.'

'What else? How many are there?'

'Quite a few. There is also an energy centre that relates to our emotions. What we feel, and how those feelings show outwardly, for example.'

'Fascinating.'

Keb smiled. 'Now, we have to think about this disguise.'

Seraphina held a hand up. 'Before that, do you think ... maybe I could stay longer? I could learn more about this energetic science you speak of.'

'Yes, but you need to be getting to your friends in Rome. Then there are the girls being held in that prison you told me about.'

Seraphina sighed. 'You are right. Perhaps I could come back?'

'Perhaps. I am going to give you some exercises to do. You can practice these wherever you are.'

'And?'

'And they will give you what you need.'

Seraphina shook her head. 'I don't understand.'

'One of the most important things for you may be letting go of the need to understand everything.'

Seraphina looked at him, frowning. Her eyes were narrowed in concentration.

'Trust me, Seraphina. We'll get to those exercises later. For now, let's figure out this disguise. You won't last long looking like that.'

'I'm sure I can defend myself, Keb. I did escape a group of ruthless pirates, you know.'

'Yes, but from what you told me, you didn't need to fight them. It's best we do as much as we can, so fighting becomes the absolute last resort if you encounter any danger.'

'I like the sound of that,' said Seraphina, a smile returning to her face.

'With any luck, you'll be able to avoid any dangers that come your way without needing to defend yourself.'

'I like the sound of that even better.'

Keb rubbed his hands together. 'Let's get started, then.'

TWENTY EIGHT

Keb stood back and admired the transformation. Seraphina's mouth was bent into a strained expression. She felt her hair with her fingers. It was much, much shorter. She felt almost bald, but actually, a thick layer of hair remained. A long, wide piece of fabric had been wrapped tightly around her chest, flattening her breasts. A long, heavy tunic replaced the dress the Greek village women had given her. The metamorphosis was completed by a thick robe covering her entire body.

'I feel … strange,' said Seraphina.

'I'm not surprised. You look like a young man,' Keb replied, rubbing his chin. Then he pointed. 'Try running to that tree and back.'

Seraphina launched into a sprint as Keb watched. With little effort, she dashed to the tree and back.

'It looks like your running is unaffected.'

She smiled and shrugged, unsurprised. If there was one thing she was confident of, it was her athletic ability. Seraphina shook her body, settling into her new clothes.

Keb walked to a nearby tree and crouched down to retrieve something. 'I found something in your supplies that might be of use,' he said as he held up a thick leather belt. The guard's club was attached. 'I hope you don't mind.'

Seraphina could see that the dried blood on the club had been cleaned off. 'No, not at all.'

Keb tied the belt around her waist. The club hung from it, next to her right hip.

'Thank you, Keb.'

'My pleasure. Now, you can wear it like this. Or if you think it better to conceal the weapon, you can put the belt on underneath the robe.'

'Which do you think is better? asked Seraphina, gripping the club.

'Fighting is a last resort, right?'

Seraphina nodded. 'Underneath.'

'Good thinking. In the morning, I will give you some supplies for the journey. Mainly food that you can keep that will sustain both you and Luna for the journey from here to Rome.'

'Thank you, Keb. I really do appreciate you helping me like this.'

'Now it's time for me to give you what will really help you.'

'You're going to teach me those exercises?' Seraphina said with wide eyes and a smile on her face.

Keb nodded. 'Take off that heavy robe and your weapon. Sit here.'

Seraphina was on the ground in a couple of seconds. She looked up for her next instruction.

'Calm yourself, Seraphina. Now, you've mentioned that you meditate. How often?'

'Here and there. Either when the mood strikes, or when I've been in a place that gives me a calm sensation.'

Keb nodded. 'Well, I'm going to show you a series of exercises that will maximise the benefits of meditation.'

'Benefits? You mean I'll be able to conjure food as well?'

'The ability to conjure a plate of food is meaningless when compared to the true power of these practices.'

'Really?'

'Let me come at this another way,' said Keb, laughing. 'I will teach you to prepare yourself for meditation, and you are to follow these exercises daily. At least once a day. In the early morning is best. It will help you to sense, and later control, the flow of energy within you. Over time, you will notice yourself getting very strong senses about your surroundings—people, places, and events that may occur.'

Seraphina nodded. Keb got her to stand and asked her to follow the movements he made. As she did, he gave various instructions on how to breathe during certain movements. This went on for some time. Standing movements. Movements while lying down on her back. Seated movements. Each set of movements included certain positions that were held for a fixed number of breaths. Seraphina did her best to follow and listen. Sure enough, during some parts of the exercises, she felt various sensations throughout her body.

'Just notice that feeling,' Keb would say. 'Notice that thought, and don't try to do anything with it.' He said that one several times. By the time the exercises were over, Seraphina was exhausted. It wasn't the physical effort; rather, trying to follow Keb's instructions not to analyse and latch on to her thoughts was a significant challenge.

Keb counted as they sat and breathed together. Inhaling, then exhaling. Inhaling, and holding the breath in. Exhaling, and holding the breath out. After some time, Seraphina managed to sink into it. After the breathing, they sat in meditation.

TWENTY NINE

'What did we do after that?' asked Keb.

Seraphina had no idea she would be tested. After she came out of their meditation, everything had felt pulled to the ground. Her body, her eyelids. It took some time before she got up. Now he was asking her to remember the entire routine of exercises, most of which she had not even understood.

'I don't know, Keb.'

'Stand up, Seraphina.'

'Why is this so important?' she asked. 'Shouldn't you be telling me about the roads and trails between here and Rome?'

'I've already written all that down for you.' Keb held a scroll of what looked like freshly made papyrus up in the air. 'You need to focus on this.'

'I don't understand why.'

'Trust me, Seraphina. I don't know exactly how this will be of use, but I do know it will be of use.'

That gave Seraphina an idea. She walked over to Luna and dug her hand into one of the pouches hanging off him. Returning to Keb, she sat down and laid down her tools. Some papyrus, an inkwell, and a pen. A gift from one of the Greek women in the village.

'Tell me why we did each of those exercises. Every movement, and every position we held. I want to know where in the body it moved energy, what the purpose of each movement was, and what type of energy we moved. Same for the breathing at the end ...'

Keb raised his eyebrows at Seraphina.

'... and what types of energy we move during these exercises,' said Seraphina.

Keb looked at her for a moment. The girl clearly wanted to learn, and there was precious little time. He proceeded to do exactly as she asked, and Seraphina took it all down. She made notes, drew diagrams of positions, or poses as Keb described them. She took note of how to count her breath for each exercise, and all the types of energies they had worked with. There were five.

There was so much information. Seraphina focused on committing it to papyrus. She could question it all later if she wanted to. Halfway through Keb's summary, she stopped writing.

'Is something wrong?' he asked.

Seraphina shook her head. 'No. It just occurred to me that this is the first scroll I've ever written on.'

Keb raised an eyebrow at this remark.

'I mean, I've written before. I made lots of notes whenever I would study in the library. It was always on scraps of papyrus, and merely my own thoughts on whatever I had been reading ...'

'And?'

'Well,' said Seraphina, 'this could actually be useful. Someone could read this and know how to do these exercises. They could learn the science behind it and know all about the principles behind each of these movements and positions. I mean, poses.'

Keb nodded. 'Right you are, but given the current situation, may I make a suggestion?'

'Of course, Keb.'

'Keep getting this all down. Your future as a scholar may await, but for now, I want to make sure you are able to practice this every day. Especially during your journey to Rome.'

'You think I'll be able to smell the bandits coming in the darkness?' joked Seraphina.

'Who knows, but you will be energising yourself and the nature around you. Every day, you will heighten your senses. In time, you may find you are more able to sense the right action to take. To be more certain of following your instincts. And—'

'I'm sorry for joking, Keb. I know you're trying to help me.'

'It's alright, Seraphina. And, as I was saying, most importantly, to know the difference between when heartfelt instinct is at play, and when your fears are driving your actions.'

Seraphina regarded Keb for a moment. Gisgo would have loved Keb. She imagined if she could go back to Alexandria. Her, Khay, Gisgo, and Keb. Talking in the gardens of the museum. For hours and hours.

'… you're daydreaming,' said Keb.

'Sorry, excuse me?'

'I said that perhaps the biggest benefit of all this would be a cure for your distracted daydreaming. If you are to make this journey, you must focus, Seraphina. These exercises will give you the power and presence necessary for your mind to remain focused.'

'I'm sorry, Keb. Let's go through the rest of the exercises.'

And go through them they did. For hours, Seraphina quizzed Keb on every aspect of the practice they had gone through. Some were questions that Keb had never conceived of. Yet, resting in each of those questions, he was able to give an answer that satisfied his new student. When they had finished, all but one of Seraphina's sheets of papyrus were filled. Once they were dry, they were rolled in the same way as she had rolled so many scrolls in her former home. After tying a small leather cord around the pages, she couldn't help but wonder if she had just penned her first scholastic text.

Keb was usually rigid about bedtime. Seraphina had so much

to ask him though. Over a hearty dinner, she peppered him with questions until the night was well and truly upon them. Her energy was contagious, and Keb spoke to her not only about the science of energy but also shared many of his personal adventures with Seraphina. In turn, Seraphina talked in much more detail about her recent exploits, including her brief encounter with Caesar.

'You've met Julius Caesar?' asked Keb.

'I have.'

Keb laughed as she told him the story. The two of them, teacher and student, continued to talk and talk. The stars danced above them, and morning had almost arrived before the pair succumbed to the need for rest. Both had fallen asleep on the edge of the circle, opposite one another, in an almost perfect symmetry.

THIRTY

Seraphina had been up for hours. Luna was prepared, and she had gotten into her disguise. She thought it a good idea so she could get used to it. Keb had been sitting in the clearing, meditating for hours. She knew better than to interrupt him, but now she was just waiting to say goodbye.

She watched as he raised his hands into the air, palms pressed together. He would do this at the end of his practices each morning. Into the air, then to his forehead, his lips, and finally, in front of his heart.

'How was your meditation?'

'It felt wonderful, thank you for asking. I deliberately took some extra time today, to pray for you and Luna on your journey.'

'Do you pray while you meditate?' asked Seraphina.

'Yes. In fact, meditation is a form of deep prayer.'

'Another thing I didn't know. It's time for me to go, Keb.'

'Yes, but please, wait just a moment.'

Keb walked to one of the trees surrounding the clearing. He came back holding two large pouches, and another item slung over his arm.

'This one is for you, Seraphina,' he said, handing her the first pouch. 'It is a mixture of seeds, nuts, and dried fruit. A handful will sustain you for a day. Eat more if you need extra strength. There's plenty there to get you from here to Rome.'

'Thank you so much, Keb.'

'Here is something similar for Luna. Leaves, roots, and a mixture of other things. All very nourishing, and it will give him everything he needs for the journey. Same as for you. A handful a day will be more than enough for him. On the days you notice him tiring, give him an extra handful. There should be more than enough.'

Seraphina nodded and glanced at Keb's shoulder. 'What's that?'

Keb lifted the strap off his shoulder, and held a leather sheath in front of him, with an ornate handle coming out of it. Then he unsheathed a long dagger. The blade was thick and sharp, and Seraphina took a step back.

'It's for you, Seraphina. I know we said fighting would be a last resort, but I want you to have this. That club is unwieldy and may not be the best thing should you find yourself in trouble. You can wear it under your robe, just like the club.'

'Um, thank you,' said Seraphina, putting the dagger back in its sheath.

'There is nothing wrong with protecting yourself from danger. Certainly, do all you can to avoid perils on your journey, but do not hesitate to protect yourself or Luna if there is no other choice.'

Seraphina nodded, as she carefully hung the leather strap and the sheath on her body.

'I guess that's it, at least for now,' said Keb.

'Will we meet again?'

'I'm sure if we are meant to, we will. Have you thought of a name?'

'A name?'

'Yes, Seraphina doesn't make a very convincing boy's name. I'd recommend a Greek name, given the direction you are travelling from to get to Rome. It will arouse the least suspicion.'

'Seorsa,' said Seraphina. 'I read a story about a Greek farmer named Seorsa once.'

'Seorsa,' repeated Keb. 'I like it.'

'I'm so glad I met you, Keb. Thank you for everything, especially for teaching me.'

'Try to practice those exercises every day. I'm glad I met you too. Start to sense as much as you can about anyone you meet on your journey. Actually, anyone you meet from this point on in your life.'

'How do you mean?' she asked.

'Have you ever met someone and had an instant feeling about them?'

'Some people, yes.'

'Practising and meditating every day will help harness your ability to get a feeling about each person you encounter in your life. For this journey you are about to take, it could make the difference between knowing who you can trust and sensing if you have met someone you can't trust. Am I making sense?'

'I think so.'

'I'm sorry if I'm rambling on about this. I just want you to get to Rome safely. I'm sure once you're there, you will find your Quintus, unharmed.'

Seraphina hugged Keb. 'I'll come back and see you again. There's so much more for me to learn.'

Keb simply nodded and smiled. He watched as Seraphina got on to her horse and rode away.

'Do you have the directions on how to get to Rome?' Keb shouted, his hands either side of his mouth.

Seraphina held up the scroll without turning around then raised her hands into the air, palms together in a prayer gesture.

THIRTY ONE

Luna had travelled for two days without any problem. Seraphina was learning his rhythms—when to have him gallop, cantering over more uneven ground, and of course, letting him rest when necessary. Between the food Keb had provided and that provided by their surroundings, he seemed very well fed. The coastline to her left had made it an easy journey to navigate so far. The landscape of fields and forest to her right was a beautiful accompaniment.

The journey had also passed without incident. Seraphina had stopped passing through any towns or settlements after the first day. Given that she had enough food and the directions from Keb, she had no need to visit those places. She was still getting used to lowering her voice and adopting the mannerisms of a young man. A few odd looks had come her way so far.

As she saw a port settlement in the distance, Seraphina noticed the coastline of the sea bending around to the left. Following the coast would take them south, and they needed to continue west. This was the part of the journey where Keb said things could become more dangerous. Looking ahead, green dominated the landscape. Hills and mountains abounded between here and their intended destination.

I'll get to the other side of that settlement and find somewhere to camp for the night, she thought. Stroking the back of Luna's head for a moment, she raised the reins, and set off. Seraphina kept the speed to a slow gallop and was happy with how quickly she had taken to horse riding. Not to mention, how quickly Luna had taken to her. She wondered about what Keb had said about energy. *Would animals have the same kind of energy flowing through them?* She supposed so. Keb had said, after all, that energy flowed through all things.

She continued, cogitating about such things. Her thoughts vacillated between dismissing what Keb had said and having a fresh perspective on her surroundings. Seraphina remembered feeling the truth in Keb's words. She looked at the natural world around her, in all its stillness. There was life there. No doubt about it. In the sea, the trees, even those mountains in the distance. They were not dead things. That much she knew from her studies. Keb had said that everything has life force energy in it. Something about how this energy flowed through all things. No exceptions.

Was that the same energy he had been talking about the other times? Most likely, she thought. She had so many questions for him. More than a few times, she had considered riding back to spend more time with him. Seraphina knew that getting to Rome was important for now. Her thirst for learning had not diminished, and it probably never would. She had to know if Quintus was alive and well, and Cicero too. She wondered if she would meet a teacher like Keb in Rome. *Surely in such a great city, someone had to have knowledge of this mysterious science?*

Her mind drew back to the Hindu texts she had read. They were full of principles that related to this science, yet there was nothing in those scrolls about the practices and exercises that Keb had given her to do. Maybe the Hindus had a unique way of doing things. Maybe they kept them a secret, and these teachings about energy were only to be passed from certain teachers to certain students.

She smiled at that thought. Maybe Keb had picked her for a reason.

Seraphina took a moment to consult the directions and made sure they were going the right way. Bringing her mind back to the present, she could see the sun starting to set behind the mountains. The habit of travelling only by day was one she thought best to continue. They were almost at the outskirts of the port settlement.

Seraphina snapped the reins, and Luna accelerated. The ground was flat and hard. She kept a good distance from the settlement, only catching a few idle looks as she whizzed by. Once they were well clear of it, Luna sniffed out a thickly covered area of grassland. Seraphina looked around for a moment. The sod was lush and thick, and Luna started to chew at it. They both decided this was their spot for the night.

THIRTY TWO

Seraphina had studied Keb's directions in detail. She didn't want to be continually stopping. Over the past few days, three separate hordes of bandits had chased her. In each instance, she had not seen them coming. Fortunately for her, in each instance, she had also managed to outrun them. Luna was proving to be a valuable companion. The chases may have even been to her benefit. Judging by Keb's calculations, they were at least a day ahead of where they were supposed to be.

Maybe they could be riding faster. Seraphina preferred to pay attention to Luna's comfort. There was no sense in tiring him out or risking injury to him. So far, the only damage had been an arrow wound to his side. Seraphina had cleaned and bandaged the wound. The animal seemed unaffected. It would take a lot longer to make it to Rome without Luna. Those hordes of bandits would be much harder to deal with as well.

After a few hours, the sun was high in the sky. Despite this, there was precious little light in the forest ahead. Keb had spoken to her about this part of the journey. The bandits and brigands in this stretch of forest were notorious, he said. The instructions were to keep in the light as much as possible and ride fast on flat ground. Beware of traps, he had warned.

They eased into the forest, and the cool air made Seraphina grateful for the heavy clothes of her disguise. At each stop since leaving Alexandria, the weather had cooled a bit more. She wondered if Rome was a warm place or not. This cold, dark forest was a far cry from the blazing heat of her home city. She pulled the hood over her head, and then put it back down. The wind would knock it back anyway, and Seraphina wanted to see as much as possible.

Slivers of sunlight helped her and Luna along their path. After some time, she saw a flat track of land. It extended as far as she could see. The forest was full of strange noises. When they sounded like wildlife, Seraphina was not too bothered. Luna was undeterred. She cantered the horse into line with the even terrain then snapped the reins. Hard.

Luna bolted, and Seraphina kept whipping the reins. She had not ridden the horse this fast. The sounds around her seemed to get louder. The wind hitting her face was freezing and damp. She pressed on, with limited visibility of what was ahead. She whipped the reins harder and harder and scanned the ground for any obstacles. After a good fifteen or twenty minutes, her shoulders began to tire. Luna seemed to also. Just as she was about to slow down, she could see daylight in the distance. Small rays of light were poking through the tree heads, and this gave her the encouragement she needed.

She whipped as hard as she could and encouraged Luna to keep going. Seraphina saw the beginning of a huge field approach. Then a beautiful, big, blue lake. As more sunshine hit her face and Luna's body, she slowed him down. As they cleared the last edge of the forest's shadow, Seraphina slowed the horse down to a trot. Luna was grateful for the respite.

'Look, Luna. Water, and grass. All the grass you can eat.'

Seraphina could have sworn the horse picked up his pace after she said this. *Funny animal*, she thought. After a few moments, she hopped off the horse and led him by the reins. He didn't need much prompting.

Sensing this, Seraphina let go. Luna broke into a short gallop towards the water and dunked his head in. Seraphina let out a giggle and rubbed her shoulders. The warmth of the sunshine was more than welcome. Looking back into the forest gave her an eerie feeling. Hopefully another dash like that would not be necessary.

Her stomach rumbled. Holding her hand over it, she walked over to Luna. The silly creature still had his head submerged in the lake.

'Come on, you funny horse,' she said, pulling him by the reins.

He resisted for a moment and then allowed Seraphina to tie him up to a nearby tree. He could still reach the water, and this pleased him.

Seraphina reached into one of the pouches. She had been eating the same thing for days now. It was still fresh, and surprisingly satisfying. She wondered what some of the seeds were. She would ask Keb when they met again. The occasional animal had crossed their path, and Seraphina had missed those hot meals by the side of the sea with Keb. Even the meals in her captivity near Tanais had been very good in comparison. Regardless, she couldn't quite bring herself to catch and kill an animal. Even if she did, she had no idea how to skin and prepare it. There was enough on her mind without having to worry about this, and she had food to sustain her. Besides, she had mostly seen wild boars. Her sense was that they were not to be trifled with.

Once she had eaten enough, she fed Luna. Looking at how much water he had drunk, Seraphina thought he'd be full to the brim. Not so. He ate triple what he usually would. He had just put in a huge effort though, and Seraphina thought him deserving of the reward. When he was full, she stroked the front of his face and said, 'Thank you.'

He lay down on the grass and Seraphina could tell he needed a rest. She, on the other hand, was still riding the wave of adrenaline from their sprint through the dark forest. Luna wasn't going anywhere for now though. She reached inside another pouch and poked around with her hand. Her fingers wrapped around the rolled papyrus sheets, and she pulled them out. Unfurling the notes she had made, she started to review everything that Keb had taught her.

She started doing some of the exercises and could see Luna was asleep. Seraphina got distracted, and wanted to keep reading. Understanding all the details about the exercises and poses before trying to go through them was important. Once she was done, she committed the sequence to memory.

Standing up, she began. It felt weird, but she persisted. The breathing, the movements, and holding herself in those positions. Seraphina needed to look down at her notes once or twice. After a few minutes, the motion began to have a calming effect on her, and she noticed that she was breathing much more deeply. At the end of the routine, she sat cross-legged and formed a mudra with her hands. A much more familiar position.

Before long, she was deep in meditation. The sparse sounds of nature around her faded into nothingness.

THIRTY THREE

The bandit was a tall, wiry man. His hair was thick and black, both on his head and above his top lip. His long tunic was black too. His pale skin was the result of living in a region often devoid of sunlight and heavy on cold, grey weather. Like many others who roamed these lands, he was Germanic and a wanderer. His tribesmen were perpetually involved in one battle or another. He had long since left that life, preferring to eke out his existence by robbing travellers who had the misfortune of crossing his path.

He had been running for almost an hour. His tunic clung to his body, courtesy of the thin layer of sweat that had formed from his exertions. The cool air provided some welcome relief. At least he had found the boy. He and his small troop of bandits had been waiting in their usual hiding place. Then the boy had flashed past them. He had never seen a horse move so fast, and he was curious. The others had told him to forget about it, and that another target would come along shortly.

He knew better though. Fewer and fewer travellers were daring to brave the forest. They needed to rob whatever targets they could. Otherwise, they would be forced to move into other areas. Territories that other bandits controlled. There would be fights and inevitable bloodshed. The boy was tall but lean. If he wasn't on his horse, he would be an easy target. He looked behind him and cursed the rest of the group. It would take him a couple of hours to get them and come back.

The boy looked like a worthwhile target. The horse alone would net them enough to eat for a week, and it was loaded with saddlebags. There had to be something valuable in them. They could even sell the boy. It would make a good haul, and a few hours work was worth the trouble.

He should have been running back to fetch the others, but he instead watched as this boy did some strange exercises by the lake. The horse was asleep, and the bandit watched as his target moved very slowly for nearly half an hour. The bandit did not know what to make of it. The boy finally sat down and was still. In the distance, it looked like his eyes were closed. Maybe he was asleep. He sat there so long that the bandit thought of sneaking up on him by himself.

The sound of steps behind him broke his concentration. He swung around and drew his sword. Three of the other bandits had followed on horseback. He smiled. Maybe he was having good luck today, after all.

'What on earth is that boy doing?' asked one.

'I have no idea,' said another.

'Well, let's not let him get away,' said the first bandit. 'If he gets on that horse, he's as good as gone. You three, ride up to that tree line at the foot of the mountains and take positions along it. I'll sneak up on him while he's sitting there like that. If he somehow manages to get on his horse, cut him off in whichever direction he goes.'

'If we're on the tree line, he could still evade us.'

'He's not going to go back into the forest. Now go.'

The three rode away as instructed. He watched as they got into position. Returning his attention to the boy, he was still sitting with his eyes closed. Whatever he was doing, he was taking his time about it. He ran out into the open field, keeping his steps light, staying directly behind the boy. Once the boy was directly in front of him, he sprinted up. He barely made a sound through the thick grass. He was standing above him. The horse was still asleep.

He wrapped one arm around the boy's neck and held the point of the sword to his chest. The boy woke with a fright but did not make a sound.

'Don't move,' grunted the bandit.

Seraphina opened her eyes without moving her body. She had no idea what he had just said, but it didn't sound good. In one swift movement, she whipped out the dagger from under her right arm and slashed it at whoever was holding her. The dagger pierced the bandit's arm that was holding the sword. The bandit howled in agony and recoiled, seeing the dagger buried almost to the hilt in his arm. Seraphina pushed herself free. Panting, she whirled around, snatching up the club off the grass. With all the force she could muster, she swung it as hard as she could at his face. She gritted her teeth and squinted her eyes as she felt the crash of the club into the bandit's head, crunching bones and mangling his skin. The bandit fell, yelling for help. Seraphina, now breathing rapidly, turned her neck this way and that, scanning her surroundings. There was no one else in sight. As quickly as she could, she pulled her dagger out of the semi-conscious bandit and took his sword. She felt her heart pound in her chest as she looked down at him, and a slight shiver came across her body thinking of how much she had hurt him.

Then she heard them. Seraphina looked up to see three horses charging at her. The men riding them were dressed similarly to the bandit lying on the ground. She dashed towards Luna to untie him. Beads of sweat trickled down her forehead as she finally released Luna's reins from the trees. The bandit was still on the ground, and the others were almost upon her. She jumped on Luna's back and got him moving westward. She was still shaken up but narrowed her eyes and whipped the reins hard.

The bandits gave chase, and Seraphina dared not look back. With tears streaming back across her face, she rode Luna as fast as he would go. She blinked, trying to see clearly through the tears, and finally took one hand off the reins to wipe them away. Poor Luna was still waking up from his nap and trying his best. Suddenly, something crashed into her right side, and she felt a dull pain in her hip. One of the bandits had ridden around and flanked her, catching her unawares. Seraphina fell to her left, and the impact of the crash threw her far enough that Luna did not crush her. The bandit in the distance was coming to his feet, and the other three circled her on their horses.

She felt her heart pump even harder, and her eyes cleared and involuntarily widened. Seraphina was still armed and had no plans to be taken as a prisoner again. Rolling over, she jumped to her feet. She brandished the club and jumped up at the nearest one. Seraphina knocked him right off his horse. He tried to get up, and she slammed the club into his knee as hard as possible. Her face scrunched again as she felt the club meet the bandit's flesh, but part of her marvelled at the efficacy of the weapon. The other two sat frozen on their horses, though the blood-curdling screams of their friend jarred them out of their trance and they jumped off their horses.

'Help him, you idiots!' shouted the leader in the distance. He was running towards them, holding the deep gash in his arm with his other hand.

Seraphina went into a frenzy, charging at another bandit as he raised his sword at her. She brandished the club towards him to distract him while she held the dagger in a reverse grip in her other hand. Her attacker focused on the club and did not see the blade. She crashed into him as he tried to slash at the arm wielding the club, plunging the dagger into his chest. Leaving it there, she pushed herself up off his body and in one movement lunged at the last one with the club. She was fighting like a man possessed, and the bandit stepped back to avoid her attack.

She looked over to Luna for a moment, and the poor horse was still on his side, coughing and sputtering. The bandit who had first attacked her was getting closer and closer. Seraphina lunged again, and the bandit landed a blow on her arm. She dropped the club, gripping the cut with her hand. Keeping her eyes on him, she drew the sword from her belt. She swung it at him repeatedly as hard as she could. He easily deflected her blows, pushing her to the ground. She tumbled and fell face down near the body of the dead bandit.

The bandit, sword in hand, grabbed the scruff of the boy's neck and pulled him up. He went to turn him around, and as he did, he could see the dagger was no longer in the chest of his dead friend. As his eyes went back to the boy, he felt the stab. Searing heat engulfed his stomach, as the boy plunged the full length of the blade into his gut. He fell to the floor, screaming.

Seraphina wasted no time. She ran to Luna and pulled on the reins, trying to get him up. She could see him trying to step with his hooves and gave up on the pulling. Crouching down, she got as much under his body as she could, trying to prop him up. The bandit was still coming across the field. Looking at the others, two were not moving, and the third was breathing but unable to stand up because of his leg. Seraphina pushed harder at Luna's body, picturing herself as a boulder underneath him.

'Come on, boy. Get up!'

She heard his hooves scraping against the ground, but he still felt heavy on top of her.

'Luna! Get up!' she yelled.

Then, she felt his weight lighten. The horse was scrambling to his feet! He cantered in a circle, whinnying loudly. Seraphina looked over to the bandits. One was still struggling to get to her, disarmed and blood gushing from his arm. The other three were of no concern. She ran over to them, retrieved her club, her dagger, and two of their swords. Her palms were so soaked with sweat that they almost slipped from her fingers as she ran back to the horse.

As she jumped on Luna's back, her body quivered as she tried to hold back a new set of tears. She snapped the reins and got out of there as quickly as she could.

THIRTY FOUR

The thick clothes clung to her sweaty body and she rocked back and forth on Luna, riding as fast as she possibly could. Their little dash through the forest had been nothing compared to this. For a good hour, Seraphina pushed the horse to get as far away as possible. Luna was starting to quit, though. She threw the reins down a few more times, but he had nothing left in him.

The horse slowed to a trot, and Seraphina took some deep breaths. The scenery had changed drastically. The colour of the open fields now gave way to darker shades of green. Thick mountain pine trees painted these shades all around them, and Luna's steps were louder on the hard ground. She could see the foot of a mountain not more than twenty steps away. Seraphina looked around for a covered spot to take rest. Seeing a darker area up ahead, she rode into a clearing surrounded by tall trees. Low hanging branches and bushes conspired to keep the clearing well concealed.

They would not ride any more today and this was perfect. Seraphina dismounted and tended to Luna. She gave him long strokes down his face, saying encouraging things to him. Thank the gods he had managed to get up, although part of her had wanted to attack that last bandit again. She had been shaking and could feel her nerves burning in that moment. The cool air had the same arid quality as a crisp, Alexandria evening. It dried her perspiration and Seraphina felt her heartbeat ease.

She started to feed Luna, replaying the events in her head. She had killed two of the bandits, without a doubt. The other two were gravely injured. She wondered what would become of them. Her head dropped, and her arms felt as though they were made of lead. For a moment, Seraphina felt guilty. She had been so scared though. That rush of energy that had come over her. The thought of being a prisoner again. Back there, on that field with those bandits, she had told herself once again that she would rather die than be held captive.

Seraphina felt her throat jerk, and she dropped the handful of food she was holding, rushing to move away from the horse. Her body doubled over, and a stream of vomit rushed up her throat and out of her mouth. The muscles in her stomach contracted and her whole face tensed up. As her body purged, water spewed forth from behind her eyeballs. A minute or so passed. She stood there, forearms resting on her knees, allowing her body to relax after the convulsions. She blew her nose, rinsed her mouth, and noticed her breathing return to normal.

It had been a last resort, she told herself. The man had a sword pointed at her chest, and the others had charged her down with swords drawn. She tried to tell herself she had done the right thing, but the guilt nagged at Seraphina. Tears now trickled down her still sweaty face. She wiped them away and noticed Luna looking over at her and then down to the spilt food on the floor. She smiled at him, cleaned herself up, and went back to feeding him. He was devouring the handfuls of food. Not for the first time, he had saved her from a terrible fate. She checked the pouch that contained Luna's food and saw it was half full.

That was enough for now. Turning her attention to herself, Seraphina removed the bulky robe and hung it over a thick, low-hanging tree branch. She did the same for the rest of her clothes. The frigid air immediately soothed her naked body. Before long though, she was shivering. Quickly grabbing hold of a strigil and some oil—more gifts from the Greek women—she scraped her entire body clean. Then, she applied a generous amount of the oil and gave it a few minutes to set in. After she used the strigil a second time, Seraphina felt a whole lot better. She rubbed down her arms, feeling the smooth, clean skin, and let out a contented sigh.

The clothes were still drying, and she was only getting colder. She rummaged around in the bags that Luna had been carrying. To her dismay, his fall had crushed the sheets of papyrus, broken open the inkwell and snapped her pen in two. Fortunately, the bottom of the bag had absorbed most of the ink. Her notes remained intact, and she held them to her chest in relief. The other bag, which had held the strigil and the oil, seemed to have something thick in the bottom of it. It felt like some kind of fabric.

Pulling out, she saw it was the dress she had worn at the prison. It had been neatly cleaned, folded, and placed into the bottom of the bag. Seraphina wondered if it was one of the village women who had done this, or if Keb had performed this courtesy. Regardless, she was thoroughly grateful. Whatever had happened, she had met some truly kind people through this ordeal. Rhea, the women in the village, and Keb, of course. She put on the dress. Then, with her eyes closed, she said a short prayer of thanks to those who had helped her on her journey.

Night was falling. She wrapped herself up in her blanket and stayed close to Luna for warmth. For a few moments, Seraphina's thoughts drifted back to the bandits. She had been surprised at her own violence but was glad she had defended herself. Still, she had killed two men. *Did they have families? Children even?*

Exhausted both mentally and physically, she finally fell asleep.

THIRTY FIVE

It had been a blissfully uneventful morning. Almost expecting to wake up to trouble, Seraphina was grateful to rise well-rested. Her clothes were dry, and everything was as she had left it the night before. Luna was in good spirits. She had practised her exercises, and a feeling of deep peace remained with her after completing the meditation.

The landscape was beautiful. The deep grey of the mountain rock blended with the dark green of the trees. A perfect blue sky appeared overhead. Seraphina could smell the musky fragrance of the trees, and there was just a hint of the sun's warmth in the early morning air. She smacked her tongue and could feel the dryness in her throat. Before she even checked the water skins, she remembered they would be empty. At the lake yesterday, she intended to refill them. Then along came the bandits with their own plans.

She looked over at Luna. He looked fine, but he would need water before they could get very far. She wrapped the now dry fabric back over her chest. Seraphina marvelled how some bulky clothes and a crude haircut could help her pass for a boy. She reminded herself to keep her voice low if she spoke. With her costume restored, she mounted Luna who trotted out of their hiding place. Seraphina turned her neck from side to side. The movement of her muscles felt good, as did the heat of the sun shining behind her.

After a few minutes, Seraphina heard flowing water. Luna accelerated into a canter instinctively, and Seraphina had to do very little to guide the thirsty horse to the water. She filled both water skins first, and then drank alongside Luna. When she saw she was downstream from Luna, Seraphina jerked her head away from the river. The horse was not about to move for her, so she walked around him. She took a few more handfuls of water and watched as Luna tried his best to drain the river.

The river was wide, and there was no obvious crossing point. She tried to remember what Keb had advised, and looking to her right, she had her answer. At an elevation on the river further upstream, there were several large stone surfaces. Once boulders, the gushing water from the river had eroded them over time. They would have to be careful, but Seraphina was confident they could cross without issue.

Turning her gaze forward, a white horse slightly smaller than Luna was drinking from the other side of the river. The sight startled Seraphina, and she reared back for a moment. Luna was utterly indifferent, continuing what seemed to be more of a head bath than quenching his thirst. Looking back across, Seraphina saw a man sitting on the horse.

The stranger had a distinguished look to him. He was much older, though not elderly. His chin was strong, with a well-groomed beard and moustache of hair almost as white as his horse's. A long toga flowed down to his legs. Long, lustrous hair flowed from his forehead, back and down to his shoulders. A pair of serene aquamarine eyes watched her from across the river. Seraphina was not threatened by his sudden presence, but she did feel uneasy. Perhaps the sword on his hip was what caused the concern. Then she reminded herself she was carrying no less than three weapons herself.

Their eyes met, and he offered a friendly wave. She went to raise her hand in response, and something in her hesitated. Seraphina then tugged at Luna. It was time to go. Riding up a slight hill, she focused on the crossing. The man and his horse had moved to meet them on the other side of the river, and Seraphina felt the skin along her spine crawl. *Maybe they are crossing too*, she thought, hoping for the best. Seraphina held the reins tightly, guiding Luna to pace across the rushing water at a snail's crawl. His footing was sure, and he completed the crossing with ease.

'Good morning,' said the stranger, in Latin, spoken with clear diction.

Seraphina nodded in his direction without stopping, barely glancing at him.

'I saw you yesterday,' he continued. 'Fighting off those bandits.'

Seraphina stopped her horse, without turning. She looked at the man but did not say a word.

'Are you alright?'

She nodded, still yet to speak. *He seems kind and is perfectly polite*, she thought. *What is wrong with me?*

'What's your name, young man?'

'Seorsa,' she said. The words came out as a croak, due to the lump in her throat she only then just felt.

'Excuse me?' said the man.

She cleared her throat and remembered to deepen her voice. 'Seorsa.'

'Where are you headed? You are a long way from anywhere here.'

'Just heading west,' said Seraphina, trying to keep her voice as even as possible. 'Looking for work.'

'Well, you seem pretty handy in a fight, Seorsa,' said the man, chuckling.

Seraphina replied with a straight face. 'Those bandits, did you know them?'

'No,' said the man. 'Nothing but troublemaking scum, I suspect.'

Seraphina raised her eyebrows. 'How did you see? What are you doing out here?'

'I keep a mountain home in these parts. A small village where I grew up. Very few people know of it. I was looking down from the mountain yesterday when I saw you being attacked.'

Seraphina nodded.

'I was going to ride down to help you, and then realised it would do no good. You see, it takes a long time to come down from the top of these mountains,' said the man as he nodded towards the closest peak.

'What's your name?' asked Seraphina.

'I am Faustus. Look, Seorsa, if it's work you are looking for, I can offer you some. If you are willing to travel with me back to Rome …'

'You're going to Rome?' interrupted Seraphina, her face softening for a moment.

Faustus nodded with a smile. 'Yes, that is where I live. As I was saying, if you can travel with me there, I could give you some work.'

Seraphina was about to ask what kind of work, but she held back for a second. She grimaced as she tried to think of what was bothering her, but came up with nothing.

'I have a proposal. Do you want to hear it?' she asked.

'Please.'

'I will travel with you to Rome. When we are there, I have to see someone.'

'Does this someone have a name?'

'Yes,' answered Seraphina. 'His name is Cicero, and he is a member of the Roman senate.' She didn't want to tell this Faustus too much but decided that, for now, invoking the senator's name could only help her.

Faustus nodded slowly. 'The senator, Cicero.'

'Yes.'

'You know Cicero?'

'I didn't say that,' said Seraphina. 'I said I have to see him. If you can get me safely to Rome and help me find Cicero, I will happily work to repay you.'

'Very well. How many days work do you propose, young Seorsa?'

'Three full days.'

Faustus nodded. 'Not a bad offer.' The truth was he would have helped this young boy anyway. He admired the boy for offering such a fair deal.

'That we arrive in Rome and find Cicero is key to this bargain,' said Seraphina.

'Well, safety won't be a problem,' said Faustus. 'I have a small detail of warriors waiting just over that hill. I wanted to come and talk to you, you see, but I was worried that the sight of me and ten large guards might be worrisome. As for finding Cicero, that will be easy. He is at the Forum almost every day. I have even met him once myself.'

Seraphina rode to Faustus and extended her hand. 'Then it's a deal.'

'Yes indeed,' said Faustus, shaking the boy's hand.

Seraphina watched as Faustus whistled and signalled his men. A very large man on a horse emerged at the top of the hill in the distance. Seraphina was shocked at his size. Two more appeared behind him. Then another three. Once it looked like there were no more to come, she took a count. Ten warriors, huge and well-armed, on horses as well kept as their master's. *They all look quite similar*, thought Seraphina. Lean and muscular, sitting tall on their horses. They were as fearsome as her captors back at the prison but clean-shaven and more graceful in their movements.

Faustus was right. If she had seen all eleven of them at the same time, she would have been considerably more nervous. A broad smile came across her face. If these men were to escort her to Rome, she doubted safety would be an issue. The looks she received as they came closer were neutral. The men kept straight faces as Faustus introduced everyone. One of the warriors, who seemed like the leader, smiled when Faustus spoke of how the young boy had fought off four bandits, killing two of them. He glanced at Seraphina and gave a little nod of admiration.

She simply nodded back, as she did with the rest of the men. Their names were not given, and conversation was evidently not expected. Their presence comforted her, but something continued to irk her about Faustus.

'Let's begin our journey,' said Faustus. 'Seorsa, you will ride next to me in the middle of our convoy. If you like, you can give your supplies to the men in the front. Towards the end of each day, they will ride ahead and set up camp for us.'

'I appreciate that,' said Seraphina, in her lowered boy's voice, 'but I can set up for myself each day.'

'As you wish.'

The warriors fell into line and began to ride. Five in front, in two rows as a three-two formation. The same for the five men behind them. Faustus and Seraphina rode side by side, as Faustus chattered happily, asking her plenty of questions. Seraphina kept her answers short but cordial and, after a while, Faustus was content to ride in silence. She looked around at the warriors and felt a deep sense of relief.

Seraphina raised her head to the sky, her heart filled with gratitude.

THIRTY SIX

Nearly a month had passed. Faustus said they would reach Rome by nightfall. Seraphina had not aroused suspicion in either Faustus or the warriors, and she suspected this was at least in part by how well she had handled the long rides each day. They had been friendly but distant, and this suited her perfectly. The occasional thought about Faustus' motives passed through her mind, but she had dismissed such apprehensions as paranoia. Each day, she either bathed or used the strigil in solitude. No one had made any comment on her need for privacy. As far as they were concerned, she was a young boy who was very capable in a fight.

They had crossed so much ground since she had met them, and with relative ease. The leader of the warriors, Darius, was clearly an expert navigator. He was also an immense man. She reminded him a little of the leader of the pirates. Minus the oversized belly, unkempt facial hair, and menacing eyepatch. His hair was of a similar style to his master's but was a dark, woody brown. The colour of his eyes almost matched his hair, and they were regularly scanning their surroundings. His natural expression was not a friendly one. After all, he was a warrior.

The group had not encountered any bandits. Seraphina suspected that any who might have spotted their little convoy had thought better of attacking them.

The day was fading fast. Usually, by this time they would be arriving at camp. That half of the warriors rode ahead each day and set up camp was something Seraphina had not stopped marvelling at. At the end of each day when they stopped, everything was prepared. Areas to sleep, places to hang clothes, food to eat. Even the horses were catered for. She had shared their food with the others. Most had given it a reluctant look before declining. One or two of the warriors, along with Faustus, had tried some. They had all commented on how filling it was.

She saw Darius accelerate his horse to a gallop. The rest followed his lead, as usual. Farmland passed on the right, and before long, they saw some small homes in the distance. *They look like some of the homes in Alexandria*, thought Seraphina. As they galloped further, the homes got bigger, and these were markedly different. Longer and much more ornate, she wondered who lived in these decadent palaces.

They were now on paved streets, and much larger buildings loomed ahead. Darius put his hand up as a signal for the group to slow down.

'Welcome to Rome, Seorsa,' said Faustus.

A wide smile came to Seraphina's face at the knowledge that she had arrived. She couldn't see much in the darkness though. She would get up at first light to look around. From what she had seen, the city was much bigger than Alexandria. Aside from those first homes on the outskirts of the city, everything looked different to the only other city she had known. She was aching to explore, but more pressing matters were at hand.

'When can we go to see Cicero?' she asked.

'It's too late for that tonight,' said Faustus. 'Though I know you must be eager to see him. We will go to find him first thing tomorrow morning.'

Seraphina nodded and smiled. She had made it. The group arrived at Faustus' home, which dwarfed the others that had impressed Seraphina earlier. The warriors said good night and rode around the side of the house to what looked like their sleeping quarters in the rear. A servant or two milled about, but the household seemed largely deserted.

'Who else lives here,' asked Seraphina.

'Just me and my wife.'

Seraphina wanted to ask more, but there would be plenty of time for conversation. She was not tired at all, but she sensed the best thing to do was to retire for the night. *Let Faustus sleep*, she thought, and early in the morning, she would see Cicero. There were far more important questions to ask him. She hoped he had found his way back to Rome safely. She had no idea what she would do next if she was unable to find the great senator.

THIRTY SEVEN

For a moment, Seraphina thought she was dreaming. The short, portly woman was standing at the end of her bed. She wore a warm smile and a simple dress.

'Yadira?' asked Seraphina, thinking for a moment she was back in Alexandria with her mother's best friend. She even used her normal voice.

The woman gave her a quizzical look, and Seraphina realised she was not dreaming at all.

'Sorry,' said Seraphina, lowering her voice. 'I thought you were someone else.'

The woman nodded. 'Not a problem, young sir. Master Faustus sent me to see if you were awake.'

'Only just. May I have a few moments please?'

'Certainly, sir. I am sorry if I disturbed you. I will be just out here. Do call out if I can bring you anything.'

'I will,' she said assertively, wanting the servant to leave at once.

That was close, she thought. To have come all this way only to give up her secret identity now. Seraphina shook her head. She had thought of revealing herself to Faustus and the other men but decided it would only complicate matters. The safest thing was to get to Rome. She hoped to meet Cicero in private. Then she could reveal her true identity. Any residual matters with Faustus could no doubt be worked out, so long as she had the support of the senator in doing so. Faustus had a kind nature and she was not overly worried about how he might react. Still, she wanted to keep things as simple as possible. Seraphina's life had been complicated enough for quite some time now. Avoiding any further difficulties, either real or perceived, was a priority.

Setting these thoughts aside, she sprang out of bed. The servant had left the door slightly ajar, and she closed it. The room darkened, but she could see enough to get her clothes on. She opened the windows, and light flooded into the room.

Seraphina looked out into the atrium. A nicely paved path ran through the centre of the courtyard. A tall, elegant woman was slowly walking along it. Her head was bowed towards the ground, and her steps were slow. Her dress was of a more refined style than anything Seraphina had seen before. Made of a brilliant white fabric, it hugged her voluptuous body and extended from her shoulders to just short of her feet. A heavy sash, seemingly part of the ensemble, was draped over one of her arms. Her hair was a golden blonde, and the long strands continued halfway down her back. It looked beautiful against her milky-white skin and the white dress.

Seraphina leaned forward, hands underneath her chin, watching the woman who was deep in thought, and Seraphina wondered what was on her mind. Perhaps this was Faustus' wife.

The woman must have felt her stare because she turned at that moment and noticed she was being watched by the boy in the window. Seraphina noticed her bright, amber eyes glaring at her for a moment. Then a voice from the other end of the courtyard stole her attention.

'Good morning, Seorsa,' said Faustus.

Seraphina shifted her gaze away from the woman, who was still glaring, albeit less intensely.

'Good morning, Faustus. Did you sleep well?'

'I certainly did. Were you comfortable?'

'Yes, thank you,' said Seraphina, looking out of the corner of her eye at the woman. She was walking towards Faustus.

Faustus gestured in her direction. 'Seorsa, this is my wife. Her name is Antonia.'

Seraphina bowed her head deferentially. Looking up, she saw that her frown remained. Nevertheless, she managed a polite nod and mumbled something to her husband. With that, she walked away, back to the courtyard and her thoughts.

'Before we go to the Forum, I think it is wise for us to speak,' said Faustus, as if there was nothing unusual about his wife's behaviour. He gestured towards the large patio adjacent to the gardens. 'Come out when you are ready and join me.'

Seraphina checked her things. There was not much else to get ready. She was finally going to see Cicero and, with any luck, her dear Quintus as well. She wanted to go and check on Luna, but she preferred not to keep Faustus waiting. He had helped her greatly, and after the little incident with Antonia, she thought it wise to follow his lead.

She found her way through the large house to where Faustus was waiting for her. A tray sat on a table in front of him with two amphoras. One seemed to contain water and the other wine. Faustus offered her a drink, which she politely declined. Seraphina watched curiously as he mixed a little wine and a lot of water into his cup. He finished it off with a generous dollop of honey from the bowl that sat next to the amphoras.

'You haven't yet told me how you know Cicero,' said Faustus. The question was implied, but Seraphina said nothing in response. 'If we go to the Roman Forum and ask for one of the most important senators in the republic, it might help for us to have a reason.'

Seraphina nodded in agreement.

'Can you tell me how you know him?' he asked.

'If you remember when we met, I never actually said I know him. I said I needed to see him.'

'Very well. Why do you need to see him?'

Seraphina decided to stop playing games. Faustus and his men had shown her nothing but kindness and generosity. Perhaps when they had first met, she was right to be cautious. Now was a different story. After all, she had spent the night in his home. There was little to be gained from being cryptic.

'Faustus, I do know Cicero,' she said, her voice coming out a little high. She cleared her throat, noting the puzzled look on his face. 'I am sorry for being vague. I am still waking up, and if I told you the full story of what has happened to me over the past weeks, you wouldn't believe it.'

'You can tell me now, if you wish.'

'Perhaps later. Right now, it is imperative that we go to find Cicero. He is a friend. I met him in Alexandria with a few acquaintances of mine. We were to come here together, but our group got separated.'

'Your group?'

'Yes, there were three of us,' she said, speaking quickly. 'We were separated, and I found my way to Tanais and kept heading west. I had my encounter with the bandits. Thankfully, after that, I met you, and here we are.'

'You said Alexandria. You mean Alexandria in Egypt?'

Seraphina nodded. 'Yes.'

Faustus took a sip of his drink and leaned back. It was quite a story, and his hunch was that many of the details were being omitted. Helpfulness came naturally to Faustus, and he was all too happy to have assisted in bringing this young Greek boy to Rome safely. Requesting an audience with a senator was no small thing, however, and Seorsa's story was peculiar, to say the least.

'So, you have met Cicero personally?'

'Yes, sir.'

'And he will know you when he sees you?'

It will probably take him a few moments, she thought as she nodded. 'Most certainly.'

Faustus finished the rest of his drink with a long gulp. 'Very well. We can take my chariot to the Forum.'

Seraphina jumped to her feet and followed Faustus to the front of the house.

THIRTY EIGHT

Luna was in good spirits. He trotted over to Seraphina when he saw her and waited for her to give him a few strokes down his face. Faustus had plenty of land behind his house. The horses enjoyed the open space, each having found their own patch of grass to chew on. In the distance, she saw some of the warriors training with various weapons.

'Are you coming?' asked Faustus, beckoning her into the chariot.

Rome was spectacular. She had wanted to visit Rome from the first moment she heard of its existence and, despite her setbacks, Seraphina was thrilled to be there. It did not disappoint. Ornate buildings of every variety lined the paved streets. The morning was already somewhat busy, with people making their way in different directions. Some were on foot, others on horseback and in chariots. The men wore togas, and the women wore dresses like the one she had seen Antonia in. Seraphina admired how graceful they were in their movements and speech. The contrast with the noisy chaos of Alexandria was stark.

'Is it your first visit to Rome?'

Seraphina nodded without turning to face Faustus. She was mesmerised. A long building with high walls ran along the street they were on. It was seemingly without end.

Faustus chuckled at the boy's wide eyes and open jaw without him noticing.

'That, my dear Seorsa, is the Circus Maximus.'

Seraphina took her eyes off it for a moment and looked at Faustus. 'Really?'

Faustus nodded with much amusement. 'Yes. All sorts of events are held there. I take it you've heard of it?'

Seraphina could only nod slowly, returning her attention to the street. The great Circus Maximus. Where gladiators battled. Where games were held. Where the Roman Republic showcased its greatest spectacles. She had heard the stories since she was a child. Most who had spoken of the place had never been there. This added a layer of reverence to their tales. The place was one of legend throughout the Roman world.

'Maybe you will fight in there one day, young warrior,' joked Faustus.

Seraphina smiled and looked ahead. They were turning, and after a few more minutes, Faustus slowed down the horses.

'Is this it?' she asked.

'Yes, indeed. The Roman Forum.'

Seraphina marvelled at its splendour. Majestic basilicas lined the wide streets as people darted this way and that, conducting their business and rushing to wherever they needed to be next. Chariot drivers sped along, and Seraphina saw one barely miss an absent-minded pedestrian. The driver didn't miss a beat, and Seraphina realised that the pedestrian had been oblivious as well. The sun shone down from a clear blue sky, and she felt the corners of her mouth turn upwards as she drank in the scene before her.

Until a few months ago, her ambition had been to live a life outside the confines of the library. Never in her wildest dreams did she imagine she would be standing here. In Rome, at the home of the republican senate, reading the Latin inscriptions that decorated its walls. Not for the first time, she was grateful for her command of the Latin language.

Without it, she may not have been able to enlist Faustus' help. *Then again*, she thought, *perhaps he speaks Greek.*

Faustus was walking up the stairs. Once again, Seraphina had become distracted. She scurried after him, taking in all the buildings around them. How she would love to run the streets of Rome by night! Maybe she would get a chance to. As they neared the top of the stairs, she could hear several voices. When she joined Faustus on the platform, she was greeted by the sight of scores of senators discussing various matters with each other. She could tell by the purple edge of their togas. Cicero had worn the same style, and he had explained the significance to her during their first day at sea.

One of the senators waved Faustus over. He was a portly, jovial type who seemed to be entertaining several of the other senators with his remarks. Seraphina followed Faustus, reminding herself to speak in her boy's voice. She stood tall and stayed a little behind Faustus out of deference. The senator had a smug look to him, his lips smirking as he looked Seraphina up and down. Avoiding eye contact, she noticed the few thin strands of hair pulled back over his otherwise bald head.

'Greetings, brother Faustus,' said the senator. 'What brings you here today?'

'Ave, Senator Felix,' replied Faustus. 'I am here looking for Senator Cicero.'

'Ahhh,' said Felix, 'the great Cicero. The senator, the consul, the traitor.'

The other senators laughed, as one jokingly admonished Felix for his impertinence. Faustus remained silent, as a slight grimace came to Seraphina's face.

'All in good humour, my dear Faustus,' said Felix, placing a hand on Faustus' shoulder. Then, looking back at Seraphina, he asked, 'and who might this be?'

'This is Seorsa,' explained Faustus. 'He is an acquaintance of the senator.'

Felix and the other senators looked Seraphina up and down. The

Greek name, the slightly unkempt hair, and the common clothing did not meet with their approval. Seraphina gave a nod that was more of a bow.

'I see,' said Felix, unsure of what to say next. He glanced at Seraphina and then addressed Faustus, 'I was only joking about Cicero. He has regained Caesar's favour after his recent travels, and all is well. I think I saw him a little earlier, just over there.' The senator pointed to a group of men in the far corner from where they were standing.

Faustus held his hands up, to show he had taken no issue with the senator's words. 'I completely understand, dear Felix. A good day to all of you, sirs. Please excuse us.'

The two of them crossed the courtyard and made their way into the corner. Seraphina saw Cicero and for a moment, went to run towards him but she maintained decorum, and let Faustus lead the way. As they got closer, Cicero was distracted from his conversation and looked towards her. He examined her clothing and hair closely, and his colleagues wondered what he was looking at. Cicero excused himself from the group and stepped towards the man and his friend, who looked very familiar to him. The other senators who had been talking to Cicero were very curious. They watched while appearing to remain engaged in their own conversation.

'Ave, Cicero,' said Faustus. 'I am Decimus Faustus Metellus.'

'Greetings, Faustus. I am pleased to meet you.'

'Thank you, sir. This, I believe, is a friend of yours, Se—'

'Seraphina!' he exclaimed, realising at that moment why she looked so familiar.

'—orsa' finished Faustus at the same time.

Seraphina widened her eyes at Cicero, as Faustus looked between the two, thoroughly confused.

'Yes, Seorsa. How are you, dear friend?' said Cicero, recovering quickly. The surprise of seeing her, and looking so different, had overtaken him for a moment.

'I am quite well,' said Seraphina in her disguised voice. 'I am glad to see you.'

'Well,' said Cicero, 'shall we take some time to talk in my offices? I have some matters to discuss with you.'

Seraphina nodded. 'Yes, sir.'

As the two began to walk, Faustus joined the other senators in the strange looks they gave the pair. Seraphina looked back for a moment, remembering the agreement she had made.

'What is it?' asked Cicero.

Seraphina gave a quiet, concise explanation of how Faustus had brought her to Rome and her agreement to work for him in return. Cicero gestured for her to wait where she was, and asked Faustus to join them in his offices.

THIRTY NINE

Cicero closed the door to his rather humble office and looked at Seraphina, who was sitting in front of his desk. Faustus had graciously refused to accept Cicero's offer to pay for the three days' work that Seorsa owed him. Both Seraphina and Cicero had thanked him profusely for his generosity. It had been quite evident that Faustus would have loved to stay and hear their conversation, but Cicero had bidden him farewell after just a few moments of idle talk.

'Well,' said Cicero, clasping his hands together, 'you must have many questions to ask, and many things to say.' He walked around to the other side of his desk, able to look Seraphina in the eyes now. 'I am so glad to see you alive and well, Seraphina.'

Seraphina smiled brightly. 'Thank you. I can't believe I made it here. Where is Quintus?' she said, asking the question that had been on her mind for months.

'Quintus? My dear, the men who took you took him as well. You don't remember?'

'No. I remember the pirates attacking our ship and wanting to take me. Then, Quintus started fighting and that is all I recall. I was knocked unconscious.'

'I am so sorry, Seraphina. We weren't in any position to fight those men.'

Seraphina shook her head. 'It's alright, Cicero. I don't hold you responsible. I hold them responsible. If you had tried to resist them, you would all have been killed.'

Cicero took a deep breath and felt relief in her words. 'I've been feeling guilty ever since it happened, but I had no idea of how to even send people to look for you. Unfortunately, I've been dealing with other difficulties here in Rome.'

'It wasn't your fault, Cicero.'

'But if I'd been travelling with proper guards, as I've been told to so many times ...'

'Those pirates did this, not you.'

Cicero nodded. He was not one to indulge in emotions, and he was glad his young friend was safe in front of him. The mystery of Quintus' location was of some concern though.

'I take it you saw no sign of Quintus where they took you?'

Seraphina shook her head.

'Did they ever mention him?'

'No. Most of the time they were speaking a language I did not understand. The—'

'Sarmatian,' interrupted Cicero. 'I recognised it when they attacked us. They spoke to us in Greek, but in Sarmatian to each other.'

'Sarmatian ...' repeated Seraphina, finally learning the name of the language those wretches were speaking. 'I overheard some of their private conversations, and they spoke Greek then too. Probably because most of the girls they were holding were Greek.'

'Most of the girls?' asked Cicero.

'Yes, they were holding a total of forty girls in a makeshift prison. There was a whole cadre of guards. The leader was a huge man who wore an eyepatch.'

'Over his right eye, correct?'

'Yes.'

'I remember him. He was standing on the bow of the ship when they approached us.'

'I am missing parts of my memory from the attack,' said Seraphina, hanging her head.

'We'll find out what happened to Quintus.'

Seraphina nodded, her head still hanging down.

'I promise, Seraphina,' said Cicero.

Seraphina looked up and smiled. 'Thank you.'

'That is quite a disguise,' he said, and the laughter lightened the mood between them.

'There is quite a story behind it.'

'I would love to hear it, but first, tell me about these girls.'

'Thirty-eight of them remained at the prison. When I escaped, I managed to take one with me.'

Cicero shook his head in disbelief. 'How did you escape?'

'That is a long story,' said Seraphina, getting up and taking off her robe. 'I've been wearing this thing every day for nearly a month.'

'Please, make yourself comfortable. I have plenty of time to listen to what happened.'

'You are very kind, Cicero. How was the rest of your trip to Rome after the attack?'

'Aside from being in shock and worrying a lot about the two of you, it was uneventful,' said the senator.

Seraphina nodded. 'I am glad for that and happy to see you safe.'

'Thank you, Seraphina. Now, tell me everything.'

Seraphina started with her failed escape attempt and took it from there. Her eventual escape from the prison, and how she had managed to take Rhea with her. Their encounter with the villagers outside Tanais. Then, meeting Keb, which took quite some time to explain. Cicero was fascinated with Keb and commented that he sounded a little like Khay. They talked for hours, and there were a few moments of laughter as Seraphina told her tale.

Cicero assured her that he would take care of her, and there was nothing for her to worry about. Seraphina was appreciative, but she knew in her heart that she would not rest until two matters had been put to rest. She had to find Quintus, and she had to stop those pirates from what they were doing.

FORTY

If Faustus' home was palatial, then Cicero's resembled a small empire. It stood high on the Palatine Hill overlooking Rome. A wide frontage of stone steps, high columns, and triangular top plates made up the façade. The side walls ran almost as long as the front itself, enclosing the massive centre building, which was in turn flanked by two halls with only slightly lower ceilings. Surrounding the buildings were spacious, well-manicured gardens.

The Forum was in plain view, as was the Circus Maximus. Seraphina was particularly excited about being able to see into the circus from her new home. It was empty for now, but she imagined there would be a magnificent view of games and fights when they were held. *If she was around long enough for that to happen*, she thought.

Yesterday had been long. It was a relief to find Cicero and talk to him about everything. She was also glad she no longer had to be in disguise. The disappointment of not finding Quintus cut deep. Seraphina had hoped her arrival to Rome was the last step of them being reunited. Now, she had no idea where he was. *Was it possible he was being held in the same prison with the rest of them?* That thought tormented her. That he could have been so close, and she escaped without trying to free him too.

She knew her imagination was running wild, and she willed herself to stop. For now, she was safe. She could wear normal clothes again and dispense with the carrying of weapons. Her hair would even grow back. She could not hope for a better protector, other than possibly Caesar himself.

Most of the previous evening revealed just how well-regarded Cicero was. As they walked to his chariot, many men, commoners and senators alike, greeted him formally. Quite a few of them used his full name, Marcus Tullius Cicero. *Quite a mouthful for a simple hello*, she thought. Cicero had laughed when she had addressed him as such. He directed Seraphina to simply call him Cicero. The senator seemed to enjoy the informality they shared.

Once they were home, she had been surprised. Aside from a few servants, there was only one other person in the household. Her name was Publilia, and Cicero looked after her, he explained. Riding the chariot home had reminded her of Luna. She would have to figure out a way to get him back from Faustus. Seraphina was confident she could reveal her true identity to him, and that he would understand. Perhaps she could visit with Cicero, just to be safe.

She enjoyed watching the city from her vantage point. Pedestrians, horses, and chariots mingled below. The streets resembled a maze. A light breeze swept across her face, and the scent from Cicero's flower gardens flooded Seraphina's nostrils. The buildings were grey and distinguished. Their varying heights once again sparked the idea of a nighttime run throughout the streets. Then again, she didn't need to hide here. *Why not a daytime run?*

Quintus would have loved this. He had not returned to Rome since birth and had no memory of his years there as a baby. The sky seemed to dim as she considered his fate. Knowing that the pirates had taken him made matters a lot worse. Seraphina almost craved the uncertainty she had felt previously. She could feel her heart beat in her chest, and her skin tingled with goosebumps. Maybe there was still hope.

She stopped examining the city and looked up. The sky was a perfect blue, with bright white clouds resembling brushstrokes on a blank canvas. One covered the sun at this moment, and the rays began to sneak out as the cloud moved to the south. Seraphina thought of Rhea and hoped she was safe in Byzantium by now. Maybe she was even looking up at the same sky. She feared what fate the other girls had come to. No doubt the pirates had done their deal and sold them to the Greek slave trader by now.

'Enjoying yourself?' came a voice from behind her.

Seraphina turned around and saw Publilia standing there. She was a petite girl, probably around Seraphina's age. Her hair was a pinkish red, not unlike the bulbs of the fragrant narcissus flowers. A pair of big, brown eyes was her most striking feature, and these contrasted with small lips that naturally pouted. She was wearing a simpler version of the dress worn by Faustus' wife, and her hands sat on her hips as she waited for Seraphina's response.

'Just enjoying the view, and …' started Seraphina, but holding off from finishing her sentence.

'And?' said Publilia. One hand had come off her hips now, and she turned her palm towards the sky as if to ask Seraphina what the hell she was doing.

It was not yet clear to Seraphina what Publilia's role was. The last thing she needed right now was any kind of conflict. 'Thinking,' she said, softening her tone, and offering a smile.

'Thinking about what?'

'Nothing important,' said Seraphina. With this, she went to walk back towards the house. This involved walking past Publilia. As Seraphina passed her, Publilia folded her arms and moved to her side. This caused Seraphina to nearly fall over to avoid a collision. She recovered and kept moving as if nothing had happened, wondering if the girl was mentally stable. Far from a big girl, Seraphina still had several inches and quite a bit of weight on Publilia.

She put it out of her mind as she walked into the house. There was enough to worry about already. A young servant girl smiled pleasantly at her, and she inquired as to where she might find Cicero. Seraphina followed her down a few wide halls and entered a lavish room where Cicero was sitting at an imposing white marble table. The room resembled his office at the Forum somewhat but was at least triple the size. There were different areas for sitting and studying. An easel sat in one corner of the room with a canvas that Seraphina could only see the back of.

The senator was reading various documents and making notes. She was unsure whether to interrupt him or not. The servant girl went to leave when she saw Seraphina tilting her head and looking to the ceiling.

'If you need to speak to him,' she whispered, 'the best thing is to say something. He'll be in here all day if no one interrupts him.'

Seraphina smiled and nodded at the girl. As she walked closer to Cicero, she noticed the mosaic on the floor. In the centre was a winged creature with a long tail holding a harp. Four grand chalices pointed towards the creature, and surrounding them were four winged animals, half-horse and half-snake. Seraphina raised her eyebrows then noticed the marble on the walls. On the surface, it appeared as though rough cracks ran across the wall, but as she leaned closer, she could see how smooth the marble was. It was beautiful to look at. *Imagine having such lavish quarters to study from*, she thought. For a moment, she thought of her old room in Alexandria and all she had learned. Like so many things in her life, it was only a memory now.

'Hello, Seraphina,' said Cicero, finally looking up. 'I didn't notice you come in.'

'I hope I'm not interrupting you, sir,' she said.

Cicero laughed. 'Not at all, and you need not call me sir unless we're in public.'

'Thank you.' Seraphina continued looking around the room, and then back at Cicero. Her weight shifted from one foot to another.

'May I ask what's on your mind?' he asked, putting his pen down.

'Come and have a seat.'

'Well, sir,' she said before correcting herself. 'I mean, Cicero, sorry, sir.'

'Seraphina, may I say something?'

'Please.'

He leaned forward, placing one hand on top of another as his arms rested on the thick marble. 'You have been through quite an ordeal. In fact, that was the case when I first met you. With everything that has happened since, I think you would do well to take some rest. You are safe now and can stay here as long as you wish.'

Seraphina thought of Publilia and wondered if she shared her master's sentiments.

'I had several ideas in mind when I invited you and Quintus to join me in Rome.' Noticing her face drop at the mention of Quintus' name, he added, 'and I don't think we should give up hope that we will see him again.

Seraphina nodded, her eyes remaining downcast.

'Seraphina look at me.'

She looked up, her bottom lip quivering.

'The opportunities I envisaged for you will still be there in a month.'

'A month from now?'

'Yes, or longer. I have a lot of influence in this city, despite a few setbacks of late. The most important thing for you now is to take some time and recover from what has happened.'

She flinched at the word 'recover'.

'If nothing else, we should let that beautiful hair of yours grow back,' chuckled Cicero, and Seraphina managed to let out a soft laugh as well. She felt herself wanting to correct Cicero immediately. That she did not need any time. Or recovery, for that matter. The words failed her. Perhaps he was right.

'What do you think?'

'I think ...' said Seraphina, '... that you may have a point. Maybe some rest is what I need.' She thought of Keb and the exercises she had given her to do. Besides, Cicero had a rather impressive library she could no doubt study from if she wished.

'But?'

'I keep thinking of those girls trapped in that awful place.'

'Yes, but didn't you say they were to be sold?' asked Cicero.

'I did, but they will no doubt take more girls who will suffer the same fate. And ...' Seraphina's voice trailed off.

'And?'

'Quintus might be there. I had no idea they had taken him, but maybe he was being kept in another room there.'

Cicero's composed posture now gave way to him holding his chin in his hands. 'What are you suggesting exactly, Seraphina?'

'The girl who I managed to escape with, Rhea. She was taken from Byzantium, where her family lives. Her family is quite wealthy, as I learned. These men seem to be kidnapping girls and selling them into slavery.'

Cicero nodded but did not say anything.

'That would have been my fate, had I not escaped,' she said, raising her voice. 'I know Tanais is outside the republic, but these men attacked your ship. Surely that would be of interest to the Roman Army?'

It was now Cicero's eyes that lowered to the ground, as he leaned back in his chair.

'You haven't told them?' asked Seraphina. 'Have you told anyone?'

Cicero shook his head. 'Look, Seraphina, I am glad that you managed to get away. Matters here in Rome are not simple for me at the moment. Before my visit to Alexandria, I was outside of Rome and made some regrettable alliances. As it stands, I am back in Caesar's good graces. But what you're asking—'

'I am asking that we go and stop these men who are selling young women into slavery,' interrupted Seraphina.

Cicero sat up straight in his chair and held his hand up. 'Stop, Seraphina. Even putting aside my personal issues, this would not be a simple request. Marching Roman soldiers outside the borders of the republic would have repercussions. Potentially grave repercussions.'

Seraphina folded her arms and did her best not to glare at Cicero. She thought of rebuking him as a coward, and then a more useful thought crossed her mind. 'What about Quintus?' she asked.

'The place you're talking about is still well outside the borders of the republic. In any event, we can't be sure he's there.'

'Yes, but Quintus is the son of a Roman general,' she said, smiling.

Cicero returned the smile. 'Right you are. Rufio may have been disgraced, but he was still a general. The most highly decorated in the entire army, in fact. Before his sudden demise, that is.'

'Quintus could still be alive in that prison.'

Cicero nodded. 'I'll talk to some colleagues of mine.'

'Do you have contacts in the army?'

'Some. It will be of more benefit to speak to some senators first.' At this, Seraphina cocked her head a little. 'Allow me to explain. If girls and young women are being systematically sold into slavery by these men, it is not something the senate would want to ignore. While slavery certainly exists in the republic, the kidnapping of girls from free families and selling them into slavery is against our laws, and punishable by severe penalties. The issue is one of politics. Exacting justice outside our borders is something we must approach carefully.'

'Who has authority over those lands?'

'It is the land of the Bosporan kings. We have excellent relations with them and they are in many ways subject to Roman authority.' At this, Seraphina sat up and began to smile. 'Yet,' continued Cicero, 'that does not mean we can simply march soldiers in there and do as we please. At the very least, the matter will need to be discussed.'

'With whom?' asked Seraphina.

'Firstly, amongst some colleagues here at the senate. Then, the ranking general here in Rome. Caesar may also need to be consulted.'

'Caesar?' said Seraphina. It was not so much a question. Seraphina had not yet told Cicero that she had met Caesar back in Alexandria. *It would be of no concern,* she thought. It was doubtful that she would be meeting him.

'Yes, Caesar.' He watched Seraphina as she looked at her feet. 'Finally, an emissary may need to be sent to the Bosporan King. Kings have been fighting and dying in those lands for decades. I believe the current monarch is a very reasonable man, who will follow Caesar's commands.'

'That all sounds like it could take a lot of time.'

'Usually, yes. I hope to make the issue of Quintus a major one. One that will expedite matters.'

Seraphina nodded. 'Is there anything I can do to help?'

'Not at this stage, Seraphina. Leave this with me. You can trust me.'

'I do, Cicero, and I thank you. My apologies for behaving poorly before. It upsets me to know that Quintus and those girls are still in captivity.'

'I understand, Seraphina. Is there anything else?'

She was about to get up and say no. Then, she thought of her encounter with Publilia. 'Is there anywhere in the house or grounds I should not go?'

'Aside from the private sleeping quarters, no. You are free to be anywhere in the house and to explore the grounds as you see fit. Why do you ask?'

'I simply wanted to be sure. One other thing.'

'Yes?'

'I know you're a very busy man, but could you come with me to collect my horse from Faustus? I will be appearing to him as a young woman for the first time. Although I don't anticipate there will be a problem, I would prefer to have you with me.'

He was about to decline her request. Then, he realised it would only take a little of his time and thought of how much this young woman had been through. 'I'd be happy to, Seraphina. We can go in the next day or two.'

FORTY ONE

Seraphina had started to notice the effects of Keb's teachings. She had been doing the exercises every day, and twice on some days. Her body felt lighter, her mind clearer, and her moods calmer. She had also gone out into the city last night. Publilia had caught her leaving and tried to start an argument about it. When Cicero had come out, Publilia's demeanour became much more pleasant. Cicero told Seraphina to do as she pleased. If she were to meet anyone who asked questions, she was simply to say she was staying at Senator Marcus Tullius Cicero's house as his guest.

The incident had amused Seraphina. She had gotten so used to sneaking out of the library back home in Alexandria. It had never occurred to her that here, she was free to go where she wanted and do what she pleased. She had caught a few looks from soldiers as she ran across the city. While sitting on a rooftop taking in the view, two soldiers had looked up in her direction. Initially startled, she froze. Then the two men waved at her and smiled. She barely raised her arm to wave in reply.

She longed to see Keb again. Despite everything that was going on, it was a thought that kept coming to her. The man had taught her so much in such a brief time. He had arguably saved her life through the assistance he had given her. Seraphina wondered if she would ever get to go back to that clearing by the sea. She wondered if she would even find him. Then again, Keb did say it was his home.

Her thoughts moved to Quintus and the girls she had been held captive with. *How quickly would Cicero act? Would they still be there?* Seraphina knew they had probably been sold by now. There would surely be more. Maybe there were even more prisons. She thought of Rhea, safe in Byzantium, and this made her smile. She would ask Cicero if it was possible to send a letter, although she had no idea how she would address it even if she could.

Aside from being absorbed in Keb's teachings, Seraphina had noticed the effects of being in Rome. There was very little she was obligated to do. Servants prepared her food. She could take Luna and ride around the city and its outskirts. She had even been invited back to visit Faustus and his wife. He had taken the news of her secret identity with great humour and grace. His wife Antonia had laughed and, now she knew Seraphina was a woman, seemed much more convivial. Antonia had even apologised for how she had behaved when they first met.

She had resolved to train herself into a routine. There was reading each morning, and she was devouring Cicero's collection by the day. While it was no doubt impressive for a private library, it was meagre when compared to what she had been used to in Alexandria. She would take Luna for a ride, and by afternoon explore the vast house and its grounds. She kept out of Publilia's way, except when Cicero was also present. The stunning architecture of Cicero's home gave her much to inspect. Seraphina had planned to ask Cicero about libraries in the city as well.

While there was still a lot on her mind, Seraphina was very much enjoying the freedom and safety of her current existence. Every day, she asked Cicero how matters were progressing. The senator remained hopeful and had spoken to several senators. Plans were being made with the army as to how the approach would be made, and Quintus' name had been waved like a flag whenever there had been resistance or a lack of enthusiasm. The late General Rufio had many friends in the senate and the army. Few people knew about the exact circumstances of his death or the crimes he had committed.

Seraphina had let the memory of Rufio go some time ago. For now, it was to their advantage for the truth about the general to remain concealed. She had started to wonder if she might be a part of any mission. The location of the prison was a secret; the women in the village had given no indication that they knew about it. *How else would the soldiers find it, short of marching around the region for days on end?* Maybe she would have to don her disguise again. The thought excited her, but she did not want to cut her hair like that again. It was just starting to grow back.

She had wandered outside amid her thoughts. It was a beautiful day in Rome. Living up on the Palatine Hill gave Seraphina some splendid views of the city. Today was no different, except for the Circus Maximus. A huge crowd was congregating at the eastern entrance. It looked as though preparations were being made inside the arena. Seraphina's eyebrows rose, and the corners of her mouth turned upward. She looked over at Luna, who was happily tied up and chewing grass as usual.

Looking back down at the Circus, she called out to Cicero. She simply had to go and see what was happening. By the time he came out, she was already mounted on Luna.

'Yes, Seraphina, what is it?'

'May I go to the Circus Maximus? I don't know what is happening down there, but it looks very exciting.'

'You need not ask me permission when you want to go somewhere,' said Cicero, 'and as luck would have it, I have already planned for us to go to today's events at the circus. Have you ever seen gladiators fight?'

Seraphina shook her head, as her jaw dropped. Cicero laughed. 'Well, you will today.' He decided to keep the animals a secret.

'Come on then,' said Seraphina.

'It may be more practical to take my chariot.' Cicero gestured for

Seraphina to come down from the horse. 'I'm glad to have the company. Publilia detests the circus, and I am usually required to go in an official capacity.'

'Does that mean …'

'Yes,' said Cicero, finishing her thought. 'We will be sitting with other senior members of the senate, and Caesar himself will be there as well.'

Seraphina slowly got down from the horse. Surely the great dictator would not recognise her.

FORTY TWO

It was a spectacle unlike anything Seraphina had ever seen. Even the most lavish of festivals in Alexandria paled in comparison. She had a tough time taking everything in. The sheer size of the crowd was overwhelming. There were thousands of people in the grand stadium, and the noise they made was deafening at times. It looked much more crowded on the lower levels.

Cicero had given her something more formal to wear, a dress of the same style worn by Antonia and Publilia. It was called a stola, she was told. It certainly helped her blend in. She had seen Caesar from a distance, but there had been nothing to worry about. He was busy being attended to by servants and had quite an entourage surrounding him. Occasionally, he would make an announcement to the crowd, or command the gladiators below. His words resulted in huge cheers.

The spectacle itself was brutal. Men of all shapes and sizes fought one another. They wore armour and face masks that varied in style and efficacy. Some of the battles were surprising too. It was not always the biggest and the strongest men who were victorious. Seraphina was not accustomed to the violence, and it dredged up memories of the soldiers fighting on the streets of Alexandria. She noticed her back hunch and her chest contract during some of the killings in the arena. It made her think of the bandits she had fought, and, finally, it brought up a thought of Quintus. Her body then shook, and Cicero asked if she was all right. Seraphina turned to him and nodded with a smile. She tried to focus away from the arena. She admired the elegant outfits of those around them. They seemed to be other dignitaries and members of the Roman gentry. Several of them introduced themselves and talked to her during lulls in the action. *These are worldly people*, she thought. They were all supremely friendly and respectful. The benefits of being friends with Cicero continued to accrue, and Seraphina lapped it up.

She had managed to ignore the fighting quite successfully. However, after several phases of battle between gladiators, the stakes were raised dramatically. The large gates leading into the arena had remained shut since the fighting began. They were now opened again. A large number of bears, leopards, and elephants charged at the fighters as Seraphina held a hand to her open mouth.

It was pandemonium. Some of the gladiators charged towards the open gates to escape. They were pushed back by men with long spears. The gates rolled shut, and those attempting to flee made for easy prey. Several of the bears mauled them. The leopards and the elephants charged at those who stayed to fight. In the ensuing fracas, all but the most dextrous and cunning of the creatures below were torn apart. As the animals attacked the absconders from behind, some of the gladiators attacked them. The elephants charged indiscriminately, and they seemed more panicked than aggressive.

The leopards were by far the most vicious. In small packs, they mutilated anything in their path. Elephant. Bear. Human. It did not matter. As the battle was nearing its close, a group of six gladiators formed a circle in the middle. Facing outwards, they struck anything that came near them. Initially mesmerised by the spectacle, Seraphina had closed her eyes and turned her head down, bringing a hand over her forehead. She stood there, listening to the wild jeers around her, wondering how long this would take to end. Finally, a loud horn sounded, and the crowd became quieter. Seraphina looked up.

Swarms of smaller men ran out. They were armed with whips, ropes, and chains. Seraphina stood frozen as she watched what they were there to do. Working in groups, they tamed and led the animals back out of the gates. This by no means went smoothly. One or two of the men were viciously mauled. For the most part, they were very efficient. In a matter of minutes, only the six gladiators in the middle remained. Them, and a huge pile of dead bodies strewn across the vast stadium floor. Seraphina's hand was over her chest, as she shook her head at the carnage.

She was about to close her eyes again, and then Seraphina observed Cicero's expression. It contrasted with most of those surrounding them. He remained straight-faced while their neighbours laughed, shouted, and cheered. This noise gave way to a chant, and at first, she did not hear what they were saying.

'Kill! Kill! Kill!' came the chorus from the crowd. All eyes in the stadium turned to Caesar. The gladiators separated, putting plenty of space between them. They also looked up as they did this. One or two lifted their face masks off, to watch the great man. The chanting continued. Finally, Caesar stood up and raised his hands to the sky. The entire arena was silent. The dictator brought his arms back down then extended one hand forward. His thumb was up. Then, with great drama, he pointed his thumb down.

The crowd went wild, as the gladiators rushed towards each other. Some worked together, and men fell in quick succession. The final two remaining could not have been more of a contrast. One was a behemoth who resembled a much larger version of Darius, the leader of Faustus' warriors. The other seemed to be no bigger than Seraphina—a wiry man about half the height of his opponent. The battle was fierce, and more than once the smaller man was thrown to the ground, as the crowd cheered 'Albus!' repeatedly.

Albus was large but too slow. Each time the giant warrior brought either his axe or his sword down and hit only dirt, the smaller man would roll away, inflicting a deep gash to either Albus' leg or arm. There was a pattern to their movements, and Seraphina noticed it before long. Albus was wearing himself out. The clever tactics of his opponent were to blame for this. First, he would run away then stop. He would then dodge a blow or two and inflict as much damage as possible on Albus before running away again. After a few rounds of this, Albus was slowing down, and holding one of the wounds to his side.

The smaller fighter sprinted away, gaining nearly the length of the stadium on his opponent. Then he turned around. Albus was charging straight at him, while his opponent dropped all his armour and weapons, except one. It was a long, sleek sword. No one, not even Albus, had even seen the weapon. It was cleverly hidden inside his armour.

Then Albus saw the man run towards him. He couldn't resist a smile and swung his huge axe down at him. What happened next astounded Seraphina, as well as the entire crowd. He took a leap off the ground and pushed off Albus' axe with his foot to jump over him. As he came to land, his body turned mid-air. He slashed his sword at Albus and landed in a perfect three-point stance.

Seraphina had dropped her head for a moment when she heard that flash. She looked up with the rest of the crowd, and Albus was still standing. He was not moving though. The giant's ear then turned towards the sky, and his head rolled off the top of his body. It made little more than the sound of a pin drop as it hit the floor. It was followed by Albus' decapitated body, which caused a much larger thud.

The warrior rose to a stunned, silent crowd. There were whispers of what this man's name was. The silence quickly gave way to the cheers of the crowd. Before long, the entire arena was applauding. They watched the victor walk towards the edge of the arena. Caesar looked down on him, offering a congratulatory gesture. The man ran around the edge of the arena, with his sword raised. The crowd appreciated the showmanship.

The senators around them talked about the victory. Seraphina just stood there, processing the entirety of what she had just witnessed.

Cicero spoke to a few of his colleagues, before noticing how quiet and still she was.

'How did you enjoy that, Seraphina? Quite something, wasn't it?' asked Cicero.

Seraphina started nodding her head. It took about four or five nods of the head before she managed to get a word out. 'Yes.' She kept nodding and looked up at Cicero with glazed eyes 'Can we go?' she asked, her voice faltering.

Cicero nodded and placed a hand on her shoulder. 'Good idea. From previous experience, I know it's best we leave quickly. This entire crowd will be on the streets soon.'

The two of them exited through a private corridor. It was intended only for those of a certain status. Cicero certainly qualified. A polite young legionary helped them into the chariot and held back traffic, so they could come out on to the street. Seraphina stood next to Cicero as he guided his horses through the congestion. Once out of the Circus, she took a few deep breaths and noticed her heart rate return to normal. The sun felt good on her skin, and she tried to forget what had happened in the arena. There was a festive mood in the air, and this helped. She watched Cicero and the horses. More than a few times, she thought of asking to take the reins.

She started to smile at the thought of driving the chariot. *Perhaps I can ask another day.* A familiar face flashed past her. Seraphina looked back and stared in disbelief. *Was that Korinna, the obnoxious girl from the prison?* Cicero was moving slowly through the streets, and Seraphina had plenty of time to look. It certainly looked like her. She wore simple clothes and followed an elegantly dressed woman. She was carrying quite a few different items. They looked to be weighing her down. Then she stopped, as she caught Seraphina's stare. Her eyes widened, and she stood up tall.

It was definitely Korinna. Seraphina was unsure of what to do. As they neared a corner and turned, she saw Korinna being scolded by the woman she had been following.

FORTY THREE

Cicero guided the horses into the entrance and looked to his side. The young woman's spirits seemed to have dipped on the ride home. She got off the chariot without a word and dragged her feet as she walked into the house. He went to ask her what was wrong. Just then, a servant came running out of the house.

'Master,' he said, 'Caesar has sent for you.' He was clutching a note.

Cicero was surprised, having just seen Caesar at the Circus. Then again, the dictator was famous for thinking ahead of time. Summoning Cicero had probably been planned days ago. He read the note, noting its obvious lack of detail. 'Who delivered this?' he demanded.

'A Prefect,' said the servant. 'I dared not ask his name.'

A Prefect? Why would a Prefect be dispatched? And to deliver such a vague note? *It must be of some importance*, thought Cicero. He turned the horses back around, clutching the note. He snapped the reins and sped towards the Domus Publica, which was not far away. Cicero racked his brains, thinking only the worst. When he arrived, a centurion approached his chariot.

'Master Cicero, Caesar is expecting you.'

'Ave, centurion,' replied Cicero.

He was led through the halls to Caesar's private office. The dictator had his back to the doorway, looking out of a window into the distance. The office was sparsely furnished and decorated. The same style was evident throughout the rest of his official residence. Cicero admired the simple approach that Caesar took to matters. That simplicity could extend to his ruthlessness as well, and Cicero was well aware that he should remain on the dictator's good side.

'Ave, Caesar,' said Cicero.

Caesar turned around and smiled warmly at Cicero. *Maybe it was not unwelcome news after all*, he thought.

'So,' started Caesar, 'I hear your latest idea is to march outside our borders on to the lands of the Bosporan King.'

'My lord—'

'Please, have a seat.'

The two men sat down. A servant came to offer refreshments. Cicero took a sip of his drink and breathed more easily. The combination of water, wine, and honey soothed him.

'Cicero, you seem nervous.'

Cicero looked up from his cup, not saying anything in response.

'Tell me about these discussions you have been having with Gaius and the other senators.'

Cicero shifted in his seat. 'I recently received some information that a band of pirates is operating in those lands to the east of the republic. After my recent visit to Pompey, I went to Alexandria to consult with an old friend.'

Caesar raised his eyes at the mention of Pompey. Cicero regretted mentioning it but continued. 'The friend advised me of some matters he was aware of. These included the misdeeds of a certain high-ranking general—'

'Rufio,' said Caesar.

'Yes, General Rufio. As it happened, I met his son and a young woman who he had become acquainted with.'

'What's the son's name?' asked Caesar with widened eyes.

'Quintus. A fine young man.'

'What does he have to do with this?'

'On my way back to Rome from Alexandria, these pirates attacked my ship. As you may know, I do not often travel with soldiers as guards. The need has ne—'

Caesar sighed loudly enough to interrupt him. Then he spoke through gritted teeth, giving equal weight to each word. 'I have told you repeatedly to travel with a proper armed escort. As of now, I am making it an order. When you travel, you will go with the standard detail of guards from the army. Is that understood?' The dictator's voice rose as he asked this.

'Yes, my lord.' Cicero hesitated for a moment. 'May I continue?'

'Please,' said Caesar, leaning back, and waving his hand dismissively.

'The pirates attacked my ship. They wanted to take the girl.'

'What girl?' asked Caesar.

'The one who Quintus had been acquainted with.'

Caesar shook his head. 'What was she doing there?'

'The two wanted to be together,' said Cicero. 'She seemed a fine young woman, so I thought there would be no harm.'

Caesar gave Cicero a little smirk. 'You were wrong about that, weren't you? By Jupiter, it sounds like you allowed these children to command your ship to have passage to Rome.'

Cicero resented the last remark, though he tried his best not to show it. 'My lord, the boy and this young woman impressed me greatly. I offered to bring them both here as they are fine young people and—' Cicero stopped himself. He had said too much.

'And?'

'And the pirates took them both,' finished Cicero. Caesar could tell it was not what he originally planned to say, but let it go for the time being.

'I don't understand. You said they wanted to take the girl.'

'Yes.' Cicero nodded. 'We were in no position to resist. The boy fought them though. They ended up taking both the boy and the girl with them.'

'I see.'

'As luck would have it, the girl escaped and made her way to Rome.'

Caesar's raised his eyebrows but did not say anything. 'She found me and told me everything she could, though she had no memory of what had happened to Quintus. She was knocked unconscious during the attack.'

Caesar rubbed his chin and looked over at Cicero.

'I need not remind you, my lord, that Quintus is the son of a highly decorated general. These men may still be holding him.'

Caesar could see why Cicero was such a valued statesman. He was principled, and precious few men who walked the floors of the Forum were. He was also tactical. Using the general's son to justify what was a quest to free slave girls. It was a bold move. Caesar knew much more than he had let on. He knew that if some of these girls were being kidnapped from wealthy families, then it was in his interest to stop these pirates. Quintus was a crucial factor too. Rufio may have disgraced himself in losing the battle in Alexandria, but he was still a general. He had lost his life in that battle. The accusations made against the late general were yet to be substantiated. There was enough at stake, Caesar decided, to proceed with the mission being proposed.

'Very well,' said Caesar. 'I will dispatch an emissary from our settlements in the east to King Asander.'

'I appreciate that, my lord. If the king agrees—'

'Asander will do anything I ask, Cicero. You know that.' The two shared a smile at this. 'Once the emissary returns, we will have the necessary authority to cross into their lands. To find these villains.'

'Thank you, my lord.'

'I am glad you brought this matter to my attention, Cicero. I am also glad our differences have been resolved. Let's move on, and never speak of that Pompey debacle again.'

'It is agreed. I thank you for your grace.'

'This girl, do you know where she is now?'

'Yes, my lord. She is safe and staying at my home.'

Caesar nodded. 'Escaping must have been some ordeal, and then to make her way here. Tanais is a very long way from Rome. The lands between here and there are treacherous, to say the least. She must be quite a young woman indeed.'

'Yes, my lord. That was the impression I formed when I first met her. She has only continued to impress me. At some point during her journey from Tanais, she fought off several bandits.'

'Will she be able to meet with our soldiers?'

Cicero flinched. 'Yes, but why, my lord?'

Caesar frowned and gave a little shake of his head. 'So she can give them an idea of where to find this place, Cicero. This prison.'

'Of course, my lord.'

FORTY FOUR

Seraphina found some interesting variety in Cicero's personal library. She had completely devoured everything she could find on philosophy. Cicero had penned many of those texts himself. She was now dying to engage him on the subject. He was a busy man though, and Seraphina remained mindful of that fact. The remainder of his shelves contained texts on government and law. These were far from Seraphina's most cherished subjects, but she found herself developing a new interest in them.

The Romans took a different approach to the Egyptians when it came to these areas. Certainly, the Romans had all but taken over Alexandria. However, their formal customs were yet to fully permeate Egyptian culture. She had now been in Rome for several weeks and seen some measure of how the city operated. The Forum was just down the hill. She was living with a senator. The texts gave her an insight into how the institutions of Rome operated. Seraphina noticed how her interest had spiked. Learning deeply about what she observed on the surface every day was wondrous to her.

Besides, one of the things she missed most about her old life was unlimited reading material. She was almost finished with what Cicero's library had to offer. Then, she hoped to visit the city's repositories of knowledge. She had overheard something about libraries at the Forum. Seraphina wondered if she would be allowed in.

Cicero walked in and glanced around.

'Seraphina,' he said. 'I thought I would find you here.'

'How are you today, Master Cicero?' She had taken to calling him 'master' jokingly. He had recognised the affection and gave up asking her to stop.

'Very well. I see you have found more to read.'

'Your library is impressive, but I used to live in a much better one.'

Cicero let out a loud chuckle. 'Yes. I do hope they have the foresight to rebuild that beautiful place.'

Her head dipped for a moment as her gaze shifted to the ground. Seraphina nodded. Cicero decided to change the subject.

'It seems that Caesar learned of my enquiries.'

'What enquiries?' she asked, getting up from her chair.

'I have been talking to several senators about the place where you were held. About Quintus and the girls. Remember?'

'Yes, of course,' she said, shaking her head. 'Sorry, my mind was elsewhere.'

'I don't blame you if you were reading that.' He pointed at the thick volumes on the table. 'Roman Law and Government? You must be terribly bored.'

'It's actually quite intriguing. I would not normally be interested in such a topic, but I've run out of material to read. Almost. It helps me learn a little more about Rome as well, which can only be a good thing.'

Cicero nodded. 'Yes. Now, back to what I was saying.' He relayed the conversation between him and Caesar, leaving out the parts about their political quarrels.

'It seems he took to the idea, after all,' said Seraphina.

'Yes. There is one thing, though.'

'What's that?'

'He wants you to meet with the soldiers who will carry out the mission. To guide them to their target.'

Seraphina's eyebrows raised and she bounced lightly on the balls of her feet. 'You mean I will go with them?'

'That's not the impression I formed, given the way he said it. I think he wants you to somehow give the soldiers the best possible idea of where to find these men and their captives. Perhaps on a map, but to be honest, I'm not quite sure.'

She became still. 'I never used a map.'

'What about the directions you said your friend gave you? What was his name? Keb?'

'Yes, Keb. He gave me various notes on landmarks to follow and where I could expect to end up each day. He based it on the fact that I was travelling with Luna.'

'Who?'

Seraphina shook her head. 'Sorry, the horse.'

Cicero nodded. 'I see.'

'Looking at a map would likely mean very little to me. I didn't even need all the guidance that Keb gave me. A few days into my travels, I met Faustus. One of his men guided us through the rest of the journey, and I paid very little attention. I was just happy to be safe and headed here, to Rome.'

'Perhaps I could speak to Faustus. We could see if his men can guide the soldiers back to where they found you. Then, between the notes and you speaking to them, they would be able to find the place.'

Seraphina had been hoping to return with the army if it was decided they would go. She understood full well that they were the soldiers, and she wanted no part of any fighting. She did want to see if Quintus was there though. This single thought consumed most of her waking hours when she wasn't distracted with other matters.

'This makes no sense, Cicero. If they're serious about finding this place, then why not just take me with them?'

Cicero hesitated, raising his eyebrows for a moment with a little frown. 'Well … they may not wish for a young woman to accompany them on such a dangerous mission.'

Seraphina's jaw dropped. 'We're not going anywhere I haven't been already.'

'I understand that, but these are Roman soldiers. They may not see it that way. Besides, you may find yourself the object of some, shall we say, unwanted attention.'

Seraphina scanned Cicero's eyes for a moment, and her own eyes widened and turned away once she realised what he meant. 'Oh, I see. These soldiers are professionals, surely.' She shook her head at such an absurd thought.

'You're being naive, Seraphina.'

'What if I went in disguise again? You barely recognised me when you first saw me. You thought I was a young man, did you not?'

'I did, but either some or all of these men already have the full story. If you go to meet with them, even to tell them what you know, they'll be expecting a young woman. Besides, your hair has finally started growing back.'

Seraphina folded her arms, thinking how unfair this was. 'I understand what you're saying. I am not one of these women, strolling the streets of Rome in my stola. I can handle myself. You can ask Faustus. That's how we came to meet. He saw me fight four bandits by myself, killing two of them.'

This was part of the story Cicero had not heard. 'You mentioned you fought them off. I had no idea you had killed two.'

'Killed two and debilitated the other two,' she said.

Cicero was impressed. 'Well, as remarkable as that is, I'm not sure it will sway these men. They, especially the commanding officers, tend to think in an old-fashioned manner.'

Seraphina's head tilted downwards for a few moments. She took a deep breath in. Cicero thought for a moment she may have given up. Then she looked up with big eyes and a wide smile on her face.

'You said something about Faustus' men showing the soldiers where they met me.' She tapped a finger against her cheek, as she looked up in the direction of the ceiling.

'What are you thinking?'

'I have an idea. What if I met the soldiers, and gave them as much information as I could? I'll hand them Keb's directions and tell them what I can about how to find the place from where I met Faustus and his men.'

Cicero nodded, though he knew that was not the end of it. He waved her on, urging her to continue.

'I could tell them how Darius, that's the leader of Faustus' personal guards, guided us expertly from where they found me to Rome. They may be inclined to take Darius with them. He was very familiar with the terrain, and seemed to navigate us from memory.'

Cicero was nodding, and a smile had started to form on his face. 'He's a formidable warrior too,' she continued. 'At least, he looked it. He was by far the largest of Faustus' men, and they were all sizeable fighters. I doubt the soldiers would have any concern taking him with them.'

Cicero turned his hands upward, dying to hear the last part of her plan.

'I could go with Darius, as an assistant. In disguise of course. Faustus seems to be quite fond of me, and I'm sure I could persuade him. He, more than anyone, knows how well I can handle a dangerous situation. If we come across one, that is. Once we got to the prison, I wouldn't need to be part of the attack.'

'That might just work,' mumbled Cicero, thinking out loud.

'If Quintus is there, I really want to be there when they free him. Please, Cicero. Please help me do this.'

FORTY FIVE

The meeting with the soldiers had gone to plan. The commander was pleased with the information that Seraphina provided and was confident in leading the mission. Cicero had gone with Seraphina to meet Faustus and explain their idea. He was initially reluctant to send Darius with them. Once he heard the story about Quintus and the young girls, his hesitation melted away. Faustus and his wife had told no one that Seraphina and Seorsa were one and the same person. After some consideration, it had been decided not to deceive Darius, and he was told. The warrior took to his new assignment with great enthusiasm. He was surprised at the revelation that Seorsa was a young woman. It took several explanations and Seraphina putting on her disguise before he completely believed it.

It was agreed by all that the top priority for Seraphina was to stay safe. If there was any type of fighting, she was to retreat and remain hidden until it finished.

'Fighting is to be an absolute last resort,' said Cicero and Faustus repeatedly.

'Where have I heard that before?' mumbled Seraphina under her breath, thinking fondly of Keb.

Seraphina knew what she had to say and do to go on the mission. She had no problem telling them what they wanted to hear. She had been rearmed with the club, sword, and dagger. Her rationale was that if anyone spotted them, she should look exactly as she did when travelling to Rome with Faustus and his convoy. The three men reluctantly accepted this justification. The truth was, she wanted to be armed, just in case. Seraphina preferred to rely on herself. In addition, her own experience had shown how quickly a situation could become dangerous.

The decision to use soldiers from the east of the republic had been considered and dismissed. Caesar's advisors had suggested when the emissary was dispatched to King Asander, that troops from nearby could be prepared. The commander had quickly said no to this. He was in charge of the mission, and he had received the intelligence first-hand from the young woman. Aside from that, the soldiers in that part of the republic were not nearly as well trained, and he had no interest in working with them.

The commander, Paulus, was a striking man, a little younger than Faustus. He was almost as tall as Darius but slimmer. Yet there was something about him that exuded strength. He had short, straight hair that was such a dark shade of brown that it seemed black. The tanned skin was a result of many years spent away from Rome in battle, and one could be forgiven for thinking he was not Roman. His eyes were blue and never seemed to blink, not that Seraphina saw anyway. There was a firmness to his voice that remained whenever he spoke. Paulus gave the impression of a man in charge, an impression that matched his reputation.

Based on the information Seraphina had provided, an elite unit of thirty men had been selected. Paulus had selected mostly centurions and tribunes. They were well-ranked officers, and Paulus never settled for anything but the best. The fact that Caesar was aware of this mission only harnessed his focus. Only one legionary had been included, an excellent young warrior named Vitus. Seraphina had informed them that the band of pirates was no more than eight. Including Darius and his young assistant, a total of thirty-two would travel to Tanais.

Paulus had expressed his reservations about the young assistant that Darius insisted on bringing. He was confident of Darius' value to the mission but did not see why there was a need to bring this young man along. He was young and of slight build. Darius assured the commander that Seorsa could handle himself in the event of a fight, and that he would be of great use in finding their way to their target. At Cicero's suggestion, Seraphina had worn a stola and a wig when going to meet Paulus initially. Disguised as Seorsa, the commander had no inkling that this was the young woman who had briefed them.

The morning had come. Darius and Seraphina prepared themselves to meet the other soldiers. Paulus had ordered that they would meet at the Temple of Jupiter. He wished to offer prayers and ask for blessings on their mission.

'Have you ever done that before, Darius?' asked Seraphina. 'Gone to pray before going on a mission?'

'You mustn't speak to me like that,' answered Darius. Seraphina gave him a confused look. 'Get in the habit of using your disguised voice when talking to me. Even when we're alone.'

Seraphina nodded. 'I understand. Sorry. I'll do that from now on.'

Darius almost laughed at the change in pitch when she spoke in disguise.

'Well, you can't ask me to do something and then start laughing at me when I do it. Are you going to be able to go along with my act?'

'Of course,' he said, barely suppressing another chuckle. 'It's quite an adjustment, but I'll get used to it. To answer your earlier question, I suppose not. Accompanying Faustus is rarely dangerous. I'm sure some of the men pray and ask for blessings, but never at a temple and as a group.'

'Does it strike you as odd?' she asked.

'Not at all. This Paulus, the commander, is very professional. It doesn't surprise me at all that he is a religious man. I'm glad we're doing it. We can always use the help of the gods, especially on a mission like this.'

'Have you ever done anything like this before?'

'Not for many years.'

Seraphina was waiting to see if he would say more. Her curiosity was piqued, and as she was about to say something else, he cut her off. 'No more questions for now. Check your supplies. This journey will be different than when we brought you to Rome with us. Each man will be expected to set up his own camping quarters each night, look after their own water supply, and so on.'

'May I ask one question about that?'

Darius nodded.

'What about food?'

'I'm quite sure that some of the soldiers will be assigned to gather and prepare food each day.'

'How do you know so much about this?'

'I used to be a soldier. Now, are you ready to go?'

'Yes, sir.'

Seraphina had already said her goodbyes to Cicero, promising she would return safely. Darius bid his master farewell, and Antonia hugged Seraphina tightly. She stepped back, beholding the costume.

'It's hard to believe that's you under there, Seraphina,' said Antonia.

'When I come back, I'll put the stola on and we can wander around Rome together.'

Antonia laughed. 'Maybe, though it could be funny to walk around with you dressed like that.'

Faustus lifted his hands up. 'Alright, ladies. That's enough. Seraphina, do you have everything you need?' He spoke to her like a concerned father.

'I do, Faustus.' Seraphina looked as though she was going to say something else for a moment, and then stopped.

'What is it, my dear?' asked Faustus.

'I want to say something to you. I am so grateful that you helped me when you found me. I wasn't sure whether to trust you when I first met you, and you showed me such kindness to simply bring me to Rome safely. Then you helped me find Cicero and forgave the debt of work I owed you. When you found out I had deceived you, you were so gracious. Now, you have once again helped me by allowing the leader of your personal guard to go on this dangerous mission. Thank you, Faustus, from the bottom of my heart.'

With this, she hugged him tightly and caught him by surprise. Antonia and Darius couldn't help but smile.

Faustus held her, patting her on the back. 'Seraphina, you're most welcome. I believe in giving. Whenever I can, and as much I can. So, I'm honoured to be able to help you. As for Darius, he is more than capable of handling himself. He'll protect you should any danger befall you. Now, the two of you best depart. You don't want to keep the commander and his troops waiting.'

They said their final goodbyes and began the short ride to the temple.

FORTY SIX

The Temple of Jupiter was an exceptional sight. More Greek than Roman in its architecture, its majesty caught the eye of anyone who happened to pass it. Even though it was close to the Forum, Seraphina had not yet seen it. Beholding the impressive columns and the wide hallways on either side of the temple, all she could think about was wanting to explore it thoroughly and of course, to ask questions. That would have to wait. Paulus and the men were already assembled on the steps of the temple. A strangely attired man stood above them at the top of the steps.

He was wearing a toga, but that was about all that seemed usual about him. A thick red tunic was wrapped around his shoulders and dropped to his legs, like a cape. He wore a helmet of brownish red colour, on top of which sat what looked like an upside-down spinning top. Seraphina stopped and stared at the odd ensemble until Darius pulled her out of her trance.

'Come on,' he said, 'that's the priest. They're waiting for us.'

She looked at Darius as if he must be joking. He gave her a stern look, and she realised she was oblivious to the gravity of the occasion. They joined the soldiers, who were lined up like clones. Right knee to the stone of the steps, left knee bent at a right angle with both hands over the bent knee. The priest started giving his blessing, an interesting ritual where he held flaming wooden torches over the soldiers. The words were rapid and mumbled, but sounded Latin. After that, an assistant of some variety came to collect the torches. They were then led in prayer. At intervals, the priest stopped so the men could repeat the words.

Of course, she had no idea what was going on. After a few rounds of this, she caught on and started repeating. Darius and the soldiers seemed to know the prayer by heart. The ceremony ended, and the priest was about to go back into the temple.

His gaze lingered on Seraphina. The boy seemed very much out of place. The priest wagged a finger at Paulus, summoning him for a conversation. Seraphina could not hear what was being said, but it was obvious that she was the subject of their discussion. After a few moments, she decided it was best to look away. She mounted her horse, just as Darius had done. Seraphina then had a funny feeling about Darius, and it reminded her of how she had felt about Faustus for most of the journey to Rome. She brushed her thoughts aside, reminding herself that both Faustus and Darius were helping her. Then she remembered what Keb had told her about sensing peoples' energies, and she looked over at Darius. The same sensation returned, and her chest involuntarily rose as she took in a deep breath. Suddenly, she was very happy that Luna was coming along with them. She checked her weapons.

The other soldiers were indifferent to Darius and his young assistant. They had clear roles, and that was to guide them through the territory they would cover in the coming days. The soldiers had a job to do too, and everyone seemed focused on what they needed to do. Once Paulus had conferred with his men, the group rode out of the city. Before long, they were surrounded by plains and farmland.

The landscape was somewhat familiar. Seraphina had seen it when arriving into Rome. Now, a mere few weeks later, she was leaving, headed back to the exact place she had escaped. The irony was not lost on her. She turned her mind to enjoying the countryside and rode alongside

Darius. Much as he and his warriors had done on the trip to Rome, Paulus and his soldiers surrounded the two of them in a protective formation. Instead of ten men, there were thirty formed around them. To say she felt safe was an understatement.

As the last farms and homes were left behind, Paulus ordered the convoy to stop. Even Darius seemed surprised by this. Not one of the men moved, however. Paulus rode by himself to the side of the road. As Seraphina looked in the direction he was walking, she saw a very small altar. It was formed by nothing more than three pieces of stone. There were a few small items on top of it. She craned her neck to get a better look and wanted to get closer. None of the others had moved though, and she knew better than to step out of line.

She listened as Darius asked the man closest to him what was going on.

'It's a small shrine to Mars,' said the officer. 'One like it can be found in most directions leaving Rome. The senior officer will usually stop and give a small offering.'

Seraphina found these traditions fascinating. She had certainly read about such rituals, but to see a highly ranked member of the Roman Army observing one was most interesting. Noticing that the other men had their heads forward, she looked in the same direction. Paulus returned to his horse as if nothing had happened, and they rode off in silence.

FORTY SEVEN

The contrast of the return trip stood out in many ways. Whereas Seraphina preferred the luxury of travelling with Faustus—riding alongside him with very little care, waking and retiring for the day at a leisurely hour, having camping grounds and delicious food prepared—the Romans were regimented. A certain amount of ground had to be covered each day. Seraphina was not sure how this could be measured, but Darius had remarked once or twice that they were travelling an identical distance each day. He said this with a tone of obvious respect for the Roman commander. They woke early, ate to a schedule, and rode with a purpose.

The discipline enthralled Seraphina. She kept up with them in every way and was quite proud of herself for doing so. No type of danger had come their way. From time to time, Seraphina's mind turned to the bandits she had encountered before meeting Faustus. If the idea that bandits would attack Faustus and his men was funny, the notion that this group of men would be attacked was downright ludicrous.

Darius was far from amused. There had been some dispute between him and Paulus about the route they were taking. Paulus preferred to take the most direct route and shorten the distance they needed to ride. Darius advised how treacherous this could be and advised the commander to take a southern route. The reason, Darius said repeatedly, were the Germanic tribes that roamed the more northern lands. He had voiced his protests loudly, telling of how fierce and indiscriminate the Germanic tribes were. Darius also mentioned more than once how they took to trespassers.

Paulus had not heeded his advice. In a final effort to convince him, Darius had reminded the commander why he had been asked to join this mission. In an emphatic rebuke, Paulus reminded Darius that he was the one in charge. That settled the matter. Darius was no coward and remained, but it was easy to see that he was worried.

Seraphina had stayed out of it. Of all thirty-two, she was the last whose opinion would be valued. She tried to remain optimistic and uncharacteristically kept her thoughts to herself. Instead, she daydreamed of Quintus, hoping that they would find him at the end of their journey. If she had managed to survive that terrible place, she knew he would too.

A few more hours passed, and the trees became more spaced out. In the distance, Seraphina saw water. She could not be sure to begin with, but it looked to be the same sea beside which she had found Keb's home. *Could it be?* She tried to count the days. They had been riding a lot more each day than when she travelled with Faustus. One and a half times as much, Darius had noted. If she was right about their position, then Keb was less than half a day's ride.

Just then, she felt a searing pain in her chest. Something had hit her. She fell sideways off her horse, and the last thing she felt was something dull hitting her head.

When she came to, Darius was holding a broken clove of garlic underneath her nose. She pushed his hands away and looked up at him. Then something else caught her eye. It was the long shaft of an arrow, and she could feel its head buried in her chest, burning. Darius put a finger to his mouth. She saw that the other soldiers were completely still, looking to the trees around them.

A few minutes passed that felt like an eternity. Darius looked in Paulus' direction and said, quietly, 'that was a warning. Come on.' He snapped the long end of the arrow's shaft off and asked Seraphina if she could get back on her horse. Just for a few minutes. She nodded through gritted teeth. The convoy rode off to their right, following Darius for now. The forest became thicker, and they came to a stop.

Wasting no time, Darius cleaned the wound with alcohol. He put a thick piece of wood between Seraphina's teeth, then gently pulled and coaxed the arrowhead free. It was painful, but it only took a few seconds. Paulus then directed one of his soldiers, the one with medical training, to patch up the young man's wound.

Darius stood up and showed what remained of the shaft to Paulus.

'Sir, do you see this?' said Darius as he pulled an arrow from his own quiver. Not the pine that we use, but oak. These trees cover most of Germania. It is heavier wood, so the arrows don't stay in the air as long. Whoever fired it was not far away.'

Paulus nodded slowly, taking what remained of the bloodied arrow for a closer look.

Darius continued. 'It was either a scout or a group of warriors. Regardless, we should take it as a warning and stay as far south as possible until we get to the edge of that sea. From there, we can skirt the shore and safely make it to our destination.'

Paulus still had not uttered a word. He looked down at the boy and felt guilty for his pride. The wound had been attended to, and he was sitting up. Thankfully, it was not serious. Paulus nodded, looking at no one in particular.

'We will do as you have said, Darius. I'm sorry I didn't listen to you before.'

Darius and several of the soldiers were taken aback by this. Even though the commander had decided to listen to Darius, none of them anticipated an apology. Paulus crouched down to speak to the wounded young man.

'How are you feeling?'

Seraphina looked at her wound, careful not to reveal too much of her body. A neat line of stitches had replaced the deep, bloody wound. The alcohol had helped numb the pain.

'I'm alright, I think,' she grunted, clearing her throat. She sat up against the tree and tried to get to her feet.

Paulus patted her on the shoulder. 'Just sit for now. Remind me, what's your name?'

'Seorsa,' she said in her deepened voice.

'You're doing very well, Seorsa.' Then, turning to the others, he pointed at a spot further south of their position. 'We will set up camp there for the night. Get to work.'

The soldiers moved out, while Darius and Paulus helped Seraphina back on to her horse. Darius instructed her to simply hold herself up on the horse. He took both sets of reins, for his horse and hers, and followed Paulus at an easy canter to the campsite. As they regrouped with the other soldiers Darius began to look around. His eyes were still darting when he helped Seraphina off her horse.

'What is it?' asked Seraphina.

'I'm not so sure about this,' said Darius. The two spoke in hushed tones, at a distance from the soldiers.

'What do you mean?'

'This isn't a safe place. Wolves have been known to live and hunt around these parts. Packs of vicious wolves.'

'Why don't you say something? I thought you said it would be safer further south.'

Darius nodded. 'Safe from those wild Germanians, yes. My plan was to meet the sea at a much further point south.' He pointed as he said this. 'Where this part of the forest thins out on the other side, that is where we should be. Then we get to the sea and follow it almost all the way to Tanais.'

'We should tell Paulus,' said Seraphina.

'I don't want another argument with that man.'

Seraphina glared at him for a moment, then looked over at Paulus.

Marching over to him, still wincing a little from the wound in her chest, she asked to speak to him.

'Yes, what is it? Are you feeling better?'

'I am, thank you,' said Seraphina. 'Listen, I don't think we should camp here.' A few of the soldiers overheard this, and most had already set up their places for the night.

'May I ask why?' The commander had his hands on his hips as he looked down on the young man.

'Wolves, sir. Wolves are known to stalk these parts. I think it unwise to sleep in an area where we could be vulnerable to them.'

'How do you know that?' he asked, glancing in Darius' direction. Darius was facing away but shot a look in their direction.

'I'm familiar with these lands,' lied Seraphina. 'I've come across them once or twice and have long since learned to travel further south of this place.' She pointed and moved her finger as she spoke. 'Here, where this forest thins out again, then across to the edge of the sea, and around its shore.'

Paulus looked up at the sky. It was almost dark. He looked back down at Seorsa. 'I think you two are worried about nothing. Wolves aren't going to attack men who are sleeping. In any case, it's too late for us to move camp now. By the time we take a new position, it will be pitch-black.'

'But, sir—'

'Set up camp, Seorsa. Tell him if your wound starts to cause you more pain.' Paulus walked away, pointing to the soldier who had treated Seraphina.

Darius shook his head, and Seraphina was unsure whether he was annoyed at her impertinence or Paulus' obstinacy. They prepared their places for the night without further discussion.

FORTY EIGHT

The night passed without incident. Seraphina woke up a little groggy, but it was when she moved that the real pain set in. The entire right side of her upper body felt as though it weighed a ton. The sky was still dark, tinged with only a faint hint of the morning's light. A breeze from the east swept the natural fragrance of the land towards her, and Seraphina breathed it in. She coughed as soon as she moved her chest. Pressing her hands on the ground, she forced herself to her feet.

She was about to start doing her exercises, the ones Keb had taught her, when she noticed movement around her. The soldiers were all awake. Someone approached her in the semi-darkness.

'Good morning,' said the voice. It was Paulus. 'Get yourself ready. I want to get away from here as soon as we can. Be quiet about it. No questions.'

Darius was next to her, and he looked to be asleep. She woke him, and as he stirred, she relayed what Paulus had said.

By the time they were on the move, there was only a little more light coming through the trees. The soldiers looked only half-awake. After a few minutes, Seraphina leaned towards one of them.

'What's going on?' she asked in a whisper.

'Those wolves you were talking about. They were here last night. Some food was eaten out of one of our bags. It was shredded to pieces. Now keep quiet.'

A big, black silhouette flashed in front of her, and Seraphina saw a horse and a soldier knocked over. Then another. She couldn't make out the shapes in the dark. Then, menacing growls and the piercing scream of the soldier. The wolves were coming from the right and knocking the men off their horses. Paulus was about to jump off his horse to aid them, and Darius yelled at him.

'Fighting wolves in the dark, are you crazy? Ride!'

Darius turned his horse and snapped the reins. Those who remained on their horses did the same, galloping away as fast as possible.

Seraphina did not look back. She whipped the reins and rode. Luna hit his stride, and outran the rest of the convoy. She didn't care. The sound of the horses behind her was still there. The others would catch up. Luna began to slow down, as they came to a steep hill.

'Seorsa,' called out a voice. It was Darius, and she could barely hear him.

Seraphina looked up the hill. They were out of the thick part of the forest, and the morning light helped her see more. She turned around and could see Darius and several of the soldiers in the distance. Darius waved for her to come back. Glancing up the hill, she sensed it was a good idea not to go further. Darius and the others seemed calm, and Seraphina made her way over to them. As she got closer, she saw Paulus had his sword drawn. It was covered in blood, dark and heavy, dripping off the blade like a paste. Deep claw marks disfigured his thigh.

'We have to go back for them,' said the commander, limping.

Darius lowered his voice. 'Sir, look at you. You can barely walk. It would be suicide. Even now that we can see them, they would rip us to shreds.'

Paulus gazed into the distance, wincing at the pain in his leg. He had felt the wolf force his skin open when it clawed at him. He had managed to fight it off but knew the reason they were no longer being chased. His men, his comrades, his friends were being dragged away by the wolves. He was furious. At himself, and at this Darius telling him what to do. The commander knew the warrior was right, and that he should have listened to him from the start. He came down to one knee, almost falling, plunged his sword into the ground, and covered his eyes with his hand. Gripping his temples, he shed a tear for his brothers.

Darius was still breathing fast, and Seraphina watched him. It seemed wise to follow Darius' lead at this point. He had a scared look on his face, and she knew something was wrong because it was not a face he wore often. Looking around, Seraphina noticed some of the trees looked familiar. She thought for a second they might be close to where she had been shot yesterday, but she couldn't be sure. Her memory was still hazy from being knocked off her horse by the arrow. Her eyes met with Darius', and they wore the same blank expression.

'How many lost?' said Paulus, struggling to get back on his feet.

'Ten men, sir,' answered one of the soldiers.

'Darius, will it be safe to go back there at any point? Even to recover their bodies?'

Darius' head dropped. 'No, sir. I'm afraid not.'

'Then let's move out. Lead the way, Darius.'

Darius hesitated, eyeing the other soldiers. They were unsure of what to do. With a shrug of his shoulders, Darius led them off to the east. They could not quite see the shoreline yet, but Darius knew it was close. Seraphina waited. She could see Paulus was in pain as he tried to get his injured leg over the horse to mount it. His eyes remained pinned to the south, a tortured look on his face as his thoughts fixated on the men he had just lost.

The group was a little disoriented, with Darius at the front and the commander at the rear. They pressed forward, their minds heavy with the gore of what they had just witnessed. The breeze from the sea was getting stronger, yet the water itself was still out of sight. Seraphina wondered how far they must have ridden off course yesterday, after her incident with the arrow, and this morning when escaping the wolves.

Whoever had fired at Seraphina was back, and he had brought friends. Their arrows pierced the silence, and more men fell. After the initial wave, shields went up to protect them from further barrages. Darius immediately called for the men to ride faster, but the Romans had reached the end of their tether. Riding back to the north, their horses and shields formed a moving wall, charging towards their hidden assailants. More arrows were fired, and their shields held true.

Darius screamed at the men to retreat, but they were not listening. They followed their commander, his actions ill-advised by pain, adrenaline, and emotion. Darius told Seraphina to ride southeast until she reached the seashore, and to not look back. She did for a few moments but was mesmerised by the attack formation of the Romans. Darius held his position, watching to see what would happen. He was torn between wanting to pull them back and staying close to Seraphina. He knew what awaited the Romans, and he was not that eager to follow. He called out after them again, the impetuous fools.

Paulus gave no sign of slowing down, and the arrows kept coming. They were well trained enough with their shields, but Seraphina counted five more casualties from the surprise attack. She dismounted Luna and tied him up, going to check on the fallen soldiers. Nothing. One of the dead was the soldier who had sewn up her wound. Seraphina said a short prayer for him, as she looked back towards Darius and the Roman soldiers in the distance.

Although they had sustained no further injuries, they also had not found their attackers. Even Seraphina could tell they were either high up in the trees or behind the crest of the hill in the distance. Something was coming down that very hill as they watched. A black swarming mass of something. At first glance, it looked as though the ground was being swallowed up by this darkness. Seraphina lifted a hand to her gaping mouth, realising it was a horde of men. Darius knew full well what it was, and she watched as he galloped towards the besieged Roman soldiers.

Seraphina wondered what on earth Darius was thinking.

FORTY NINE

The barbarians did not attack. Nor did the Romans, but for different reasons. Their shields were covered with arrows, and their numbers had further dwindled. More of Paulus' men had succumbed to the precise strikes of the Germanic archers. They were surrounded by at least a hundred to one. Their assailants encircled them just as Darius approached. The Romans formed a circle of their own, facing outwards. One or two of the men looked to Paulus, but most stared blankly as the barbarians repeatedly chanted their unintelligible war cry.

The leader raised his hands to the sky, and there was silence. Clad in black leather, he wore a heavy silver chain around his neck. Hanging from the chain was a talisman—three interlocked triangles. He wore a thick helmet, black like his clothes. Two horns protruded from the top of it. Everything about him seemed to cast a thick shadow—his clothes, his helmet—so much so that the Romans could not make out much of his face. There were deep-set dark eyes, a thick black beard, and teeth gritted so hard that the grinding was almost audible. It was easy not to notice his size, but only because each member of the horde was gigantic.

Every single eye was on him, including Seraphina's in the distance.

His horse took two steps forward and he drew his heavy sword from its scabbard. Then he snapped the sword in Paulus' direction, pointing its tip at him. He grunted a string of words that the commander could not understand. Paulus apologised, for no offence in particular, and he did so with great deference. The barbarian knew the Roman was speaking Latin, but the language barrier prevented any discussion.

Bowing his head downwards and in Paulus' direction, Darius whispered, 'allow me, sir.'

Paulus nodded without saying a word. The pain in his leg was still fresh, and now they were facing another disaster. The other men remained frozen as Darius started speaking to the leader of the horde. His tone was much softer than usual, and he kept his distance. They were very sorry, he explained. The group had gotten lost while fleeing a pack of vicious wolves. He pointed to the wounds on Paulus' legs as he said this. All eyes moved to the commander's legs. The barbarian leader was having none of it. You were here yesterday, he said. Were you fleeing wolves then?

No, Darius said. Gesturing towards the Romans, he explained the confusion about which route they were to take from Rome to their destination. They had not intended to cross into Germanic lands. The sword went back in the scabbard, which allowed the group to take a collective breath. The barbarian folded his arms and continued to glare at Darius. Most of the other barbarians had their weapons drawn, and the Romans had certainly taken note of this.

You are within our borders now, explained the leader, and we will deal with you as we please. A warning shot had been fired yesterday, he said. The barbarian's expression seemed to soften when he asked about the boy they had shot. The boy was fine, Darius said. The Romans followed the conversation, understanding only the body language. The leader seemed to have the coolest head; the look on the faces of the barbarians, and the way they brandished their weapons made their desires very clear.

'May I ask your name, my lord, so that I can address you properly?'

asked Darius. His tone remained soft, and his palms held forward in soft surrender.

'Adalwin,' grunted the barbarian.

'Thank you, Lord Adalwin. As I said, we offer our most sincere apologies for having trespassed on your lands. I assure you it was not inte—'

'What are you doing here?' Adalwin asked abruptly.

'We are on a mission from Rome.'

'To where?'

'Tanais is our destination.'

A nasty little smile crossed Adalwin's face, as his arms lowered slightly. 'That's also outside of your territory. Is it to be more trespassing?' He paused for a moment, then asked, 'what is your name?'

'I am Darius, sir.'

'More trespassing, Darius?'

Darius shook his head and tried to return the smile. 'No, not at all, my lord. We have permission to cross into those lands.'

Adalwin simply grunted at this. The Bosporan king and queen were no friends of his. He regarded them as stooges to that troublesome Roman leader, Caesar. He looked around at his men and thought for a few moments. This slaughter would be easy, but he knew it would not end there. Adalwin had no desire to incur Caesar's wrath.

'What is your mission?' asked Adalwin.

The Romans had started to relax, and Paulus made the mistake of shifting around on his horse and grimacing at the conversation between Darius and Adalwin. He had lost many men since this time yesterday, and the wounds in his leg required attention. His movements caught the barbarians' attention. Darius turned and lowered his eyebrows at the commander as if to ask what the hell he thought he was doing. Unbeknownst to anyone, Seraphina had inched closer to hear and see what was going on. She understood about as much of the conversation as the Romans did. Keeping a safe distance, she could not believe the scene that was unfolding before her eyes.

'It is a rescue mission, my lord,' said Darius.

'Rescuing who?'

It's a good thing the Romans can't understand, thought Darius. Paulus would no doubt be shouting and trying to assert his authority by now.

'A young Roman, the son of a general.'

'And you believe he and his kidnappers lie in those lands to the east?'

'Yes, sir.'

Adalwin looked around at the Roman soldiers again. They looked exhausted but sat at full attention on their horses. None of them looked directly at him or his men, which was a wise move on their part.

'Then go,' he said, once again drawing his sword, and pointing to the southeast. 'Leave our lands, and never dare trespass here again.' He looked at all of them as he said this, and Darius nodded in solemn gratitude.

'Thank you, my lord. You are most gracious.'

Darius turned to Paulus and nodded in the same direction that Adalwin's sword pointed to. The barbarians looked disappointed. They opened space for the men to pass, glaring and mumbling sarcastic pleasantries as the Romans left. The soldiers kept their gaze straight ahead and dared not react.

FIFTY

After a mile or so, Seraphina rejoined the group. She had watched as the barbarians disappeared back over the hill, then told the soldiers they were gone. They were now down to a group of twelve. Little was said. One or two of the soldiers had quietly expressed their thanks to Darius, but they remained in shock. Vitus, the military prodigy, asked if they were going the right way. Not a bad question, given the circumstances.

The only response he got was Darius pointing to the now visible sea. The group galloped to the water's edge, dismounted, and tied their horses. The medical supplies had been recovered, and Paulus' wounds were attended to. The others spoke amongst themselves in small groups, checking each other for wounds and injuries. The mission had not been spoken of, and everyone was wondering what Paulus' next order would be. Darius was particularly quiet, having spoken more than he typically would in a week during his conversation with Adalwin. He was still in disbelief that they had been allowed to leave.

More than anything, Seraphina wanted to do her exercises and meditate. There was so much going on in her head, and she was craving calmness. She was worried about what the men would think.

None of them were paying any attention to her. Seraphina started to walk, occasionally looking back at Darius and the soldiers. They were indifferent and seemed pleased to rest, for now. She found a spot, partially concealed by the trees, and started stretching and breathing as Keb had taught her.

One or two noticed the boy and his strange movements in the distance. Nothing was said. They were much more preoccupied with the fact that twenty of their comrades had died in the past day. A few of them stretched their own bodies out, and it felt good.

Paulus sat and faced the sea, his weight resting on his hands behind him. Darius crouched down next to him and asked how his leg was feeling.

'Never mind the leg, it is fine. Darius, I really am grateful for what you did back there. I don't understand a word of what you said, but I know it saved all of our lives.' He said this without turning his gaze from the sea, then added, 'those lives that are left, anyway.'

Part of Darius wanted to scold the commander. If he had listened from the start, they would be peacefully riding around the sea and approaching their target. With three times as many men. Darius' life, not to mention the lives of Seraphina and the soldiers, had been put at risk by the commander's arrogance. Indeed, most of their party had paid the ultimate price for his mistakes. Looking at him, he could not bring himself to say any of it. Gone was the pompous attitude and dominant presence. He just looked out over the sea, wearing a sad, almost indifferent expression.

'A pleasure, sir,' said Darius. 'Commander, I think the men want to know how we're going to proceed from here.'

Paulus took a deep breath, not taking his eyes off the water.

'Sir?' asked Darius.

The commander began shaking his head and jumped to his feet. There was a slight limp in the wounded leg, but it barely slowed him down.

'We will continue,' he said to Darius, and loud enough for the others to hear. 'There are supposedly eight men at most holding that prison. Including you and the boy, there are twelve of us. Your master mentioned that the boy is more than capable in a fight.'

Darius could not think of anything to say to this. He looked around at the other men, and then at Seraphina in the distance doing her odd exercises.

Paulus continued, now talking to the group. 'Given the intelligence we have on this prison and the fact that we still outnumber them, this mission can still be a success. Men, ready your weapons and make sure you have what you need. We're not far from our target. We'll take today to rest and recuperate. Tomorrow, we'll set off.' He pointed at two of the younger men. 'You two, gather some food for us to eat while we are here.' He then turned to two others. 'You two, check that the horses are well fed and patch up any wounds.' Finally, to another pair, he said 'you two, scour in the nearby area to see what dry food you can collect. It is a good idea for us to have some extra sustenance in case things don't go to plan.' Then he added, 'needless to say, do not stray too far to the north, and keep the sea in sight.'

He sat with the remaining three soldiers, all of whom were senior officers. They went back a long way and talked amongst themselves while the others went about their tasks. Darius stared at the commander. He could not believe they were going to continue the mission.

One of the officers said something, and the rest of the men laughed. They all turned to look at Seorsa in the distance, doing his strange exercises. Paulus caught the end of Darius' stare and raised his eyebrows. 'Is everything alright, Darius?'

'Yes, sir,' he thundered as if acknowledging an order. Clearly, all was not right.

Before Paulus had a chance to respond, Darius turned and walked away from the commander and his colleagues.

'Darius,' said Paulus, calling out after him, 'thank you again for your efforts today. From now on, you will be navigating our route. Are we clear on the route from here to this prison we're looking for?'

Darius did not break stride. 'Yes, getting there will not be a problem.'

'Glad to hear it!' Paulus shouted, but only because he sensed Darius' defiance. The brave warrior had certainly helped the Romans out of a tricky situation, but Paulus was still the commander, and he was still in charge.

FIFTY ONE

True to his word, Paulus deferred to Darius' guidance for the remainder of the journey. Darius had in fact deferred himself, to Seraphina's knowledge of where the prison lay. He simply spoke to her in private, so he could lead the soldiers. Darius correctly assumed that they would not take kindly to a boy leading the way. *Imagine if they knew she was a young woman*, he thought.

They arrived at the edge of the forest without any further surprises coming their way. Paulus was grateful and said a short prayer to Mars and Jupiter to give thanks. The men hunkered down at the edge of the forest and watched the prison. From the outside, it certainly did not look like a prison of any variety. For three days and nights, they watched. At times, it appeared that the place was deserted. They did see men in the distance at times, and they matched the descriptions of those they were looking for. Casting his mind back, the commander thought that the descriptions given by the young prisoner, Seraphina, were remarkably accurate. She had definitely been here.

There was only one problem with what she had told him. There were no girls, no young women whatsoever. On the first day, they had expected to see a group of young women marched into the field for their daily meal. It did not happen. *No matter*, Paulus had thought, perhaps they don't do it every day. After three full days and nights, something was amiss.

They had come a long way, but Paulus was loath to simply attack the men without cause. He thought about arresting them, but for what? That idea raised another issue. King Asander had given them authority to enter his lands to affect a rescue. *If no one was being held, then who was there to rescue?* The Roman soldiers could not simply assume the authority to arrest and question anyone they pleased. Suddenly, Paulus felt just how far they were from Rome. The presence of Darius and his assistant, Seorsa, only complicated matters.

It was decided that the Roman soldiers would ride out from the forest, in full regalia, and speak to the men, the supposed pirates and slave traders. Darius and his assistant were told to wait behind.

As Seraphina watched the soldiers getting ready, an uneasy feeling brewed within her. Yet, she could not think of what was bothering her. She had been disappointed a few days ago when they passed Keb's clearing and he was not there. To be honest, it was probably a good thing. Seeing him there, with a cadre of Roman soldiers and the gigantic Darius, would have been complicated to say the least. Maybe it was just nerves at being back here again. She certainly wondered why the routine at the prison had changed. It had been several weeks since she had escaped. *Surely they would have taken a new batch of girls by now?* That was the impression Seraphina had gotten from the conversations she overheard during her captivity.

Darius and Seraphina both looked out from behind the thick green foliage as the soldiers rode out. First Paulus, then the remaining soldiers after him, forming a triangle as they rode towards the prison.

As they neared the building, Paulus had a similarly uneasy feeling. They had been spotted, without a doubt, but there was no discernible reaction. Paulus would have thought that in such a remote location, well outside the republic's borders, a troop of Roman soldiers in full battle gear may have been some cause for concern. Apparently not. The horses came to a halt. A door at the front of the building opened. Out came a very tall, very thick man, wearing a black eyepatch. *He certainly looked like a pirate*, thought Paulus.

'Ave,' said the pirate, with a smile on his face.

'Do you speak Latin?' asked Paulus.

The pirate waved his hands and replied in Greek. 'No, no. I just know that's how you Romans like to be greeted.'

Fortunately, Paulus had been stationed in Greek regions early in his career. 'Very well. Thank you for that. What is your name?'

'I am Karsas.'

The uneasiness was only deepening. This man seemed very calm. Maybe he overestimated the power of the Roman military uniform. They were a long way from home, after all. His hand rose to his chin, and he tapped his cheek with his index finger. Paulus inspected the building. It was exactly as described. Made of thick wood, matching the trees they had been surrounded by during the past three days. Pragmatic construction, with no thought given to appearance. A big wooden box, built on this vast green field, next to a thick forest. Virtually in the middle of nowhere.

His eyes came back to Karsas. He had not moved and seemed content to wait as Paulus looked around. It disconcerted Paulus that he had not even asked why they were there. It was time to simply come out with it.

'Well, Karsas, we have received reports that people are being held here against their will. That you and your men have kidnapped them, and we are here to investigate.'

Karsas stood still, his hands sitting comfortably on his navel, one over another. He let out a brief laugh and shook his head while still smiling. 'Sir, I'm not sure where you have received this information. I assure you that nothing of the kind is going on here.' He gestured with his hand around the field and continued, 'this land, all of it, belongs to my master. It's being cultivated for farming. As you can see, this is fine farming land. It's flat and well kept, and the soil is highly fertile.'

The explanation was perfectly reasonable, thought Paulus. 'Very well, but you don't look like a farmer to me, Karsas.'

The smile remained, and now Karsas nodded in agreement. 'Right you are, sir. My master hires me as a warrior, not a farmer. My men and I make sure his land and properties are protected. A group of farmers has been hired. They're on their way from Apollonia, where my master lives. We're here to keep the land secure until they arrive.'

Whoever this Karsas was, he was remarkably candid. Paulus was becoming less sure of what to do. 'What is your master's name, if I may ask?'

'Theos. Sir, I'm sorry, I don't know your name?'

'It's Paulus.'

'Sir, Paulus, is that how I may properly address you?'

'Either Paulus or Commander is fine, Karsas. I thank you for your respect.'

Karsas opened his arms and bowed his head. 'But of course. Commander, would you like to come inside and inspect the building? These are just our living quarters, with some rooms for storage.'

For a moment, Paulus suspected an ambush. Then Karsas called into the doorway and asked for his men to come outside so the soldiers could go about their inspection without them being in the way. Paulus glanced to each side of the building, looking around the edge of the walls.

'Commander, you and your men can tie your horses up here,' said one of Karsas' men, leading the way.

Paulus eyed Karsas and the other men as they came out of the building. They were formidable men, dressed as warriors. Their manner was perfectly calm and friendly, and Paulus wondered what on earth was going on. *What was this story he had been fed by Seraphina, back in Rome?*

The rest of the soldiers were baffled, and happy to follow their commander's lead. As they stepped into the building, one by one, the rich smell of wood and soil struck them. It was not an unpleasant smell, but rather rustic. The light from the doorway did little to affect the darkness inside, and Karsas stepped in after them.

'My apologies, Commander. We are yet to have windows in this place. The farmers will decide on that. Here, take these.' Karsas took down the two torches on either side of the doorway and handed them to Paulus and another soldier. 'We'll keep this door open, Commander, so call out if you need anything.'

Paulus just nodded at him and proceeded inside. It was almost pitch-black, but nothing else seemed to be amiss. There were living quarters, a kitchen, a room that resembled an office of sorts. Then there were two other rooms, one large and one small. Both had heavy bolts, which were locked into place. The soldiers followed their leader, looking for anything that seemed unusual. They noticed the torches mounted on the wall throughout the building. If they were all lit, there would be plenty of light throughout the farmhouse.

The rooms with bolts on them concerned Paulus. Seraphina's description of the farmhouse was accurate, and if she was right, these rooms are where prisoners were being held. Two of the soldiers opened one of the bolts and pulled open the heavy door. Paulus peered in with the torch, expecting the worse.

FIFTY TWO

Nothing. The room smelled of hay, which lined the floor. There were a series of hooks along the wall, where Seraphina said the young women had been chained up. She was right about the hooks, but there were no chains, no prisoners. What Paulus was looking at resembled a typical room for keeping animals in a farmhouse. He shook his head and came out of the room.

'Vitus, go outside and see what those men are up to,' he whispered in Latin. 'Stay near the door and act as if you are just getting some air.'

Vitus went and reported back that the men were standing in a circle near the doorway. They were talking amongst themselves, and nothing more.

Paulus shook his head again. 'You two, open this door.' He pointed at the bolted door to the smaller room. The bolt seemed to be jammed and they got nowhere with it.

'Karsas,' called out the commander in Greek. 'Please come here for a moment.'

Karsas came jogging into the building. 'Yes, Commander, what is it?'

Paulus' eyes bulged out of his head, and he glared at Karsas. Pointing to the bolt, he said 'that will not open.'

'That's strange.' Karsas looked at each of the soldiers, one by one, as if he was looking for something.

'What is it?'

'Nothing, Commander. Let me see what I can do here.' Karsas pushed and pulled at the bolt, but it would not budge.

Paulus smelled blood, and his hand instinctively moved to the hilt of his sword.

'Just a moment, Commander,' he said, taking a few steps towards the front door. 'Ourgious!' he called out. Coming back to the soldiers, Karsas said, 'Don't worry, sir, Ourgious will get it open.' He glanced down at Paulus' sword as he said this, but only for a moment.

Ourgious appeared behind Karsas. 'Yes, my lord?'

Karsas swung around and shouted. 'Get this door open. We are keeping these men waiting, and they need to finish their inspection!'

'I'm sorry, my lord. Of course.' Ourgious pushed and pulled in the same way that Karsas and the soldiers had, but to no avail. He looked at Paulus and the other soldiers, seeing the blank looks on their face. All eyes were on the door. 'Do not worry, good sirs. Sometimes this lock is a bit stubborn.' He unsheathed a heavy dagger from his belt, the blade pointing in the direction of the floor. Ourgious then bashed against the bottom of the bolt a few times, and something seemed to release. He unlocked the bolt and opened the door. Ten Roman heads peered in at the same time, and none were surprised by what they saw.

It was as bare as the last room. Paulus stepped in for a moment and, realising there was nothing to see, bowed his head to the ground. All this way, and all those dead men, for nothing. He would find that Seraphina when he returned to Rome, and there would be hell to pay!

'Thank you for your co-operation,' he mumbled to Karsas, handing him the torch.

'You're most welcome, Commander.' Karsas and Ourgious followed the soldiers back out into the field. A few of them flinched at the sunlight. Compared to the darkness inside the farmhouse, it was blinding.

Paulus was about to ask why they kept it so dark inside, but he let it pass. He walked around the building once. Nothing but horses and a few bales of hay. His mind started to turn to the long trip home. Fierce words began to build in his mind for both Seraphina and Cicero. As he came back to the front of the building, Karsas approached him. The same smile was on his face.

'I trust that everything is in order, Commander?' Karsas offered his hand to Paulus.

Paulus shook it. 'Yes, I'm sorry for any inconvenience.'

'No inconvenience at all, Commander. We're always happy to help the authorities. I just hope it wasn't a waste of time for you.'

Oh, it was, thought Paulus. But he didn't share this thought with Karsas. He had been very helpful and understanding. Too helpful, perhaps. He hadn't even questioned what Roman soldiers were doing so far outside their borders. The query would have been resolved with a quick invocation of King Asander's name, but nevertheless, Paulus thought it somewhat odd. Maybe they were just friendly, helpful warriors.

In any case, there was nothing to do but leave. Karsas' men helped them untie and mount their horses, and they wished the soldiers well on their journey. Paulus took one last look at the farmhouse, the field, and surrounding territory. It was a beautiful place, and any man would be grateful to have such fine land to farm on. He turned and led his men away, back to the forest.

FIFTY THREE

Seraphina had watched with eager anticipation as the soldiers approached the prison. After a few minutes, Paulus looked to be having a friendly chat with the leader of the pirates. She was sure that once they went inside, the pirates would be arrested. Instead, the soldiers remained in there for some time. Then they left, without so much as a raised voice and were riding back towards her and Darius.

She was enraged and waited for a similar reaction from Darius. There would not be one. He had watched the same sequence of events without so much as a change in expression. He had mumbled something about Paulus being foolish to want to continue the mission in the face of so many casualties. Other than that, he had not said a word or moved a muscle.

Seraphina was at a loss about what to do. Darius was acting somewhat aloof, and the soldiers were about to return. She couldn't very well curse and yell at them; so far as they knew, she was a young man, and Darius' assistant. So, she stayed quiet and tried to think of what to do next.

The soldiers entered the forest and moved away from the tree line, so as not to be seen.

'So, what happened?' asked Darius.

'You saw, didn't you?' said the commander, throwing his helmet to the ground. 'Nothing! There isn't a soul there. The rooms, the supposed prison cells, were empty. Not so much as a single chain, not a shackle, nothing. Wait until I get my hands on that girl, that Seraphina!'

Seraphina flinched at the sound of her name, but everyone was too captivated by the commander's tantrum to notice.

'They're securing the home until some farmers arrive!' Paulus threw his weapons and armour on the ground, only because he was sure he could not be heard. 'The land belongs to their master, or so he said.'

Darius smirked, but only for a split second. Seraphina caught it and thought it odd. However, she was more concerned with what was going to happen next. The other soldiers removed some of their gear, but in a calmer fashion. They were frustrated too, but more than that, they were surprised to see their usually composed commander acting this way.

'All those men!' said Paulus, revealing the true source of his anger. 'Dead, and for nothing.'

Darius took a step forward and folded his arms. 'It's a farm? They didn't look like farmers.'

'Of course they're not farmers!' shouted Paulus. 'They're warriors. Just like you're a warrior for your master. Keeping the place secure until the farmers arrive to start running the place.'

'This doesn't make any sense,' said Darius, shaking his head. His arms were still folded, and he looked to the ground as he spoke.

The commander, out of things to take off and hurl, threw his hands up in defeat. 'Well, that's what they said. He answered all my questions, with generous candour, I might add. Aside from one or two oddities, everything he said makes perfect sense.'

Darius had walked away and started to feed his horse. The other soldiers were either indifferent or suppressing their own anger. Knowing no one else was going to speak, Seraphina asked, 'What oddities, Commander?'

He glared for a moment at the young man, and then remembered he had nearly suffered a mortal wound for this mission as well.

'The farmhouse, the prison, whatever it was, it was very dark. There were no windows. No way for light to get in, except for the doorway.'

Seraphina nodded, urging him with her eyes to say more.

'But then again, there were unlit torches throughout the house. So what if there were no windows? Maybe the farmers will attend to that when they arrive. It is to be their home, after all. These men are just guarding the place until they arrive.'

'What else, sir? You said oddities.'

Paulus was no longer facing the young assistant. He jerked his neck in the boy's direction as if to say how dare he question a Roman commander, but kept speaking nevertheless. The man with the eyepatch. He had been calm, and friendly. Too calm, and too friendly, given the circumstances. A group of highly decorated soldiers from the Roman army arrive, miles outside their borders, and he greets them with smiles, courtesy, and almost undue honesty. The commander realised the folly of such suspicion, but he couldn't shake the idea that something was amiss. Right now, he preferred to be suspicious about everything. He was angry, but he had exaggerated his tantrum for the sake of his audience. Some of his men were clearly upset, but some also indifferent. Darius seemed more incredulous than concerned and made no comment about the mission being a complete waste. Seorsa, the young assistant, seemed unusually interested, for one who had largely remained silent so far.

The commander stopped and took a breath. He looked at his armour and weaponry, scattered on the ground. Similarly, his men were strewn across the forest floor. Some lying down, some sitting up, and others looking blankly into the distance. Darius was feeding his horse and ignoring everyone. Seorsa was staring down at the ground like Paulus was. As he looked over, there was something familiar about the boy. He had seen him before. For a moment, Paulus thought he could place him, and then the memory escaped him.

'Alright, men.' The commander clapped his hands loudly. 'We are not staying here to lick our wounds and mourn what has passed. We must make our way back home.'

No one said a word, although Paulus had their undivided attention. He clapped twice more to get them moving. 'Get yourselves ready,' he said, raising his voice. 'We are going home to Rome. Darius, you will ride next to Seorsa in the centre as we have thus far. Two men in the front and rear, and three to each side. We will follow your navigation without exception.'

The words were crisp and decisive and spurred everyone into action. Darius walked over to Paulus and suggested they visit a nearby Greek village on the other side of the forest. He knew it to be friendly to travellers. There, they could replenish their supplies for the journey home. Anyone with injuries could also have their wounds checked. Seraphina overheard part of what was said, and Paulus thought it an excellent idea. They talked more, and Darius said they would reach the village by nightfall.

FIFTY FOUR

As fate had it, Seraphina found herself in the very same house she had been in with Rhea. The village Darius had led them to was Tamura's village, the exact place they had escaped to after fleeing the prison. None of the women recognised Seraphina in her disguise. She gave no indication that she had been there before, not even confiding in Darius. At this point, Seraphina was grateful for a bed, a hot meal, and a good night's rest.

She had managed to bathe herself in private, having thus far been restricted to using the oil and strigil to take care of her hygiene. She observed that the Roman soldiers did not make their hygiene a high priority. Then again, they were soldiers, and they were focused on their mission.

Seraphina felt the stillness and quiet around her. Everyone had gone to sleep, she was sure. She was nowhere near slumber. Today she had hoped to gain some vindication, and perhaps even be reunited with Quintus. The disappointment of what happened at the prison had crushed her. When Paulus recounted his conversation with the pirate, for a moment she had doubted herself. As if it were possible that she had imagined the entire episode. She had no idea what to do next. Even in disguise, once they returned to Rome, Paulus wanted to have words with Seraphina. Considering how that conversation would go was beyond her at that moment.

She tore the sheet off her body and walked out into the night air. It was a little cool, but the freshness of the forest calmed her a little. One thing she had enjoyed about her ordeal and the subsequent mission had been the presence of nature. Seraphina felt calmer when surrounded by greenery and water. It had always been the case, since she was a little girl. Hidden away by day in the library in Alexandria, most nights she found herself sitting by the sea. As she reminisced, Seraphina realised there was a sense of freedom on those nights that she had not felt in quite some time.

Voices jerked her attention away from the stars and the memories they inspired. Not everyone was asleep, it seemed. She made her away towards those voices, careful not to make a sound. The damp soil and grass squished under her bare feet. As the voices became louder, Seraphina took smaller steps. Her heel slipped on a patch of mud, and for a moment she lost her balance. The front foot slipped forward, and she leaned back to make sure she did not fall. Holding her arms out, Seraphina managed not to hit the ground.

Nothing but her eyes moved. She scanned from left to right, making sure no one had woken up. The conversation continued without interruption, and she focused in the dark to see where it might be coming from. Tamura's tent was up ahead. Whoever they were, they were still talking. In complete darkness. She lowered her eyebrows for a moment. Then, Seraphina crept towards the edge of the tent, careful not to touch it. The faint light of the stars helped to guide her steps. She crouched down, a foot or so from where the tent opened.

'What do you mean, she's here?' came a woman's voice.

'She's here with us. The boy, that is her. Seraphina.' Seraphina was shocked to hear her name. She was also surprised to hear Darius speaking in Greek. *Why was he telling her this?*

'I don't believe it.' Seraphina could now recognise the gruff voice. It was Tamura.

'Well, believe it.'

'That girl is nothing but trouble, Darius. I let her go because I recognised that, and now you've brought her back here.'

'Let her go?'

The voice rose slightly. 'She was here. After she escaped Karsas, she and another girl came here. Rhea, I think her name was.' Seraphina covered her mouth with her hand when she heard her friend's name. *What had they done to Rhea?*

'I don't understand why you let her go. Look at all the trouble this has caused. It could've been avoided. You sent the other girl back?'

'Of course. Karsas demanded it, and we have a strict arrangement.'

Darius' tone lightened, and he chuckled. 'I know, I know. You co-operate with him, and the women here are spared.' Then after a few moments, he added, 'and you get a nice pouch of coins each time you deliver.'

'Shut up, Darius. Now, what are we going to do?'

'I still can't believe you let her go.'

'It was a smart move, given the circumstances. How was I to know that this girl would make it back to Rome, that she was friends with a high-ranking senator, and would convince the Roman army to come here on a liberation mission?'

Seraphina listened as nothing was said for a moment. Then, finally, 'you're right, Tamura. We'll have to take care of her.'

'What do you mean?' Tamura sounded frightened, as her voice took on a quality Seraphina had not heard before.

'You say she is trouble, and she is. The commander doesn't know she is here in disguise. When he gets back to Rome, he wants to talk to her about the supposedly false information she gave.'

'Faustus played this brilliantly, Darius. Getting you to join the mission and bribing the emissary to warn Karsas. I wish I could have seen the faces of those soldiers when they went in there and found nothing.'

The two shared a laugh, and Seraphina felt a pit forming deep in her stomach.

'Between here and Rome, I'll dispose of the girl. I'll find a way to do it. The commander, Paulus, has proven adept at making mistakes. I cannot believe we lost twenty men. That was not part of the plan and was only due to his own arrogance.'

Seraphina gulped and held her hand to her throat. Her first instinct was to run, after hearing plans for her murder so casually discussed. She did not move though, wanting to hear more.

'Just make sure you don't arouse suspicion. There are already going to be a lot of questions asked when you return.'

'I can handle the girl, Tamura. Once we leave, you can send word to Karsas that it has been taken care of.'

'Very well.'

'And Tamura, never let one of these girls go again. You'll regret it if you do.'

Darius walked out of the tent, so close to Seraphina that she felt a breeze of air as he rushed past her. She waited a few minutes, not making a sound. Tamura had either gone to sleep in the tent or left through the opening on the other side. Seraphina inched towards a nearby building and sat against the wall.

Two things were clear. She was in grave danger while she was near Darius, and the pair of them were working with the pirates. Seraphina shook her head as she realised the entire scene at the prison today had been staged. If anyone was being held there, they had been moved, along with all the chains and shackles. The fact that they had known when the Roman soldiers were arriving was chilling. Then there was Rhea. *What had happened to her?* Seraphina cursed herself for leaving her friend behind.

There was no time to dwell on things. It was still dark, and she could not wait for the morning light. She got back to her room without incident. Fortunately, most of her supplies were still in the bags hanging over Luna. Trusty Luna, how grateful she was for her horse. He had gotten her out of more trouble than she cared to remember in the past several weeks. Fumbling in the dark, Seraphina gathered what few possessions she had in the room and went outside.

She stirred Luna from his slumber. In a sleepy, crawling trot, Luna eased away from the village and into the darkness of the forest.

FIFTY FIVE

The slow movement helped Seraphina think. She was still wary of being heard, and Luna plodded along, almost tiptoeing his way through. Seraphina could barely see, but Luna seemed able to detect his surroundings with ease. He stepped around trees that were barely visible to her.

Where would she go now? Seraphina knew she had to get away from Darius. For a few moments, she had considered rushing to Paulus and telling him what she had heard. She would have no credibility though, especially once her true identity was revealed. After all, Paulus was furious at her regarding the failed mission. Darius would have an easy time painting her as a self-interested liar, and who knows what her fate would be. No, she decided, the Romans could not help her. At least, not for now.

She thought of going back to Rome and speaking to Cicero. It was not a bad idea, but she knew first hand of the dangers of riding through these lands. Seraphina wasn't sure if she had another fight in her. Besides, killing those bandits, whilst absolutely necessary, was still bothering her.

The first rays of morning light began to penetrate the forest. Her thoughts wandered for a moment, thinking it strange how familiar she was with her surroundings. They were a good distance from the village now, and she urged Luna into a brisk canter.

Maybe she could go to Keb. He wasn't home on the way to the prison though, and she could not know for sure where he was. Seraphina also did not want to bring any trouble to Keb. Darius' words rang in her head, and she knew he would not think twice of killing an old man if it furthered his agenda. She was still bracing from the shock of having overheard their conversation. Darius had been protective of her throughout the trip, and she remembered the sense she'd had on the steps of the Temple of Jupiter. It had all been a ruse. Now, here she was, alone in this forest once again, fearful for her life.

She stopped in her tracks. *The prison!* That is the last place anyone would expect her to go. As soon as the men woke at the village, no doubt Darius would be in pursuit of her. *Would he possibly conceive that she went back to the prison? Perhaps*, she thought, *but unlikely*. Seraphina had to see for herself if there were women being held there still. Maybe she could somehow convince Paulus to return covertly and see the truth of what was going on.

It was as good a plan as any in that moment, and there was now enough light that Seraphina could see. She spotted the lake where she and Rhea had first stopped to rest after they escaped. Her heart was filled with sadness, and she felt her chest rise at the thought of Rhea, chained up and no doubt being mistreated.

Luna was fully awake now, and Seraphina rubbed his head a little. Then she started whipping the reins, and the pair of them tore through the morning air, heading back to Karsas, his band of pirates, the prison, and whatever else awaited them there.

FIFTY SIX

It was midday by the time Seraphina arrived at the edge of the forest once again. The sun was high in the sky. Seraphina rubbed her arms and let out a gentle moan as the sunlight penetrated the trees. Everything was still, just as they had left it. She waited and watched because there was nothing else to do. Seraphina looked up to the sky, almost willing the sun to move.

A few hours passed, and the time was right. *If it was going to happen, it was going to happen now*, she said to herself. Her gaze locked in on the thick wood of the front door. Sure enough, a few moments later, it moved. One of the pirates came out and looked around nonchalantly. Seraphina leaned forward as if moving would somehow enable her to see more. No one followed, and the man rode off on a horse. Towards the back of the building, and off into the distance he went. She wondered where he was going.

Those thoughts did not last long, as the door opened again. The soldier she had spoken to, and attacked, came out of the prison. Ourgious. She remembered the name now. Seraphina was breathing heavily. After he came out, she held her breath, and then became aware that she was doing so, exhaling loudly. A small, familiar figure followed him out. *It was Rhea!* There were a few more women behind her, but Seraphina recognised none of them. *A new batch*, she thought to herself. Beads of sweat began to trickle down her forehead and the tiny hairs on the back of her neck stood tall.

Seraphina watched them come out. Her hand felt tight, and she looked down, realising she was gripping the handle of the club on her belt. Her teeth were also gritted so hard that they were practically grinding. She loosened her grip and relaxed her jaw. *Calm down*, she told herself. *They are here, just as you knew they would be. Now what?*

Nothing of note happened. Rhea's face looked as downcast as ever. A solitary guard came to feed the five girls. The usual trio of knapsacks was not needed, obviously, as there were fewer women. Thoughts raced through Seraphina's mind. *How long have they been doing this? Have they ever come close to being caught before? Do they just cycle through batches of women, selling them off and then refilling their prison?* It only enraged her further. She gripped her skull tightly, wanting the thoughts to stop. Finally, she calmed herself, realising it did no good for her to get angry and upset.

She looked around. Only a few of the guards seemed to be there. Then again, the rest could be inside. They talked amongst themselves, the occasional laugh coming from their direction. Casting her gaze back to the women, they looked so tiny in the distance and against the vast backdrop of the field, the prison, and the expansive sky. *No one would ever find them here by chance*, thought Seraphina. As much as she despised these men for what they were doing, she had to admit they had picked the perfect spot to do their dirty work.

Seraphina weighed up her options. None appealed to her at that moment. Going back to find Darius and the Romans had plenty of pitfalls. It would no doubt result in all sorts of difficulties for her at best, and death at worst. She thought of Keb, but there was little he could do to help her in this situation. The thought of making her way back to Rome had her shaking her head before she could even finish the thought. She stared at the prison, and her gaze was soon lost in its outer walls.

There was one other option. Wait until nightfall and try to enter the prison. She looked away, chastising herself for her silliness. The thought returned, and she gave it more consideration. Seraphina knew that there were fewer men in the prison late at night, and possibly none. That night, the guard had been in her cell only to feed her in her solitary confinement. Ourgious had only been there to take Rhea to the toilet and back to the cell with the other girls.

Her arms folded underneath her chest, and her brow furrowed. *The cells may not even be locked*, she thought. She remembered the heavy bolts being pushed into place each day. From the brief glance she had managed during her escape, Seraphina could not recall a lock. She smiled to herself. *Was she really going to do this? Was it even so crazy, given the circumstances?*

Danger had been a familiar state of mind as of late. Fighting pirates. Riding through dangerous forests. Defending herself from bandits. Fleeing a warrior four times her size who wanted to kill her. That was to say nothing of the challenges in Alexandria before she left. Maybe she could free Rhea and rectify her earlier mistake. If she hadn't overheard the conversation between Darius and Tamura, she might be dead by now. Though this thought sent chills running down her spine, Seraphina couldn't escape the thought that she'd be given this chance for a reason.

She was armed, and she had Luna to make a quick getaway if needed. It was the best option, and really the only one that Seraphina felt comfortable with. *Enough running*, she thought, as she watched the guards lead the young women back into the prison in their chains and shackles. To be chained up once again in their dark, lonely cell.

FIFTY SEVEN

It had been dark for a few hours. Each time a man left the building, Seraphina could not be sure if it was the last one. She had kept track of the horses by the side of the prison. The last guard to leave the prison had taken the sole remaining horse. He had also blown out the torches inside the front door, and lit a torch on the outer wall, just above the front door.

Now is the time, she decided. She and Luna crossed the field, but not too fast, as there was no need. The horse's strength may be needed for a speedy getaway, and Seraphina was mindful of conserving his energy. Luna slowed as they got close to the prison, and Seraphina listened for any sounds. Aside from the cicadas' gentle song from the nearby trees, there was silence. Jumping down from Luna, Seraphina's hand went straight to her club. The sword and dagger remained at hand, but the club had proven most effective in the past.

Her body shook with each step. She could feel her hand trembling around the handle of the club, and she gripped it tighter. Locking her jaw, Seraphina reached out with her free hand and pulled at the door. At first, she thought it was locked, but it was just heavy. She set the club down and heaved. It needed to be lifted off its hinge. Once it was free of the frame beneath it, the door swung open with ease.

She stopped again, seeing only as much as the fading torch could reveal. Returning the club to her belt, Seraphina retrieved the torch from its holder and stepped inside. She pulled out the dagger, and walked through the prison, checking all the rooms at the front. No one was here. She allowed herself to smile for a moment, and her breathing slowed. Her head was covered in sweat, and she dragged her forearm across her brow to wipe away the perspiration that was now trickling down over her eyes.

Seraphina moved more easily now and mounted the torch in the hallway. She heard some movement. Just chains, and the girls were probably wondering who was there.

'Rhea?' said Seraphina.

A throat cleared to her right. The small cell, where she had been held. Seraphina stepped to the door, trying to peer inside and repeated, 'Rhea?'

'Who is that?' came a croaked whisper.

'It's me, Seraphina.' She pressed her hands against the door, trying to catch a glimpse of her shackled friend.

Rhea cleared her throat again, coughing. 'Seraphina? Is that really you? How can this be?'

Seraphina was already at work on the bolt of the door. 'It's a long story.'

More noises behind her. The other girls were waking up, and their chains and shackles moved with them.

'What is wrong with this bolt?' said Seraphina. It was not moving. She brought the torch down and could see the problem. The jagged edge of the bolt handle was caught on the other part of the locking mechanism. Seraphina returned the torch to the wall and pulled out her club. She swung it upwards, hard, no longer concerned about making noise. The bolt released, and Seraphina opened the door.

Her friend managed a weak smile. Now that she was up close,

Seraphina could see she had lost a lot of weight. 'What have they done to you?'

Rhea shook her head, mumbling under her breath. Seraphina caught 'beat me' and 'that big man,' but little else. She was focused on removing Rhea's restraints. Once she got them free, Rhea collapsed. Whatever they had done, her friend was waifish and barely able to stand.

'Rhea, you have to get up.' Her arms tensed for a moment as Seraphina tried to help her to her feet, and then she fell back. 'Rhea!' She was shouting now. Rhea was awake, but only barely. Seraphina crouched and wrapped her arms around her friend in a tight bear hug. Throwing her weight back, she jostled Rhea to her feet and held her up. *Thank goodness she is a small girl*, thought Seraphina. She could see far too many of Rhea's bones than was healthy, but right now, it helped for Rhea to be as light as possible.

The other girls were awake now, but no one had said anything. They probably thought it was a guard. Seraphina had hoped to at least try to free the rest of them, but she was now saddled with Rhea's almost dead weight.

FIFTY EIGHT

Seraphina looked up as Karsas just stood there. His men were behind him, all glaring down behind folded arms and snarled little smiles. Seraphina dusted herself off after falling through the front door with her friend. Then she looked at Rhea, who seemed to be worsening, and shot daggers from her eyes at the pirate leader.

'What did you do to her?' said Seraphina.

The burly pirate laughed at her. 'I must say, Seraphina, you look ridiculous.' He gazed up and down her lean body, hidden underneath the crude outfit she wore as her disguise.

Seraphina cringed at the way he looked at her. 'I asked you a question,' she said.

Karsas was impressed with her defiant attitude. 'Well,' he said, stroking his beard and smiling even wider at Seraphina, 'after she was returned to us, we had to teach her a lesson. You know, you're the first of these girls to ever escape from here.' He looked down at Rhea's body. 'I suppose she was the second, but we got her back. So, she doesn't really count.'

Seraphina wanted to hit him, but she just grimaced. She finally heard the sound, but only she did, and only because she had been waiting for it. Her face relaxed, as her stern expression was replaced by a smile as wide as Karsas'. She checked on Rhea, making sure she was as comfortable as possible. Then she got to her feet. She took two steps towards him and was so close to Karsas that she could smell him.

'Well, you're going to pay for what you've done to her.'

His instinct was to grab her neck and squeeze until she screamed, and the very life was drained from her. Something was not right. *Why would this girl be so daring when they had her surrounded, and outnumbered?* Then he heard what Seraphina had been listening out for, and his heart sank. Heavy cavalry riding towards them, and far more than the ten soldiers who had visited earlier. Before he turned around, Karsas saw the smile on Seraphina's face get even wider. She began to giggle at them as they squirmed, as her plan to capture them alive and without resistance came to fruition perfectly.

Out of the darkness came Adalwin and his horde. Except, this was a much bigger group than the one Seraphina and the Romans had met in the forest. Karsas could not believe his eyes. He and the other men stood there, frozen. Their eyes darted this way and that, taking in the sheer number of men, and they quickly lost count. Adalwin dismounted his horse, his eyes never leaving Karsas. His men were still riding up from the rear. The sound of galloping horses mingled with the clanging of heavy armour and weaponry.

'Don't say a word' said Adalwin. His Greek was rough, but Karsas understood. He hadn't thought of speaking. Seraphina noticed a very slight shake in Karsas' legs, and it amused her greatly. Adalwin strode towards Seraphina, letting each step be heard. Then he stood even closer to Karsas than Seraphina had. Their noses were almost touching. 'Do everything this girl says, and you might live.' Karsas nodded slowly, and Adalwin stepped away. He knew if Karsas was within reach, he would kill him within seconds. Adalwin stood behind Seraphina.

Seraphina let the moment set in for Karsas. She had come across Adalwin in the forest after fleeing the village. Initially, she was terrified she had once again set foot in their lands without knowing. Adalwin assured her she had nothing to fear. His manner towards her was much gentler than it had been to the Romans, and he confided in her that he could tell she was a girl. Seraphina, still worried, was ready to run at that point. Adalwin spoke quickly about why they were there, and he shared with Seraphina that many Germanic women had been kidnapped from their villages.

They had tracked the kidnappers to that region, he told Seraphina, and that is why they had crossed paths in the forest. Seraphina told him how she had been taken to the prison, and that she knew where it was. She also told him of the plot involving Darius and Tamura, as well as Faustus and others in Rome.

Together, they had come up with this plan. Now, the pirates were at their mercy. 'You,' said Seraphina, pointing at Ourgious, 'patch up her wounds.' She pointed down to Rhea. 'Feed her and make her as well as you can. You had better hope she lives.' Ourgious did not even look to Karsas for approval; he went straight for Rhea and started attending to her.

'Now, you,' she said, looking straight at Karsas. 'You tell us everything. How you find these girls, how you bring them here, who you sell them to, and where they end up. Tell us if this is the only prison or if there are others, and before you say a word, heed this. If you tell a single lie, or if I even think you might be lying, my friends here will inflict a lot of pain on you, for a very long time. At least as much pain as you have inflicted on me and these other girls. Do what I have said, and you may be spared that punishment.'

Karsas hung his head. He thought for a moment of just how this simple Hebrew girl had enlisted the help of these barbarians. He even thought about asking, but knew better. Karsas was defeated. There was little point in doing anything other than cooperating fully.

Seraphina had nothing more to say, and Adalwin took over from that point. The other pirates were taken away. Towards the forest, towards the darkness. Her head dipped as the pirates were led away. She knew what was going to happen to them, and why it had to happen. She even knew they probably deserved it for all the suffering they had inflicted. Nevertheless, Seraphina could not escape the small tinge of sadness she felt for them.

Karsas and Ourgious watched in silence as their comrades were taken away. They would not see them again.

FIFTY NINE

Once Rhea had been patched up, she was reunited with the other girls. The door to the prison cell was unlocked, and their restraints had been removed. Seraphina briefly explained that they were free but said little more than that. After one or two questions, the group decided to stay together and wait so they could leave with Seraphina and their liberators. They were unsure of where they were and finding their way through the forest by themselves did not appeal to them.

A minor but lengthy disagreement also ensued at this point. Once Ourgious had attended to Rhea, Adalwin did not see why he should not join the rest of his cohorts. It was not said exactly where the remainder of the pirates had been taken, though Seraphina expected they were dying slow, painful deaths in the nearby forest. She knew she was letting her compassion get the better of her. After all, it was not as though Ourgious could be trusted. She did, however, know that Karsas trusted him implicitly, and she explained this to Adalwin. Karsas had initially scoffed at this. After a short while, Seraphina had made it quite clear just how much she had overheard while locked up in the smaller cell. Karsas' eyes bulged out of their sockets as he listened.

Adalwin wanted blood. It made Seraphina wonder if some of Adalwin's kin were amongst the women who had been kidnapped. She dared not ask. The barbarian leader had been composed and even calculating when they spoke in the forest and formulated their plot. Now, he was anything but. After a long discussion, Seraphina convinced him that Ourgious may be of use if there was more than one prison. She consoled Adalwin by reminding him that he could kill Ourgious any time he wanted.

They spoke in basic Greek as it was the only language they both understood. It also meant the pirates could understand them. Both Karsas and Ourgious were sitting on the ground, crouched over their knees. They had taken to burying their heads between their arms. Each time they looked up, they were not met with any positive reaction. At best, Adalwin's men glared at them while they brandished their weapons. At worst, they shouted all manner of epithets and slurs. They didn't understand the language, but there was little doubt as to the crux of the message. It could be worse. They had heard the screams of the other pirates from the forest. Neither wanted to think about what the barbarians were doing to them.

Seraphina felt her body shudder at the screams. She took a deep breath and tried to think of something else. Her thoughts drifted, as they often did, to Quintus. *Quintus! One of them must know what happened to him.*

'You!' she said, pointing at the leader.

The once proud Karsas looked up. 'Yes?' he said, barely making a sound.

'Do you remember when you took me? When you attacked our ship?'

Karsas kept his head up and nodded.

'There was a young man with us. The others didn't fight you, but when you took me, he did. I was knocked out and don't remember. Tell me what happened to him. He wasn't with the others when I returned to Rome.'

Karsas still could not believe this girl had escaped and made it to Rome. It was even more of a shock that she had made it back here and had brought them to their knees. He shook his head and wanted so badly to lie. Then he remembered her warning. These barbarians were not to be trifled with. As he took a breath in, his chest rose. Then he exhaled, and all his weight dropped into the ground.

'He fought. He fought as fiercely as he could. We tried to restrain him, but he just flailed wildly and kept calling your name. Seraphina. I didn't know it was your name at that point. He was acting like a crazed man.'

Seraphina folded her arms and looked down at both Karsas and Ourgious. 'Well, that's not really surprising, now is it? He and I were travelling together, and along you come.' She pointed at Karsas first, and then Ourgious. 'You kidnap me and knock me out, and then think he is crazy for wanting to defend me. To protect me. Tell me what happened to him.' Seraphina's voice gave even weight to each word, with very little tone or inflection. As she spoke, she did not blink.

'He fell overboard. He had managed to wound a few of my men. Nothing serious, but we weren't interested in pulling him back up for more. We left him there.'

She felt the dryness in her throat. This evil pirate's words replayed in her head. She stared at the wall of the prison because if she kept looking at Karsas, she worried she might draw a weapon and kill him. Seraphina saw Ourgious raise his head and look at her. She was in no mood to look down at whatever expression he was wearing. Her knees wobbled, and for a moment, she thought they might buckle. She felt the tears coming, threatening to mingle with the sweat already covering her flushed skin. Turning around, she looked out into the blackness of the night. Morning was coming, but it was not there yet. Though she could not see it, she knew the water was in front of her, somewhere in the distance. Seraphina just kept looking, knowing that somewhere out there, her dear Quintus was resting in a watery grave.

Her fists and jaw clenched, and she could feel her whole body moving with each breath. *It wouldn't take long,* she thought. The weapons were on her belt, and she glanced at them for a moment. Even if they resisted, the barbarians would hold them down. She shook her head and tried to remember what she had learned. What she knew to be true. That the anger would stay with her. That nothing would change. Seraphina tried desperately to cling to something. To think of Keb. Afiz. Gisgo. These teachers who had passed on so much to her. To remember what she had been through with her parents.

In that moment, it all failed her. She could physically feel the rage rising inside her. It was so much rawer and more palpable than the anger she had felt towards her parents' murderers. Seraphina's hand went to the club hanging on her belt, and she turned to face Karsas. Brandishing the club, she went straight for him. Karsas leaned back, and his one exposed eye widened. Adalwin stepped in front of her.

'You can't, Seraphina. Not yet.' She had raised the club, and his thick hand gripped her wrist. 'You can kill that one if you want.' He nodded in Ourgious' direction. 'Though you told me we need him if we are to learn everything about this.'

Seraphina dropped the club and fell to her knees. She glared at Karsas through soaked, glazed eyes. Then her head fell to the ground, followed by a loud, dull wailing. She cried without restraint, mourning her dear Quintus, and wishing, at least in that moment, that she was dead and gone too.

SIXTY

The barbarians were not accustomed to wailing women. Such a display by their own women was completely unusual for their culture. Their master was content to let her continue, so they would too. It was a strange situation. Hundreds of warriors gathered around a girl crying her eyes out. The girl herself in disguise and plotting with their leader to take down a band of pirates who apparently were also kidnappers and slave traders. This was to say nothing of the five girls who remained inside the prison.

At that moment, one of those girls came outside. Rhea was finally awake, having heard her friend's cries of anguish. With one foot outside the door, she glanced around before deeming the situation safe. The two she recognised as her captors were on the ground, unarmed and not moving a muscle. There were hundreds of men she had never seen before, and Seraphina was on the ground. Sustained by the food and what little rest she'd had, Rhea stepped out and went to Seraphina's side. She placed her hand on her back and told her she was there. It seemed to calm her for a moment, as the cries died down. Then she listened as Seraphina coughed and spluttered. Rhea patted her back as Seraphina cleared her throat. Finally, Seraphina rose. She kneeled on the ground, wiping her face and nose with her sleeve.

'Very ladylike,' said Rhea, and the two of them shared a much-needed laugh as they embraced.

A familiar voice then spoke from behind Seraphina. 'So, you are a woman.' She turned around to see that it was Paulus. Rhea just stared at him, trying to comprehend what was going on.

Before Seraphina could respond, another familiar voice rang out. It was Darius, shouting in Germanic. Adalwin would later tell her that he was demanding to know what was going on. As planned, several of Adalwin's men had ridden to Tamura's village. They had woken Darius, Paulus, and the other Romans with the ruse that they had found the young Seorsa, dead. They had also discovered that Seorsa was not a boy, but a young woman.

Paulus and the other soldiers stared at Seraphina, unable to speak. Darius' eyes darted left and right, and he ran towards his horse. He barely made it two steps before several of Adalwin's men tackled him to the ground. The Roman soldiers went to his aid, but they stopped when a thick line of the barbarians got in front of them. The other men piled onto Darius, delivering punches to his face and body. For a few moments, Adalwin was content to allow the maiming. He looked over at Seraphina, and then back towards Darius. He stepped forward and raised his hands. Then he commanded his men to get Darius on his feet.

'Whatever she has told you,' he screamed, 'they're all lies!'

Adalwin sneered at Darius, as Paulus and the other soldiers tried to gather what exactly was going on. While Adalwin screamed back at Darius, Seraphina walked over to Paulus. She stepped past the barbarians to get to him, and Paulus noticed they made way for her to pass.

'Seraphina,' said Paulus. 'It was you the whole time.'

'Yes, sir.'

'Can you please tell me what is going on?' As Paulus asked this, Darius was thrown to the ground next to Karsas and Ourgious and told to stay quiet.

'It would take some time, Commander.'

Paulus smiled. 'Take all the time you need.'

'Well, everything you knew about me back in Rome was true. I was taken from Cicero's ship on the way from Alexandria to Rome by these men.' She pointed at Karsas and Ourgious. 'They brought me here, and when I came to, I was chained in a room with a group of young women. There were forty of us in total.' As she said this, she pointed into the prison.

Paulus nodded. 'Yes, yes, I remember what you told me before we left Rome.'

Seraphina sniffled. 'Remember the young Roman man I told you about? The son of the general?'

'Yes, I do. Quintus was his name, correct?'

'Yes.' Seraphina wept a little at the mention of Quintus' name. 'Well, we were together. We were in love. That's why I wanted to come on this mission. I'd managed to get myself to Rome using this disguise, and if there was any chance we were going to find Quintus, I wanted to be here.'

'A very dangerous move, Seraphina. Brave, but dangerous.'

Seraphina nodded. 'I know, but I'd managed to defend myself before. I didn't think I'd be putting anyone in danger. I knew I'd be of help in finding this place.'

Paulus glanced at Adalwin, who looked as fierce as ever. Then he looked down at Darius and the other two men sitting against the wall of the prison. 'Why are they so angry at Darius?'

'It turns out that Darius was sent not to help navigate, but to sabotage our mission.'

'What do you mean?'

Seraphina folded her arms and glared at Darius. 'I overheard him talking to Tamura. The woman from the village. I heard how he, or maybe his master Faustus, had bribed the emissary that was sent ahead of us.' Seraphina pointed at Karsas. 'The emissary warned this man that we would be coming. His name is Karsas, and he is the leader of these men. Pirates, and slave traders.'

Paulus looked at Darius with raised eyebrows, then at Adalwin, and then back to Seraphina. His eyes softened, and his expression went blank.

It was as if he had not absorbed what Seraphina just said. 'So, Darius' master, Faustus.'

'Faustus is the one who helped me get back to Rome. I was in disguise at the time, and he probably didn't realize he was helping someone who had escaped from this place. When I spoke to Cicero about the mission, we came up with the idea that Darius could join to help find the way. I would come, in disguise, as Darius' assistant, so as not to arouse suspicion. Cicero thought there was no way you'd allow a young woman to join the mission.'

'What did you hear them say? Darius and this woman, Tamura?'

'I overheard them talking about how the emissary had been bribed. They also spoke about killing me, in a way that avoided suspicion.' They both turned to look at Darius. 'Why?' asked Seraphina. 'What did he say to you?'

'This morning, before these men arrived, Darius told me you had attacked him and fled the village. He said we had to find you, and make sure you didn't cause any more trouble. It didn't make complete sense to me. I was going to ask him about it, but then the barbarians arrived and spoke to Darius. They led us here.'

'Very well. Where do they come into this?' Paulus gestured in the direction of Adalwin and his men.

Seraphina told him the story of how they had met in the forest, and the plan they had come up with. As Paulus listened, he and the other soldiers pieced together the story. Paulus could not help but be impressed with Seraphina. He could also see the silver lining. A few hours ago, his mission had been a complete failure. Now, they not only had the men they had wanted to apprehend, but they also had uncovered a conspiracy involving corruption and bribery.

As Seraphina continued to speak, it was clear to Paulus that she had a plan for what was next.

SIXTY ONE

They were reeling from what they had heard. For hours now, they had interrogated Karsas, Darius, and, to a lesser extent, Ourgious. There were seven prisons in total, flung across the lands to the east of the Roman republic. Darius confessed that Faustus was one of many prominent men in Rome affiliated with the network, as he described it. Whereas Karsas and Ourgious were completely resigned to their fate, Darius still held out some hope. Hope for what, he did not know, but he remained defiant in providing only a few details.

Paulus was not having it. As the story sunk in, his anger towards Darius had only risen. He understood that the mistakes he had made were his own and that his men had paid for it with their lives. Despite that, he would not move past the fact that Darius had joined his mission for the sole purpose of ensuring its failure. Seraphina and Adalwin were exhausted. They had been up all night, and the adrenaline had worn off some time ago.

The commander reached down and grabbed Darius by the throat. He flung him on to his back, drew his sword and held the tip to his neck. 'Do you think your master can protect you? When we return to

Rome, he will be the first one arrested and put on trial. Then we will find every single other person involved in this and do the same.' Darius smiled up at Paulus and did not say a word in response.

Paulus' eyes bulged and he fumed. He lifted the sword and swung to his right. The commander's intention had been to cut off Darius' left forearm. The strike was not clean, and a small fragment of bone held Darius' arm together. The smile was gone, replaced by wild screaming. Paulus commanded one of the officers to hold Darius' arm up, at least what was left of it. He mercilessly sliced the forearm clean away from the bicep. Blood poured out.

Seraphina vomited. Adalwin remained still and watched. In truth, both had been ready to get some sleep. To gather their thoughts and plan the next move. They were wide awake now.

'Don't any one of you help him,' said Paulus. Then he pointed at the officer, the same one who had held up Darius' arm only a few moments earlier. 'You tell him everything, and I mean everything. Everyone you know who is involved, and everything you know about how these women are kidnapped and sold to households in Rome. When he's satisfied that you have no more to tell, then one of my men will sew up your arm. Not a moment before.'

Paulus had to almost shout these words because Darius was crying out in agony at the top of his lungs. He waited for him to quiet down, and then added 'if I were you, I'd speak fast. You're losing a lot of blood.'

Seraphina had cleaned herself up and now stood, her hand practically glued to her cheek. Her mouth gaped open, and she watched the soldier take notes as Darius spoke. To say he was speaking fast was an understatement. Eventually, the officer had two of his colleagues come and take notes. Darius was laying out the operation, and the details were scintillating. He named senators, other officials, and numerous wealthy families in Rome. He told how much slaves were sold for, and how buyers contacted brokers in the network to arrange a transaction. Slavery was far from illegal in the republic, but women of such grooming were rarely available in the slave trade. Thus, a premium was paid. Their appearance was also dulled—their hair was tied back, and they were dressed in loose, common garments from head to toe. He did not know for sure, but he believed a similar system was adopted in the Greek and other non-Roman cities where the trade was conducted. He disclosed the exorbitant prices for which each girl was sold, with more exotic women being sold for even more.

Karsas listened with great interest. He had given every bit of information he had without hesitation. He had no desire to follow the fate of his comrades, who were by now dead in the nearby forest. However, Karsas knew nothing of what happened to the girls once they were handed over. He was shocked at the part about the prices. The seven prisons made a tidy profit, but the brokers in Rome and Greece were making much, much more from their endeavour. He said nothing as Darius spoke, and did not move. Hundreds of men were still nearby and could be observing him, not to mention the Roman soldiers and this damn girl, Seraphina. He was still trying to fathom how she had gotten the best of him, but Karsas had long since decided to cooperate as much as possible. He had money hidden away in various places, with people that none of his fellow pirates knew. People who could be relied upon. He would try his best to avoid death, serve time in a prison somewhere, and hopefully find himself a free man someday. Free with plenty of money.

Adalwin was impressed with Paulus. No stranger to brutality himself, he had flinched when the commander mutilated the stubborn Darius. He had threatened and intimidated, all to no avail. The free flow of Darius' tongue had Adalwin admiring the efficacy of the Roman commander's methods. He knew enough about Romans to know that he could not get away with such methods in Rome. Yet here, many miles away from anyone who had authority over him, and in these circumstances, his actions were perfect. After a few minutes, Adalwin laughed at the sheer speed of Darius' words.

Seraphina did not miss a thing. Quintus' demise would not be in vain, she had decided. With everything she had heard in the past twelve hours, there was much to do. Prisons would be stormed, and many high-profile individuals in Rome would be arrested. The same would happen in other cities throughout the republic, and in Greek cities too.

Darius spoke until he could speak no more. He started to stutter, and then faded in and out of consciousness. The officer was more than satisfied with the information and called out to Paulus for approval to stitch up the wounded man. Paulus nodded, and two of the soldiers began the gruesome task of sewing up Darius' arm. He would never again be the mighty warrior he had been. Seraphina watched in muted horror.

She stretched her arms into the air once it was over. At the same time, she turned her neck from side to side. The movement felt good, and she even moved into a few of Keb's exercises. She wasn't about to sit down and meditate in front of hundreds of barbarians, but the breathing and stretching felt good.

'I've been meaning to ask you. What are those exercises you do?' Paulus was standing next to her, with a slight smile on his face.

Seraphina laughed. 'Another long story, Commander. I promise to tell you when this is over.' She nodded over at Darius. 'Are those standard interrogation techniques?'

Paulus was looking at Darius too. The smile vanished from the commander's face and he shook his head. 'No. I shouldn't have done that. I lost my temper, but he just made me so angry. To dare to come on our mission, to see to it that we failed. Then to threaten to kill you.' He looked back up at Seraphina. 'Look, Seraphina, I was very angry at you. I thought you had sent us on a wild goose chase. I'm sorry I doubted you.'

Seraphina placed her hand on the commander's shoulder. 'There's nothing to apologise for. You have done what you believed to be right at every turn. I was as fooled as you were by Darius. I'm just glad I overheard that conversation.'

'I bet you're happy you ran into them again too.' Paulus tilted his head towards Adalwin and the barbarians, and they shared a laugh.

'What is his name, the leader?'

'Adalwin,' said Seraphina. 'Yes, I'm very glad I crossed paths with them in the forest. None of this would have happened but for their help.'

'Did I hear him speaking Greek?'

Seraphina nodded. 'Very basic, but yes. A good thing too, because I have no idea how to speak their language.'

Paulus stood up straight and folded his arms. The serious commander was back. 'This is serious business, Seraphina. We are a long way from home, and this situation is unprecedented. We need to plan what to do next.'

Seraphina had been thinking of little else. 'I have an idea of where to start.'

'What's that?'

'Tell Adalwin everything we have learned from these stinking pigs. Then listen to what he has to say. I have a feeling he will want to help.'

Paulus' hand came to his chin, and he tapped his index finger thoughtfully against his cheekbone. 'From what I've seen, I know you have more of a plan than that.'

'I do, but let's start by hearing what Adalwin has to say.'

'Good idea.'

SIXTY TWO

There were going to be no quick decisions. A committee of sorts was forming, and several parties made up the circle. Seraphina sat with Rhea and the remaining four prisoners behind them. These girls had not been held for very long and were in good spirits given their sudden liberation. Paulus and two of his tribunes took up another corner of the circle. Then there was Adalwin, with five of his men.

Seraphina knew nothing about the hierarchy of barbarian hordes, but she suspected these men were very loyal to Adalwin. She had seen them talking to him at various stages of the morning. They seemed relatively calm in contrast with the bloodlust evident on the faces of most of Adalwin's army.

Like so many important meetings, the decisive conversations had been conducted beforehand between the major players. Seraphina found herself in the middle of the situation, and thus her viewpoint was both respected and demanded by Adalwin and Paulus. They sat and ate in silence, surrounded by beautiful blue sky and numerous shades of green. The prison, now relieved of its purpose, looked rather picturesque in the background.

During her better days in captivity, Seraphina had basked in the natural beauty of this place. Being there now, free of shackles, only enhanced her nostalgia. It certainly helped that Rhea was next to her, unharmed. The fresh air from the sea swept over the perfectly flat field. A flock of birds momentarily interrupted the stillness but at that moment, everyone Seraphina cared for was as safe as they could be. Except Quintus, but there would be time to mourn later.

Ourgious had prepared them a fine meal. He had offered to do so, and, initially, Adalwin had chained him with the same shackles used on the girls. After a few moments of watching Ourgious trip and fall, then spilling boiled water all over himself, the barbarian leader relented. He promised Ourgious a swift axe chop to the neck if he misbehaved in any way whatsoever. There had been no issue, and everyone was grateful for the food.

Seraphina watched the young pirate as he went about his tasks. There was a gentle quality to him, one that she had observed before. That night, when he foiled her escape attempt in the forest. He moved gracefully, and almost everything about him stood in stark contrast to Karsas and the rest of his men. She was far from liking him but sensed there was more to his story. These thoughts took her mind to Keb, and she wondered if this is what he had been talking about. *Getting a specific feeling about certain people*, she said to herself, Keb's words ringing in her head. As her thoughts drifted, she noticed Adalwin on the other side of the circle. He was looking straight at her with raised eyebrows. Seraphina glanced around the circle and saw that all eyes were on her.

Adalwin had come up with a plan, but he had decided that Seraphina would share it with the group. Paulus had initially baulked at this but wisely thought better of challenging Adalwin's authority in the present situation.

Seraphina patted Rhea's knee and swallowed the food she had been chewing. 'Adalwin has decided we will visit the rest of the prisons. We are told there are six more, and that some are much larger than this. Adalwin has committed a total of six thousand men to destroy these prisons, and free anyone being held captive in them.'

While Adalwin spoke some Greek, his lieutenants did not. He whispered a translation to them as Seraphina spoke. Seraphina looked towards Paulus, and then Paulus glanced at Adalwin. Once Adalwin nodded, Paulus had the floor. 'Six groups, each of one thousand men, will march towards each of these prisons. Each group will be accompanied by at least one Roman soldier, and Adalwin and his, uh, chiefs here, will lead each of the six forces.'

Paulus noticed Seraphina and Adalwin nodding, so he continued. 'No one is returning to Rome at this stage. We can trust no one for now, and thanks to Adalwin, we have more than enough men to execute these plans. From what the pirates have told us, their friends holding each prison will be severely outnumbered. We expect that they will surrender rather than be slaughtered.'

Everyone seemed pleased by the plan and all were either nodding or smiling in agreement. Except for the five girls next to Seraphina. They remained still. Paulus, thinking quickly, gestured towards them and said, 'Getting these girls home safely is a priority,' and continued, turning towards them 'and we will make plans depending on where each of you need to go. We will need to do the same for the girls we rescue from these other prisons. Is that acceptable, Adalwin?'

Adalwin nodded, and his men nodded with him.

'Very well,' said Paulus. 'Seraphina will determine where each of these young women need to be escorted to. We will depart at first light.'

Rhea leaned over and whispered in Seraphina's ear. 'You said there was a prison near Byzantium?'

Seraphina nodded. 'Yes, why?'

'Will these men take me with them? So I can get home to my family?'

Seraphina turned and smiled at Rhea. 'Yes, and I'm coming with you.'

Rhea's eyes widened, and a smile formed on her face. 'You are?' she said, loudly enough that it got everyone's attention. Rhea noticed everyone looking, and blushed. Then she leaned back towards Seraphina and whispered, 'Really?'

Seraphina laughed. 'Yes, I'm not leaving you again until you're safely home. Besides, Adalwin said that he will lead the force heading to that prison. I told him I wanted to come too, and I don't even have to wear that ridiculous disguise. Paulus, the Roman commander over there, the one who just spoke, will also come on the mission to Byzantium.

'Thank you, Seraphina,' said Rhea. 'But …'

'What is it?'

'Are you going to fight the pirates in this other prison?'

Seraphina shook her head. 'It's unlikely. Adalwin and Paulus both said they would not have me anywhere near the front line when we attack. They said I should be allowed to come because of how much I've helped. I'll be safe, don't you worry.'

Rhea wrapped her arms around Seraphina and hugged her, while the two remained sitting on the ground. 'I'm so glad I met you, Seraphina. Thank you for everything you've done for me.'

Seraphina returned the embrace. 'Thank me once I have you home safe, alright?'

SIXTY THREE

The flames and smoke rose high into the blue sky. Seraphina, Paulus, and the other soldiers had been woken by the crackling roar of the fire. Adalwin and his men evidently rose before dawn. They had decided the prison should be burned to the ground. What Seraphina and Paulus did not know is that the Germanic leaders had debated whether to throw their prisoners—Karsas, Darius and Ourgious—in with the fire. Cooler heads had prevailed.

The plan was for everyone to get ready for their journey, but the fire proved too distracting. So, they stood and watched, as the wooden fortress was reduced to ash. One of the barbarians thought it fitting to line up the two pirates and their conspirator to witness the destruction. Thus, all three sat and watched the fire do its work. They were all shackled, although Darius obviously could not have his arms shackled together. Adalwin had chained his good arm to his legs and done so with great amusement. Darius had not spoken since his rapid-fire confession the day before.

Seraphina was amazed at her ability to feel sympathy for any of them, especially the mutilated Darius. There had been a discussion late the night before as to the fate of the three prisoners. Darius must return to Rome, Paulus had insisted. Adalwin seemed uninterested in holding any of them. He knew that the prisons were going to be destroyed, and the women freed. That was all he cared about. Darius was not faring well, and riding a horse was out of the question. He had been sick several times and looked dangerously pale. One of Paulus' men examined him and pronounced him fit enough to travel. He was thrown in a cart, so he would be able to travel with them to Byzantium without needing to ride a horse.

Given Adalwin's apparent indifference to keeping them, Paulus said that Karsas and Ourgious would also travel with them. First to Byzantium, and then to Rome, where they would stand trial for their crimes. Given her history of escapes, Seraphina was charged with ensuring the two pirates were shackled, chained, and otherwise restrained so that they had absolutely no chance of getting away. *Overkill*, thought Seraphina. Each of them was going to be surrounded by twenty of Adalwin's warriors throughout the journey. Both had adopted a strict policy of speaking only when spoken to, and their body language was thoroughly subdued. Seraphina restrained them and had them put in the cart with Darius. She took a few extra moments with Karsas, ensuring his discomfort.

It was time to leave. Destinations for the other girls had been determined. Both Paulus and Adalwin made their men promise to make it a priority that they got home safely. Under no circumstances were they to attack their target prisons until the girls were safe with their families. The girls said tearful yet joyful goodbyes, and all of them hugged Seraphina tightly, thanking her over and over. Seraphina simply nodded and smiled. Inside, she felt deep gratitude that she had been able to spare these young women from a terrible fate.

Rhea was a new woman. Happy and energetic, she wanted to ride her own horse. Two of Adalwin's men had spent the morning teaching her, and she was loving every minute. She talked Seraphina's ear off with tales of Byzantium, her family and all the things she wanted to show her once they arrived. Seraphina grinned at her enthusiasm but hoped she didn't keep up the same level of chatter all the way to Byzantium.

As each of the forces prepared to leave, Paulus said goodbye to his men as well. He gave strict orders. They were all going to be crossing the borders of various kingdoms without permission. They were to tell anyone who stopped them the nature of their mission and to proceed by force if necessary. Paulus was clear on this point and assured them that he would bear any responsibility for the consequences. Paulus just hoped that Caesar would be on his side if anything went wrong. The last thing he wanted to do was start some regional war but storming these prisons and freeing these young women had become something more than a mission to him. It was the right thing to do, and he would pay whatever cost was required to do it.

Paulus and Seraphina took up a position behind their three prisoners. They were in the middle of the convoy, but no one was moving. Voices moved back from the front towards them, and one of the barbarians spoke to Seraphina. She had no idea what he was saying, but he pointed at them and then to the front of the group. Seraphina and Paulus exchanged looks, with neither having any idea what was going on. After a few moments, Adalwin rode down to them.

'What are you doing back here?' he asked.

Paulus started to say something about it being the safest spot, and Adalwin laughed at him. He explained that they needn't worry about any danger. When Paulus hesitated, Adalwin asked him 'how many men are in the Roman Army?'

'Twelve thousand, give or take.'

'There are a thousand men here, all far fiercer than your precious soldiers. What are you worried about?'

Paulus didn't appreciate the remark, but Adalwin was speaking in good humour. He also made a valid point. Paulus and Seraphina followed Adalwin to the front.

'Isn't this better?' asked Adalwin. 'Back there, you have to ride with my smelly warriors and those evil pirates.' Seraphina laughed at this, and

Paulus started to relax. Even if they ran into any trouble, he doubted it would be a force unwise enough to attack a thousand barbarians.

At that moment, Rhea came charging along with her horse. She was having a wonderful time, and nearly fell off as she screamed to a halt next to them. Her horse touched noses with Luna, and Seraphina was laughing hard. 'Are we ready?' she shrieked in excitement. 'I'm going home!' Even Adalwin was amused, and Seraphina caught a rare smile on his face. Paulus shook his head, wondering what was going to happen next.

Rhea was still learning to control the horse and she took off almost as quickly as she had come. Adalwin told Seraphina not to worry. She was heading in the right direction, for now, he said. Rhea's antics brought a much-needed lightening of mood, and Seraphina realised it was the first time she had laughed since she found out about Quintus.

They began to ride, and despite the circumstances, Seraphina felt a tinge of excitement. She was so relieved to be out of disguise. Her friend was free, and clearly having a great time. Seraphina was riding between two experienced leaders, both of whom had shown her a lot of regard and respect in the past day or so. She talked to Paulus about what life was like back in Rome for him, and what would likely happen once they got back there. He spoke in detail, and it was obvious he had been thinking about it non-stop. He planned to arrest and put on trial everyone who was involved, including any senators and soldiers who were involved. He was particularly keen to get his hands on the emissary who had been bribed.

Listening to the way he spoke, Seraphina felt sorry for that emissary. Thinking of Darius' severed arm, she was quite certain that many more were going to feel Paulus' wrath before this was over. Seraphina had come to respect Paulus deeply. His reverence before the trip started, and his dedication to the mission were admirable. The way he had apologised to Darius, back when they thought he was an ally, showed great humility. Now, he had taken it upon himself to continue the mission far beyond what was originally imagined. The look in his eye was one of sheer determination, and Seraphina got the idea that he would follow this through to the very end.

'May I ask you a question, Paulus?'

'Of course.'

'What was going through your mind when you severed Darius' arm? What's going through your mind now as you come with us to Byzantium? Won't your commanding officers be expecting you back? I mean, aren't you going to get into trouble when you return to Rome?'

Paulus laughed. 'Well, there are four questions there, my dear.'

Seraphina nodded and smiled.

Paulus sighed and looked away from Seraphina, in the direction they were riding. 'I rarely lose my temper like that, Seraphina. The truth is, when I first heard about this operation, it upset me greatly. I was impressed, as we all were, that you had somehow managed to escape and return to Rome. The idea that more girls like you were being held in places like that, and then sold into situations of slavery ... well, it disgusted me.'

Seraphina watched him speak and could see that his eyes were a little wet. His normally strong diction faltered at times. She resisted the urge to reach out and comfort him, as she felt it would not be appropriate.

'You see, Seraphina, I was not born into the privilege that you see in today's Rome. I grew up in a village on the outskirts, and we were not a rich family. My father was a soldier. When I was young, he was killed in battle, and I watched my mother and sister work to make sure we had enough. I often saw them mistreated by the wealthy families who employed them. They weren't quite slaves, but their situation wasn't far off. One day, I went to the house where they worked at the end of the day. I would usually go there and the three of us would walk home together. I found my mother being beaten by the woman she worked for. My sister was trying to help, but one of the woman's sons was holding her back and hurting her too.'

Seraphina's own eyes were watering now. Paulus needed to clear his throat to finish the story.

'I was only a small boy, and there was nothing I could do. When my mother finished taking her beating, she took my sister and left with me. The next day, she had no choice but to go back to work there. Things didn't get that bad very often, but when I thought of the girls at the prison, no doubt waiting to be sold into an even worse fate, it just made me so angry and sad at the same time. So, I said I would lead this mission. Then, when that awful Darius refused to tell us what he knew, I snapped. I know it was wrong to cut his arm off, but this whole time I've just kept thinking of my mother and sister.'

Seraphina shook her head. 'I'm really glad you are here with us, Commander.'

Paulus wiped his tears away with the back of his arm and chuckled. 'I think we've been through enough that you can call me Paulus.'

Seraphina smiled. 'Okay, Paulus it is.'

'Can I keep calling you Seorsa?'

They both shared a laugh at this, and Paulus added, 'that was an incredible disguise. How did you come up with it?'

'You wouldn't believe me if I told you. Can I ask one more thing?'

'Please.'

Seraphina took a deep, heavy breath. 'What ended up happening to your mother and sister?'

Paulus' head nodded slightly. 'Well, my sister lives with me in Rome. She never married or had a family, but she is very comfortable there and seems happy most of the time. Being a highly decorated commander comes with a pretty good life. As for my mother, unfortunately, she died without knowing any other life than the one I just told you about. She worked hard so we could have opportunities.'

'You must be very grateful to have had a mother like that.'

Paulus nodded. 'So, what about you, Seraphina? Where are your parents? They must be worried about you.'

This time, it was Seraphina who turned her head away. They rode along for a minute or so, and she had not said anything. When Paulus looked over, he could see she was crying.

'I'm sorry, Seraphina. I didn't mean to upset you.'

'It's alright. I think it has been quite an emotional few days. Maybe I should tell you the story of the disguise first.'

'Go ahead. I'd love to hear it.'

Seraphina wiped her own tears away and launched into the story of how she met Keb. She added very early on that they would be passing his home, and they might even get to meet him. Starting with the story of waking up to Keb prodding her with his staff, Seraphina told him everything. Adalwin overheard and became interested in the story. Seraphina switched to Greek, and both men were fascinated. As Adalwin asked questions, Seraphina told of her escape from the prison, and her journey into the forest before she met Faustus and Darius. They both looked back at Ourgious when she told of her failed escape attempt, and later of maiming him when she successfully escaped with Rhea. They glanced at Rhea when Seraphina spoke of her. Rhea was oblivious and being chaperoned by four of Adalwin's men as she rode haphazardly—a mixture of learning to ride the horse and the excitement of getting the horse to gallop fast as she could.

'I've heard many stories,' said Adalwin. 'This is one of the best.'

Paulus nodded in agreement, and Seraphina beamed with pride. After some time, Rhea joined them. She wanted Seraphina to tell the full story of how she and Adalwin met and came up with their plan. Seraphina had the rare sensation of being tired of talking, and Adalwin's entire face lit up. Seraphina deferred to Adalwin to tell the story. Paulus and Rhea listened intently as he spoke, with Seraphina adding a titbit or two here and there. She laughed when he talked about surprising Karsas and their men from behind. The mood was solemn when he spoke of taking Karsas' men to their demise in the forest.

'Why are you sad?' he demanded, seeing their faces downcast. 'These men have taken many of our women. Sold them for money. Death is too good for them.'

None of them disagreed. All three nodded, but Seraphina and Rhea had both heard the screams of the pirates as they met their end.

It was a difficult sound to forget. Adalwin was unimpressed with their compassion. Seraphina changed the subject, asking how long it would take them to reach Byzantium. When Adalwin and Paulus agreed that it would take the better part of a month, Seraphina dropped her head a little.

Adalwin and Paulus were both unconcerned. Between them, they were aware of many friendly cities and villages where they could stop, rest and resupply. Their journey would be a safe one. A protocol had been agreed upon. Under no circumstances would they disclose the nature of their mission to anyone, unless it was necessary in order to continue towards Byzantium. Adalwin seemed particularly keen to encounter anyone who dared stop them.

They continued talking into the day. While Seraphina was dismayed about how long the journey would take, she was grateful for the friends and allies she was now surrounded by.

SIXTY FOUR

Seraphina told them they could not all go. Paulus and Adalwin and Rhea had all been fascinated by her tales of Keb, and Adalwin had even told a few of his men. Seraphina would not take a thousand men to visit Keb though. *Who knew if he would even be there?*

In the end, it was agreed that only the four of them would go. Adalwin made his men promise two things. One, that they would not follow. Two, that they would not do any harm to the prisoners. The barbarians reluctantly agreed.

Darius was starting to get some of his strength back. He was a different man though and frequently looked at his amputated arm, weeping at times. Ourgious shot a look of alarm at Seraphina once it was clear they were leaving them. Like Seraphina, Ourgious and Karsas had no understanding of the Germanic language. They began to panic and pleaded for their lives to be spared.

Darius spoke his first words in days. 'Calm yourselves. They're not going to kill us. He just made them promise not to harm us while they're gone.' The voice was much more faint and gentle, and a few of them did a double take as to whether it was actually Darius who was speaking.

Karsas turned with as much ferocity as his shackles allowed. 'Don't you talk to me, you fool. If I weren't in these,' he said, holding up his arms in chains, 'I would come over there and rip your other arm off. Then your head.'

Darius returned his gaze to the floor and resumed his silence.

Ourgious shook his head at Karsas and gave a roll of his eyes. He also remained silent. Meanwhile, Seraphina watched as Karsas continued to shout at Darius. It was as if he was oblivious to his situation. At one point, Adalwin joked about setting Karsas free so he could finish Darius off. Paulus and Seraphina, both starting to sympathise with the pathetic Darius, gave polite smiles in response. Seraphina quipped that Paulus was becoming more lawless by the day. They all laughed at this.

Adalwin thought of a better idea. He stood over Karsas, glaring down at him. Then he retrieved the huge axe that sat on his back. The handle was long and thick, wood bound with black leather. The axe head itself was heavy and its edge glistened in the sunlight. Seraphina wasn't sure which was more frightening—the weapon itself, or the fact that Adalwin could brandish it with such ease.

'Do you want to keep shouting, or do you also want to know what it's like to be without an arm? Or maybe a leg?'

Karsas gave no response, and not a single person there doubted Adalwin's resolve. He kept glaring down at him, daring any kind of response. He wanted Karsas to give him an excuse. Part of him was still jealous that Paulus had the pleasure, as he saw it, of chopping off Darius' arm. Karsas became as quiet and still as the other two prisoners, and they all breathed a sigh of relief when the axe was returned to Adalwin's back. He crouched down and whispered into Karsas' ear that his men had axes, swords, and plenty of other weapons capable of separating his limbs from his body.

Adalwin got back up and mounted his horse. Then, looking at the other three, he said, 'Well, Seraphina, let's go meet this friend of yours.' As they rode off, Seraphina could not help but think what an odd sight they made. A Germanic barbarian chief, a Roman commander, a Greek girl from Byzantium, and a Hebrew girl with Egyptian blood from Alexandria. She wondered what Keb would think when he saw them. If he was even there.

She had asked the rest of their group to camp well into the forest. Adalwin assured her they would not follow them, but Seraphina wanted to make extra sure. She did not know how Keb would react to the presence of the other three, let alone hundreds of warriors. Before long, Seraphina caught a glimpse of the sea in the distance. As they got closer to the water, Luna started to navigate more so than Seraphina. She smiled down at the horse as he picked up the familiar surroundings. She started to notice parts of the woodlands—trees, bushes, clearings—that she had seen before. In the distance, Seraphina could see Keb's clearing, where the two of them had meditated.

She leaned forward and squinted into the distance. Keb was most definitely there, and he was not alone. As her eyes focused, she could see a lot of swift movements.

'Is that your friend?' said Paulus.

'Yes. Is he—'

'I think he's in trouble,' said Rhea.

The four accelerated into a gallop to go to Keb's aid. As they got closer, it became evident that no such aid was necessary. Keb was in the process of dispatching his attackers, all three of them. He wielded his staff nimbly and had drawn blood. He dodged their attacks by ducking, weaving, and jumping. The old man counterattacked with ease and before Paulus had even gotten off his horse, Keb was standing over all three men. They lay there, writhing. The old man leaned on his staff and looked down at them with a warm smile on his face. He looked over nonchalantly at his visitors and, noticing Seraphina, beamed in her direction.

'Well, hello, my dear Seraphina,' said Keb. 'Who are your friends?'

Seraphina was dismounting her horse and panting. 'Keb … what … are you okay?'

'Oh, yes, quite fine,' he said. He stood tall and held his staff to his side. There was no indication of exertion on his part. In fact, he looked perfectly calm and relaxed. He was speaking Coptic, and the other three simply turned their heads back and forth from Seraphina to Keb as they spoke. Seraphina asked Keb to speak in Greek, so everyone could understand.

'Who are these men?' asked Paulus, gesturing towards the pitiful trio on the ground.

Keb's hand stroked the beard on his chin. 'I don't know, actually. They were here waiting for me when I came back from my walk. They threatened me and demanded money from me. When I told them I had none, they attacked me. Bandits, I presume.'

Seraphina looked down. No, she didn't recognise any of them from her encounter in the forest.

'Where did you learn to fight like that?' asked Seraphina.

Keb laughed. 'You're not the only one with abilities, my dear. Now, are you going to introduce me?'

Seraphina was still reeling from seeing the old man move so fast. She shook herself out of it and introduced Adalwin, Paulus, and Rhea to Keb. The four exchanged pleasantries. Keb gave Adalwin's amulet a long glance before returning his attention to Seraphina.

'What brings you all here?' he asked.

As Keb knew about Seraphina's escape from the prison, the entire story did not need retelling. She filled him in on what had happened since she last saw him. Keb listened, fully engaged, though the only reaction he gave was the occasional raising of his eyebrows.

'Just a moment,' said Keb, interrupting Seraphina. Then he looked at Rhea. 'You're Rhea, correct?' Rhea nodded, to which he said, 'I thought you were being taken home to Byzantium.'

Rhea then told Keb of her betrayal at the hands of Tamura at the village, and Seraphina joined her in telling the rest of the story. The men remained remarkably quiet and deferential. They looked Keb up and down as the conversation ensued, interested in his style of dress, and thoroughly impressed by his fighting ability. The bandits were still laid out on the ground and in a lot of pain.'

'Well, a lot has happened then.'

'Yes, and I've been trying to do my exercises every day, but it hasn't always been possible.'

Keb smiled. 'In the circumstances, I think that's very understandable.'

'Wait,' said Paulus, 'those exercises you do. He taught them to you?'

'That's right,' said Seraphina.

'What are they exactly?'

'Well,' said Keb, 'I doubt you have time to get into all that, but broadly, they are energisation exercises.'

'Energisation?' asked Adalwin.

'Yes,' said Keb, turning to Adalwin. 'They help reenergise the body by using movement and breathing. Just as food and water help infuse our bodies with energy, so too can these exercises and practices.'

Paulus and Adalwin nodded, though they weren't entirely sure they grasped what this old man was saying. Rhea did not have the slightest clue but noticed how Seraphina was smiling as Keb spoke.

'So, you're on your way to Byzantium to liberate more prisoners?' he asked, to no one in particular.

'Yes,' said Seraphina. 'Seeing as we were going to pass through here, I wanted to come and see you. We came through here on the way to the prison near Tanais, but you weren't here.'

Keb nodded. 'From time to time, I take long walks in these woods. So, you can't always find me, but I'm glad we have met again today. May I offer you and your friends something to eat or drink?'

SIXTY FIVE

'It's so quiet here,' commented Paulus. The four were sitting in a circle around the centre of the clearing. The others nodded their head. They noticed the quietness, looked out at the sea, and watched Keb as he went about preparing a meal for them. Seraphina was determined to ignore any questions that came up. Paulus watched, noticing that Keb had pots of food cooking on a fire. There were no vegetables or animals in sight.

It was peaceful, he thought. Then he said, to no one in particular, 'what are we doing here?'

'You all wanted to meet Keb,' said Seraphina, 'so I brought you here.'

'Very well, but after we eat, let's get back to camp. We have a long journey ahead of us, and it won't help any of us to delay it.'

Adalwin nodded in agreement. Rhea did too, but the smile on her face contrasted with the serious frowns worn by the men. To say she was in good spirits was an understatement. She was like an excited child, and Seraphina suspected this was her typical nature. *Good for her*, she thought. She had survived being captured twice by the pirates and was now on her way home to Byzantium. From all accounts, there she had a loving family and a wonderful life.

Adalwin kept an eye on Keb while trying to look as uninterested as possible. The Germanic people were no strangers to mysticism, and Adalwin could sense the power this old man wielded. Keb was so far from his homeland too, and Adalwin wondered what business he had here. It was not, strictly speaking, anyone's territory, but the situation was unusual. He sat there, rubbing the amulet he wore around his neck, his talisman, and remained silent.

'There's nothing to worry about,' said Keb, surprising Adalwin from behind. The barbarian shook, and Keb laughed loudly as he slapped him hard on the back. 'Seraphina, the food is ready. Why don't you take your friends, the commander and Rhea here, and serve them?'

Adalwin looked at each of them as they got up and walked towards the food. It sat neatly in three pots under a nearby tree. Keb's hand rested on Adalwin's back, and he whispered to him as the others went to get their food. By the time they returned, the two were whispering and smiling at one another. Adalwin let out a hearty laugh and went to get something to eat for himself.

'What was that all about?' asked Paulus.

'Nothing at all,' said Keb. 'I just wanted to make sure he felt comfortable here.'

'Right,' said Paulus, raising his eyebrows.

Keb ignored the sarcasm and with his guests' plates now full, he went to serve himself. 'Please, eat up,' he said as he rose to his feet. When Keb rejoined them, they all thanked him and complimented him on the delicious food. A hearty duck stew, with plenty of vegetables and rice. As they savoured the rich flavour of the food, one question was on their minds. *Where had the food come from?* Seraphina, of course, had an explanation, but she was unsure as to how Keb did the things he did.

'So, Seraphina,' said Keb, breaking the silence, 'it seems like the exercises have been working.'

Seraphina gulped her mouthful down. 'What do you mean?'

'Well, from what you've told me, you've achieved some rather miraculous feats, wouldn't you say?'

'Yes, but—'

Keb put his plate down. 'Fighting off bandits, staying safe from men who would do you harm, enlisting those men as allies, finding your way back to Rome, convincing senators and high-ranking members of the army to launch this rescue mission, surviving an arrow shot to the chest, foiling a well-laid plot of sabotage, allying yourself with a barbarian horde, and planning the liberation of many young women in prisons scattered across these lands.'

The words Keb had chosen did indeed make it sound miraculous.

'Did I miss anything?' he asked as he took another mouthful.

'She probably saved our lives too,' said Paulus. 'When she made sure that Darius thought she was dead. Who knows what he might have had in store for us.'

Keb nodded. Seraphina looked at the old man and was astonished. She had done all those things because she was capable. Then again, she had virtually no experience in dealing with such matters, and a lot of things had gone right for her.

'Are you saying that doing the exercises is the reason why everything has turned out the way it has?'

The other three were following this conversation with fascination. 'I can't say that for certain. What I do know is that when you regularly practice these habits, new and wonderful things start to materialise in life. It's all a matter of what you believe.'

'What do you mean by that, Keb, sir?' asked Rhea. She had put her plate down and was very interested in what the old man was saying.

Keb's palms turned upwards and he held his shoulders up in a shrug. 'Well, let's say you believed that all men with weapons were dangerous. You might never talk to such men, and that could have all sorts of follow-on effects. In your situation, Seraphina, it might mean that you would never have asked Adalwin here for his help. That's a very practical example.'

Four blank stares were the only responses he received. 'You might believe that if you energise yourself daily and take the time to meditate and connect with nature, that nature will act in a way that serves you. That's something I believe, after all.'

Seraphina started a slow nod, while the others remained still. Their food was going untouched too. 'The sequence of events seems to have helped you along in a positive way, wouldn't you say, Seraphina?'

'I suppose so.'

'Just look at this delicious food we are eating. Connect with nature, and nature provides.'

'Alright, I have to ask' said Paulus, waving his hands, 'where did this food come from? There are no animals here, and I don't see anything edible in these plants. Yet here we are, eating a veritable feast. What did you do, fish these ducks out of the sea when we weren't looking?'

Keb laughed so hard that he almost choked on his food. Once he swallowed what was in his mouth, he thought for a moment. 'Maybe this is too much to explain for now. You all have something important to do, and I don't want to keep you from it.'

'You conjured it,' said Adalwin, still holding his talisman. His food was largely untouched.

'What was that?' said Keb.

'You conjured the food. The same way you fought those bandits.'

'Where did those bandits go, by the way?' asked Rhea, looking around.

'I let them go,' said Keb. 'Tell me what you're saying, Adalwin.' He looked at the barbarian with a wide smile on his face.

'You let them go?' asked Rhea, with more than a slight trace of concern. 'What if they come back?'

Keb patted her on the knee. 'They won't. Even if they dared, we're more than safe here, I assure you.'

Rhea relaxed, but only because she happened to be surrounded by four people who were very capable of protecting her.

'The exercises,' continued Adalwin. 'They manipulate and harness energy, correct? Energy from nature.'

Keb nodded, and Seraphina looked over at Adalwin. He had

not let go of the talisman the entire time they had been having this conversation.

'My people do such things. They know how to sense and work with the energy around their bodies, and in plants and throughout nature. I don't know much about it, but they have a lot of power.'

'Yes, one thing that these exercises and practices do is cultivate power. Over time, a great deal of power.'

'The power to conjure food out of nothingness?' asked Paulus.

'Well, yes, but that's not a sign of anything important.'

'I don't understand what we are talking about,' said Rhea. Her voice was cracking, and she moved closer to Seraphina.

'It's alright,' said Seraphina and Keb to her at the same time. Then they both laughed.

Keb explained how the practices were indeed about cultivating power through the harnessing of energy. The practices were also about calming the mind. It was very important not to use that power selfishly for one's own ends, Keb said. The exercises he had given Seraphina were about calming the mind and activating the energy that comes from the heart. Doing those things together was very important.

Adalwin looked down at the ground. 'Some of our people use powers like these, but not always for good. They use it for themselves only. It can cause problems.'

'Yes,' agreed Keb. 'Responsibility around these powers is very important. As you build your ability to work with energy, these practices will also build calmness in your mind. It is the calmness which instils the necessary responsibility.'

'Interesting,' said Paulus. 'Could you teach me?'

Keb was on his feet, clearing away the food. 'Seraphina will be able to show you, I'm sure. Now is not the time for you to be here. You have a mission to complete, and it's an important one.'

Paulus was slightly miffed, but he was not about to argue. 'You're right, Keb. Thank you for your hospitality. We should be getting back now. I think it's best we get an early start tomorrow. What do you say,

Adalwin?'

Adalwin nodded, neither taking his eyes off Keb nor his fingers off his talisman. He wore an easy smile on his face now though, instead of the grimace and furrowed brow that he had regarded Keb with for most of the encounter.

'Thank you for your time, Keb,' said Seraphina. 'I hope it wasn't too much of a surprise that we came here.'

'Not at all, Seraphina. I'm glad I got to see you again, and it was a pleasure meeting your friends. Share what I have taught you with them if they're interested. Come back and see me any time.'

Seraphina rose to her feet and gave Keb a hug. Adalwin and Paulus both opted for an arm grabbing handshake, as was custom. Rhea said thank you to Keb, flashing him the big, bright smile that had been on her face for a few days now.

Keb held her shoulders. 'You have great spirit, Rhea. I see so much joy and vibrancy in you. May you have a blessed life.'

'Thank you, Keb,' said Rhea, smiling, and blushing at the same time.

The four mounted their horses and rode away from the sea, back into the forest. Keb watched as they left and gave Seraphina a little grin and a wave when she turned back to look at him.

SIXTY SIX

The long journey to Byzantium caused everyone to fall into a routine. Not all were the same though. Adalwin's men rode in a huge pack, surrounding their three prisoners and generally keeping in good spirits. A mixture of scouts, warriors, and archers rode ahead each day. They looked out for bandits and any other signs of danger and made quick work of whatever they found. It was not unusual for the main group to see what was left of anyone or anything the reconnaissance party had come across. Seraphina was sometimes horrified at the brutality. The typical response from Adalwin and the other barbarians was jealousy that they had not been able to join in.

Towards the end of each day, a large contingent of warriors rode ahead and prepared a campsite. Sleeping areas were laid, and food was prepared. It was like what Darius and his men had done during Seraphina's journey back to Rome. As for Darius, he seemed stronger and was adjusting to life minus one forearm. He had asked to ride on a horse and was happy to be shackled while doing so. Paulus let him try for a little while, but he was not able to and it was more out of pity than discipline when Paulus returned him to the cart with Karsas and

Ourgious.

As time often does, the duration of their journey had calmed the barbarians' hostility towards the prisoners. It was understood by everyone that they and their comrades would not be marching upon these prisons, if not for the information given by Darius, Karsas, and Ourgious. So, they were left alone for the most part.

Rhea only got more excited with each day that passed. She told Seraphina, Paulus, Adalwin, and anyone else who would listen about her life in Byzantium. Her horse riding continued to be a regular source of entertainment, both to her and everyone else. While she talked an awful lot at times, for the most part, her joy was infectious and provided some welcome laughter and smiles. The barbarians did not naturally tend towards outward expressions of happiness, but they could not help an occasional smile or chuckle at Rhea's antics.

Adalwin's mood remained sombre throughout the trip. After a few days and some gentle prying, Seraphina discovered why. Many women had been kidnapped in the preceding months, and he had been frustrated by their inability to catch the perpetrators. Karsas, when questioned, claimed not to know specifics of women who were brought to the prison. His other men handled such things, and Karsas did not need to remind Adalwin that all those men were now dead. Adalwin believed him and was upset at himself for allowing the other men to be slaughtered before they were questioned.

To make matters worse, one of the women who had been kidnapped was his niece, Saxa. The daughter of his brother. His brother had gone mad with the loss of his only daughter, and when his wife succumbed to consumption shortly thereafter, he reached his breaking point. Adalwin had told Seraphina the story with tears in his eyes. One day, he had gone to visit his brother, and found him hanging in his house. He had killed himself, and Adalwin had lived with the horror ever since. Even if Saxa was found, Adalwin would have to break the news that she was now an orphan.

Seraphina decided to keep the story to herself. She doubted he would want her telling anyone else about it.

As for Paulus, he became more energised as they drew closer to Byzantium. The visit to Keb had piqued his curiosity, and Seraphina had taught him the exercises and practices that Keb had shared with her. He had formed the habit of doing them daily, and his military discipline meant he never missed a day or night without doing them. His regimen and consistency inspired Seraphina and, before long, the two were practising together, day and night. Adalwin never participated, but always wanted to sit nearby and watch. Most of the barbarians thought it odd, and even a little funny. Given their leader's apparent interest, however, the men never engaged in any overt mockery.

Almost a month passed. There were never any serious skirmishes or dangers. One day, Rhea began to recognise some of the areas they were passing through. As did Paulus. He had been stationed near Byzantium earlier in his career, and he was sure they were getting close.

Once Karsas was informed that the journey was almost complete, his nerves began to show. He did not know exactly where the prison was, but he could lead them to a man who did. Karsas' head would always shake whenever he spoke of him. Everyone, including Darius and Ourgious, was curious about who this man might be, for a giant and brutal man like Karsas to be so afraid of him. Karsas knew he had no choice, but he would be betraying a man he both feared and loved. Feared, because he had seen his ruthlessness. Loved, because he had helped raise him. His Uncle Gadas was still married to a woman he loved and maintained a veneer of respectability for the sake of appearances.

Despite the size and strength of Adalwin's forces, Karsas knew this would not go smoothly.

SIXTY SEVEN

According to plan, the first task upon arrival in Byzantium was taking Rhea home. The thought of a thousand barbarians riding into town appealed to no one, so Paulus agreed to escort Rhea and Seraphina. Adalwin wanted to stay back with his men and formulate a strategy for what was going to happen next.

Seraphina marvelled at the wonder of Byzantium. It was only the third city she had ever seen, and the distinctions that showed in comparison to Alexandria and Rome were remarkable. She had read a little about the city, but nothing compared to the awe of it in person. Whereas Alexandria and Rome were distinct symbols of Egyptian and Roman culture respectively, Byzantium was undeniably Greek. The buildings were characterised by thick columns and clean, polished stone. It was much calmer than Rome, which made the ride into town even more enjoyable.

Rhea pointed at buildings and monuments as they rode past. She could tell how interested Seraphina was, and she tried to give her as much information as possible.

Paulus' mind was elsewhere, on the mission that would no doubt follow in the next day or two. As he rode behind Rhea and Seraphina, their chatter became background noise. *How many women were they holding here? Was the force bigger than what they encountered at Tanais?* He knew that a thousand men would easily overpower whoever was guarding the prison. Nevertheless, he wanted everything to go smoothly.

A loud, piercing scream interrupted his thoughts. By the time he looked up, someone was pulling Rhea off her horse. He was about to spring into action when he saw Seraphina smiling.

They had arrived at Rhea's home, and her mother was beside herself. Mother and daughter were going through a tearful reunion, and more family members were running out of the house. There was quite a commotion, which only increased once the neighbours realised that Rhea was home.

For a moment, Paulus was going to suggest that they move inside the house. It wouldn't have done any good. Rhea's mother had fallen to her knees, overcome with emotion. Rhea crouched down to hold her. Her father and other siblings encircled them and they became one big, crying, wailing mass.

Seraphina's smile gave way to tears and laughter, and Paulus smiled. A seemingly endless stream of people brushed past Seraphina and Paulus and stood around the reunited family. It had been months since Seraphina was taken by the pirates at sea; she wondered how long Rhea had been away from her family.

Now was no time for questions though, and Rhea's family refused to let go of each other. They stood, and still holding one another, began to walk Rhea into the house. Rhea turned her head over her shoulder and locked eyes with Seraphina.

'Wait,' she said, untangling her arms from her mother and father. She skipped over to Seraphina and flung her arms around her. A giggle turned into a cough, as Seraphina felt Rhea's arms clamped around her torso. She wrapped her arms around Rhea, giving her a few well-spaced pats on the back. Rhea's shoulders relaxed, and Seraphina's breathing returned to normal. Rhea let her go and took a step back.

'I'll never forget you, Seraphina,' she said. 'Thank you for being a loyal friend, and for risking your life for me … twice.'

'I'll miss you, Rhea. Please stay safe and take good care of yourself.' Then she laughed, gesturing at Rhea's family and neighbours. 'Though it looks like you have plenty of people around to look after you.'

Rhea nodded and brushed away her tears with the side of her hand. 'Listen to me, Seraphina. Don't take any more risks. Let Adalwin and his men do what they are there to do, and let Paulus protect you. There's no need for you to go rushing into a battle, so please don't.'

The corners of Seraphina's mouth stretched to the sides and she folded her arms.

'Promise, Seraphina.'

Seraphina nodded as her face relaxed. 'I promise, Rhea.'

The contingent of family and neighbours overheard the conversation. They rushed to Seraphina, thanking her, and bowing at her feet. She was frozen for a moment, unsure of what to do. Rhea just laughed at her as she squirmed at the barrage of gratitude.

'You'll have to get used to this, you know,' said Rhea.

Seraphina was standing with her arms held up. She was looking down at the crowd at her feet and looked at Rhea with her eyebrows raised.

'By the time this is over, think about how many young women you'll have returned to their families.'

The eyebrows remained raised, but her eyes looked up and to her right, away from everyone. *I'm not going to personally deliver each one*, thought Seraphina. Then she laughed at herself, and the present situation.

'We had best be going, Rhea,' said Paulus, who had remained on his horse.

'Thank you, Paulus, for everything.' Rhea was helping to unhook hands from Seraphina's legs. 'Come on, come on, she has to go now.'

Seraphina managed to get free, and the two young women shared one last hug. Rhea and the rest of her family behind her waved as

Seraphina mounted Luna and rode away with Paulus.

'How did that feel?' asked Paulus.

'Quite overwhelming, but …'

'But?'

'Absolutely amazing.'

Paulus smiled. His thoughts exactly.

SIXTY EIGHT

Leaving the city, they arrived at a tense scene back at the campsite. Adalwin was shouting at Karsas, who was shouting right back. As Paulus and Seraphina dismounted their horses, still riding the high of seeing Rhea reunited with her family, one of the barbarians charged at Karsas, his helmet striking his navel. Karsas fell back, winded.

'What have we interrupted here?' asked Paulus, keeping his distance from the melee.

'We need him to tell us exactly where his uncle's house is, and he wants to come along with us.'

Paulus and Seraphina both turned towards Karsas. In the background, they could see Darius and Ourglous looking at the ground or off to the distance. Anything to avoid making eye contact with Adalwin or his men.

'It's not what you think. I'm not trying to get away. What you need to understand is that this isn't a simple matter of walking up and knocking on a door. My uncle's home is a compound, guarded by walls and armed men.'

Seraphina watched Adalwin, and it was clear that some of Karsas' words were being lost in the language barrier. They both were speaking Greek, but Adalwin's command over the language was limited. Seraphina put her hands up as another round of shouting was beginning.

'Let's try to work this out,' she said, turning to Karsas. She spoke slowly, for Adalwin's benefit, and asked Karsas to slow down his speech as well. 'Your uncle's house is guarded, you say?'

Karsas nodded. 'Yes.'

'And if we were to approach the gate, what would happen?'

'These men are not fools. You are a Hebrew woman. They are Germanic barbarians.' Then he nodded in Paulus' direction. 'Even though he is not wearing his uniform or armour, anyone can see he is not from here. Besides, you'll want to be wearing your armour if you're going to this place.'

'Why didn't you tell us any of this earlier?' asked Paulus.

Karsas shook his head. 'I was telling you everything I knew when we were at Tanais. If you recall, it was you and the barbarian who decided I'd told you enough.'

Paulus opened his mouth and held up a finger. Then he realised the pirate was right.

'Very well.'

There was silence for a few moments, and no one made eye contact with anyone else. Karsas pushed himself back with his legs, breathing heavily. He pushed his back up against a tree. Using his feet as leverage, he stood back up. 'He should apologise.'

'Excuse me?' said Adalwin.

'Him,' said Karsas, nodded at the barbarian who had charged him to the ground. 'I'm trying to help you as much as I can, and that brute attacks me while I'm chained up like this.'

Adalwin looked at the man who attacked Karsas, and then back at Karsas. He pointed a finger straight at the pirate, and said, 'Don't push your luck.'

Adalwin kept his finger pointed, and all was still. Adalwin was thinking how the pirate was right, and he probably didn't deserve to be attacked in the circumstances. This was followed by another thought—*to hell with him, he was a kidnapper and slave trader.*

'I have an idea,' said Seraphina. She walked over to Adalwin, looking him up and down, and then side to side.

'What is it?' asked Paulus. He watched as Seraphina walked over to Karsas and did the same thing.

'They favour each other, wouldn't you say?' said Seraphina.

Adalwin and Karsas both stretched their necks forward, each examining the other. Paulus folded one hand underneath the other elbow, his free hand covering his mouth and chin. He looked to his left at the barbarian, and then to his right at the pirate. Paulus started to nod. 'His stomach is a little bigger,' he said, pointing at Karsas. 'Other than that, you're right.'

Adalwin smiled at Karsas. The smile was not returned, but the pirate had nothing else to say. Seraphina pulled Adalwin closer to Karsas. 'We shave your beard to match his. You take his clothes and the eyepatch of course. His weapons, and his horse. We bundle some clothing to make your stomach look bigger.'

Seraphina took a few steps back. 'Look, they are even the same height. Oh, and we'll have to cut your hair.'

Adalwin winced at this and shot a glare at Seraphina. She put her hands up in mock defence. 'Only a little.'

Paulus started to laugh and kept nodding. 'That's brilliant, Seraphina.' Adalwin just kept looking at Karsas, who was not amused. He started to ask some of his men if he looked like the pirate. A few made the same observations, and before long several of the barbarians were falling over each other, laughing.

Seraphina put her hands on her hips and looked at Karsas. 'I assume you can tell us how to find your uncle's house.' Karsas nodded without moving his eyes from the ground.

Several of the men unshackled and stripped Karsas. A large tunic was wrapped around him, and the shackles put back in place. As Adalwin put on the clothes, one of his men stared at Karsas' face for a minute or so. He then retrieved a sharp piece of flint and motioned for Adalwin to sit down.

Paulus put his hand up, and the barbarian waited. He retrieved something from one of his bags and walked back to them with it. Holding it out, it was an iron contraption with two finger holes and a sharp blade along its edge. Both Adalwin and the barbarian holding the flint looked at it, and then looked at Paulus with matching smirks. Paulus shook his head and said, 'Here, I will show you.' He looped his fingers into the holes and set the surface of the blade on his forearm at a slight angle. Then, with a simple drag of his wrist, he shaved a small section of his forearm.

The barbarian took the razor and put his fingers into it. Paulus held his index finger up, and both men watched to see what he would bring next. It was a small glass bottle with a pale liquid in it. 'In case you cut him,' said Paulus. The barbarians' eyes met, and they nodded in approval.

As Adalwin had his beard shaved to match Karsas,' Seraphina emerged in her old disguise. Adalwin said nothing, as he didn't want to risk being cut while his face was being shaven. Paulus immediately started shaking his head. 'There's no way you are going, Seraphina.'

'Why not?' she asked, turning her eyes to each hip, admiring her own outfit. 'I'm armed, and this disguise fooled all of you. I just need a haircut. Adalwin, perhaps your man can help me when he is finished with you? What do you say?'

Adalwin remained silent, his eyes moving from the blade only for a moment to Seraphina.

Paulus had plenty to say. 'What's the point of risking your safety at this juncture?'

Seraphina put her hands on her hips. 'Look, Commander. We wouldn't even be here if it weren't for me and the choices I've made. Besides, we can't very well let Adalwin go all by himself, now can we?' She smiled at Paulus, raising one palm into the air as she asked.

Paulus opened his mouth, then moved forward, and even breathed out. There were no words though. The current plan was wanting. Adalwin was to pose as Karsas to try and get the gate open, at which point several men would storm the building.

'He looks the part, but it won't take long before they realise it is not him. His voice is different, and his Greek isn't so good.' Adalwin was standing up now, relieved that the shaving ordeal was over. Seraphina put a hand up in his direction. 'No offence to you, Adalwin. What I mean is that your spoken Greek is unlike Karsas'.'

'What good will it do for you to be there then?' asked Paulus. 'It's not as if you can speak for Adalwin.'

'True,' said Seraphina, 'but I can speak better Greek. I don't know, perhaps he can say he is not well, and I can do most of the talking at the gate. I don't know what's going to happen. Even if we have to charge the gate down, two horses and two attackers are better than one.'

Paulus looked at Adalwin, who simply gave a shrug of his shoulders. 'She may be right, Commander. You can't go. You'll stand out like a sore thumb. Even though I feel ridiculous in this costume,' he said, patting his belly, 'at least I look like someone they might be expecting. Obviously, none of my men can go. She fooled everyone here into thinking she was a Greek boy at one point or another.'

'What about him?' asked Paulus, pointing at Ourgious.

'You'd rather send a prisoner with Adalwin than me?' asked Seraphina. 'How's that any better than me going?'

'I'd prefer not to go alone,' said Adalwin. 'I don't know exactly where this house is, but my men will have some distance to travel between where they're hidden and the gate. Karsas says there are at least three or four men at the gate at all times.'

Seraphina looked over at Ourgious. 'This Gadas. Does he even know you?'

Ourgious shook his head. 'No. He may know of me, but we've never met.' He did not seem overly eager to get involved.

The matter was settled, and Paulus knew it. 'Alright, but just focus on getting that gate open. We'll be as close by as we can. And get that hair of yours cut.' Paulus pointed at her as he spoke then threw his hand up as he finished. He walked away, hands on his hips and shaking his head.

'He'll calm down,' said Adalwin. 'It's a good idea, Seraphina.' He pointed at Karsas, continuing, 'I think the idea that he would come all this way alone would be suspicious. You've acted like one person's assistant. You can do it again.'

Seraphina smiled and thanked Adalwin. She crouched down in front of Karsas. 'Now, tell us exactly where your uncle lives.'

SIXTY NINE

The house turned out to be more vulnerable than they had thought. There were high walls and several guards, but it was on the edge of the city, making it relatively isolated. When taking positions, Adalwin's men noticed a hill. They started debating the distance between the hill and the walls, and whether their archers could get within range. Paulus thought it was about a tenth of a mile. More debate ensued, and it descended into an argument about different types of measurements. With Roman, Egyptian, and Germanic standards being discussed, it was a good thing that there were no Greeks contributing to the argument. The prisoners were left at camp, far away from the city, guarded by a small contingent of Adalwin's men.

The argument was settled when Adalwin's most reliable archer said they could hide behind the hill and be within range. He was, in fact, the archer who had struck Seraphina in the chest from a much greater distance. Even Adalwin did not question the man. Twenty of the finest archers were dispatched to the hill with orders to shoot anything on the wall once the signal was given.

Paulus resented being out of the front line. Seraphina quipped, 'Feel free to storm the house with the rest of them once the gate is open,' and he did not like it.

'So, what's the plan exactly?' asked Paulus.

Adalwin shook his head. 'I thought we'd been through this.'

'I just want to confirm before you two ride up there and all hell breaks loose.'

Seraphina took a deep breath and did her best to hold her tongue. Then Adalwin asked Seraphina to explain the plan. Both were losing patience with the commander. They understood he didn't like having only a small role in the operation, but he was starting to become obstructive. Seraphina repeated the plan that had been discussed at least ten times. She skipped any further opportunities for cheek, not wanting to bruise the commander's ego any further.

Paulus nodded. 'So, when the red cloth flies into the air, the archers let loose from the hill and we charge the gate.'

Both Adalwin and Seraphina nodded. Adalwin mounted his horse, and almost tripped as he did. He was still getting used to the eyepatch. Seraphina patted Luna, thinking how she couldn't wait to get him home, so he could relax and graze all day long. *Where is home*, she thought. Then she shook her head. There were far more pressing matters at hand. She jumped on Luna's back, stroking the back of his neck. She watched Adalwin shuffle to get comfortable on the horse, and he began a slow trot towards the house. It was barely a third of a mile away, but they were behind enough buildings and trees that no one could see them.

Seraphina followed directly behind Adalwin, and she felt a lump in her throat. The reins felt a little slippery in her hands, and a trickle or two of sweat dripped from her forehead. It was just nerves, she told herself. Everything is going to be fine. The walls of the house were visible in the distance. Seraphina could see a man patrolling the top of the wall and another standing by the gate. There was no one else in sight. The nearest house was a mile away. Seraphina noticed nothing but flat plains and one or two wayward goats. The hill where the archers were hiding looked small from there, but even that stood out a little.

A perfect place to hide away, thought Seraphina. As they neared the gate, Seraphina rode alongside Adalwin. The man on the wall saw them and gave a friendly wave and a smile. If only he knew.

'I'm here to visit my uncle,' grunted Adalwin. 'Open this gate.'

'Karsas, is that you? It has been a long time. How are you?'

Adalwin mumbled something unintelligible in response. Seraphina's hands were gripping the reins so hard that her knuckles were white. *Why had they not asked Karsas about the men at the gate?* It would have been useful to know their names.

'My master is not well,' she said in her disguised, deeper voice. 'Is Gadas in?'

The man on the wall nodded for his colleague to open the gate. 'Of course,' he said. 'Welcome.'

Once they had both peered beyond the open gate, Adalwin threw the red cloth into the air. Before Adalwin even had time to kick the guard in the face, an arrow rang out from the hill. It struck the man on the wall in the side of the neck. Seraphina heard a gurgling, choking sound as he fell. She turned around to see Paulus and the barbarians charging at full gallop towards the gate. In front of them, two more men in the courtyard were calling out for help and rushing towards Adalwin. They could not yet see the force that was converging on the house.

As agreed, Seraphina moved to the side of the gate. The two guards sprinted from the house to the gate, and they saw Adalwin smiling at them. Then hundreds of men filled the courtyard, and they stopped dead in their tracks. So did the men behind them who had just rushed out of the house. Adalwin and Paulus rode past all of them, heading for the front door of the house.

The barbarians rounded up the shell-shocked guards, bound them at the wrists, and lined them up against a wall. They had no clue what was going on. The one that Adalwin had kicked in the face was coming to, and he was retrieved and reunited with his comrades.

Paulus and Adalwin waited by the front door for a few moments. They weren't about to knock but thought that the commotion would have drawn out whoever was remaining in the house. After a few minutes, it was clear that no one else was coming out. The guards were being kept quiet, and the barbarians remained silent.

Paulus looked down at the door. A round bronze ring was attached to the thick wood. He gripped it and rotated his wrist. It moved clockwise, and he felt a latch releasing on the other side. He looked at Adalwin and drew his sword. The barbarian unsheathed his weapon and nodded. Without making a sound, Paulus turned the handle the rest of the way, and both men stepped into the house.

SEVENTY

The marble floor rendered their attempts at silence futile. The house was lavishly decorated, with lots of opulent furnishings visible from the entrance. Beautiful rugs appeared in each of the rooms they could see, along with various ornaments and other possessions that gave an air of serious wealth. A long cursory glance by both men upon entering the house revealed no one. Several rooms fanned out from the foyer of the house. Adalwin wondered why the guards would say he was home if he wasn't.

Paulus held a finger to his lips and gestured for Adalwin to check the rooms on the left. He would go to the right, he said by pointing at himself and the rooms on his side. Adalwin nodded and stepped towards what looked like a sitting room. As he entered the room, he spotted a tall woman to his left. She was nearly as tall as he and stepped sideways, her hands held behind her back.

Paulus found a young woman cowering in the corner when he walked into the dining room. He didn't spot her at first, as her body was obscured by the long, ornate table that sat in the middle of the room. She was curled up in the corner, clutching her knees to her chest. Her fair-skinned face was wet with tears, and she was shaking. Long auburn hair was braided to each side of her head. Even with the braids, her hair touched the floor. She wore a common-looking grey dress, and her piercing blue eyes shot a look of terror across the room at Paulus.

Adalwin held his sword towards the ground and he turned, continuing to face the woman squarely as she stepped sideward. She kept her distance from him.

'Who are you, and what are you doing in my house?'

'We're looking for a man named Gadas,' he replied.

'Oh, why didn't you say so?' she said, smiling, and bringing a hand to her chest. 'That's my husband, and this is our home. You scared me, with that sword and all.'

Paulus held up his free hand to try and calm the girl.

'Are you alright?' he asked.

'Who are you?'

'I am here looking for someone. Your father perhaps? His name is Gadas.'

'He's not my father,' she spat out in disgust.

'My husband is in the back of the house, let me go and find him. You know, you look just like my nephew Karsas!' The woman shouted the last word as she lunged at Adalwin with a knife she had been holding behind her back. Adalwin swung his sword as the knife flashed in front of him. He hit something, but he was not sure what.

'Then who is he to you,' asked Paulus.

'My master, I suppose. I'm a servant here.' The girl had not moved, although she seemed calmer.

Paulus held his gaze on her for a moment. 'Are you here against your will?'

The girl looked back at him with a blank stare.

'I mean, were you brought here by force?'

She nodded and flinched as she heard a voice cry out. Paulus heard it too. It was Adalwin. 'Just wait here,' he said, holding his hand up to the girl. 'I'll be right back.' Paulus ran out into the hallway and saw Adalwin on the floor. He was sitting up, clasping his upper arm with the opposite hand. His sword was on the ground. An elegantly dressed, dark-haired woman was sprawled out on the floor, apparently unconscious.

They heard the stomping of his feet before they saw him. Gadas rushed into the house from the back, wielding both an axe and a sword, demanding to know what they were doing in his house. He looked down at his wife as more of Adalwin's men entered through the front door, having heard the ruckus inside.

'What have you done to my wife?' Gadas shouted, more at Paulus and the other barbarians. 'Karsas, is that you?'

He was just as Karsas had described—identical to him, but older, with greying hair, and no eyepatch. Adalwin shook his head and pulled off his eyepatch.

'Your wife nearly cut my arm off,' snarled Adalwin. 'We're here for you, you miserable wretch. We hear you like to kidnap and sell young women.'

Gadas was taken aback, but only for a moment. *Where were his guards? How had these men found their way in here?*

'And what if I do?' he asked, showing the same nasty smile Paulus had seen when he first encountered Karsas. His eyes turned to his left, as the servant girl came out of the dining room. She looked at the soldier she had spoken to and noticed the other men standing in the house.

'Oh, I forgot to mention,' said Paulus, looking back at her. 'He's keeping one of them here, no doubt for his sick enjoyment.'

'Saxa!' shouted Adalwin.

The young woman recognised her uncle and ran towards him. Gadas was in between Saxa and the rest of the men, and he seized the moment. He dropped his axe and grabbed her. Holding his sword across her throat, he took a step back. Gadas shouted at them to drop their weapons and get back.

Adalwin was barely gripping his sword, due to his wounded arm. He dropped his sword without hesitation and told his men to do the same. They all did, but Paulus continued to brandish his weapon.

'That's my niece, Paulus. Put it down.'

Paulus gritted his teeth and turned his body so he could keep Gadas in sight while looking at Adalwin. 'I know, but we can't let him get away. We have to find out where that prison is.'

'I'll kill her!' shouted Gadas, taking another step back.

'Then do it. You're outnumbered, and you'll not get away.'

Adalwin held his injured hand up towards Gadas. 'No!' He turned to Paulus. 'Keep your mouth shut, Roman. Hear me, do not say another word.' The other barbarians snarled at Paulus as these words were spoken.

Paulus took a deep breath and held both his weapon and his position.

'Well,' said Gadas, 'what's it going to be, gentleman? Does she live, or does she die?'

Seraphina leaped through the doorway next to Gadas and plunged her dagger into the arm he was holding his sword with. He howled in pain and, as a reflex, smashed his elbow against her head. Seraphina fell to the floor, and Saxa got free. Paulus, Adalwin, and the rest of the men rushed across the room and tackled Gadas to the floor. Four of Adalwin's men held down Gadas.

Adalwin got up and embraced his niece Saxa, who was in tears. He could barely hold her, given the deep gash to his arm.

Paulus rushed to Seraphina's side and rolled her over on to her back. He pressed his ear to her chest, and then to her mouth.

'She's not breathing.'

SEVENTY ONE

The woman was hysterical. Despite having a huge bruise on her head from Adalwin's sword, she screamed and shouted at the intruders who were holding her husband down. Even when confronted with the reason why they were there, she mustered an impressive amount of indignation. It was obvious that Gadas' wife knew how he made his living, and she was not the least bit ashamed.

'Get that witch out of here,' shouted Paulus. 'Adalwin, is there a physician amongst your men?' Seraphina was still not moving, and he feared the worst. He tried to resuscitate her, doing what little he had learned in the field of battle. They had all heard the crunch when Gadas smashed his meaty arm into her head. Adalwin shouted out the front door in his native language. A few moments later, a short, stocky man came sprinting into the house, a black knapsack flung over his shoulder. He came straight to Seraphina's side and started asking Paulus questions ... in Germanic.

Paulus then shouted at Adalwin, who was elated with the discovery of his niece. His arm was also in need of medical attention. Right now, having the one-armed Darius around to translate would have been a blessing.

'Adalwin, get over here. I don't understand what this man is saying.'

Adalwin walked over, already shouting orders at the physician. He pointed at his head and made the gesture of an elbow hitting something. Apparently, this was enough for him to understand, as he immediately started applying ointment to a large bump on Seraphina's head.

'Girl, or boy?' asked the physician, switching to Greek while scratching his head.

'Just get on with it!' screamed Paulus.

The physician flinched and told the commander to relax. She was going to be fine. *How is she going to be fine*, thought Paulus? The girl is not breathing and had been unconscious for several minutes. With all the chaos going on around him, Paulus would have given anything to have his own medic there.

Seraphina was completely still, and her eyes were closed. She had a large bump on the back of her head, where it had crashed into the wall. A rough graze adorned her forehead, where Gadas had struck her. To her credit, she had plunged the dagger in to the hilt. It was in so deep that they had not even tried to remove it yet. The pirate's medical needs were a low priority at this stage.

Paulus looked at Seraphina, and then back at the physician. He was mixing a concoction in a small glass bottle. Nothing seemed to be happening, and his frantic looks to and fro were being ignored.

When the physician was good and ready, he plunged the neck of the bottle into Seraphina's nostril. Her back shot up, and her eyes snapped open. Her pupils looked dilated, and she looked from left to right rapidly. The bottle was still wedged in her nostril. The physician got up, patting her on the back, and went to examine Adalwin's arm.

Paulus placed his hand behind Seraphina's back. 'Are you alright, Seraphina? Do you know where you are?' He moved his hand slowly towards her face and plucked the bottle from her nose.

Seraphina nodded, and slowly moved her hand to the back of her head. 'Ouch, that hurt.' She rubbed the back of her hand against her forehead, and the graze smarted from the contact of sweat with the wound. She hissed and pulled her hand away.

Paulus shook his head and smiled. 'I've never been on a mission like this,' he said, almost to himself.

'I came around the back when you all attacked. Something told me it was a good idea. Now, I'm not so sure.' She chuckled, keeping her hands down, afraid to touch anywhere that was hurting.

'How did you manage to do that? Look how far this doorway is from the window.'

Seraphina shook her head. 'I saw him holding the girl through the other window. I could see him moving backwards and shouting at you. I couldn't see any of you, but I assumed he must be shouting at you, or Adalwin, or one of his men. When I saw he would keep moving back, I gave myself some distance from the window.'

Just listening to the story was causing Paulus stress. His palm was pressed against his mouth, his thumb and fingers squeezing both cheeks.

'I just thought, as soon as I see any part of him in that doorway, I'm going to run and jump through the window. I had the dagger in my hand and was determined to stab him as hard as I could … in the arm, of course. After all, we need information from him.'

Paulus laughed and shook his head. 'Telling you to stay out of danger was a complete and utter waste of my time.'

'It was a last resort, Paulus. He was going to hurt that girl.'

'I know. You did very well. It's Adalwin's niece, you know. The girl you saved.'

'Saxa?'

Paulus nodded.

'Let's go outside and talk to that evil pirate,' said Seraphina, rising to her feet.

SEVENTY TWO

There was a demilitarised zone in the middle of the courtyard. On the right, Adalwin stood with his arm around Saxa, along with the rest of his men. On the left, Gadas sat on the floor, tied up just like his guards alongside him. He was also gagged. Evidently, he had not been wise enough to shut his mouth voluntarily.

Another disturbance caught Seraphina's attention and she looked to her right. Gadas' wife was being held down as Adalwin's physician tried to treat the wound to her head. She was a tall, powerfully built woman. Her muscles strained against the pressure being applied by Adalwin's men. She spat at all three men, including the doctor, who was only trying to help. Her high-pitched screams, laced with profanity, launched insults at those trying to help her, as well as Adalwin and Saxa. As Paulus and Seraphina came out of the house, she gave them a good dose of her foul tongue as well. Her straining finally paid off, as she got a foot loose. She swung her thick leg and kicked the doctor in his ribs, knocking him over.

'That's it,' said the doctor. 'Tie her up and put her with the rest.' He pointed at Gadas and his men across the yard. 'Gag her as well.

Wretched woman!'

The men were very happy to comply. They were already confused by their leader's mercy towards the enemy in this situation. One man reached down to the lower part of her dress and tore it. He deftly detached a long strip of material. It was tied around her mouth as a gag while another man bound the woman's arms behind her.

Seraphina watched as the barbarian dragged Gadas' wife across the courtyard and threw her next to her husband. Gadas' eyes narrowed at the barbarian as he walked away. Seraphina noticed her dagger was still plunged into his arm, and she felt herself retch at the sight. Once she composed herself, she and Paulus walked over to Adalwin. As they got closer, they could see he was shaking.

'Hello, Saxa,' she said. 'I'm Seraphina.'

'You really are a girl,' said Saxa. 'Thank you for what you did in there.'

'It's my pleasure. I don't know if you were properly introduced, but this is Paulus. He is a Roman commander.'

Germanic women had learned to be suspicious of Romans, especially Roman soldiers. Saxa was no exception. She just nodded and looked at Paulus. It wasn't quite the same look of terror from inside the house, but it was obvious she was afraid.

'Don't worry, my dear,' said Adalwin. 'He's a friend and has been helping us. He helped us come here to find you.'

Paulus smiled at the generosity of Adalwin's words. 'I'm glad you're safe,' said the commander because he felt he should say something.

'Excuse me for a moment, my dear,' said Adalwin to Saxa. He stepped away with Paulus and Seraphina, so the three could talk in private. 'You two will have to interrogate him. If I'm near him, I'll kill him. Saxa has been telling me about some of her ordeals since she was taken. In particular, what he has done to her since having her here as his personal slave.' Adalwin clenched his fists to stop the shaking and locked his jaw.

Seraphina noticed his eyes were moist, and she felt for him. 'Of course, Adalwin. I'm sure we can find out what we need to know. He seems a stubborn one though. It might take him a bit longer to realise he has little choice.'

Adalwin barely heard her words. 'I haven't even told Saxa about her parents yet. I don't know how I'm going to do that.'

Paulus placed a hand on his shoulder. 'I don't think that's something you need to do straight away. Give it time. She has just been freed, and no doubt is relieved about that. More traumatic news at this point would be no good for her.'

Adalwin nodded.

Seraphina looked over at Gadas. 'Why does he still have that dagger in his arm?'

Adalwin shook his head, looking over at the wall where Gadas and the rest of them sat. 'You saw how his wife was behaving, didn't you? He was ten times worse. He tried to bite my men and the physician when they tried to remove the dagger. In the end, they tied him up and left it in him for punishment.'

Seraphina recoiled at this. 'I'm all for punishing him, but I want my dagger back, and not sitting in that disgusting man.'

'Well, he's tied up tight, so you can go over there and take it. Find out where the prison is, Seraphina. He must die, and the sooner the better. We'll get what we need from him, and he'll live no longer.'

Seraphina and Paulus exchanged glances upon hearing this, but neither saw the use in discussing the matter at that point. Paulus happened to agree. He would happily see both Gadas and his vile wife executed, just for what they had put Saxa through. They both walked over to the other side of the courtyard. Gadas' wife was still struggling, but she had been tied so tight that she could barely move. She was either too arrogant or too stupid to realise her efforts were in vain. Despite all this, Seraphina's stomach turned at the thought that the two would shortly be put to death.

Seraphina pulled the dagger out of Gadas' arm, thinking he must be just as stupid as his wife. She knew the truth of why Adalwin had wanted to tend to their wounds. It was only to make sure they were fit to be interrogated. The premature execution of Karsas' men back at the forest had weighed heavily on him. She admired the barbarian's restraint, especially given Saxa's involvement.

Gadas didn't make a sound when the dagger was removed, but he squinted, and Seraphina saw his jaw move through the gag. He was doing his best to show no pain. He went berserk when she wiped the dagger clean on his tunic. *What's the problem*, she thought? *It's your blood.*

Paulus swung his right shoulder back and flung his arm at Gadas' head. In quick succession, he punched him in the face three times. Hard.

Seraphina felt her body harden and flinched away from the violence. It had been a purely instinctive reaction, and she was ashamed to look weak in front of the others. Even though she had seen a lot of brutality, she had the inkling she would never get used to it. Paulus seemed to become calm, and Seraphina's muscles relaxed. Notwithstanding her reaction, she had no love for Gadas.

Paulus untied the gag and asked him if he wanted more. No response from Gadas, except to spit blood on Paulus' tunic. 'You're right,' he said to Seraphina. 'He is a stubborn one.' Paulus started punching his face with a rhythm. He was a strong, fit man and it looked as though he could go on punching Gadas all day without much strain. Seraphina stood up and took a few steps away, her back to Paulus and Gadas.

After a few moments, Gadas' wife calmed down and looked with concern at her husband. 'Stop,' she screamed, although the word was muffled under the gag.

Gadas had one hell of a hard head. He just glared at Paulus, continuing to spit blood. *This was going nowhere*, thought Seraphina. She decided to try a different tactic and reached out to stay Paulus' arm. 'Listen, Gadas, we have your nephew Karsas. I am sure you've worked that out by now, given we have his clothes, weapons, and eyepatch. We also have your wife here, and we know there is a prison of some kind near Byzantium.'

Gadas looked away, his mouth empty of blood to spit. He found a spot on the ground to focus his attention on. Seraphina turned to face him and pointed at Saxa across the courtyard. 'You see that woman you were keeping against her will? For your twisted pleasure, I might add. The man next to her is her uncle. The reason he is not over here is because he fears he'll kill you if he can reach you. Do you understand all this?'

'What do you want?' said Gadas, finally looking at Seraphina.

'We need to know where that prison is.'

'And if I don't tell you?'

Seraphina looked over at Paulus, who huffed at this response. He wanted to resume his punching, if for no other reason than to inflict pain on this awful man. He could see, however, that Seraphina was making some headway. So, he restrained himself.

'Then I don't know what will happen,' said Seraphina with a shrug of her shoulders. 'Look across at those men, Gadas. I think they'll give you a very slow, painful death. I've heard them do it to others already.'

'Karsas' men, I presume?' asked Gadas.

He was not stupid, Seraphina had decided. He was just ruthless and determined. She nodded, with a slight shudder as she remembered the screams of those men in the forest.

'You don't have the taste for this, do you, child? This brutality?'

'Maybe not, but that seems to be all you understand. Let's not forget that,' she said, pointing at the wound in his arm. 'Do you want someone to bandage that up? That is, without attacking them?'

He nodded, and Paulus called over the physician.

Seraphina looked at Gadas, who had resumed staring at the floor. His eyes looked softer, and he was blinking more often. She sensed his resolve waning. His wife was now silent and looking at him for guidance.

'Here's what I think,' said Seraphina. 'They want to kill you. Probably all of you. If you don't help us, they'll do so brutally. They'll torture you until you tell us where the prison is, and if that doesn't work, they'll torture your wife here. Then maybe your nephew will be brought here for more of the same. Even these guards may happen to know something. It will be long, and painful, and you'll end up telling us anyway.'

'Maybe,' he said, 'but if we're all going to die anyway, why would I want to help you?'

Seraphina knew she was getting somewhere now. She also knew that it would do no good to try to appeal to any sort of kind or decent nature in this man. He had none. He was only concerned with what might be of use to him.

'If you tell us where the prison is, and where the rest of their people are,' she said, nodding towards Adalwin and Saxa, 'then maybe we could persuade them to spare your lives. I'm not promising anything, but it's possible.'

'It makes sense, Gadas,' added Paulus. 'They're here because you and your men kidnapped their women. If they're all returned, unharmed, then it may temper their anger. A little.'

Seraphina and Paulus were content to let him think. Seraphina locked eyes with Adalwin across the courtyard and gave him a little nod.

'I'll tell you everything I can. You must spare my wife and nephew. These guards know nothing. You could torture them for days and realise that.'

Seraphina nodded and gave him a little smile, thanking him. 'Alright, tell us everything.'

'I want to at least see my nephew first.'

Paulus stood up, glad to get away from Gadas. He walked over to Adalwin and asked him to have Karsas brought over.

SEVENTY THREE

Uncle and nephew, who were more like father and son, were allowed to reunite. Paulus and Adalwin both insisted they remained shackled, so they could not embrace. It was peculiar to Seraphina and the others to see the warmth between these otherwise callous, arrogant beings. They had witnessed Gadas' strength first hand and given that Karsas was younger and seemingly stronger, there was not the slightest hesitation in keeping them shackled.

Paulus allowed them a few minutes together, and then took Karsas away. It was time for Gadas to talk. He gave him a similar warning about lying or any omissions he might make. If there was even the slightest suspicion that Gadas was withholding any information, Paulus promised to hand him and his wife over to Adalwin and his men with no indication they should receive any mercy.

Gadas nodded his understanding. His warmth towards Karsas seemed genuine, and he had quietly asked for his wife to be given some medical attention. The loud, boisterous voice was gone, replaced by a gentle, almost whispering tone. The more he thought about it, the more he was sure he could give these people enough information to stay alive.

He kept looking at his house, dreaming of returning to it. *Maybe it would be nice to have a simpler life*, he thought. He had enough money, and there was no chance of returning to a life of slave trading after this. He would stay alive, and if there was the slightest chance of escape, he would take it.

The girl sat down in front of him with the Roman commander, and they started asking him questions. He wondered who this girl was, that she would be interrogating him alongside a highly decorated soldier. *What was she doing in disguise when she leapt through the window and stabbed him?* Gadas had many questions, but he was in no position to ask them. He knew there would be no answers. *Stay alive*, he kept telling himself. He had been in equally perilous situations before.

The only thing he would lie about was his money. He doubted they would ask about that anyway. He helped the Roman draw a map from his house to the prison.

Paulus' knowledge of Byzantium proved very useful. He knew the area where Gadas claimed the prison was. He asked as many questions as he could to verify that Gadas was telling the truth. The answers fit, and he told Seraphina as much.

Seraphina acted as scribe and made notes of everything Gadas said. He believed some of Adalwin's women were at the prison, but he could not be sure. Like Karsas, he was rarely involved in the kidnappings themselves. The men at the prison would be able to say where some of the women came from, and he advised that they not be killed or harmed before questioning them. Seraphina felt that Gadas was genuinely trying to help, or at least being genuine in giving all the information he could. They were pirates after all, and no one expected them to show compassion or loyalty to one another.

Gadas was only concerned with his own neck. To a lesser extent, he wanted to save Karsas. Then maybe his wife, although he suspected she would be spared. These Romans were weak when it came to women, and he believed that Paulus would intervene if his wife was about to be harmed.

Paulus asked more questions about the number of men guarding the prison, and how well they were armed. Gadas laughed at this, promising that a thousand men would be more than enough to overwhelm them. He even gave them advice on where the guards would be positioned, enabling them to take the prison by surprise.

The girl then asked him about how the women were sold, and to whom, and for how much. She wanted all the details. Gadas tried to resist smiling. Many years ago, he had envisaged this scenario. He had kept a set of records for just this moment.

'I can give you details of who these women are sold to. I can tell you which city each broker takes them to. I can tell you the names of numerous people involved in our network. All are very respectable families in cities throughout the Roman republic and the Greek nation. I can even tell you the names of officials—politicians and high-ranking soldiers—who are paid off to keep this quiet. Of course, some of them have their own slaves as part of the bargain.'

Paulus' jaw dropped. Gadas looked over at him and said 'yes, Roman, some of your colleagues and maybe even your superiors are involved with this.' Paulus shook his head, not in denial, but in shock at the notion that his fellow officers, colleagues and men he revered, could be involved. Darius had mentioned other officials, but the idea that Roman soldiers could be involved in such a thing was unthinkable.

Seraphina, on the other hand, was excited. 'Tell me everything,' she said, pen in hand and eyes focused on Gadas.

'You won't need to write it down. I have it all recorded.'

'Where?'

'Before I tell you, do you think that might be enough to keep your friends over there from killing me and my family?'

Seraphina thought 'family' an odd word to come from the lips of this man. She looked over at Paulus, who was regaining his focus. The scope of this scandal continued to expand in his mind after listening to what Gadas had just said. 'We should talk to Adalwin,' she said, in Latin instead of Greek.

'In the spirit of honesty, I should tell you that I understand Latin.'

Seraphina stood up and pulled Paulus with her. 'What's the matter?' she asked.

Paulus shook his head. 'I'm sorry. I'm just shocked at the extent of this problem. Just think, if we had never met, no one would have known about this. It was sheer luck that this all happened.'

'Yes, but we did meet, and I'm not sure I'd call it luck.'

'Maybe, Seraphina. It's just amazing how deep this runs. Let's go and talk to Adalwin, and let's move as far away from them as possible. I don't want them to hear this.'

The conversation did not last long. The moment Adalwin heard that Gadas was trying to negotiate, he stormed across the courtyard. As he neared Gadas, he pulled out his axe and rested the blade just beneath the pirate's meaty knee.

'How dare you,' said Adalwin, in a throaty whisper that only Gadas could hear. 'I'm going to take this leg first, just for punishment. Then wait and see what happens.'

As he raised the axe, Gadas held up his shackled arms and shouted at him to stop. 'It's in the house, it's in the house, it's in the house,' he said repeatedly.

Adalwin stood, axe raised, with half a mind to bring it down. The nerve of this swine. He was lucky to be alive, and here he was trying to exchange information for mercy.

Time stood still. Then Seraphina calmly crossed the courtyard and asked where in the house his records were. Gadas promised he would show them and apologised 'Anything you want,' he said.

Paulus couldn't help but laugh. Adalwin's rage had reduced this fearsome man into a whimpering child. Adalwin still had not moved, and Paulus got two of his men to help Gadas to his feet. Paulus placed a hand on Adalwin's shoulder, and he lowered the axe.

'Come on, show us where these records are.'

SEVENTY FOUR

The raid was almost anticlimactic. Between the information provided by Gadas, and the sheer size of their force, the prison was taken in a matter of minutes. A number of women were freed, and it so happened that a few of them were indeed Germanic. Adalwin did not recognise any of them personally, but some of his warriors recognised the women. One of the barbarians was reunited with his wife.

The mission was complete, and now their minds were elsewhere. A significant problem was the number of prisoners. They could not travel with so many people, and decisions had to be made. Gadas' house guards were interrogated for a couple of days, and it became clear that Gadas was telling the truth about them. Their only job was to guard the house against intruders. They were the least of the group's worries, and Paulus let them go with a stern warning to keep out of trouble. The men happily agreed and ran off. Paulus got the distinct impression that they didn't enjoy serving their master and were glad to be free of him.

Next were the guards at the prison. The women they freed were not in good condition, and this pleased no one. Adalwin knew his men would slaughter the guards for sport, and while he thought they deserved it, he was tired and wanted to go home. Enough blood had been shed for now, he said. Paulus and Seraphina faced an even longer journey back to Rome. They had no desire to take the prison guards with them. In the end, they were handed over to the Athenian authorities in Byzantium. Full details of their crimes were disclosed, and the Athenians were happy to throw them in their gaol.

That left Gadas, his wife, Karsas, Ourgious, and, of course, Darius. Paulus insisted that Darius return with them to Rome. He was key to unravelling the network of people involved there, and Paulus said this was non-negotiable. Adalwin smiled and reminded Paulus that he was in no position to demand anything. It looked as though an argument was going to follow when Adalwin assured Paulus that he had no interest in holding Darius. That was 'Roman business' as he put it, and Adalwin had no interest in unravelling a scandalous conspiracy in Rome.

'Those three must come with us,' said Adalwin, pointing at Karsas, and then Gadas and his wife.

Paulus had little idea of how Germanic barbarians settled serious crimes. Somehow, he imagined there were no courts involved. He shrugged and looked blankly at them. Paulus could only imagine what their fate would be, and he didn't dwell on it for long.

No one said a word about Ourgious, and he was, unfortunately, sitting right next to Karsas. Seraphina watched as his eyes shifted towards Karsas and then the barbarians. He did his best to avoid eye contact and stay as still as possible. Seraphina was still uncertain about Ourgious, and noticed the mixed feelings swirling about inside her.

'Adalwin, we should take the other one with us.'

'Why?' asked both Paulus and Adalwin in unison.

'We, or rather you, Paulus, are going to spend a long time explaining this situation. To your superiors, to members of the senate, and perhaps even Caesar himself. It would be wise to have one of the pirates with us. To give them a first-hand idea of what we have been dealing with. There may even be questions for him.'

Ourgious remained still, but his gaze moved in Paulus' direction.

His glance was like that of a frightened dog looking at his angry master.

Adalwin threw his hands up in the air. 'I don't care. Take him. But Paulus, we must talk about where the rest of our women are.' He pointed at Gadas. 'How long is that list he gave you?'

'Very, and it isn't just Rome. It could take a very long time to track down all of these girls.'

Adalwin folded his thick arms across his chest and looked at the ground, tapping one of his feet. 'We must return home. I'll see to it that the women rescued from the other prisons are safe. Once those missions are complete, your men will return home.'

'That's very generous of you,' said Paulus. 'Thank you.'

'There is something else. I want you to take five of my finest archers. Actually, make it ten. A small detail of my scouts as well. I don't want you having any problems with these two,' said Adalwin, pointing at Ourgious and Darius as he glared down at them. 'This isn't over for us until every single one of our women is brought home, but there is nothing more to be served by us remaining so far away from our lands. As your investigation unfolds in Rome, you must keep my scouts informed.'

'I don't understand. Informed of what?'

'Of whether you find any Germanic girls working as slaves.'

The complications in what Adalwin was asking were numerous, but for now, Paulus gave the only response there was to give. 'Of course, Adalwin. I'll make sure they're told.' He meant it, but at that exact moment, he had no idea how it would happen.

'Thank you. You're a fine soldier, Paulus. Maybe there's hope for the Romans yet,' he said, laughing as he mounted his horse. 'Seraphina, I thank you for your help. If you ever decide to return to see your friend Keb, or are near us, come and visit.' He lifted the heavy silver chain from his neck and rubbed the talisman with his thumb for a few moments. 'Hold this up, and our people will allow you to pass safely.' He handed it down to her.

All the barbarians who saw this raised their eyebrows in unison, staring at the talisman as he passed it down to the girl. Even Paulus was taken aback.

Seraphina took it in her hand, looking down at the three interlocking triangles. She dragged her fingers across the smooth, silver surface. She beamed a huge smile up at Adalwin and put the chain around her neck. Her neck jerked a little. The weight would take some getting used to. She looked back up at him and felt a tear forming at the edge of her eye.

'I owe you my life, Adalwin. Thank you, for everything.'

He nodded down at her. Paulus extended his arm and the two gripped arms as they said a brief goodbye. There were no goodbyes between the prisoners, and they all mounted their horses.

As Seraphina was making sure Luna was ready, she felt a tap on her shoulder. She looked up and followed the direction that Paulus was pointing in. The barbarians were congregated behind Adalwin, exactly the way they were when she first saw them come over the hill in the forest. They were all looking straight ahead. Adalwin smiled, a rare sight, and raised a hand to the sky. One thousand men then thumped their chests with a single fist and brought the fists away from their chests. All then chanted a word in Germanic. Seraphina could not tell if it was one word or more, but it only lasted a moment. Then Adalwin gave them a nod and rode away with his men behind them.

One of the archers would later tell them it was a gesture for saying goodbye to comrades.

SEVENTY FIVE

Seraphina missed Adalwin and the barbarians. There had been a couple of scuffles with bandits on the long ride back to Rome, and more than once she yearned: yearned for their fearsome presence, yearned to be back in Alexandria, and yearned for her Quintus. There had been no time to properly mourn, and the journey back to Rome had involved many teary nights.

Both times they had been attacked, neither Darius nor Ourgious had tried to escape. There had been an opportunity on both occasions, but they probably realised their fate at the hands of bandits would be no better, and likely far worse, than whatever awaited them in Rome. Darius was still in bad shape, and knew he would not fare well in the wild by himself.

During the second fight, a bandit had been standing over Seraphina, ready to plunge his sword into her. Ourgious, having fallen off his horse, tripped the bandit, giving one of the archers enough time to take him down. He had risked his life to save hers, and it only deepened Seraphina's curiosity about him.

She had spoken to him in the days following that ambush, and learned how he had come to be involved with Karsas and their operation. His story was like Tamura's. In the beginning, the pirates had come across the small port town he was from. He had struck a deal with them to leave the women in his village alone. In exchange, he would give them information on boat movements in and out of the port. Over time, Karsas offered large sums of money if he guided travellers, male or female, in their direction. He had become corrupted by greed. Many times he had wanted to leave, he told her, but it was known that you did not simply walk away from that type of life. He knew of others who had tried. His voice trailed off when he spoke of them.

Seraphina knew well enough to keep their conversations to themselves. Paulus would feel no sympathy for the man and in all honesty, neither did Seraphina. She did, however, remember his kindness to her and the other girls in the prison. Then there was the fact that he had saved her life. Her mind was not made up about him, but her suspicion that there was good in him had been confirmed.

When he wasn't talking to Seraphina, Paulus spent his time with Darius. The saboteur became increasingly concerned with his fate with each passing day. He had begun asking questions, and Paulus told him what he would need to do. It would involve betraying his master and compromising as many people involved as possible. Darius' attitude had changed markedly, and he seemed willing to help. Paulus reminded himself not to trust him, and he couldn't help but cringe every time he looked at Darius' amputated arm.

'I'm sorry about your arm.'

Darius raised his eyebrows for a moment, and then his head dropped towards the ground.

They continued riding in silence. After a few minutes, Darius said, 'I'm going to help you get all these people, Paulus. I know there's no way you can trust me, but I will.'

Paulus nodded and continued to look straight ahead.

'All I hope for,' said Darius, coughing to clear his throat, 'is not to be executed.'

A few more moments of silence.

'And maybe, just maybe not to spend the rest of my life in gaol.'

Paulus didn't respond.

'Alright, everyone, it looks as though we're half a day away from Rome. We'll camp here tonight.'

The archer who could speak Greek translated for his comrades. One thing Seraphina had enjoyed was the proficiency of the men in setting up camp and preparing dinner. They were the same ones who had done that job on the way to Byzantium. She longed for a bed and to eat at a table, but she remained grateful.

While the others set up camp, Paulus gathered Seraphina, Darius, and Ourgious. The four sat in a circle, the latter two still in chains. For good measure, one of the archers stood nearby, an arrow loaded into his bow.

'We will reach Rome tomorrow,' said Paulus. He turned to Darius. 'You'll go home to your master, Faustus. When he asks about your arm, you are to say you lost it in a fight with bandits. You'll tell him that the mission was a failure, as you had both plotted to make it. We found no prison and no slaves. Only a farmhouse with a group of men guarding it.'

'What am I to say of how long I have been away?' asked Darius.

'That many of our men were wounded in the fight with the bandits. We had to stay with them, to see if they would recover.'

'But Tamura—' began Darius.

'Tamura has been taken care of,' said Paulus, cutting him off. 'Adalwin sent some men to the village after we left Tanais.'

Seraphina had known of this and had extracted promises that no one except Tamura was to be harmed. Unless, of course, it was discovered that the other villagers were also helping the pirates.

'Now, do you have that clear, Darius?'

Darius nodded.

'You'll come to meet me three nights from now at the temple of Jupiter for further instructions. After the sun has gone down.

Understood?'

Darius nodded again.

'People will be watching you, Darius. If there's any indication you've told Faustus the truth of what has happened, there will be trouble. Not just for you, but for anyone you care about. Anyone who has benefited from your treachery. Basically, anyone who has the slightest connection to you.'

Seraphina looked at Paulus. There was such a dichotomy to him. Most of the time, he was the epitome of a soldier; professional and honourable. Then there were those other moments when a ruthless streak surfaced. She wondered if it was a technique, or if, on some level, the angry young boy who saw his mother being beaten was still inside.

'I'm not stupid enough to betray you now, Paulus. I shall do as you have said.'

'Good. Now, Seraphina, come and walk with me.'

The archer stepped closer to the prisoners, making his presence felt. The head of his arrow was only a few inches away from their necks, and they were acutely aware. They sat still and silent, looking at the ground as had become their habit.

'What do you think, Seraphina?'

Seraphina shook her head. 'No matter what he says, we can't trust him. Don't you think giving him two full days with Faustus is too long?'

Paulus smiled. 'I made arrangements with my men before we left them in Tanais. At least one of them, if not more, are already back in Rome, but in hiding. They had instructions to contact Caesar. The finest spies in the republic will be surrounding Faustus' house the moment Darius rides in there tomorrow.'

Seraphina folded her arms. 'What? How? Why didn't you tell me?'

Paulus lowered his head. 'It wasn't an issue of trust, Seraphina. Don't take it like that. We had more than enough to worry about at the time. I'm telling you now.'

'Very well, but Caesar? How do we know that Caesar himself is not involved?'

'Well, nothing in what Gadas gave us indicates that he is. Besides, if Caesar is involved, we'll all be dead before the week is out.' Seraphina felt that lump in her throat again as Paulus said, 'so let's hope he isn't.'

'Yes, let's.'

'Do you trust Cicero?' asked Paulus.

'Why do you ask?'

'Well, for one thing, you'll be going back to stay at his home. The other reason I ask is because we may wish to confide in him about the senators who are involved.'

'I'm not sure. I do trust him, and he is the one who set this whole mission in motion. It was important enough to him that he used his influence, but …'

'But what?'

'He only decided to help when he knew the son of a Roman general was involved. I don't think he is part of this, but I don't think we should rely on him. Those senators are his colleagues. We can't trust that he'll betray them.'

Paulus nodded. 'Very well. Then tomorrow, you'll go and tell him the same story that Darius is going to tell Faustus. The mission was a failure. We lost men, and some were wounded. This necessitated the delay in our return home.'

'What happens next?'

Paulus shook his head. 'I honestly don't know. I must regroup with my men and find out what they learned from their raids on the other prisons. This could go even deeper. I must talk to Caesar myself, and your presence will only complicate matters at this stage. I'll get word to you when the time is right. For now, just go back to Cicero's house, and live life as normally as you can.'

Seraphina set aside her disappointment. Rome was Paulus' turf, and he seemed sure of what he was doing. She nodded and said she would do just as he had instructed.

SEVENTY SIX

'So, what of your mission, Commander?' asked Caesar. 'Your men have already briefed me on their efforts since they split off from you.'

Paulus was standing in Julius Caesar's private office. It was only a few moments after dawn. The faint morning light penetrated the office somewhat, and Paulus noticed sparse yet elegant furnishings – a table and chair, two larger chairs in a corner, and a set of shelves. The dictator was already working when Paulus had arrived. It was a well-kept secret that Caesar was often the first person to reach the Forum each day and the last to leave at night. The commander was there most of all because he needed to tell someone the story, but he was having trouble deciding where to start. He stared at his feet and the marble floor beneath.

'Commander?' asked Caesar again, raising his voice slightly.

'Yes, my lord.'

Pen in hand, Caesar spread his arms out. 'Well, how was your mission? Is that what you're here to talk to me about?'

Paulus nodded, his eyes having returned to the floor.

'You're acting very strangely, Commander.'

'It has been a strange few weeks.'

'Weeks? You have been gone for months.'

Paulus reached into his satchel and retrieved the records. He stepped forward to Caesar's desk and said, 'Here.'

'What is this, Paulus?'

'Details of a very broad conspiracy, I believe.'

'Conspiracy? What type of conspiracy? Political?'

'Not exactly, my lord.'

Caesar picked up the thick scroll of papyrus sheets. He read through them, pausing intermittently to look up at Paulus. The commander wore a nervous look on his face.

'You had better start talking, Commander. If this is a list of conspirators, it includes many officials, known personally to both of us. Not to mention some of your army colleagues, and two senators.'

'Two that we know about, sir.'

'Your mission was to rescue the son of a general, was it not?' Caesar had put down the scrolls and laid his palms flat on his table.

'That was part of it, sir. We were hoping to find him. We were also investigating the allegation of a slave prison.'

'Where?'

'Tanais.'

'Yes, Tanais. I remember now. Cicero came and spoke to me about this. If I recall, he was the one who pushed the idea of a mission to begin with. All on the word of some girl, was it not? A girl who had supposedly escaped this prison?'

At least he remembers, thought Paulus. 'That is correct, my lord.'

'Get Cicero in here this minute!'

Paulus hesitated for a moment, unsure if he was expected to go and fetch the senator.

'Guard! Guard!' shouted Caesar. A guard rushed in, and Caesar shouted across the room at him. 'Go to Senator Cicero's office and tell him to come here. If he's not there, search the grounds. If you don't find him, go to his home. Do you know where that is?'

'Yes, Lord Caesar. He lives on the Palatine. I will not return without him.'

'Go,' he said to the soldier.

'While we're waiting, Paulus, tell me exactly why you're here. Trading in slaves is no crime.'

Paulus gritted his teeth and did his best not to show any outward reaction. 'Of course not, my lord. There's evidence that these people have been kidnapping young women and selling them into slavery.'

'And?' asked the dictator, now standing with one hand on his hip.

Paulus didn't miss a beat. 'Our investigation shows that many of these women are from wealthy families. Our investigation also shows that the people on that list are part of a network that benefits from the kidnapping of these girls. Some of them are here with families in Rome.'

Caesar walked around to the front of his table and leaned against it. His hands rested on its edge and he smiled at Paulus. 'Enslaving others is not necessarily a crime, but kidnapping and false imprisonment are. That is your thinking, correct, Commander?'

'Yes, sir, it did cross my mind.'

Caesar laughed. 'I'm sure it did. I would wager that no tax is being paid on these slaves by their owners.'

'Well, I'm not sure, sir, but legally they don—'

'Yes, yes,' said Caesar, waving his hands in Paulus' direction. 'They don't own the women, because of the way they obtained them. But there would be an issue of failing to pay their taxes.'

'I see your point, sir. Yes, there would.'

'Let's have a look at this list again.' Caesar turned around and scanned the lengthy list of names. Paulus watched his face as he did so. Some got a raise of the eyebrows, others got a little grin.

Paulus spoke slowly as Caesar still had his attention on the list. 'That's only part of it, my lord. I have here more records, obtained by my men during our investigation.' Paulus handed an even thicker bundle of documents to the dictator.

'Put them on the desk,' said Caesar, shaking his head, and showing Paulus his full hands.

'Yes, of course, my lord. My apologies.'

Caesar walked back to the other side of his desk and sat down, throwing the scroll he was holding on to the table. The guard returned, panting, and said, 'My lord, the senator, Cicero, has arrived.'

'Show him in, please.'

After a few moments, Cicero joined them, and pleasantries were exchanged.

'Have you seen any of this?' asked Caesar, waving at the pile of documents now covering his table.

Cicero scratched his head. 'My lord, I'm not exactly sure what those documents are. This is the first time I have seen the commander since he returned.'

'I'll take that as a no then,' snapped Caesar. 'Look, Cicero, I need an explanation for all this. This mission was your idea, after all.'

'Yes, my lord, but the mission was a failure as I understood it.'

Paulus held his forehead, closed his eyes, and bowed his head towards the ground.

'What do you mean, a failure?' asked Caesar, grinding his teeth in Paulus' direction.

'I was informed that there was no prison, no women being held, and no general's son.'

Caesar went to say something then leaned back in his chair. Folding his arms, he smiled at both Paulus and Cicero. 'My dear Cicero, if this is the first time you're seeing the commander since his return, how did you know that the mission had been a failure?'

Cicero just stood there, unable to speak, and unable to look away from Caesar.

'Commander?' said Caesar.

'My lord, it's going to take a long time to explain what happened on our mission.'

'In that case, the two of you had better sit down. Whatever this is, at least two senators are implicated in what I have read of these documents so far. Cicero, why don't we start with you? How did you find out that the mission had supposedly been a failure?'

Both men were wise enough to opt for complete disclosure. After Paulus finished his account of their lengthy mission, he was exhausted and felt as though he had lived it a second time.

'Well,' said Caesar, 'you've been on quite an adventure.' Then he turned to Cicero. 'Listen, Senator, it seems some good was done here. The main objective of the mission was to recover General Rufio's son. Instead of coming home when he was not found, it looks as though the good commander here has gone on some righteous crusade beyond our borders, losing some twenty men in the process. You set all this in motion, and I'm holding you personally responsible for this mission. You had one thing right when you walked in here—the mission was, in fact, a failure.'

He returned his attention to the commander. 'As for you, Commander, I'm not sure what to say. I have known you as a reliable and professional soldier until now. Why you would pursue this, staying away from your station of duty for months, and going far beyond our borders, is a mystery to me. The mistakes you made have cost Roman lives, lives you were duty bound to protect as part of your oath as a soldier. Allying yourself with barbarians and riding far and wide? For what?' Caesar picked up the documents and threw them across his table. 'This is no tangible evidence. This is merely a list of prominent people, written in Greek I might add, provided by a source that is dubious at best. May I remind you that we have courts, and those courts have procedures. Even if I wanted to, and I don't in this instance, I cannot override their authority.'

Caesar paused for a moment, in case either of them had something to say. Both men were silent, but at least did him the courtesy of maintaining eye contact.

'It's not completely in vain, Commander. From what you've told me, all seven of these prisons have been destroyed. The men perpetrating these crimes have faced justice, and the women have been freed. You should be proud of that. The pirate you brought back with you to Rome will be thrown in gaol, and you have my leave to arrest this Darius, who seems to have acted alone. Your actions are perplexing to me, Commander, and perhaps unreasonable, but I'll not punish you for them.'

'That's very gracious of you, my lord. Thank you.'

'A pleasure, Commander. Now take these papers off my table. That is all, gentlemen. Please, excuse me.'

Paulus and Cicero exchanged glances, but only for a moment. Both promptly rose to their feet and walked out of the office.

'Oh, and gentlemen,' said Caesar, returning to his work, 'I don't want to hear about this again.'

SEVENTY SEVEN

It was still early in the morning, and yet both Paulus and Cicero felt it had already been a very long day. Cicero wanted to ask why Paulus had not trusted him but thought better of it. Instead, he invited him back to his home for some refreshments and a further debriefing.

The pair took the short ride very slowly, both processing the browbeating they had just received from Rome's leader. When they arrived, the sight of Luna, Seraphina's horse, brought a welcome smile to Paulus' face. They walked into the courtyard and Paulus saw Seraphina doing Keb's exercises, which they had done together many times.

Maybe Caesar was right, he thought. He had lost two-thirds of his men, failed to find the boy, and gone gallivanting with a horde of barbarians. He had even ordered his men to do the same. Then he shook his head. This was no time to doubt himself. Everything had happened for very good reasons. They had marched on the prisons because it was the right thing to do. Word had not been sent to Rome because they could not know who to trust. They had brought back what evidence they could find of a scheme that deliberately left no trail.

Cicero had yet to say a word to either Paulus or Seraphina. The two watched her perform her exercises, breathing and bending herself into all manner of positions.

'I don't suppose you know what she's doing, do you?' asked Cicero. 'I would see her doing this occasionally, even before she left with you. Now she does it twice a day, without fail.'

'I do,' said Paulus, smiling, 'but that is the least of our concerns right now.' He turned to Cicero. 'I know you're upset with me for not telling you about the mission. We just weren't su—'

'I understand,' interrupted Cicero, 'but it may have helped your cause if you'd told me beforehand. The senators who have been named are both men I know. Perhaps ... well, it doesn't matter now. Caesar's mind seems made up.'

Seraphina opened her eyes when moving into another position and saw the two men standing there. She raised an eyebrow as she glanced at Paulus, and stopped what she was doing.

'Good morning, Paulus.'

'Cicero knows all about what really happened on the mission, Seraphina.'

'I see ...' said Seraphina, turning towards Cicero.

'Don't worry, Seraphina. After all, we did deceive Paulus by sending you on the mission without him knowing. I suppose this makes things even.'

Seraphina just nodded, unsure of what to say.

'In any case,' continued Cicero, 'Caesar has also been informed and has made up his mind about what we are to do, which is nothing.'

'What!' shouted Seraphina.

'Lower your voice,' said Cicero. 'He has no confidence in the "evidence" you brought back with you. The two of you should've told me the truth. I know both Porcius and Felix. There was a chance I could've had them incriminate themselves before we went to Caesar.'

'Can't we still do that?' asked Seraphina.

'No,' said Paulus, shaking his head as he looked down. 'We have our orders. Well, Cicero here is not a soldier, and Caesar is not exactly my commanding officer, but he has authority over us. We are not to pursue this investigation any further. I'm to arrest Darius, who Caesar believes acted alone.'

Seraphina put her hands on her hips. 'How can he decide that? We know what we heard, and what Darius told us. Faustus is his master!'

Paulus shrugged. 'Caesar has spoken. He is the dictator of Rome, and his word is final. He was quite clear in his directions to us. This would be like me disobeying a superior officer, Seraphina. Please try to understand.'

'Cicero? Can't we do anything about this?'

'I'm sorry, Seraphina. This has gone as far as it can. I have only just regained Caesar's favour after some previous matters went awry. It would do no good to anyone for me to defy Caesar.'

Seraphina kept quiet. She knew they were looking after their own interests, but she sympathised. She could only imagine what the consequences would be if either of them defied Caesar.

'I understand,' said Seraphina. Looking at Paulus, she added, 'We saved a lot of women and destroyed those prisons. That's something.'

'It is, but I would've loved to arrest the devils involved here.'

'Paulus ...' warned Cicero.

'I know, Senator.'

'Then it's over,' said Seraphina.

Cicero smiled at her. 'If you like, once some time has passed, we can move on to the reason you came to Rome in the first place.'

'You mean ...?'

'Yes, I have a number of people I'd like to introduce you to. Scholars, writers, and scientists. Then there are some colleges you might want to see.'

The word 'colleges' triggered a memory of Quintus. *This was his dream too*, she thought.

'Let some time pass first. Where will I stay?'

'Here,' said Cicero, gesturing at the house and its grounds. 'This is your home now, at least until you find another one you want to move on to.'

'That's very kind of you. Thank you, Cicero.'

'Well,' said Paulus, 'I'll be seeing you from time to time, then. At least when I'm in Rome. I had best be going for now. Caesar has at least authorised me to arrest Darius.'

'When will you do that?' asked Seraphina.

'Tonight, when I meet him at the temple as planned.'

SEVENTY EIGHT

Seraphina had no intention of letting things go. She knew it would do no good to tell Paulus and Cicero. Right now, they were not able to help her. She had vowed back in Tanais to do whatever she could do to give Quintus justice. These people in Rome, in Athens, and in countless cities elsewhere – they were the reason that this slave trade even existed. Seraphina could not believe that Caesar had decided to do nothing about this. She remembered his arrogance from their brief encounter in Alexandria, and it matched what Paulus and Cicero had told her.

She walked outside into the courtyard, kicking off her sandals, and letting the green grass massage the soles of her feet. She closed her eyes and took a deep breath in. Like Keb had taught her, she allowed the sun's light to hit the spot between her eyebrows. A light breeze brushed her cheek, and she spread her arms out. Breathing in and out, she focused on that same spot in between the eyebrows.

I could visit Faustus. The thought came but unlike many others she was having, that one remained. *Visit Faustus*, she thought. *Why? What good would that do?* She returned her head to the same position and continued breathing. The words rang in her mind, again and again. *Visit*

Faustus. Visit Faustus.

She came to a normal standing position and brought her hands to her hips. Seraphina nibbled on her top lip, wondering why on earth she would go and visit Faustus. She walked around the courtyard, still barefoot, trying to remember what Keb had said about that spot between the eyebrows. Something about clarity of mind, perhaps. Seraphina looked up at Luna, who was looking right back at her.

Slipping her feet back into her sandals, she walked straight over to Luna, untied him, and jumped up on to his back. As she began riding out of the gate, Cicero called out to her.

'Off anywhere interesting, Seraphina?'

'Just for a ride around the city. Some fresh air will help clear my head.'

Cicero nodded and waved.

As Luna trotted along, Seraphina wondered what she would say, or do, once she saw Faustus. *Was she riding into danger? If anything happened to her, Cicero would tell Paulus*, she thought.

She arrived at Faustus' home and saw Antonia occupied in her usual pastime of walking around the courtyard. She looked up and waved at Seraphina.

'What brings you here, Seraphina? It's so good to see you.' Antonia hugged her tightly as soon as she got down from the horse.

'I thought I would come and see Faustus. To thank him again for all his help.'

'Oh, how lovely. He'll be happy to see you. I think I saw him over here near the servants' quarters,' she said, already walking away. She pointed to the front door. 'You can wait there. Have a seat and I'll let him know you're here.'

Well, if there was any danger, thought Seraphina, *it wasn't from Antonia.* She seemed happy as ever. Seraphina sat down on a bench next to the wide dome-shaped entrance to their home. Once she sat, she could hear some voices inside. She craned her neck towards the doorway to eavesdrop.

'What did you say?' That was Darius' voice, without a doubt.

'The broker said we won't be getting any more girls for a while. No one will. Some problem with the supply.'

Seraphina couldn't believe her ears. She sat near the edge of the bench, careful not to make a sound.

'I don't understand,' said Darius.

'That's all his message said. This has never happened before. He wants to meet as well, tonight, with the senators.'

'Is that safe?'

'Well, he insisted. He said they have paid a lot of money to the senators, and the—'

'Darling,' came Antonia's voice, 'I'm sorry to interrupt, but you have a guest.'

'Just a minute,' said Faustus. 'Wait, who is it?'

'It's that lovely Seraphina. She said she came over to thank you.'

Silence, and then Seraphina thought she heard footsteps. As quietly as possible, she shifted towards the end of the bench, looking around to see if anyone was watching. Seeing no one, she stood up and walked to the very edge of the patio. There, she looked out in the distance, careful not to turn around.

'Seraphina!' said Faustus. 'This is a surprise.'

Seraphina spun around and faced him, wearing a broad smile. She saw Darius behind him. He wore his signature blank expression.

'Hello, Faustus. I'm sorry for coming over unannounced, but I realised I hadn't seen you since we returned.' She looked over at Darius for a moment. 'Hello, Darius.'

Darius nodded and asked if his master needed him.

Faustus dismissed him, and he walked into the courtyard with Seraphina.

'Darius told me about the disappointments during the mission. I'm very sorry you did not find Quintus.'

Seraphina nodded thoughtfully. 'Yes, I had hoped to find him, however unlikely it was. I just wanted to thank you, Faustus. You have done so much for me. First, you helped me get here to Rome, and then to find Cicero. You were very understanding about me deceiving you with my disguise, and then you even allowed Darius to put himself in harm's way, so I could go on that mission.'

Faustus smiled and said, 'As I told you before, it's a pleasure to help you in any way I can. I'm just sorry for all you've been through.'

What a phoney, thought Seraphina. 'Thank you. At least now I can take the time to mourn Quintus. The mission was quite draining.'

'Darius told me.'

'How's he doing with the loss of his arm?'

'Darius is not one to complain. He's a warrior and will make do. I heard that you didn't find any of the women at the prison.'

'No,' said Seraphina, shaking her head. 'It was very strange. The soldiers went there and left me and Darius behind.'

'Was this before or after he lost his arm?'

'After,' said Seraphina, slowly.

Faustus just nodded.

'The soldiers came back to us and said they didn't find anything amiss. I was still in disguise, so I didn't want to ask any questions.'

'I can understand why,' said Faustus.

Seraphina hoped that what she was saying lined up with whatever Darius had told his master.

'That was really the end of it. We had already lost several men by then. The journey home took so long because of the wounded we had to look after. In the end, we lost those men as well.'

Faustus shook his head. 'What a waste. I'm sorry it was all for nothing, Seraphina.'

I bet you are, she thought. 'I appreciate that. I'm still grateful to you. You've done a lot for me, and I'll never forget it. I hope to be able to repay you someday, in some way.'

Faustus gave a little chuckle. 'There's no need for that, Seraphina. I don't help in order to create entries on a ledger that need be repaid. You're a good person, and I'm glad I was in the position to help you when I did.' They walked in silence for a few moments. 'So, what will you do now?'

'Well,' said Seraphina, 'I'll be staying with Cicero for now. I will take some time to mourn Quintus properly, and take things from there.'

'That sounds wise. Well, Seraphina, I appreciate you coming to see me, but I have some matters to attend to. Feel free to come and visit again, just let me know beforehand. Antonia is very fond of you, and we would love to see you again soon.'

'Thank you for seeing me, Faustus. Enjoy the rest of your day.'

'Good day to you too.'

Seraphina smiled and gave a little bow of her head. She rode out slowly and once outside, scanned the walls around the house, looking for good hiding places.

SEVENTY NINE

He always found peace here. He paced the smooth stone floors, circling the inner sanctum of the temple with its altars and ornaments. The chilled night air brushed the hairs on his arms, making Paulus shiver slightly. The tall, statuesque columns formed a perfect rectangle. He glanced between them as he paced, noticing the blanket of stars that lay over the dark night sky. As he walked, he offered prayers. Prayers of gratitude, mostly. That he had returned safely from another mission. He offered a short prayer that Jupiter would allow justice to prevail in the present situation.

It was always quiet around the temple at nighttime, and he loved to walk there and think. He would read some of the inscriptions on the walls and felt at ease.

He knew Darius would come alone, and this was a place he was happy to wait. The commander recited the prayers his mother had taught him, and her memory brought a smile to his face. *I should come here more often*, he thought.

Paulus was walking along the rear side of the temple when he heard three high-pitched sounds, interrupting the night. *Like whistles*, he thought. He was admiring the inscriptions on the temple wall when he recognised exactly what those sounds were.

The muscles in his legs pumped, and before he was even around the corner, he heard the dull thud. He could see the front of the temple now. His head lowered, and he swung his arms, sprinting as fast as he could. Leaping down the steps, the commander saw Darius, lying on the ground. The moon, dulled by grey clouds, faintly lit his face. Three arrows protruded from his body, their heads forming a perfect triangle in the centre of his chest.

Paulus fell to his knees and cradled the dying man's head in his arms. He looked down and saw his eyes blink. A grunting breath emanating from his throat.

'Darius, what happened?'

'Meeting …tonight …' he whispered.

'What meeting?'

Darius tried to raise his arm, pointing at something. 'Be … caref—'

The arrow struck Paulus in the shoulder, right in the gap between his plates of armour. He howled in pain, retreating up the temple steps. Another arrow whistled out and hit something behind him. When he looked out from behind the columns, he saw a fourth arrow in Darius. It was planted in the exact centre of his forehead.

Paulus' chin dropped, then he remembered Darius' last words. *A meeting tonight? What meeting?* He removed the armour from his shoulder and chest and snapped off the end of the arrow. Looking at it in the moonlight, he could see it was of Roman design. For a moment, he had wondered if Adalwin's men had decided to take matters into their own hands. The reality was much more sinister. It was one thing to assassinate Darius, who was a civilian and about to be arrested as a criminal. For a Roman, any Roman, to attempt to kill a commander of the Roman army was a serious offence, one punishable by death.

The other soldiers! All but three of his men had returned from their missions to the various prisons. Unlike Paulus, they did not live in fortified camps or in barracks. Gritting his teeth, he stumbled to the rear of the temple and whistled for his horse. He rested his body against the horse and eased on to it. Paulus lay still on the horse for a moment, listening for any sound. There was more than one of them out there, he was sure. Whoever they were, he couldn't hear a thing. Finally, ignoring the pain in his shoulder, he pushed himself up and took the reins. Staying away from the open streets, Paulus, weaved between the buildings and into the shadows.

EIGHTY

Her feet sank further into the soft earth with each passing minute. Just an iota, but Seraphina could have sworn it felt like quicksand. She didn't know how many hours she had been there, but she had arrived just after dusk. Now the pitch-black night was upon her, the half-moon dulled by a sky of grey clouds.

She rubbed her chest to chase away the chill. Despite the cold, a layer of perspiration rested on her brow. Seraphina pressed her fingers into her thighs, where she had lost nearly all feeling in her squatted position. As uncomfortable as she was, she dared not move. She was convinced that Faustus' guards were out there, watching for any kind of movement.

Seraphina's eyes turned towards Luna, who was tied behind enough trees and bushes to conceal him. He stood still and looked as comfortable as ever.

She had found the perfect place to watch Faustus' front gate, but the hours of waiting now caused fatigue to set in. *I must have missed him somehow*, she thought. She pressed her fingers into her thighs again and could feel nothing. Seraphina pressed her hands to the ground and let them absorb her weight. Lifting her chin up to keep an eye on the gate, she then pressed her legs back, giving them a much-needed stretch.

It felt so good, but she resisted the urge to sigh in relief. Then she heard a sound and dropped her body to the floor. She focused through the gap in the bushes and saw the white horse poke its nose out of the gate. Faustus trotted the horse out into the street, dressed in his usual dignified attire.

You won't get to look so fancy in prison, she thought. Then her neck jerked, as he turned right out of the gate. He was riding away from the city. Seraphina had not anticipated this. To follow, she would have to ride straight past the gate. This was not an option, as she could easily be spotted.

She reached out and untied Luna, easing on to his back. She had to be quiet, but she also had to move quickly. Luna's hooves made precious little sound in the dirt, and Seraphina got away from the house, finding a road leading off to the right. Beating the reins with her wrists to a slow rhythm, Seraphina had Luna pick up the pace, trying to catch up with Faustus and his bright, white steed.

There he was! A flash of white ahead of her and to the right. She made a turn and stopped just short of the corner. Pressing her hand against the smooth stone, Seraphina peeked around the building's edge. Faustus was dismounting his horse. She didn't recognise the building, but she could certainly count the number of rooftops between it and the one she was hiding behind.

Looking around, she couldn't see anywhere to tie Luna. There was no time to lose. She climbed on to his back, clambering to the top of the building, and as soon as her feet were on the roof, she took off. Her arms pumped as she accelerated off the building, leaping towards the next. *Two more*, she thought. As luck would have it, both buildings were of similar height. *Easy*, thought Seraphina.

As she looked down to Faustus' horse, she realised she had miscalculated. *It was the third building!* If she'd been able to slow down, she would simply have hopped down to the street and taken her chances following Faustus into the building. There was no time though.

Seraphina took her last step off the rooftop, pushing up instead of forward, her arms outstretched. She could see the bricks, far too close to eye level for her liking.

Thud! She prayed to all major and minor deities that everyone was inside. Anyone on the street would have heard Seraphina's cheek slamming into the brick wall. At the last minute, she turned her face. Her fingers gripping the stone rim of the roof were all that had saved her. Seraphina flung her other arm upwards. Then, she swung her body from side to side, until she got a foothold on the top of the building.

Seraphina crept to each of the four corners of the rooftop, listening for any voices. Nothing. Her palm pressed against her forehead. She squeezed her eyes closed and told herself how stupid she was. Empty streets and the still silhouettes of buildings surrounded her. Luna was somewhere down there, not far away. If she was lucky, she could get down and get back to Cicero's house before she got herself killed.

A voice interrupted her thoughts, and Seraphina froze. She crawled towards it, as it spoke louder. There were more voices. She pressed her head down as far as she could, straining to hear what they were saying. Seraphina was sure it was Latin, but she could barely hear. Down the wall, there was an opening, a window. If only she could get closer to it. She was sure that's where the voices were coming from.

She caught the words 'two nights from now,' and knew she had to hear more. Shuffling around on her stomach, Seraphina tried to get into a better position. As her neck turned, a sliver of the moon's light reflected on something on her belt. Keb's dagger. Pressing her fingers against the wall, she could feel the soft concrete between the bricks. Seraphina drew the dagger with one hand and gripped the top of the wall with the other. Reaching down as far as she could, she swung the dagger towards the wall once or twice, for practice. Shaking her head, she closed her eyes, praying for it to be as quiet as possible.

She plunged the dagger into the wall and buried it to the hilt. It was like a sharp knife sinking into hot, soft bread. Seraphina opened her eyes and realised they were still talking. She could only catch a word here and there, something about 'your money' and 'the last time'. Seraphina had never prayed much, but she did now, as she lowered herself down from the wall, holding on to the handle with both hands.

All the muscles in her arms and chest were flexed, and the words were now crystal clear.

'So, what happened?' asked a male voice, which Seraphina vaguely recognised.

'It's best you don't know, my dear Felix.' Seraphina nodded, remembering the senator from her first visit to the Forum.

'Don't you dare call me by name when I don't know yours.'

'Pardon me, Senator, but some details are not for your ears.'

'We'll decide what we do and do not wish to know,' came another voice. *If Faustus was there*, thought Seraphina, *he wasn't talking.*

'Is that right, Senator? Well, I think we pay you enough to decide what information we share with you, and what we keep to ourselves.'

'Well,' said Felix, 'from what you're telling us, those days are over.'

'Only for now. Don't forget how much we have paid you over the years, Felix. Choose your next words wisely.'

A bead of sweat moved down Seraphina's forehead, and it felt so loud that she had to stifle a gasp.

'How dare you threaten me! And to use my name again!' shouted Felix.

'Gentlemen, gentlemen.' That was Faustus. 'Let's all stay calm. All we have here is a minor delay, isn't that correct? Tell them, broker.'

'Yes,' answered the broker. 'What's more, the shipment you'll receive tomorrow is ten times the usual size. All top quality, as usual, though they may be a little worse for wear.'

'What do yo—' said the other senator.

'Porcius,' said the broker, pronouncing the senator's name slowly as three syllables, 'do not interrupt me.'

There was silence, and Seraphina closed her eyes, concentrating on holding her upper body firm so her entire weight was not hanging from the handle.

'As I was saying, they've had a long trip, so they may need to be cleaned up a bit. May I remind you that this comes with ten times the usual payment, to each of you.'

Felix chuckled and said, 'Dear Broker, I'm sorry if I was being impetuous. Meeting here, late at night, these changed arrangements. It's all out of the ordinary, and I simply got a bit nervous, that's all.'

'It's no problem, Senator. Be at the port at Ostia two nights from now. At midnight. You'll need to march the women on foot, so I suggest you find somewhere close to there to keep them.'

'We can handle all of that,' said Faustus.

'Until then, gentlemen,' said the broker.

Seraphina's arms were beginning to give way, and she clasped her hands even more tightly. Her forehead rested against the bottom of the handle. She kept her eyes closed for another minute or two. The footsteps of the men descending the stairs had faded, but she didn't want to take any chances. Tilting her neck upwards, the roof looked so far away. Holding her body weight up on the dagger handle had caused her muscles to cramp.

Her hand slipped off the dagger and she swung her arm, hoping to grip something. She caught nothing but air, and the dagger came loose in her other hand. Twisting in the air, Seraphina tried to land on her chest. Then something broke her fall. It was a cart of hay, but she landed at an awkward angle. The side of her head collided with the wooden frame of the cart, and her limp body bounced into the hay. Blood flowed down the side of her face, and Seraphina lay there, as still as the moon shining down upon her.

EIGHTY ONE

She had some experience as a nurse and insisted on helping him while they waited. They were safe for now, so Paulus relented and let her look. With great care, she removed the rest of his armour. She was the wife of one of his soldiers; one who was yet to return from their mission. One of her children, a young boy, moved around his mother to get a look at the gore. He rotated his stare between the wound, Paulus' armour, and his sword. Occasionally, he would look up at Paulus and offer a toothy smile. Paulus smiled back, amused by the child's antics.

'Alright,' she said, 'this may sting a little.' She poured alcohol over the wound, and Paulus flinched. He kept his body still, as he knew to do in these situations. Armed with a long knife, she poured more alcohol into the wound and dug in with the blade.

The boy recoiled but did not look away for a second. He watched as his mother pulled out what remained of the arrow. Looking up at his mother with newfound awe, he moved to the other side as her hand waved him away.

Paulus was relieved to have it out of him, and he thanked the woman. She just gave a nod and a smile, then stitched him up. When she finished, he tapped on the stitches with his fingers and was impressed with her work. He looked out of his window, watching, and listening for horses and wheels. It was late. So late, in fact, that morning would be upon them soon.

He looked around the room. Three wives, five children. He had woken all of them and brought them here. Two of the women knew Paulus personally, but the third had argued for some time. Eventually, he had prevailed and now here they all sat, safe for now.

The discoveries after fleeing the temple had been gruesome. Five of the six soldiers who had returned from their mission to Tanais had been murdered, along with their wives and children. The only one to escape this fate lived in the same fortified camp as Paulus. That soldier's house was now surrounded by soldiers, men who could be trusted, as was Paulus' home, where they waited now.

The commander had not woken the entire camp, but only those men he trusted and needed. None of the soldiers named in Gadas' records lived in this camp, but nothing seemed certain at that moment. Paulus' only thought was getting these people to safety.

His friend's name was Spurius. He was a retired centurion, who had joined the army at the same time as Paulus. They had trained together as legionaries, but he had opted for a life outside the military. Spurius had struck it rich as a businessman and now lived deep in the mountains outside of Rome. Paulus had visited his house, which more resembled a fortress, and it was the perfect place for these women and children to hide.

There was a knock on the door, and everyone looked at it. Two soldiers entered with Spurius behind them. Paulus smiled at his old friend, noticing the slight belly that had replaced the flat stomach of his military days.

'Thank you for coming,' said Paulus.

'Of course, my friend.'

Spurius had been briefed by the soldiers who had rushed to fetch him, and no time was wasted. The women and children were loaded into the cart and made as comfortable as possible. Half of the men guarding Paulus' house joined the men that Spurius had brought with him. They left the camp as quickly as they had arrived.

Paulus felt relieved as he watched them ride away. It was still dark, and this would make them harder to follow. Spurius knew the terrain between Rome and his home better than anyone, and Paulus knew that he only hired the very best to be his personal guards.

The commander weighed up his options, and he liked none of them. Exhaustion from the night's events caught up with him, and he decided to sleep until the sun came up. He gave his men orders to wake him at dawn and to arrest anyone who approached or entered the camp who was not supposed to be there.

EIGHTY TWO

The lighthouse looked so majestic, she thought. The boat rocked slightly from side to side as they sat there together. Looking down, Seraphina saw his arms crossed over her navel, and she smiled. As the boat swayed and her head rested deeper into Quintus' chest, Seraphina felt herself drifting off to sleep.

Quintus chuckled, and she felt the movement of his chest from the brief laugh. Her chin dropped, and she could feel his nose nudging the side of her face. She held his hands, and her grip loosened as she fell asleep. The blackness inside her eyelids turned to red, and then a bright orange. A light was shining on them.

'Wake up, Seraphina,' said Quintus, his nose still nudging her.

She shook her head, smiling and basking in his gentle touch.

'Wake up,' said the familiar voice once again. The orange got even brighter, and her eyes burned.

Her eyes opened and the flame at the top of the lighthouse was reflected straight at her. The white light struck her pupils and her body jerked away.

Seraphina woke up. Most of her vision was obstructed by Luna's face.

He was nudging her with his big, wet nose. For a moment or two, she lay there, wanting to close her eyes and go back to her dream. Something was in her hand, and she raised it, so she could see. The dagger. She returned it to her belt and sat up.

A bunch of hay had stuck to her head and she grabbed at it. She felt skin peel as she pulled it off, and she winced from the pain. Luna was still very close, and she pushed him away to have some space. A few cuts and scrapes on her legs, but nothing serious. Seraphina lowered her feet to the ground and tried taking a few steps. A bit wobbly, but she could walk. *Best not to touch my head again*, she thought.

Taking great care with her movements, she clambered on to Luna and rode back to Cicero's house. The day was beginning to break, and no one was on the streets. The movement and fresh air felt good, and she remembered the conversation she had overheard. Seraphina rode back as fast as she could.

EIGHTY THREE

'Well, what happened to you?' asked Paulus. He had just rolled out of bed to find two very early morning visitors in his home.

'Your soldiers are fanatics, Paulus,' said Cicero, not giving Seraphina a chance to answer. 'They wanted to arrest us.'

'They know how to follow orders. What are you doing here anyway?'

'There have been developments since we last spoke,' said Cicero.

Paulus looked at Seraphina, who wore a bandage on one side of her head. 'Come through here, please. Let's sit for a moment.'

'There really isn't any time for us to sit,' said Seraphina.

'You look like you've had a rough night.' Paulus then gestured towards the chairs in his sitting room. He winced from the pain of his arrow wound. Showing it to them, he said, 'I have too, as you can see. Why don't you go first?'

Seraphina told Paulus the same story she had told Cicero. He chastised her just as the senator had done for involving herself in the situation again, although once she spoke of the conversation she had overheard at Faustus' house, Paulus went silent. Seraphina moved her hands as she spoke and showed him the dagger when she spoke of how she had eavesdropped on the clandestine meeting.

'My goodness, Seraphina. Your head … are you alright? Why didn't you come to one of us?'

Seraphina shook her head. 'You both made it clear that you weren't able to do anything. I didn't want to get you in trouble.'

'Well, things may change now,' said Paulus.

'I should think so,' quipped Cicero. 'We are going to catch these devils in the act.'

'Yes, we are. Unfortunately, there's more to tell. Last night, I went to the temple to meet and arrest Darius as planned. I heard arrow shots and when I ran to the front of the temple, he was lying on the ground with three perfect arrow strikes to his chest. All he managed to say to me was something about a meeting. The meeting you managed to follow Faustus to.'

'He really was going to help us,' said Seraphina, almost to herself.

'Yes, he was. Whoever shot him then fired at me. I was in my armour, and the arrow hit me in between the plates. By the time I had retreated into the temple, Darius had another arrow in him. This time, in his head.'

Seraphina shook her head, raising one hand that pressed against her temples.

'He was not a good man, Seraphina,' said Paulus.

'I know, I know, but he was trying to do the right thing, telling you about the meeting.'

Paulus nodded and looked over at Cicero who was uncharacteristically speechless.

'What do we do now?' asked Seraphina.

'Before that, there's more.'

Seraphina raised her eyebrows and listened to Paulus tell the story. He told of how he had found the soldiers and their families slaughtered and getting the wives and children of the other men to safety.

'Will the men be safe when they return?' asked Cicero.

Paulus nodded. 'Yes. I've left them coded notes that they are to remain in hiding. They'll go to the same place as their families until this is over.'

'Porcius and Felix,' muttered Cicero to himself. 'I was never fond of either of them, but this is scandalous.'

'There are many more than those two.' The commander held up the records that were sitting on a nearby table. 'These mean a lot more now, and I have all of them. Including those brought back by my now dead brothers-in-arms.'

'How many names?' asked Seraphina and Cicero in unison.

'Over a thousand, at last count. In cities from here to Tanais and beyond.'

It will take forever, thought Cicero. 'What do you plan to do from here, Commander?'

'Caesar's orders still stand, at least until his mind is changed.'

Cicero shook his head and said, 'This can't depend on persuading Caesar, it's too important.' He noticed Seraphina smile widely at this. 'I know a man, one of your superiors, who is beyond reproach. He has insisted on going without a name for many years now and is simply known as The General.'

Paulus blinked and stared at Cicero. 'You're a friend of The General?'

Cicero nodded as Seraphina looked back and forth between the two men. 'I'm one of the few people who know his real name, though I dare not utter it.'

'I've met him once,' said Paulus. 'Will you talk to him about this?'

'I will. This is a special situation, and we need his help. We must not let these people get away with this.'

'Well,' said Paulus, 'technically, I shouldn't be involved. Though I may be able to round up a few allies who can help. Midnight at the port in Ostia. Is that right, Seraphina?'

'Yes,' she said, nodding slowly. Then, after a short silence, 'Who is The General?'

EIGHTY FOUR

Seraphina was going, and no one was going to stop her. She had been imprisoned, twice. She had ridden more days through more wilderness and danger and uncertainty than she cared to remember. She had lost her dear Quintus, taken an arrow to the chest, and two serious knocks to the head. She had gathered maps of Rome and the surrounding region from the Forum archives and from Cicero's personal library.

Cicero knocked on her door as she sat on her bed, the maps spread out everywhere. After a moment, he walked in, and Seraphina was sweeping her arms across the bed, collecting the large sheets of paper together. When they made eye contact, she froze and smiled at him.

'Seraphina,' he said, 'I know what you're planning to do.'

'What's that, Cicero?'

The senator smiled. 'Do I need to station guards around the house, Seraphina?'

'Whatever for, dear Senator, sir?' She had leaned back now, and rested against the wall, smiling.

'We both know where you're going tonight, and I know what you have there in front of you.'

Seraphina's smile faded, as her eyes pleaded with him across the room.

Cicero put his hands on his hips. As he watched her, he strummed his fingers against his body. Finally, he started shaking his head, saying 'this goes against every wise instinct I have, but I think there's someone you should meet.'

Seraphina pushed the maps aside and slid off the bed on to her feet. She watched as Cicero opened the door. A short, stocky man entered the room and nodded at Cicero before looking Seraphina up and down. His uniform was identical to Paulus', but that was where the resemblance ended. He was a good foot shorter than Seraphina, with frizzy, red hair that spiked out from underneath his helmet. His thick moustache was of a matching colour. From the time she had spent with soldiers, she thought it odd that he was wearing a helmet with no armour, and the only weapon he wore was a small sword that looked more like a dagger.

'So, this is the girl you have been telling me about, Cicero?' His voice was clear and elegant, in stark contrast to his appearance.

Cicero simply nodded. 'Seraphina, this is The General.'

'This is most irregular,' said The General. He was not one for lengthy introductions. They both knew who the other was. 'Young lady, this is a serious mission we're embarking on tonight. Are you sure you're up to this?'

'Yes, sir. I am.'

'Cicero tells me the same. We've learned over the years to respect each other's opinion. So, understand, you're coming tonight because he has said you should. Is that clear?'

Seraphina nodded, still taken aback by The General's appearance. He was not what she had expected.

'I've been told of your exploits. Tonight will be different. No disguises, no sword, and no fighting. You're there to watch only, and you will follow orders. Is that understood?'

Seraphina nodded again. 'Yes, sir.'

The General gave her some brief instructions on where and when she was to meet them. He said a curt goodbye to both and left the house on his black stallion.

EIGHTY FIVE

'Where are the other men?' grunted The General at one of his commanders.

All he got was a shrug in response, and he glared fiercely at his subordinate. It had been dark for hours. While Seraphina was doing as she was told and staying back, she was close enough to hear The General's grumbling. *So much for being a master tactician*, she thought. There were twenty men in total, not including her, hiding at the top of the hill, looking down at the port.

The night was cold and still, and everything at the port was as usual for such a late hour except for the presence of a large group of men waiting at the shore. They made no attempt to hide because they thought no one was watching. By Seraphina's count, they numbered eighty-five. Aside from Faustus and the two senators, all were armed warriors.

Seraphina had worn her robe due to the cold, and her dagger was underneath. She had planned on complying with The General's orders and staying out of the action. Truth be told, her head still hurt, even though the bandage had been removed. Now, she prepared herself for the very real possibility that she might have to be involved.

There was very little movement or sound by the water. The men and their personal guards waited in silence. The General anticipated the women and the broker would be arriving in one or more boats. The plan was to rush down the hill as soon as they docked. The plan also called for a force ten times larger than the one they currently had. The soldiers fidgeted with their weapons as they looked into the distance, hoping the rest of their squadron would arrive soon.

Seraphina saw the two boats first. She pointed in the direction of the water, and The General and his men turned around. They were still a good distance from the shore, but a decision had to be made. She watched as The General looked at the boats and then looked at his men. He massaged his temples with his thumb and index finger.

'Check your weapons, men. We're going ahead as planned. They outnumber us, but the surprise of seeing us may catch them off-guard. Also, do not draw your weapons until we're upon them. Seize the broker and the senators as quickly as possible and separate them from the fighting. At least two men are to guard them and no matter what happens, do not leave them to join the battle. All clear?'

The soldiers nodded, and Seraphina noticed no visible reactions amongst the men. *Four to one, and they were going to run down the hill and hope for the best?*

The General was still facing away from the water, his back up against the crest of the hill. He saw his horse and had a stroke of genius.

'You men,' he said, pointing at four of the soldiers in turn. 'Go and get our horses.'

A few of the men smiled and understood immediately. 'We'll ride over them. That should even up the odds.' He looked around at his men. 'Trot down the hill. Once you're on flat ground, accelerate into a canter, and leave your weapons undrawn. When you hear me shout 'charge,' gallop as fast as you can and ride straight over them. Try your best to avoid the senators, but if they get hurt, then so be it.'

He waved Seraphina over to him. 'Here, take this,' he said, handing her a sword. It was twice the size of the one he carried himself, but similar to what Seraphina had wielded before. 'Now, I have a question for you. Do you want to stay up here, or do you want to come down with us?'

Seraphina smiled and took the sword.

'I thought so. Listen, don't do what the other soldiers do. Stay on your horse as long as possible and use the sword. Don't get in the middle of the fighting. Stay at the edges and try to catch their men unaware. Do you understand what I'm asking?'

'Yes, sir.'

'Can you do it?'

'I most certainly can,' she said, swallowing the lump in her throat.

'Good. Stay as safe as you can. I hope the stories I've heard about you are true.'

The General peeked over the hill and could see the boats were coming close to the shore. He mounted his horse first and began a slow trot down the hill. The other soldiers followed. One of the men brought Luna to Seraphina and gave her a military tunic and a helmet to wear instead of her robe. Exactly the same as the soldiers were wearing! *Talk about a disguise*, she thought.

She followed the soldiers down the hill. They had not yet been spotted. All eyes were on the boats and the broker. However, after a few moments, she saw the broker point in their direction, and the senators turned to see The General less than half a mile from them. His horse was only cantering along at this stage, and both his hands were on the reins.

The General offered a friendly wave and said in a raised voice, 'Ave, Senators. Beautiful night, isn't it?'

A few of the guards drew their weapons, but Faustus and the senators were yet to react. The broker did not hesitate, and just as The General yelled for them to charge, he shouted at the men on the shore to attack. The battle was on.

The General's plan worked brilliantly to begin with, and Seraphina heard the screams of those men being trampled as Luna was still galloping towards the shore. Faustus' men knew what to do, and they began to duck and slash at the horses' legs with their swords, bringing them crashing to the ground.

The broker signalled his boats to turn around, but two soldiers quickly put an end to that idea. The broker lost a couple of his fingers as the centurion swung his sword, and the drivers of the boats did not move a muscle after that. They lay face down on the shore, as the broker screamed about his missing fingers. The two soldiers stood guard in front of the boats, slashing their blades at anyone who came close. After a couple of minutes of enduring the broker's screams, the centurion knocked him out with the handle of his sword.

The women on the boats had already been through more of an ordeal than anyone would ever know. The conditions at their prison had been far worse than the one at Tanais, and now they remained captive watching a hundred men try to maim and kill each other. They were not even sure which side they wanted to win. What was clear, at that moment, was that it was safest to stay exactly where they were.

Seraphina, having seen the fate of the horses that had charged before her, wanted no part of that for Luna. She did as The General said, and skirted the battle, slashing down from her horse when she could. Her heart raced, but she kept focused on helping as much as she could. She was the only one left on her horse and could see the mastery of Faustus' men as they slowly got the upper hand. One brave soldier grabbed the two senators and pulled them to where the boats were. Seraphina saw the warrior before anyone else. He was about to stab the soldier in the back. Ignoring her orders, she charged straight across the middle of the fighting to knock him over.

The soldier never saw that he had been saved, but The General witnessed Seraphina's bravery. He was fighting with a fury, dispatching enemies with single strikes from his small but trusty sword. He shouted out at Seraphina to stay on the edges of the fight.

She heard him yell something, but she wasn't quite sure what. Less than half of the Roman soldiers were left, and they were surrounded.

They continued to fight, and true to The General's orders, the men guarding the broker and the senators did not rejoin the fighting. Faustus could see what was happening, and pulled his men away, shouting at them to focus on the ones they had surrounded. Seraphina couldn't believe her eyes as the three soldiers stood there, following orders but letting their comrades fall into a deathly situation.

Seraphina galloped around to where Faustus' men were, seeing that they were the most talented fighters. As she pulled her sword back to swing at one of them, something knocked her in the chest. One of Faustus' warriors had thrown his sword. The blade had missed its mark, but it was thrown hard enough that Seraphina was knocked from Luna's back. She crashed to the floor, landing on her hands.

The warrior stepped over her and picked up his sword. As she rolled over, trying to get up, she saw him raise the sword, but not over her. Luna had fallen on his side, and the warrior was standing above the horse with the sword raised. Seraphina scrambled to her feet and screamed 'NO!' As she went to lunge at him with her dagger, something whizzed through the air. The man fell, his hands still over his head holding the sword.

Another whizzing sound, and Seraphina looked up to see where it came from. It was Paulus! He and three other soldiers – the only surviving members of the original mission – charged down the hill on their horses. Adalwin's archers stood at the top of the hill, picking off their enemies one at a time.

When Faustus saw three of his men fall in as many seconds, he put his hands up. Some of the men continued to fight, and they were put down, either by arrows from the archers on the hill or The General and his men. Paulus reached the battle just as Faustus was telling his men to surrender. He swung his leg at Faustus and gave him a swift kick to the face. Those who were still alive put their hands up and dropped their weapons. They looked down at those who had fallen, astonished by how quickly the battle had turned, and the number of arrows that had been fired in the space of less than a minute.

Seraphina ran over to Luna and saw that he wasn't hurt. He just needed some help getting up. She stroked his face and whispered some words to him and watched as the soldiers took control of the situation.

'Well, fancy seeing you here,' said Paulus.

'I could say the same thing,' said Seraphina, offering her arm to him.

Paulus surprised Seraphina by giving her a hug instead. 'Well, my men talked me into it,' he said, waving at the three soldiers who had come with him. 'They said it wasn't right for us to hide, and that orders or no orders, this was the right place to be. Looks like I showed up just in time.'

Seraphina laughed and nodded. 'Let's not forget them,' she said, pointing up at Adalwin's archers and waving at them. 'I think the one who shot me in the chest just saved my horse.'

'Well, well,' said The General, walking over to interrupt them, 'you took your time getting here, Commander.'

Paulus took a step back and stood to attention. 'Yes, sir. I had my orders to stay out of this.'

'At ease, Commander. I understand the situation, and I'm sure Caesar will too. I'll be speaking to him about this first thing in the morning, so there's nothing for you to worry about. And thank you, I think we were done for before you got here.'

'My pleasure, sir.'

'And you!' he said, raising his voice as he turned to Seraphina and pointed at her. She also took a step back. Then The General smiled, adding, 'I'm glad I listened to Cicero about you. Thank you for helping us too. You're quite the warrior.'

'Thank you, sir.'

'Is your horse alright?' he asked, looking past her to Luna, who was still lying on his side.

'Oh yes, but could your men help me get him back up?'

Five of the soldiers got Luna to his feet. As The General and Paulus focused on tying up those who had survived the battle, Seraphina walked over to the boats. Some of the women kept their eyes down, and some smiled at her as she walked towards them. She spoke to them and assured them they were now safe. If they were surprised to be talking to a dark-skinned woman in a Roman army uniform, they didn't show it. They started to get out of the boats and sat on the shore as the soldiers went about their business.

Seraphina talked to them for hours, long after The General had suggested she go home. She learned about where they were from, what they had been through, and assured them repeatedly that all would be well.

EIGHTY SIX

It was a rough day for the establishment. True to his word, The General had visited Caesar, alone, at dawn, taking with him the long lists of names gathered by Paulus and his men during their raids on the prisons. In a three-hour meeting that was tense at times, The General lay out what he had learned and the details of the mission that had been carried out the night before.

Caesar was initially surprised that the mission had taken place without him being consulted, but he knew full well that he couldn't know about everything the army did. The General was the highest-ranking soldier in the entire Roman army, and his authority was unquestioned when it came to matters of keeping the peace and preventing crimes.

The dictator could not deny the veracity of what The General was telling him, especially now that it involved eyewitness accounts of crimes committed. It turned out that several of the women were Roman citizens, and this infuriated the mighty Caesar. He authorised The General to start arresting everyone involved with 'the network', as it had come to be called, and to report back daily, either in person or through one of his commanders.

The arrests started at about the time when most Romans were beginning their day. After a few hours, it was clear that this would be no ordinary day in Rome. In addition to the names on the lists, the senators Porcius and Felix had implicated many others, including fellow senators. Neither The General nor Paulus were inclined to believe a word that came out of their mouths without proof to corroborate it, but for now, the arrests were necessary.

Rome came to a standstill as senators, high-ranking soldiers, government officials, and many members of prominent families were pulled out on to the street and arrested. The broker, still upset about his missing fingers, was threatened with much worse and began confessing all. He led a group of soldiers to those in Rome that he had sold women to. One by one, the women were freed, and all the adults in each household were arrested. Korinna, the bold girl who had been imprisoned with Seraphina in Tanais, slapped her owner as hard as she could upon being freed. The woman was knocked unconscious, and the soldiers had to spend several minutes reviving her before they could arrest her.

Paulus oversaw a lot of the chaos, and he met regularly with The General throughout the day. It became clear that completing the arrests in Rome alone would take several days, and security checkpoints were set up around the edges of the city. Many of those involved with the network were caught trying to flee Rome in the coming days.

During his lengthy interrogation, Senator Porcius gave up one of Caesar's personal guards. This guard had been on duty the morning Paulus had gone to see Caesar. It became clear that this guard had informed on the conversation between Caesar and Paulus, which had directly led to the murders of Paulus' soldiers and their families, not to mention Darius. When this got back to Caesar, he issued an unwritten decree that the guard would not be arrested, nor would he stand trial. The other guards would deal with it, he said, and deal with it they did. The turncoat was never seen or heard from again. After they had meted out justice, several of his colleagues found money at the guard's home amounting to twenty times his annual salary.

Blood money, they said. It was given to Paulus, who decided it would be given to the widows and children of the soldiers murdered as a result of his treachery. Many seizures of assets followed, and Caesar agreed that the money should go to help those who had been kidnapped and held captive. Minus a small administrative fee for Rome, of course.

Seraphina stayed home at Cicero's during most of those chaotic days. She spent a lot of time in her room, crying and grieving over Quintus. She let her wounds heal, although the scars inside would take longer than her bodily injuries. She talked and laughed with Cicero, and Publilia even thawed and the two became friends. Of course, she practised her energisation exercises and meditated daily, saying a short prayer of thanks for Keb each time she did so.

Once or twice, she went to visit the young women who had been rescued that night. They had been given fine housing, and they were joined by those freed from households across Rome. Seraphina got permission from Paulus and The General to return the girls who were from Rome to their families, but many more had a much longer journey ahead of them. Cicero helped by providing several scribes, and Seraphina began the task of documenting where each girl was from. A cursory glance at her notes by Paulus confirmed that they indeed had a long job ahead of them to get each of the girls back home.

Seraphina listened to Paulus speak about the logistics – the arrests, interrogations, returning the girls to their homes, the further arrests to be made, and so on. *It was a lifetime's work,* she thought, *but no one should be stolen from their families and have their freedom stripped from them.* She understood that slavery existed in the world, but even Caesar had made a distinction between that and what the pirates had perpetrated through their nefarious network.

She decided she would get every single one of those girls home, although, in her heart, she suspected that an even larger purpose lay in wait for her.

EIGHTY SEVEN

THREE MONTHS LATER.

Seraphina rode Luna up the Palatine hill, stopping as always to appreciate the splendid view of the city. The beautiful temples and basilicas, most of which she now knew. The clear blue sky and the shining sun. The gentle clouds of smoke emanating from the steeples of homes and workshops. She patted Luna on the head and guided him home. She had been enrolled in one of Rome's finest colleges for over a month now, and it felt just like home in Alexandria – the great teachers, the scholars who were now her peers, and endless libraries for her to read and learn from.

This is the life I've always dreamed of, she thought. Yet she often found herself looking off into the distance, wondering about what she had left behind. She yearned to return to the forest and see Keb once again. Seraphina knew there was much, much more for her to learn from him. She wondered whether that was the education she should be getting right now, and the more she thought about it, the more she felt the call to leave Rome. At least temporarily.

Seraphina was distracted from these thoughts by the sight of Paulus' horse when she arrived home. She rushed inside to find him relaxing with Cicero, enjoying a drink and a leisurely chat. She hugged Paulus, as had become her habit, and said good afternoon to Cicero.

'What brings you here, Commander?' asked Seraphina.

'I was just sharing some good news with Cicero here.'

'Oh, and what's that?'

'I've been promoted to the rank of general.'

'Well, congratulations, Paulus.'

'Thank you, Seraphina. This investigation has made me famous. More famous than I'd like to be, but for good reasons at least. The work we've done over the past months has been noticed.'

'How are the girls? Are there many left?'

Paulus shook his head. 'No, most of them have been sent home. There are only a few left, although some of them have no home to go back to. They complain at not having seen you for some time,' he said, grinning at Seraphina.

'Well, it turns out the life of a student is quite demanding. Not quite as demanding as dismantling an illegal slave trading business, but still.'

All three of them shared a laugh, and then Paulus' face straightened. 'Life may become even more demanding.'

'Why's that? she asked.

Cicero listened with curiosity, as Paulus had not mentioned this second reason for his visit.

'I've been sworn to secrecy. You are to come with me. Caesar has requested your presence.'

Seraphina raised an eyebrow at Paulus. 'What does Caesar want with me?'

'I am not to say.'

'Do I need to bring my dagger? A sword, maybe?' she said, laughing and reaching towards the grip of Paulus' sword.

'I don't think it's anything quite that dramatic. In fact, he seems rather excited to meet you.'

'Well, we'd better not keep him waiting.'

EIGHTY EIGHT

They rode out of Cicero's house and, before long, were on streets unfamiliar to Seraphina. It was clear they were not heading towards the Forum.

'Where are we going?' she asked as they continued to ride.

'I told you, I'm not to say anything. Just be patient.'

'You Romans … so odd and secretive sometimes.'

'This from a girl who hangs off buildings to spy on people.'

Seraphina grinned and said no more. She looked around, trying to work out where they were. The streets looked pleasant enough, with large homes and tall, elegant buildings interspersed together. Paulus slowed down and eventually stopped. Seraphina looked up. It was a modern building, and much narrower than the others that housed apartments.

Paulus was walking up the steps when he looked back to see Seraphina still on her horse.

'I thought we didn't want to keep Caesar waiting,' he said with a smile.

Seraphina looked down at him, dismounting the horse slowly. She wasn't afraid. In fact, she was quite curious about what Caesar wanted, and why he had brought her here. She followed Paulus up two flights of stairs, and through a door flanked on either side by a guard. They wore a strange uniform, one that Seraphina had seen before. In the palace in Alexandria. The door was unlocked, and Paulus pushed it open. Seraphina paused, and looked each of the guards up and down. They ignored her, their gaze not shifting for a moment, and she went into the apartment.

The main room was spacious and bare of any furniture. There were rooms off to each side and a balcony where Caesar was enjoying the view while he waited. Turning to face them when he heard them enter, he waved them over without saying a word.

'Thank you for being so prompt, General. This must be Sera ...' His voice trailed off as he tilted his head and stared at Seraphina for a moment. 'I have the strangest feeling that we've met ... have we?'

Paulus was taken aback but did not show any sign. He was more surprised at the smile on Seraphina's face.

'We have, sir. More than a year has passed.'

'Where, though?' He rubbed his chin as he tried to place her in his mind.

'In the palace, at Alexandria.'

Caesar shook his head, trying to jog his memory.

'I was dressed as a servant girl at the time. I told you a story you thought was quite farfetched.'

'That was you!' he exclaimed, then turning and glaring at Paulus with wide eyes.

Paulus looked at Seraphina, unsure of how to react. Seraphina realised she should have said something before this meeting started. She had been so surprised at the prospect of Caesar wanting to see her, that the importance of mentioning it had escaped her until now.

Caesar folded his arms and looked at her, tapping his elbow with his finger. 'Well, let's start with why I've asked you here. I would offer you a seat, but this place is yet to be furnished.'

Seraphina nodded, her smile disappearing.

'What you've done over the past several months is commendable, Seraphina. You've uncovered several serious crimes, and Paulus here has done some fine work. Many trials have already concluded, and we've obtained a lot more information.'

Caesar paused, and Seraphina said, 'Thank you,' to fill the silence.

'There's a lot more work to be done. As you know, this extends far beyond the city of Rome, and well beyond the borders of the republic. There are more arrests to be made, more women to be freed, and more ill-gotten funds to be seized. From what we know at this stage, the investigation could take years.'

Seraphina nodded, looking over at Paulus, who was now smiling back at her.

'I know you're studying at college now, Seraphina, and both Paulus and Cicero have given me the impression that this is quite important to you. Is that correct?'

'Yes, sir,' she answered, still unsure where this was going.

'I need someone to liaise with the senate and the army until all of this is resolved. As you know, we do have slavery in the republic, but what you two uncovered is quite different. These people traded only in young women. Kidnapping and false imprisonment are serious crimes, but the trade of young women as slaves for the pleasure of their masters is something that offends me personally. I'm not sure that this was happening in every case, but it's clear that part of their operation was conceived with this in mind.'

'I agree, sir,' she said, feeling the disgust inside at how much worse things could have been for her.

'The women who were taken have confidence in you, as do Paulus and The General, who I believe you've met. Cicero speaks highly of you too, and I believe you're the right person for this job.'

Seraphina's eyes went wide and did not blink. Her jaw dropped as she considered the implications of what Caesar had just said. *Working with the senate! And the army!*

Caesar noticed her reaction and spoke slowly as she had not moved for nearly a minute. 'You would be responsible for making recommendations on how the army is to pursue the various avenues of this investigation and will keep the senate appraised of the progress made. With regards to the number of women freed, the amount of assets seized, and who else you discover is involved in this network, which seems to be vast, you will also report directly to me.'

The only movement Seraphina had made was to turn her eyes towards Paulus for a second, and then back to Caesar.

'Seraphina?' said Caesar. 'Do you understand what I am offering you?'

She nodded her head slowly, and Paulus couldn't help but chuckle. Caesar smiled too, and Seraphina took in a long breath and stood at ease.

Caesar waved his arm across the main room of the apartment. 'This will be your home if you wish to take it. As to my offer, if your answer is no, then take it as a token of thanks. If yes, then it will be an ideal place for you to work, and to continue your studies in your spare time.' He gave Seraphina a big grin, and added, 'you will, of course, have considerable resources at your disposal.'

The remark about her studies jerked her back into reality. 'What do you mean exactly?'

'Well,' said Caesar, 'I know most of the academia in Rome. We could arrange private lessons, learning materials to be brought to and from here, whatever you wanted really.'

Seraphina was smiling so much at these words that her face began to hurt after a few moments. Then her eyes dropped, and she yearned to return to Keb and continue his teachings. She thought of Quintus, who she was supposed to be living this dream with.

Caesar watched her, and after a few moments, he said, 'Look around the apartment. Enjoy the view and think about what I've said. Excuse me and the general, we have a few matters to discuss.'

Seraphina nodded and looked over at Paulus who gave her a little smile and a nod as Caesar began speaking to him. She walked around the huge room, peering through the corridors on either end of it. *It was a luxurious home,* she thought. The balcony was spacious, and the view over Rome was spectacular. She could see the Forum, the Temple of Jupiter, and countless other buildings and monuments that she was yet to visit.

She was only at the beginning of her life here, and she wondered if she could somehow accept Caesar's offer and still go to spend time with Keb on occasion. Quintus was born in this city, she realised. In that moment, she felt how much she was still holding on to him. She had loved him, no doubt, as he had her, but he was gone, and she had to move on. She bowed her head, said a quiet prayer for him, and let him go.

'I forgot to mention,' said Caesar, suddenly next to her on the balcony, 'you will also have an office down there.' He was pointing at the Forum.

Seraphina felt dizzy. A year and a half ago, she had been living in secret in the library in Alexandria. She was content to read her scrolls and talk to Afiz at night about all she was learning. Now she was in the greatest city in the world, standing next to its powerful leader, being offered something she would have thought beyond all realms of possibility.

'There's something else I want to talk to you about.' Caesar looked over his shoulder at Paulus, who was standing by the door, doing his best to listen. 'As you said, a long time has passed since we first met. An investigation has been completed in Alexandria with regards to Rufio and the extent of his crimes. I made the grave mistake of trusting him, and one of my finest spies was involved in his efforts against you. I have learned of the late general's true nature, and I offer my apologies. I did not know him when he committed those terrible crimes against your parents and those other women, but I was a member of this government. So, on behalf of the Roman people, I apologise to you, Seraphina, and thank you for all you've done for us.'

'Thank you, sir,' she said, wiping a tear away. 'That means a lot.'

'You know, there's something you and I have in common.'

Seraphina turned to look at him, with a slight smirk on her face. 'I'm interested to know what.' She looked him up and down, wondering what they possibly could have in common.

'We've both been kidnapped by pirates, and we've both exacted justice on them after escaping their clutches. I'll tell you the story sometime.'

'I would like that.' Seraphina couldn't wait to hear it and thought of how much there was to learn about this fascinating man standing next to her. A few moments passed, and they both returned their attention to the view of the city below.

'So, would you like more time to consider my offer, or shall we get to work?'

If you enjoyed the book and would like to hear about Tiago's future releases, follow him on Amazon or Goodreads.

146-47; Convention on the Rights of Persons with Disabilities, 34, 185n8; Convention on the Rights of the Child, 80; Decade for Women (1976-85), 81; Global Commission on International Migration, 14; International Convention on the Protection of the Rights of All Migrant Workers and Members of Their Families, 13-14; policy learning and transfer, 96
United Nations Development Program (UNDP), 34, 148-51, 157, 160
United States: foreign trained nurses, 41-42, 58; global care chain, 27; migrant care workers, 11, 68; nursing shortage, 46; State Department, 148; women's labour force participation, 7, 127
United States Supreme Court, 174
universality: caring experience, 133, 184n2; development practices, 92, 93; elder care, 118; human trafficking, 141-42; preschool education, 91; public child care, 105, 107; universal breadwinner model, 184n2
USAID, 90

Van den Anker, Christien, 141-42

Wade, Robert Hunter, 92
Walker, Margaret, 134-36, 140, 164-65, 169, 172, 190n8; *Moral Understandings*, 166, 188n2
Walzer, Michael, 190nn12-13
Weitzer, Ronald, 139
welfare, 29, 82
welfare states. *See* nation-welfare states
Werbner, Pnina, 176
White, Julie, 5
Williams, Fiona, 5, 10, 21-38, 23, 92, 170, 182

women: Beijing global women's conference, 33; as care providers, 130, 158; empowerment of, 33-34; neoliberal policies, 185n10; OECD on economic role of, 79, 92; representation of Filipino women, 73; responsible for child raising, 123-24; womanhood discourses, 129, 136; women's movements, 33-34; women's rights, 141-42, 144; women's work, 127-28, 130-36, 137, 140, 141, 142, 158; World Bank emphasis on, 88-89, 92. *See also* human trafficking; labour force participation by women; sex trafficking
work/care balance: developed world, 38; gendered aspects, 36; Japan, 121-22; migrant care workers, 30-31; reconciliation efforts, 8-9, 10-11, 33
World Bank: American social policy model, 92; anti-poverty strategy, 11, 86, 87-91; on child survival, 80-81; compared to OECD, 91-93; focus of aid strategies, 93, 187n3; gender equality, 35, 87-89; geopolitical headquarters, 92; policy learning and transfer, 96, 179-80; social insurance, 82-83; social investment, 80, 81, 88-89, 91; social justice, 90-91; social policy discourse, 2, 10-11, 87-91, 92, 180; social reproduction dilemma, 138; Washington Consensus, 88, 89, 92, 187n2; work/life reconciliation, 10-11; *World Development Report*, 35. *See also* early child education and care
World Trade Organization (WTO), 99
Wren, Anne, 184n1

Yamazaki Takashi, 68, 72, 186n6
Yang, Jae-Jin, 103

Yeates, Nicola: regulation/certification of care provision, 43, 56; religious care chains, 185n6; remittances, 31; social reproductive labour, 40; transnationalization of care, 10, 12-13, 27, 42

Yoder case (*Wisconsin v. Yoder*, 1972), 174
Young, Iris, 4-5, 168-69
Young, Mary Eming, 89, 90

Zimmerman, Mary K., 41

GDP, 45-46; restructuring social expenditure, 88-89, 181; social politics of care, 178-83; social safety net, 158, 161; state policies, 8, 22-25; tax-related benefits, 8, 23, 32-33, 37, 115; techno-muscular capitalism, 137-38; Third Way policies, 103, 121-22. *See also* citizenship; ethics of care; social investment
Somers, Margaret, 96
Soros Foundation, 77
South Africa, 27
South Korea. *See* Korea
Southeast Asia, 47
Soviet Bloc countries, 79. *See also* Ukraine
Spain, 23, 26, 29
Spitzer, Denise, 55
Sri Lanka, 26, 128, 172
Stasiulis, Daiva, 44, 45, 50
Stockholm, 87
Sugimoto Kiyoe, 63
Suzuki, Nobue, 63, 68, 72, 186n6
Swaziland, 27
Sweden, 7, 8, 9, 23, 28, 29, 105
Switzerland, 28

Takagi Hiroshi, 71
Takahashi, Nobuyuki, 67
Takenaka, Heizō, 121
teachers, 26
temporary migration, 49, 52
Thailand, 156-57
Thedore, Nik, 10-11
Third Way policies, 103, 121-22
Tokyo Chamber of Commerce and Industry, 120
Torres, Sara, 55
trade unions, 29
transnational households, 67
transnationalism, 2, 24
transnationalization of care, 127-44; background, 10-14, 127-30; care commitment dynamics, 29-31; care discourses and polices, 32-33, 158; challenges posed by, 14-16; child care, 15-16; gendered globalization, 136-39; global social justice, 34-37; movement of care capital, 31-32; movement of care labour, 25-29; notions of citizenship, 12, 13, 24-25, 183; social organizations and movements, 33-34; socioeconomics, 10-11, 25-34, 178-83; transnational families, 12. *See also* commodification of care; ethics of care; Internationally Educated Nurses; migrant care workers
Tronto, Joan, 4, 5, 112-13, 131-32, 151, 162-77, 165
Truong, Thanh-Dam, 137, 143
Tsuji, Yuki, 60, 63, 111-24

Ukraine, 147-61; average annual purchasing power, 149; changing role of women, 153-54; child-care responsibility, 150; demographic crisis, 160; Environmentally and Socially Sustainable Development (ECSSD), 153; female migration, 153-59; fertility rates, 160; sex trafficking, 147-60; single mothers, 153; socioeconomic circumstances, 149-50, 152-53, 157-61, 189n2
UNESCO, 33, 77, 78-81, 80, 87, 101-2, 104
UNESCO Courier, 102-3
UNICEF, 33, 78-81, 90, 91
United Arab Emirates, 30
United Kingdom. *See* Britain
United Nations: Committee on the Elimination of Discrimination against Women (CEDAW), 121; Committee on the Rights of the Child, 84; Convention against Transnational Organized Crime,

44-45, 115-16; politics of needs, 2, 16, 35, 69-70; sex work, 135-36
prenatal care, 81
prostitution, 139, 141, 144, 147, 156
psychoanalytic theory, 3
public/private dichotomy, 133, 137-38, 181

racism: epistemological ignorance, 168; and justice, 190n7; racialized discrimination, 29, 61, 69-71, 124, 138. *See also* discrimination
Rawls, John, 90
Razavi, S., 35
ReggioEmilia approach, 83, 87
religious care chains, 27, 185n6
remittances, 12, 27, 31, 67, 154, 162, 179
responsibility concept, 169-70
Rhaguram, P., 31, 36, 43
Rhyu, Simin, 101
RNs. *See* nurses
Robinson, Fiona, 1-17, 37, 115, 127-44, 145-46, 151-52, 158-59, 178-83
Roh, Moo-hyun, 94, 100-1, 108-9
Rohatynskyj, M.A., 150-51
Rojas, Cristina, 93
Romanow, Roy J., 45, 185n4
Rose, Richard, 95
Rosemberg, Fúlvia, 11
Ruddick, Sarah, 3-4, 132
rule of law, 190n5, 190n7
Russia, 147

Sabatier, P., 96
Sainsbury, Diane, 7
Sanghera, Jyoti, 151
Sarvasy, Wendy, 13, 172
Sassen, Saskia, 12, 182, 189n6
Saudi Arabia, 26
Save the Children US, 90
Scandinavian welfare state models, 82, 83, 105
Schmidt, Vivien A., 113
self-sufficiency, 135
Sen, Amartya, 9, 78, 82, 90

Sevenhuijsen, Selma, 4, 6, 14-15, 132-33, 166
sex trafficking, 147-60; ethics of care, 129, 130, 135, 151-54; feminization of survival, 15-16; Filipino care workers, 73; global political economy, 137, 138, 139-42, 143; human costs, 159-60; narrative accounts, 156-57; socioeconomics, 153, 157-60. *See also* human trafficking
Shapkina, Nadia, 158-59
Singapore, 26, 172
Sipilä, Jorma, 8, 9
slavery, 139, 170
Smith, Susan J., 181
social democratic regimes, 184n1
social investment, 94-110; Britain, 109-10, 180; children, 32-33, 77, 79-80, 101-2, 180; developing countries, 36-37; gender/gender equality, 31, 79, 81, 180; mothers, 32-33, 85, 87-89, 91, 98; non-governmental organizations (NGOs), 96, 104, 106-8. *See also* socioeconomics
social justice, 33, 34-37, 90-91, 190n5, 190n7
social reproduction labour: dimensions of, 1-2, 10, 40, 112; gendered assumptions, 6-7, 112; global restructuring, 43, 128-29; hidden costs, 11-12; international divisions, 22, 24; investment in, 47; neoliberal assumptions, 114; World Bank dilemma, 138
social space concept, 65
Society for International Development, 80
socioeconomics: CIS states, 149-51, 157-60; gendered power structures, 42; inclusive liberalism, 92, 104; international development strategies, 29, 31; international transfer, 95-97; national contexts, 115; politics of needs, 2, 16, 35, 69-70; public expenditures as share of